Rev

Ed Jones is the author of ....
scriptwriter for television. He lives in Manchester.

·1·

THE WHOLE PARISH agreed that the bride looked lovely.

Verdicts ranged from 'very nice' to 'ethereal', through 'distinguished', 'elegant', 'magnificent', 'dazzling' and 'perfect'. Mrs Cavendish used the word 'acceptable', which for her was a spectacular compliment, and old George Duckinfield muttered something unacceptable before disappearing back down the road to the pub where, everyone agreed, he was better off.

Those who weren't invited to the ceremony gathered on the side of the road opposite the church and sighed and gossiped and generally had the best Saturday they'd had for a long time, criticising this awful hat and admiring that pretty dress, nudging each other and pointing and cooing and ahhing. Half the parish turned out on the grass verge opposite – 'half the parish' meaning, of course: 'all the women'.

Everyone understood that it was family and close personal friends only at the service. If *everyone* had been invited there simply wouldn't have been the space and, besides, it would have spoiled things for the couple; it wouldn't have been fair to crowd out the church just because it was the bishop's wedding, but everyone had to show their face. They simply *had* to. It would have been expected.

Of course it wasn't the bishop who was getting married, it was his son, but locally the event was referred to as the Bishop's Wedding. As with any other event in the life of the bishop's family, in its mind's eye the parish saw it as something that was happening to the bishop. Furthermore, as Market Cross was such a small parish and the bishop was such an important person in it, when something happened to the bishop, in its heart the parish felt as if something was happening to itself.

The grand jury of the parish women judged the ceremony to have been a great success. They knew that the groom had requested Lefebure-Wely's Sortie in B Flat for the music and that old Mrs Tottington had refused, or forgotten the music, or been unable to play the piece because of her arthritis. News had reached them that there had been some drunkenness the night before involving one of the young women – that friend of the bride's no one liked the look of. Word was that the groom had recently come home from London after having had some sort of trouble there and the bishop's family had paid for the reception because the bride had no family of her own. The couple had known each other for only six months, which meant the marriage probably wouldn't last. There had even been a puncture on the way to the church and the ceremony had been delayed by twenty minutes. But, dazed by the bright sunshine, the pealing of bells, the pretty dresses and the occasionally awful hats, intoxicated by the scent of the flowers – which was in fact the bouquet of their own liberally applied perfumes and powders – dazzled by the elegance of the guests, aroused by the beauty of the bride and most of all by the special, bewitching charm of the wedding dress itself, the jury's verdict was unanimous – the applause as the couple came out of the church was spontaneous.

The happy couple kissed and the women of the parish stood beaming, crying and clapping. Perhaps they would have cheered if not for the lumps in their throats.

There they were, the Rattigan family, the bishop's family, assembled in the sunshine like a photograph, surrounded by extended family and friends, a perfect picture of contentment and joy.

Jessica Rattigan was standing, as she should be, next to the bishop and surrounded by the family, modestly but elegantly dressed in a smart navy-blue suit with matching blouse and a pearl antique brooch, the slight breeze gently wafting wisps of her hair under the broad-brimmed hat but somehow managing not to upset a single strand. She did not stand out from the scene, yet she was the centre of it; that was her achievement.

As usual during a public appearance, Jessica Rattigan was not as calm as she looked. Today she was worried above and beyond the call of duty. The wedding arrangements had been complicated and expensive. She had had to oversee them and often had to sort things out for herself; every time she entrusted a task to someone else it went hopelessly wrong, didn't get done at all, or cost twice as much as necessary. On top of all this, Jessica was worried about her son, the bridegroom. She was also worried about the bride. She was worried about the marriage.

Edward didn't understand. Men never worried enough about things. Yet if you don't worry about things, how were things expected to work themselves out? Quite how Edward had managed to keep up his various commitments she didn't know. Well, she did. He had done it because she had been there to do his worrying for him.

She was determined, absolutely determined, that nothing was going to go wrong for their son, Gabriel.

'Mum . . .'

Gabriel was tugging at her arm. The photo session was over. Jessica's face ached with the smiling.

'Mum, I just wanted to tell you how happy I am.'

'Yes, darling. I'm very pleased for you.'

'Really, I couldn't have done it without you. I mean . . . without you I'd probably still . . . you know what I mean.'

He looked so handsome and vulnerable with his curly black hair as uncontrollable and charming as it always had been, now with bits of confetti scattered throughout, like colourful dandruff. Jessica straightened her son's tie automatically.

'Darling, you've got confetti in your hair – it's going to be in all the photographs.'

Gabriel didn't seem to care. 'I want to thank you.'

Jessica smiled. 'There's plenty of time for that.'

'Well, I wanted to say it now. As well.'

She could still smell the drink on him. 'Darling. Don't get drunk. I mean, at the reception. Don't let me down.'

'Course I won't!'

'Just stick to soft drinks.'

'I haven't had a drop. The others have been at the champagne all morning.'

'Just be careful, Gabriel, for me.'

'Trust me.'

Jessica managed another smile. 'I do.'

Funny how his eyes looked as big and as sad as they had when he was child, even when he smiled.

Dear Caroline,

   Yes it's me, Rachel, writing to you already and I only saw you yesterday!!

4

I've been married for eighteen hours and I'm miserable already!! Gabriel's being very sweet and sexy – even though he was too drunk to make love on the first night!! – and the Lodge is gorgeous – imagine – me in a beautiful little cottage in the middle of nowhere with the man I've just married who happens to be an up-and-coming (gorgeous) young artist who's just sold a painting for the incredible sum of £2,000!!! but I'm sitting here feeling sorry for myself.

I feel very sorry for myself. You know, I think was trying to pretend that I wasn't upset that Steve (my big brother – in case you'd forgotten) didn't show up at the wedding. I don't even know where he is and he hasn't contacted me for nearly nine months. What kind of family is that? It's not as if we've got anyone else – it's just me and him and the rest of the world. Poor little orphan Annie!

I think I had a fantasy about the Rattigans becoming my family. Of course they *are* my family now. But I suppose I thought I'd fit straight in. In fact, it hasn't worked out like that at all. It's strange but there's tension already between me and Jessica – that's Gabriel's mum.

At the reception – it was just after you left – Gabriel was getting more and more hammered – I was worried about him – anyway, Jessica marches up to me, takes me by the arm and says, 'You must make Gabriel calm down. He doesn't know when to stop. He's relying on you to tell him.' (!!!) I was gobsmacked. I think I managed to say something like 'OK I will', when really I should have said 'Piss off and mind your own business'. Imagine if I'd said that to her! I was livid, but I didn't say anything. I thought I was just being over-sensitive. I'm sure she blamed him getting drunk on me.

Well obviously I didn't say anything to him, and obviously he was too drunk to get it on. So maybe I should have said something. Maybe I would have if she hadn't said that and I wasn't so stubborn.

Anyhow. Here I am sitting here in the Lodge all on my own. Gabriel's gone running up to the house to see Jessica, I think he feels guilty because we skived off church this morning.

When we got here we had to go to the house to pick up the keys for the Lodge. Gabriel and I had agreed to have a nice morning unpacking and undressing each other but Jessica came on really heavy about us going to church and coming to lunch after, saying how it was expected of us. What was it she said – 'One of the pitfalls of marrying into an ecclesiastical family is that you are always slightly on show.'

Well I might sound ungrateful, I don't know, but I *didn't* marry into an ecclesiastical family. I married an artist whose father happens to be a bishop – we came here because Gabriel wanted to come here for his work and his family kindly offered to let us live here.

So here I am the big hypocrite. I wanted a family – and now they want me I don't want them any more. Proper ungrateful bitch, aren't I? Right, that does it – I'm going up to the house to look for him. Jessica or no Jessica. Then we're going to have a nice, quiet evening of sex . . . oops, I mean a nice quiet evening in.

I'll finish this tomorrow and get it in the post.

I love you,
Rachel xxx

PS Resolution (I've just read this bit back): I'm not at war with Jessica. She's the nearest thing I've got to a mother. I will be more understanding and patient of

my mother-in-law. I've actually got a mother-in-law!!!
How strange and how beautiful.

Jessica was heartily glad the wedding was over and life could return to normal.

'Normal', though, somehow didn't feel like the right word. Not any longer. Life had long since ceased to be anything resembling normal.

Exactly as she had predicted, Gabriel had been monstrous at his own wedding reception. Happily it had been immediate friends and family, but the sight of her son flailing around drunkenly, even dribbling by the end of it, before finally falling over in a heap and being carried up to his room by the best man and the bride herself had been almost too much for Jessica to bear.

The débâcle of the reception had been bad enough in itself, but what was even more galling was the fact that the spectacle could have been avoided if only Rachel had taken care of him from the start. Jessica had told her so herself and the girl had even promised to take him in hand. But then what did she do? She sat there sheepishly watching Gabriel's antics, even got up and danced with him as if there was nothing unusual or undesirable going on.

It didn't bode well for the future.

Jessica was in a very difficult position. On the one hand she was pleased that Gabriel had done the right thing and decided to settle down, in the country where he was safe; she was even pleased that he had got married, even though she really didn't think it could last – surely no marriage could last based on a six-month flirtation. On the other hand, she knew that if Gabriel was given too much of a free hand he would end up getting into trouble again, just as he had in London.

The couple hadn't gone to church that morning even

though they knew Edward would have appreciated it. Jessica sighed, and decided not to worry too much about that. It was probably a good thing they hadn't shown up at the church for everyone to see what a dreadful mess Gabriel looked after his drunken debauch. She would concentrate on getting everything, and everyone, back to normal again after the wedding had turned the world upside down. She would prepare a large family supper tonight and invite Gabriel and Rachel over. That would be a good start.

It was just as Jessica had made this resolution that Gabriel appeared in person at the house, looking for her. She was delighted to see him, but from the look on his face she could see she had something to worry about, too.

'Mum, could I have a word with you? In private.'

Charlie was leaning out of the bedroom window smoking a fag when she saw Gabriel hurrying down the path.

Officially she was sulking in her room. Really she was damn glad to be out of the way of all the housework she would inevitably be dragged into after the wedding. The row she'd had with Edward and Jessica over staying out half the night when she was 'only seventeen' had been mighty handy indeed, leaving her free to smoke cigarettes, laze about listening to music and dream about her latest obsession: Thomas Hunt.

She was totally in love.

She wanted to spray-paint his name in a great psycho-tag on the ceiling of her bedroom. She couldn't, though, she had to be subtle about it. She knew she had to play her cards right this time.

The fact that Thomas was nearly ten years older than her made it totally, spectacularly brilliant. The fact that he was Gabriel's best friend going back to when they were all young – who had only ever known her as a spotty, skinny creature who was always a nuisance because she wanted to follow them round when they didn't want her anywhere near them, but who had been amazed at the change in her and now found her irresistibly attractive – made the whole thing *mega*-spectacularly brilliant.

OK, so Thomas had been patronising to her at the end when he'd wished her luck with her A-levels and then gone off to his recording session in London, but she was old enough and experienced enough to know the signs. He had looked at her in that certain way, she had caught his eye several times and she had definitely and without doubt seen him looking at her cleavage – oh, God bless Wonderbra and all who sail in her!

She was going to have him. Then she and Gabriel and Thomas – and, she supposed, Rachel – would go out together in a four. No. Perhaps Gabriel's marriage would break up and he'd get a famous artist girlfriend and they'd all go to London together – maybe Gabriel would *move back* to London. Yes! She pictured herself and Thomas walking down a street somewhere in London with Gabriel and his gorgeous, no, his *famous* girlfriend. She visualised her clothes and what Thomas would wear and what people would say when they saw them both passing, her arm through his; she saw people in street cafés, nudging each other and pointing out the attractive couple.

Charlie threw herself on to the bed, gazed up at a poster of Jean-Claude Van Damme looking his meanest and hunkiest and went to work on the plot.

The immediate problem was how to get rid of her current boyfriend, Nick, without giving him back his *Africa Generation* T-shirt.

Gabriel sat on Jessica's bed, his head drooping, his eyelashes far too long, his big eyes sad and worried.

'She still has no idea,' he said. 'And I don't want her to

find out. Ever. I don't want to keep the stuff at the Lodge in case she finds it – that would ruin everything. I tried to think of somewhere to hide it, but then I realised that I don't want it there, I don't want it to be part of my life with Rachel. I want to leave it here and come up to the house to do my injections. Do you mind?' He looked up at her. 'Do you understand?'

Jessica nodded. 'Of course.' Her heart quailed. She felt as if she were about to meet the enemy in the flesh for the first time.

Gabriel took the little bag in which he kept everything from inside his jacket as furtively as if it were a bomb. At the same time he handled the package with all the care you would give to a baby.

Methadone. Prescribed by the doctor and entirely legal, yet to Gabriel as illicit as the heroin he had used for years when he was in London, those years when he was out of touch with the family, out of touch with himself – beyond hope, or so it had seemed to Jessica.

'If Rachel doesn't find out . . . I mean, if it doesn't become part of our life here, then I'm certain everything will work out. It'll give me something to aim for. When I'm settled, I mean, when I'm working again and feeling strong, I can start to reduce the dose. I'll get off the wretched stuff for good. And never go back to it.'

Jessica nodded again. 'Good. Excellent,' she heard herself say. Her hands were trembling, but she still managed to sound calm and commanding.

'The other thing is . . .' Gabriel again looked down sheepishly.

'What?'

'Oh, no, it's all right. I can't ask you. It's not fair.'

'What's not fair?'

'Nothing, I . . .'

'Gabriel, I'm your mother. There's no reason to hide

anything from me. Especially not now, now we're together again and you've told us everything. I'm here to help. Ask me.'

He struggled to get the words out. 'Can you . . . could you . . . be here with me . . . when I . . . inject? *Please*.'

Jessica blinked. 'If that's what you want. If it . . . makes it easier.'

'It's not necessarily easier. So much as . . .'

Again his reticence.

'Gabriel, what?'

'I can't always trust myself with it. I'm scared I'll start taking too much.' He shrugged his shoulders. 'One day I'll say, "Oh just a bit more", then the next day I'll have to take more again, and then I'll be off . . . I don't know where I'll end up.'

A cold shiver ran through Jessica. The enormity of the situation struck her. Her son was in the grip of a terrifying illness – she had heard addiction described as illness and that seemed to her a sensible way of looking at it. He was asking her to save him from himself, from whatever it was inside him that was in danger of destroying him.

'Darling, I'll be here. I'll do it for you. Whatever you want. Just ask.'

'Keep it then, in here. In your bedroom. Whatever I do or say, don't give me any more than my prescription. You have to be strict.'

Jessica thought how nothing would be easier than to be strict on that score. She was overwhelmed by a desire to protect her son. As he begged for help she had been struck by his vulnerability – it was a reminder of how things used to be. This was the tiny little being she had cradled in her arms so gently, the speck of life she had once been so afraid of, so in love with. It was as if the baby had suddenly cried out in pain and she felt her old urge to pick him up and smother him with love. Only now it was not a childish pain he was suffering; he was facing death. She looked at the cold instruments of self-destruction laid out before her on the bed like so many implements of torture. 'I'll do it for you,' she said. 'I'll give you the injection myself.'

'No, mum!'

'Why not? It's the best way, surely.'

'It'd be . . . demeaning for you.'

'No. Strangely enough, I think it would reassure me. It will feel more like treatment if someone else does it for you.'

'No.'

Jessica looked at him. 'Ga-*briel*.' It was her old voice. Her stern voice. A voice from the past.

Gabriel nodded. 'You're right. It would be better.' His nose pinched up in what Jessica took to be self-hatred.

'It's for the best,' she said, thinking how it would do him no harm to hate himself for it; how it would make him all the more keen to ditch the wretched habit.

'Yes. Yes, you're right.'

'You'll have to show me how.'

They both laughed a cold sort of laugh at the irony of it. Then they went ahead and did it, Jessica with a look of grim determination on her face.

Next day

I still haven't posted this letter off! And now I need to write some more in it.

You must think that I've forgotten you. Maybe you think I'm enjoying my honeymoon. Sorry, Caroline, forgive me, but the only reason I haven't sent it off yet is that I've been busy doing nothing very much at all.

I've just read my PS resolution about not being at war with Jessica and realised that I spoke too soon!!

12

I told you I was going to go and look for Gabriel up at the house and then we were going to have a quiet night of noisy sex by the fire – the great advantage of living in the middle of nowhere is that you can make as much noise as you like when you're coming! (I hasten to add that I've yet to put this theory fully into practice!!!)

Anyway – he'd been gone ages and when I got there Jessica gave me a look as if to say, 'What business is it of yours *where* my son is?' – then says, 'He's asleep upstairs in my bedroom.' I think my face must have said something, because my lips certainly didn't. Jessica suddenly looked guilty and said, 'Shall I go and wake him?'

When he came down he was all quiet and gorgeous – he always looks a dream when he first wakes up – I always did love that dishevelled artist look!! He looked all sleepy and vulnerable. I wanted to be cross, but it was impossible. Really I wanted to run over and kiss him – oh you feeble-hearted wimp, girl!

Next thing Jessica invites us to dinner, saying it was a pity we hadn't made it to church and lunch afterwards, yesterday – meaning: So you can jolly well make up for it now you little scumbags!!!

I think my eyes must have popped out of my head, the glare I gave Gabriel – meaning: You dare say yes, you bugger, and I'm divorcing you *tonight!!!*

And guess what? My darling boy doesn't even notice. He says, 'We'd be delighted, wouldn't we, Rachel?'

I wanted to say, 'But you said you were going to shag me senseless all round the Lodge tonight.' Instead I said, 'Yes' – which might have come out as 'Ooof.'

There's more. Oh, yes, there's always more in this

exciting country life, so stay tuned, me darling! Things can only get worse!!!

So there we are sitting round the grand dining table, me trying to sound intelligent and failing miserably, Gabriel and Jessica discussing the God-awful print she bought him in New York hung in the Lodge, Charlie – Gabriel's little sister – giving me daggers and generally being a pain, when the subject of the decorating comes up.

Let me try and remember how it went.

I think it was me who started it. 'Thank you for decorating the Lodge, Jessica, it was very kind of you.' I was desperate for something to say.

She says, 'Sorry we didn't finish it.'

Gabriel says how grateful we are and I nod again. Oh hypocrite, I'd far rather she'd left us to do it ourselves.

Then Jessica starts dropping these heavy hints. 'You know how I love designing things, I would really have *loved* to do upstairs.'

Then guess who pipes up again!

'Well, do it, mum.' Gorgeous cretin! I would have booted his shin if I could have reached it.

'I'd regard it as a marvellous challenge,' says Jessica.

Then comes Charlie: 'Rachel looks like she'd rather they did the decorating themselves, mum.'

'No!' I shout. 'No, I didn't mean to imply that . . .' grovel grovel. I wouldn't dare to imply a terrible, *awful* thing like that no no no no no. Can you believe I said that!' 'No, I didn't mean that at all,' came from my own sweet, politely smiling mouth.

Then I spend the next few minutes conspiring with Gabriel – who's totally oblivious – trying to persuade Jessica that we'd absolutely love her to interfere with our upstairs.

Oh, God, do I sound completely petty? She really does mean well. She's probably bored and looking for something to do. And I'm quite sure she wants the upstairs to look stunning. But it *is* our house and I suppose *I'm* a bit bored and looking for something to do. It's all right for Gabriel, he's got his work. I really do need to feel like I'm making some sort of contribution.

Anyhow, I've decided to take the bull by the horns and speak to Jessica about it. I'm going to be assertive. I shall step up to her and quite clearly say, 'Thank you, Jessica, for the offer, but no thank you, Jessica, I'm going to do it myself.'

And now I really am going to get this in the post.

I love you madly and wish you were here, I really do.

Your Rachel xxx

Charlie and Nick were in the woods, dressed in their school uniforms.

'Charlie, have you ever had it off in the woods?'

'Course I have.'

Nick stopped. 'Do you want to do it now?'

'No.'

Nick was exasperated. They'd been walking around for ages already and Charlie hadn't even let him touch her.

'What the hell are we doing walking round in the woods if you don't want to do anything?'

'We're bunking off school, stupid.'

'Let's go over to the old barn.'

'No.'

'Why not?'

'Because I don't want to.'

'Have you got your period?'

'Oh, for God's sake! Is that your sensitive man psychology?'

Nick kicked at the undergrowth. 'No, it's my sensitive man wants a shag and isn't going to get one psychology.'

Charlie looked at him. She was beginning to get an idea.

'What's it worth?' she said in mock-sultry tones.

He grinned. 'What do you mean?'

'Sex. What would you give for a unique experience?'

'Erm. The rest of the fags?'

'I'm having them anyway.' She grabbed the proffered pack.

He shrugged. 'What do you want?'

She pretended to be thinking hard. 'How about your *Africa Generation* T-shirt? I keep it.'

He didn't like that. 'Depends.'

'What on?'

'How unique the experience is.'

'It'll be something you've never experienced before.'

'Like what?'

'Uh-uh. You have to agree to the conditions first.'

'What conditions?'

'Well, if it's something you've never experienced before, I keep the T-shirt.'

Nick was starting to get turned on, she could tell.

'OK. If it's something I've never experienced before and I *like* it, I'll give you the T-shirt.'

Shit. 'OK, yes. You have to like it.'

'OK. Deal.'

'You are desperate, aren't you,' Charlie said, as she took hold of him where it would hurt if she took hold of him any harder.

'Yeah. I'm desperate.'

She smiled. 'Right. Wait there.'

16

'What? Where are you going?'
'Just wait there. I'll be back in five.

It took fifteen.
'Where have you been!'
Charlie grinned. 'Getting my equipment. At great personal risk, I might add. I had to go to the house. I might have been seen.'
She was carrying a plastic bag.
Nick grinned. 'What's in there?'
'The equipment. Now take your clothes off.'
'What? Why, what are you going to do?'
'Just do it. You can leave your boxers on.'
He dithered for a moment, but then went for it.
'Now lie down!'
He did so.
'Turn over and put your feet together.'
'What? Why . . .'
'Just do it!'
There was some initial protest when it became obvious that Charlie was tying his feet together with rope. Nick reminded Charlie that he had to like it and Charlie reassured him that he was going to. There was further protest when she produced the blindfold until she volunteered to stop altogether. When he declined this offer she made him promise that he would go along with whatever she said.
He said, 'So long as it's sexy.'
Then she stood him up and tied his hands together behind a tree.
'Ouch! That's too tight.'
'Shut up. It's got to be done properly, or there's no point.'
'OK . . . Ouch!'
'Quiet! And that's an order.'

17

'Check there's no one around.'

She slapped him. 'I did. Now shut up.'

'I'm not sure I like this.'

'I haven't started yet! One more word and I'm not going to.'

Silence.

'OK?'

He nodded.

'Right. First I'm going to get you nice and hard.'

He was starting to like it, she could tell.

'That's better,' she said, as she stroked him and teased him and coaxed him. Nick started to moan a little, and then quite a lot.

'There. Now you're ready.' She rustled the plastic bag so that he'd know she was fetching more equipment. 'Not a word!' she threatened. She knew Nick would think she had a whip or a vibrator or something predictable like that, but she didn't. She had a pair of scissors which she promptly used to cut off his boxer shorts, leaving him stark naked.

'Now then. Your last treat,' she said, as she started to kiss her way down his body. She could tell by the way he was squirming that he was hoping beyond hope that she was going to do what she had previously refused point-blank to do. She was.

As she approached the penalty area, she paused tantalisingly. 'Do you like it?' she asked.

He nodded vigorously.

'I'm asking officially.'

The same nod.

Then she did it to him.

It had been a spontaneous decision, to do that to him. It had also been a difficult decision, and had Nick not added the proviso that he had to like what she was going to do, she would only have done what she had originally intended – which she was now going to do when she was finished with this. But she also knew that if she was going to stand any serious chance of catching or keeping the greater, the glorious and all-important prize of Thomas Hunt, she had to hone her skills.

As soon as she'd seen Nick that day she knew she was going to have to be cruel to him so that he'd leave her alone. Then when he had pestered her for sex all morning she thought she may as well try and trick him out of his *Africa Generation* T-shirt. And then, as she ran to the house to get the rope, she suddenly realised that she might as well use this as an opportunity to get some experience that would be useful to her Thomas Hunt-wise.

The thought of doing what would be horrible to do to Nick was positively exciting when she thought of doing it to Thomas. So now, as she took the plunge and put Nick into her mouth, she concentrated hard on pretending he was Thomas. That way it wasn't as bad as she thought it would be, and she might even have started to enjoy it had Nick given her time to form a clear picture of Thomas in her head before he surprised her and filled her mouth with his stuff.

Charlie swore and coughed at the same time and then spat on to the grass, leaving Nick to give the rest of his precious flow to the woodland breeze.

When the worst of it had stopped, Nick giggled. He was waiting for Charlie to say something. He'd heard her cough and curse and he wondered if he had over-stepped the mark. It occurred to him that he should perhaps have asked permission. But he would be able to argue that he wasn't able to warn her because he hadn't been allowed to speak.

She was rustling about in the plastic bag again. He thought he was for it now, but he didn't really mind. It had been a first for both of them and even though he

19

usually felt pretty miserable after he'd come, Nick wanted to kiss Charlie to death.

Then he realised there was no reaction.

Then he thought he heard something a little way off and broke his silence.

'*Charlie!*' he hissed. 'Did you hear that?'

Silence.

'*Charlie . . .*'

Charlie wasn't replying.

'Charlie! For God's sake. What's going on? Is there someone there?'

He couldn't hear anything.

'Charlie?'

Nothing.

Nor was there going to be anything. Charlie had packed all his clothes into the plastic bag and left him there, tied to the tree.

As far as she was concerned, it was over.

Gabriel felt good that morning.

He told himself it was because he was glad to have got away from London, because he felt his life was beginning again, because he was totally in love, because he was back in the bosom of his family surrounded by people who loved him. The reasons he gave himself for his elation changed from one moment to the next, but never once did he consider that it had anything to do with the fact that, in his mother's bedroom, he had just been injected with a dose of a drug large enough to kill two or three people.

He had made his excuses first thing that morning and gone up to the house, leaving Rachel to finish off her letter to Caroline. Now he and Jessica were about to enter the Lodge. Gabriel was going to work – he felt inspired.

On the way to the Lodge, Gabriel had been improvising

in his head – creating a whole moral and artistic philosophy centred round this beautiful landscape, round sights familiar to him from his youth, the feeling of the countryside infused with echoes from the past.

He had enthused Jessica who was struck by her son's *naïveté* and his boyish charm. It was as if he had by-passed the usual stages of growing up and taken all the innocent, insistent curiosity of childhood into the body and the life of a man. Jessica, of course, was only too aware of the fact that she had just given Gabriel his dangerous, mood-altering shot, and so while she marvelled at his boyish enthusiasm, she also wondered darkly if it was that aspect of his character which had taken him close to danger and death and which, without her to protect him, might well project him back there again.

When they entered the Lodge, therefore, Jessica and Gabriel were preoccupied and neither noticed that Rachel had something of a different air about her.

'Ah, morning, Rachel. I'm going into Market Cross this morning. I thought you might like a lift.' Jessica was looking round the place as she spoke.

'That would be nice. I've not had a chance for a proper look round yet,' Rachel said simply.

'I've got a couple of meetings but I thought we could meet for lunch.'

Rachel thought how any minute now Jessica would notice that something was missing.

Gabriel had flopped on to the sofa.

'It's not London,' Jessica was saying, 'but we have some interesting shops.'

Rachel smiled. 'I'd like to see them.'

Jessica's eyes stopped flitting about the room. She looked straight at Rachel. 'Then I thought we could go and see the decorators and sort out exactly what I'm going to do.'

Ah. So *that* was it. Rachel had thought as much. She was ready. She stood her ground for a moment and then said, 'I'm very grateful for the offer, Jessica, but I'd rather we did the decorating ourselves. Me and Gabriel.'

Jessica blinked. 'Oh?'

Rachel went on, 'This is our home now and I think *we* should decide what we do to it and when we do it. You're letting us live here. That's more than enough.'

Jessica's reply was icy. 'I see.'

Even Gabriel noticed the atmosphere now.

Rachel was firm. 'It's not unreasonable.'

'Well, if that's how you feel.' Jessica looked hurt suddenly. 'I was just trying to help.' Then she looked hard again. 'Of course, *Gabriel* seemed keen on me doing it last night.'

Gabriel was looking anxiously at them both.

'But it was your idea, Jessica. Gabriel didn't have the heart to say what we were really thinking.'

'I only thought it was what you wanted.' Jessica sounded defensive. 'I wouldn't have offered otherwise.'

Rachel said, 'It was very kind of you . . .'

'But you'd like me to mind my own business.' Jessica moved towards the door.

At last Gabriel opened his mouth. 'Mum, we didn't mean that. Please don't go.'

Jessica stopped and gathered herself. 'I'm not going. I'm . . . you're right. I shouldn't have interfered.' Jessica stopped. And noticed. 'You've taken down the print from New York! I thought perhaps you'd like it there.' She nodded to herself. 'But I can see now that was rather presumptuous of me. Could you let me have it back?'

Rachel said, 'Yes, of course,' a little too quickly.

Jessica said she was rather fond of it and Gabriel leapt in. 'So are we, mum. We really like it. But Rachel wanted one of mine up there.'

'So I see.'

Gabriel sighed as his mother silently picked up the print from where it was leaning forlornly against the wall next to several of Gabriel's works in progress, and left the Lodge without saying goodbye.

Rachel and Gabriel stood in silence for a moment, Rachel feeling mean and guilty in victory.

Gabriel shook his head. 'What did you do that for?'

'Because that's how I feel.'

'She's just trying to help us.'

'Yes. So she said.'

'Don't you believe her?'

'Yes, Gabriel, of course I believe her.'

'Then why upset her over a few lousy rolls of wallpaper?'

'It's not about a few rolls of wallpaper.'

'Why didn't you talk to me about it?'

'I did. You agreed we should decorate the place. Or I should.'

'Yes, but there was no need to upset her. She's been really good to us.'

Overwhelmed by guilt, Rachel became angry in her own defence. 'I know she owns this place but that doesn't mean she owns *us*, does it? This is our home now. Don't you think we should choose what we do with it? What's wrong with that?'

Gabriel sat on the sofa and sulked.

Ten minutes later Rachel was sitting on the sofa with Gabriel.

Gabriel was being gentle. 'You mustn't get things out of proportion.'

'I didn't mean to,' she said and smiled. 'Was I terribly rude?'

'You stood your ground, that's all.'

'I just want this to be our home.'

'My mother will understand that. She's not an ogre.'

Rachel sighed, grandly. 'I suppose I should go and apologise. What do you think?'

Gabriel fluttered his extra-long eyelashes. 'I think you're the most beautiful, sexy, desirable woman in the world. Especially when you're aroused.'

'I *was* rude, wasn't I? Now I've got my own way I feel dead guilty. I'll go and see her.'

'She might appreciate it.'

'You *do* think I was rude!'

Gabriel laughed. 'Let's go for a walk. I feel like taking in some landscape.'

Ten minutes after that they were walking in the woods.

Gabriel was back into his philosophical treatise on Landscapes, Life and Memories. Rachel didn't mind, she loved it when Gabriel gave vent to what she took to be his artist's heady enthusiasm.

He was telling her about a bird he'd found as a youth and had returned to freedom in this very spot. About how he'd felt as if the trees had reached down and taken the little thing back. How the woods had always seemed enchanted when he was very young and how they'd lost their charm in his adolescence when he'd been very unhappy and bored, in awe of Edward and always arguing with him. 'Dad always seemed so perfect,' he laughed. Now Gabriel said he felt that the woods were enchanted again and he felt very in touch with his childhood, especially now he felt closer to his father again.

'He still seems pretty perfect, though,' Gabriel mused.

Rachel squeezed his hand. 'Edward is a very nice, dependable and friendly man.'

'I just wish he didn't make me feel so inferior.'

'Does he? Still?'

Gabriel sighed. 'Yes. But not as much as he used to. If I can just . . . I mean, if I can get my act together I'm sure I'll feel better.'

'Gabriel, you've got your act together. You've just sold a painting for two thousand pounds.'

'That was a fluke.'

Rachel stopped in her tracks. 'Don't be daft, no one pays two thousand pounds for a painting if they don't think it's a good painting – they probably think it'll be worth more soon, too, because you're going to be famous.'

Gabriel's mouth curled at the edges. 'Well, I'm going to start work here now. I'm going to try and get this feeling of renewal, of childhood revisited into my work. I just need to get myself together.'

Rachel squeezed his arm. 'You will. You will.'

Gabriel sighed and agreed that he might.

Rachel laughed. 'Anyway, it doesn't matter what you think. Your work speaks for itself.'

Gabriel turned to her, suddenly. Urgently almost. 'You really believe in me, don't you?'

'Of course, yes. I really believe you will be a great artist.'

'I want to be a great artist for *you*,' he said with his customary *naïveté*. 'I want to succeed so that you'll love me and stay with me.'

Rachel frowned. 'Gabriel, I love you. You being a great artist doesn't make any difference to that. I want you to be a great artist because it'll make you happy. I love your paintings, but I'd stay with you if our house was falling down and the rain was coming through the roof, so long as you were happy.'

Gabriel looked at her with his black, beautiful eyes and smiled. 'God, I want to make love to you. Let's search out some springy grass.' As he ran ahead looking for a spot, he shouted, 'That should infuse the landscape with some new feelings!'

Rachel ran after him, laughing.

They had just found a nice secluded patch of woodland turf when Gabriel said, 'Did you hear something?'

Rachel listened. 'No.'

'I'm sure I heard someone.'

Then Rachel heard it too. 'Sounded like someone calling Charlie.'

'Can't be, she's at school.'

Rachel raised her eyebrows. 'She's *supposed* to be at school.'

'Huh. Good point. Yes, there it is again.'

'*Charlie! Come on, where the hell are you?*'

They looked at each other.

'Let's go and see what's going on.'

As they got nearer, the calling got angrier.

'Sounds like Nick,' Gabriel said. 'Charlie's boyfriend.'

Sure enough, when they approached they could hear Nick cursing and swearing, but in a funny kind of subdued shout. Something in his tone made Gabriel and Rachel want to tip-toe towards him, instead of calling out to him. When they finally caught sight of him tied to the tree, stark naked and blindfolded, they fell about laughing, but quietly, which made it all the more amusing to them.

When she had recovered some of her composure, Rachel said, 'Leave this to me.'

Gabriel looked shocked.

Rachel grinned. 'I'm sick of people thinking I'm some sort of goody-goody, just 'cause I'm married to you.'

She kissed Gabriel, walked silently up to Nick and whistled gently, as if she was Charlie returning to the scene of the crime and letting him know she had come back.

Nick fell for it right away. 'Charlie, you bastard . . . I'm going to kill you ... come on, untie me ... and next time you suck me off I'm tying *you* up!' he spat out before Rachel had time to speak.

'Actually, it's not Charlie, it's me – Rachel.' Quickly she untied him and offered him her cardigan to cover some of his embarrassment.

·2·

EDWARD WAS SEATED at his desk in the office, feeling very grand.

There was something about the ancient leather and the oak panelling that was deeply satisfying. The lines of old books, the faded prints of past and forgotten bishops, the smell of polish and the great leather-topped desk, even the antique leather *chaise longue*, in the corner gave the atmosphere a grave and serious tone that Edward enjoyed. If business was grave or serious, especially if it were religious, solemnity came naturally, reverence reverberated in the very wood and dark varnish, it hung from the picture frames. Yet if affairs demanded a lighter tone, then one simple word of humour or reassurance against such a background had twice the effect. Edward knew that in the domain of his study, as he preferred to call it, he appeared larger than himself, commanding and grand, a modern version of the figures that loomed out of the great gold-patterned frames hanging on the walls of the study, the outer office and the corridors of the building itself. His relaxed manner gave his official personage the appearance of great warmth and kindness, which was, Edward felt, essential to a successful bishop.

It had been a busy day, full and eventful, one which had required his skills as diplomat, despot, husband and father-in-law. Each encounter had been a success and now, as he reflected on the day, he leaned back in his ancient office chair and sighed, thinking how the best was yet to come.

He called his secretary, Anne, asking her to make them a cup of tea and enquiring whether she could make herself available for some extra work when things had settled down and the phone had stopped ringing. She said that she had one or two things to finish off, but she would be able to stay late if that was what Edward wanted.

First had come today's diplomacy.

Simon, the parish vicar, had again gone against specific diocesan instruction – directly from Bishop Harris himself – and married a divorced couple. Edward had wanted to blow up there and then, filling his chair with blood and thunder, but, statesman-like, he had successfully held his temper in order to extract a full confession of guilt and find out if anything similar had been planned. This tactic also had the advantage of giving him a stronger hand to use against Simon later, when he had spoken to Bishop Harris himself and when Simon would not be able to blame Edward's anger only on a show of temper.

Extreme diplomacy was required with Bishop Harris, who had personally telephoned Edward the very moment he caught wind of the affair. Bishop Harris was, of course, a personal friend, but nevertheless Edward had needed to reassure him that his authority locally was intact and that Simon's action was simple, youthful idealism, in other words not an act of open rebellion against church authority.

Then came the despotism.

Using nothing more than utmost gravity, Edward had made Simon quake in his boots. He told him he had personally prevented Simon's career from being irreversibly damaged and that he hoped there would be no further examples of recklessness and stupidity on his part. He dismissed the young priest without any hint of forgiveness, judging it better to let Simon fear him for a day or so. Then, when Edward later talked to Simon in a friendly tone, he knew the young man would be very pleased to hear it. At this point they would have a friendly chat to clear the air and reassert Simon's subservience to the greater good for the church's authority. Edward liked Simon, he even admired the young priest's naïve idealism, but the bishop would not tolerate undue attention being paid to the parish.

Next, Edward had been a father-in-law.

He felt a little sympathy for Rachel and had been heartily glad she felt able to come and see him with her troubles. He thought she was a grand girl, but he knew she would have her hands full both in terms of Gabriel and adjusting to life at Market Cross.

When his secretary, Anne, showed her in, Rachel looked positively forlorn.

'I've been doing some shopping and I thought I'd come and say hello to my brand-new father-in-law.'

Edward was very pleased indeed. 'That's very sweet of you. Please have a chair. Would you like a sherry?'

'Yes, yes. I think I would, thank you.'

Edward was delighted to fuss around with the bottle and glasses while they spoke. 'So you're settling in at the Lodge?'

Rachel hesitated.

Edward nodded. 'But you're finding things a bit strange, adjusting to country life. You're a city girl.'

'Yes, but it's not just that. It's everyone knowing your business.'

Edward smiled. 'At least you haven't got neighbours looking over the garden wall.'

'No. No one except you and Jessica.'

'Yes, yes, it's nice to be so close.'

Rachel faltered. 'Yes, yes, it's nice.'

Edward's ear picked up the tremor. 'Ah. But not that close, eh? Did Jessica call on you this morning, by any chance?'

'Yes, to see how her chicks are settling into the nest.'

Edward tried to fill the room with reassuring sentiment. 'And? Come along, you can talk to your brand-new father-in-law. I can see Jessica's done something.' Rachel looked very sad and Edward's heart ached for her. 'Jessica must have *said* something then?'

Rachel was very flustered. 'Jessica said she was going to decorate the bedrooms. And I don't want her to. I'm not ungrateful. I just think Gabriel and myself should decide what we do with our home.'

Edward gave his most reassuring nod and hummed sympathetically. 'I understand exactly how you feel,' he said.

'It must sound like I'm telling tales. I didn't come here to talk about this. And I'd hate Jessica to think . . . you won't tell her I mentioned anything, will you?'

Edward could see the girl was in some pain. He told her he thought she and Jessica were going to be best of friends and explained that Jessica had some readjusting to do herself and then they chatted about nothing very much at all until her troubles seemed forgotten and Rachel went away smiling.

Then came Jessica and he was the husband again, which, as all husbands know, meant being another kind of diplomat.

'Edward I was just telling Anne that I won't be able to do the reading for tonight's service; she said you were on the phone.'

Edward had just come into the outer office. Jessica and

31

his secretary were sorting out the rota for the flower-arranging. Edward watched the two women for a moment with something of the air of a proud father, then said, 'Is there anything you want to speak to me about, Jessica?'

'No, Edward. I'll go straight off.'

'Well, I wonder if I could have a word with you before you go.'

'Ah, yes, of course. Excuse me, Anne.'

By the time Edward had seated himself behind his desk and Jessica had perched on the visitor's chair, Jessica already knew what Edward wanted to say, even though there were no more grounds for her prior knowledge than the conversation they had just had in the outer office.

She spoke first. 'I need to go so as to be there for Gabriel, Edward. He needs to feel secure.'

Edward nodded. 'And we must give him that security. I shall ask Anne to do the reading. She's working late this evening anyhow.'

Jessica nodded. And waited.

After a moment Edward went on, 'Yes, we must give Gabriel all the support we can.' He took a breath. 'I do feel for Rachel, however.'

Jessica's lips tightened fractionally. 'It was Gabriel's decision not to tell her. Not mine. He thinks it's in the best interests of their marriage. We have to respect that.'

'Yes. She's a sensitive soul. She came to see me this afternoon.'

Jessica pretended to be surprised. 'Did she? What for?'

'As a matter of fact she talked about you. I gather you two had a disagreement.'

Despite herself, Jessica was angered. She tried not to show it. 'Nonsense, Edward. The girl was foolish enough to turn down a perfectly good offer. That's all there is to it.'

'She denied it, but I got the distinct impression she felt she'd offended you.'

'How could she offend me?'

'She was most anxious that I didn't say anything to you. In case it looked as though she'd come scuttling to me behind your back.'

Jessica raised her eyebrows. 'That's exactly what she did, isn't it?'

The diplomat said, 'You've obviously made quite an impression on her, my dear.'

His wife softened. 'Yes, well. She's no need to worry. I'm only her mother-in-law. She's the wife.'

Edward smiled at her. 'I'll see you later, then, shall I? After mass.'

About half an hour later, exactly on cue, the phone stopped ringing, Edward's secretary shut down her computer and officially closed up shop for the evening.

She was a very efficient secretary and could be relied upon to protect Edward from all those unnecessary distractions that can make the life of a bishop impossible. People always asked to speak to the bishop when really, if it was an administrative matter, Anne could sort it out far more quickly herself. If it were a spiritual matter, Anne would first send people to Simon who was after all the parish priest, and only when it really was a matter for the bishop and the bishop alone, did Anne finally disturb Edward at his work.

Edward took pains to let her know that he appreciated her very much. She was a fine woman in every way. She was both young and capable. She always looked exactly right on every occasion and Edward loved to look at her as she went about her work. He appreciated her wavy red hair and the way she walked. He liked the deep blue of her eyes and the way she looked at him when he complimented her.

As he sat there thinking over the day and thinking

about his secretary, she came through into the office and closed the fine oak double doors behind her. She stood as if waiting to be given some instructions.

Edward looked at her and smiled. 'Is everything finished for the day, Anne?'

Anne nodded.

'Good. And did Jessica speak to you about tonight's reading?'

'Yes,' said Anne. 'It's a very good reading,' she said and quoted from it: '"If we say we have no sin, we deceive ourselves and the truth is not in us."'

Edward smiled at her. 'John. Chapter one. Verse eight.'

Anne returned his smile and locked the door behind her. Then she began to unbutton her dress at the front. As he watched, she gently slid the straps of her dress from her shoulders and let it slip to the floor.

Anne stood there in her underwear, while Edward came around his desk to take her in his arms and press her up against the fine oak of the double doors. Then they made love on the ancient leather *chaise longue* while grand and austere personages of a different age looked on from dark old paintings.

·3·

Dear Caroline,

It was so good to talk to you on the phone last night. I'm so glad things are working out for you in London at last.

I've decided to write my diary to you. So aren't you the lucky one! I'm going to write it when I need to talk. I'll send it off to you in weekly instalments. When I come and see you, you can show me what a fool I'm being, or preferably how I've matured and become self-aware!! You know what it's like here – I mean I can talk to Gabriel honestly about what's going on for me, but somehow I feel I need to talk to *myself* about what's going on. And that's what it's like talking to you – it's like talking to me. That's how close I feel to you, my darling friend. Gosh, I'm getting slushy, aren't I?

Anyway. I went up to the house this morning to apologise to Jessica like I said I would. Edward was there – they were both having breakfast together and it actually looked quite cosy. You know I really like Edward, he's such a kind-hearted man. Now I know where Gabriel gets his soft side.

I told you I went to see Edward in the office yesterday and he was just so lovely. The office is a very grand sort of place, very dark and there's all these old pictures all over the place and a proper leather desk – in fact the whole place is covered in leather!! (Sounds kinky doesn't it?!!) But Edward just sits there and nods and it makes you feel dead nice and calm. I'm not surprised his marriage to Jessica has lasted. I mean, she's kind of cold and fussy, but underneath she must be warm. I bet she's madly in love with Edward underneath that hard shell of hers.

Gosh, I've just read this back and it sounds like I'm in love with Edward, doesn't it? I suppose I am a bit in love with him because he's Gabriel's father and I love Gabriel so much that I love everything about him. Mind you – that doesn't seem to apply to Jessica does it!! So maybe I am a bit in love with Edward in a daughterly kind of way.

So, anyway – there they both were, Jessica and Edward, having breakfast together when I blunder in and ask if I can speak to Jessica – hinting that I wanted to see her alone. You know I'm so suspicious – I'm sure she knew I wanted to see her alone but she made me stand there in front of Edward – who was obviously in too much of a hurry to give us space. So I say, 'I've left Gabriel hard at work at the Lodge. Isn't it beautiful there? I've fallen in love with the place already . . .' and words to that effect. Edward chipped in that it was good to see the Lodge being put to good use and Jessica just ummed and smiled like she does when you know she doesn't approve of something. So I just came straight out and apologised. 'Well . . . um . . . um . . . er . . . well, I hope, Jessica . . . you . . . er . . . um . . . didn't think I was being ungrateful . . . I thought you might have . . . er . . . yesterday . . .

Anyway I'm sorry if I offended you.' By the time I'd got it out I felt like a little girl with her toes curling inwards talking to her teacher.

So then Jessica says, 'My dear girl, it's only wallpaper. It would take a lot more than that to offend me.'

And that was that. Somehow, although she didn't say anything at all other than exactly the right thing, it was as if I'd been a total and complete imbecile and made an utter fool of myself. So then I crawled back here and wrote this. I'm blushing as I write to you. It feels like I've been turned down and forced to walk around on my hands for half a morning because I decided to get humble and apologise to Jessica.

Gabriel's nowhere to be seen – he seems able to disappear here in Market Cross as easily as he did in London! – so I'm going to catch the bus into town and do something rash in a clothes shop to cheer myself up.

Oh the ongoing saga of daughter-in-lawdom!!

While Rachel was busy apologising to Jessica, Gabriel was upstairs lying on Jessica and Edward's bed, recovering from his morning injection.

By the time he went downstairs the house was empty and when he arrived at the Lodge that was empty too. So he sat and stared into space for about an hour, thinking foggily that he ought to be getting on with his work and vaguely fantasising about himself as a great modern painter with a mission to create the perfect landscape imbued with reflections of childhood – perhaps even with night-mares subtly painted into the background so that at first they weren't noticeable and everything looked perfectly normal.

37

He was awoken from his reveries by a knock on the door.

It was Charlie. She let herself in and came over to the sofa where he was sitting. 'So, get the whisky out, then.'

Gabriel grinned. 'It's funny, you know. I was just thinking I could do with a little drink.'

Charlie said, 'I'll go.' And while she poured him a drink and he rubbed the sleep from his eyes, she said, 'I feel like getting really pissed.'

'Haven't you got anything else to do?'

Charlie laughed. 'I'd rather stay here with you. How often do we get the chance to talk?'

'Oh, you want a serious discussion, do you? That's a first.'

'There's a first time for everything. You should know that!'

Gabriel smiled. 'What's brought this on? Is it the fact that you don't want to go to school by any chance?'

Charlie handed him a large glass of whisky. 'I want you to know we care about you, that's all.'

'Who's we?'

'Well. Me, mum and dad.'

Gabriel raised his glass. 'Thanks. The feeling's mutual.'

Charlie sat back. 'We were talking about you last night at tea, about mum helping you with your injections.'

Gabriel's jaw dropped.

Charlie went on, 'I think it's a really good idea.'

Gabriel managed to stay relatively calm. 'What exactly did mum tell you?'

'Everything.'

He was openly angry now. 'This was between me and her. I didn't want everyone to know.'

'It's OK, Gabriel, I'm your sister, I'm family, I can handle it. I told you, I care about you. I want to help you.'

Gabriel felt bitter and took a great gulp from his glass. 'I don't need your help. I don't need mum, either. She's just getting me into a routine, that's all.'

'Relax, Gabriel. Mum was worried. She just needed to talk it through – with dad really, but she trusted me to keep it secret.'

Gabriel looked very grave. 'You mustn't tell Rachel.'

Charlie smiled, confidently. 'I won't. Trust me.'

Gabriel took another gulp of scotch. 'I thought about telling her. But I never did. I never seemed to find the right moment. And suddenly it was too late. I love her. I don't want to lose her.'

Charlie nodded far too knowingly. 'She'd run a mile if she knew.'

'She believes in me. She believes I can achieve something. I don't want her to lose faith in me.'

Charlie was patronising. 'There's no reason she should. You just get yourself clean.'

Gabriel nodded and thought how strongly the whisky was affecting him already. 'Right. There's no heroin now. And eventually there'll be no methadone either. So Rachel need never know.'

'Exactly, bro.'

Gabriel stared at the little bit of drink remaining in his glass. 'Sorry for shouting,' he said, miserably. 'I just *hate* feeling so useless, having mum discuss me like that – I hate being a problem.'

Charlie patted Gabriel's arm. 'You're not a problem, forget it. You're my big brother, and I love you.' She knocked back the rest of her own drink. 'What I've always loved about you is the fact that you take risks. You don't give a damn.'

Gabriel realised what Charlie was saying and frowned at her, big-brother style. 'What I did, Charlie, was lose control of my life. And that's not daring or exciting. It's hell. And if you've got any sense, you won't let it happen to you.'

Charlie was indignant. 'I don't intend to! But I don't see what's wrong with a bit of danger.'

Gabriel grinned. 'That's exactly what I'm worried about.'

Charlie grinned now, too. 'Anyway,' she said settling back into her chair, 'tell me all about Thomas Hunt.'

Gabriel frowned, quizzically. 'Thomas? You know most of it.'

'OK. Well, tell me about him again.'

'What do you want to know?'

'Like, has he got a girlfriend?'

'Ha, Thomas? Na, he's far too . . . well, he just doesn't bother.'

'What, you mean he just shags girls and then drops them?' Charlie asked with a certain glint in her eye.

Gabriel shrugged. 'Yeah, he's like you. A bastard.'

'I'm not a bastard!' Charlie laughed.

So did Gabriel. 'I don't think Nick would agree with that proposition.'

'If you must know, brother dear, Nick has been on the phone three times since I abandoned him in the woods. I thought he would take the hint, but unfortunately I've got myself involved with some kind of perverted masoch-ist. He was practically begging me to meet him again today.' She shook her head dismally. 'I didn't bloody ask to be forgiven. Dick-head.'

'Why don't you just tell him it's over? I mean, then he'd know, wouldn't he?'

Charlie shrugged. 'Na. He doesn't speak proper Eng-lish. He only understands sign language.' She went to drink from her glass and tutted. 'Empty.' She went over to the bottle and held it up. 'Oh, dear. Empty, too.'

Gabriel said, 'Shit.'

Charlie suggested going up to the house for supplies. 'There's no one there.'

Gabriel grabbed his jacket. 'Let's go.'

Jessica had a few things to pick up from the office so she went in with Edward.

Edward was always flustered when he was going away, so Jessica sat quietly in the corner with her check-list, ticking off names and making the odd phone call to check availability for the coffee morning the following Tuesday.

It wasn't long before Edward was furiously stomping around the office, giving his usual pre-conference performance. Jessica wondered how his secretary put up with his tantrums. She knew that he would never dream of speaking to her, Jessica, like that.

'Anne! Anne! I told you not to worry about the monthly figures. It was far more important to type up my address!'

'The address is typed up and waiting for you on your desk, Edward.'

Jessica admired Anne's amiability under pressure.

'Ah, there it is.' Edward was back in his office now and he could be heard through the large double doors, bossing Anne about. 'Anne, why didn't you tell me you'd put it here, instead of just assuming I'd see it?'

It was always the same when he went away for a weekend – and that was quite often. Edward was a different man when his routine was upset in any way.

Jessica watched Edward and Anne together out of the corner of her eye while she got on with her own arrangements. Anne had definitely got the measure of her husband, that was for sure. Jessica had seen Edward get through quite a list of secretaries over the years. They were nearly always the same type of woman – it was as if he had a *type* of secretary. They even looked the same.

Same age, same looks, same way of doing what Edward wanted when Edward wanted it done and generally not having much of a life of their own. Quiet little mice that he could bully with impunity. Jessica laughed to herself – his secretaries were not like his wife, that was for sure.

Then Edward was ready with his coat on, his briefcase in one hand, his carry-all in the other and Jessica was the wife saying, 'Goodbye, dear,' and kissing him on the cheek. 'See you in a day or so.'

Jessica noticed that Simon was very keen to carry Edward's bag and give him a lift to the station after their little set-to the other day. Edward still wasn't giving Simon any indication that he was forgiven and Simon was practically scraping his nose on the floor in his eagerness to please.

'Here's the flower-arranging rota, all printed up,' Anne said to Jessica, when they were alone.

Jessica smiled. 'You won't have made any slip-ups, will you?'

Anne smiled, too. 'No.'

'You never do make any, do you?' Jessica said.

Anne shook her head. 'I try not to.'

Jessica was packing up ready to leave. 'You know, I admire you, Anne. I know *I* couldn't put up with him treating *me* like that. It really isn't good enough.'

'It's water off a duck's back to me.'

'Well, I admire you. And, let me tell you, so does Edward. He speaks highly of you behind your back.'

Anne smiled again. 'I should turn my back more often.'

'You'll have to forgive him. He's always been like that with his secretaries. I've seen him go through enough of you. He treats you all the same. He hasn't deserved any of you.'

42

Anne nodded at this, not seeming to want to make any comment.

'You all leave him in the end. And I don't blame you.'

'Yes, I'm sure,' Anne said, and went quickly back to her work.

'Well, goodbye.'

'Goodbye, Jessica.'

Gabriel and Charlie were well drunk now.

Charlie had found her father's very best whisky and they had not kept to their promise that they would have only one each. The bottle was nearly empty. They had both fallen into that appalling stage of drunkenness, deepest nostalgia.

Charlie was sprawled on the sofa. 'Remember that Christmas eve when I was about eight?'

Gabriel laughed. 'No.'

'I'd been allowed to stay up to watch something on TV. I was sitting here on this very sofa and there was this great bang and crash through there in the kitchen. Don't you remember, Gabriel?'

'Go on.'

'It was you. Out of your skull.'

Gabriel roared at the memory. 'I fell through the front door!'

'Then you came in here, bleeding. Staggering. Swaying. Mum sent me to bed but I sat at the top of the stairs . . .'

'Typical. You never do anything you're told.'

'I could hear her shouting at you. Screaming and shouting.'

Gabriel was still laughing at the memory. 'I remember.'

'And all you did was laugh. You just laughed in her face. And then, can you remember what you did then?'

Gabriel frowned. 'No. God, was it awful?'

'You sang "Silent Night". And yes – it was *bloody* awful!'

'It *was* Christmas.'

'Oh, you were so brilliant, Gabriel.' Charlie sighed. And drank more whisky.

Gabriel said, 'Anyway – you've got room to talk!'

'Yeah?'

'Yeah. Do you remember the time Mary had to fetch you home from school?'

'Oh, God, was Mary still having to clear up after me in those days?'

Gabriel chortled. 'Let's face it, Mary has been house-keper in this house since the medieval period.'

'But, anyway, why did she have to come and fetch me?'

'Don't you remember, Charlie, you naughty girl?' She shook her head. 'You'd hit someone.'

Charlie yelped. 'Christine Baxter! My best friend . . .'

And so it went on until Charlie was drooping over Gabriel like a tramp over a ragged friend. And, except that both wore expensive clothes and the sofa was worth over a thousand pounds, there was no difference now. Drunkards all.

In town that afternoon, Jessica had the good fortune to bump into Rachel.

Both women were ill at ease, Rachel after her apology and Jessica because there was no other family member there for her to hide behind. But Rachel had some good news, so things went passably well.

'I got a job,' Rachel beamed. She was glad to have someone to tell.

'Rachel, how marvellous.' Jessica couldn't help but think that it was a good thing because Rachel would be out of the way at convenient times of the day. She scolded herself for the thought. 'When do you start?'

'Right away. I saw the advert in the window of the insurance office and went straight in. They took me on there and then.' Rachel smiled. 'To be honest, I don't think there's much competition.'

Jessica tutted. 'Nonsense, there's plenty of girls looking for work.'

So on the strength of having something to talk about they went for a coffee and then to a few shops and before they knew it it was closing time, so Jessica gave Rachel a lift home.

It was getting quite late by the time they arrived. Jessica said she wanted to speak to Gabriel. Rachel went straight to the kitchen with her shopping, calling for Gabriel who obviously wasn't in. Jessica went into the living room and immediately spotted two empty glasses and the empty whisky bottle. She knew Rachel hadn't been drinking. Quickly she put them into her bag, made her excuses and left with her customary chilly air, which Rachel spotted immediately with a twinge of dismay.

By now, Charlie had got as far as trying to kiss Gabriel.

'You've got to show 'em who's boss, Gabriel, that's my motto. One of 'em. See, you and me – we're brilliant. You're going to be a brilliant painter and I'm . . . me, I'm just going to be brilliant.'

Gabriel was slurring awfully. 'You've had it too easy, Charlie. You don't know what it's like to *really* suffer.'

Charlie wasn't listening. 'No one's going to tell *me* what to do!'

'It's just a kid's game to you, isn't it? If you get into trouble somebody grabs you by the hand and drags you home kicking and screaming.'

Charlie couldn't believe it. 'Hark who's barking!'

But Gabriel was too far gone to notice. 'You know what I could never handle? When we were young?' he asked, miserably. 'Our Father . . . huh . . . that's what my friends used to call him. That and "God".' Gabriel raised his glass. 'Cheers, dad.'

They both drank, and Gabriel went on, 'When I was little, when I said my prayers at night, that was who I saw: God our father. Him. I always used to try and be like, like he wanted me to be, but whenever I did it was never good enough. I mean, how do you compete with perfection?'

Charlie grunted and said, 'Have another drink.' She knew how Gabriel felt all right. 'We need another bottle,' she slurred.

In a sudden burst of anger, Gabriel stumbled to his feet and hurled his glass across the room. 'To hell with it!' he growled. 'Fuck it all!'

Gabriel noticed Jessica standing at the drawing-room door just a moment before Charlie copied him and threw her glass across the room.

When Charlie noticed Jessica, she just laughed in her mother's face.

Charlie was sent to her room like a naughty child.

She was too drunk to protest for long. She fell asleep on her bed almost as soon as she lay on it. An hour later she was sick all over her bedspread and didn't wake up until the middle of the night when she had to clear it up as best she could. She was sick again then and again later.

After Charlie had been dispatched, Gabriel, although very drunk, was nearly overwhelmed by guilt as he stood, swaying, in front of his mother. He was hardly able to look at her. 'I'd better go,' he mumbled.

Jessica's eyes flashed. 'And let Rachel see you like this?'

Gabriel stood helpless, stranded. Like a child.

46

'And what happens in the middle of the night when you wake up needing your injection?' Jessica was hissing, her anger almost tangible.

Gabriel felt again that old feeling of needing to obey his mother, needing to hide from her voice by pleasing her.

Jessica went on, 'Because I can't give it to you now. Do you understand? If I gave you your injection now, you'd probably die! Do you see what you've done? You foolish boy. *Foolish!*'

Gabriel shrugged his broad, bony shoulders, wishing his mother would tell him what to do.

Ten minutes later he was lying, nearly asleep, in his mother's bed.

She was sitting on the side of the bed, stroking his hair affectionately. He felt infinitely safe, and very drunk. He wanted to close his eyes and go to sleep.

'Go to sleep, darling,' Jessica was saying. 'Go to sleep.'

Rachel was sitting in near darkness when Jessica called back at the Lodge.

'Jessica! I thought you might be Gabriel. He's not back, I'm afraid. I don't know where he is. He didn't leave a note or anything.' As soon as she'd said this, Rachel felt a twinge of regret at having shown Jessica her vulnerability, so she added, confidently, 'He'll be back soon, I'm sure,' to show Jessica that she wasn't overly concerned.

'He won't, actually. Be back,' Jessica said. 'He tried to reach you, but you were out so he left a message with Mary.'

Rachel frowned and felt suddenly resentful. 'Is anything wrong? Is he all right?'

'He's fine.'

'Where is he?'

'He's in London.'

'London? Where in London?'

Jessica shook her head.

Rachel was angry. Why was Jessica being so vague? It was as if she was trying to make the most of the fact that she knew where Gabriel was and she, his wife, didn't. 'Gabriel didn't say anything about going to London,' Rachel said, keeping reasonably calm.

'It was a spur-of-the-moment decision, apparently. You know Gabriel.'

'What's he doing there?' Rachel asked. Why didn't she just come out and tell her the whole story? Rachel felt as if she was having to screw the information out of Jessica, but decided to keep her cool at all costs.

'Do you know that friend of his? Runs a gallery? You know, they were at school together?'

Rachel didn't know, no.

'The gallery's been going through a rough patch. No?'

Rachel still didn't know, no.

'They're particularly anxious to exhibit some of Gabriel's paintings. They have a long-standing agreement.'

Rachel shook her head. 'I still don't understand. Why did he go today?'

Jessica waved a hand. 'Gabriel's very excited about the work he's doing here . . .'

'He hasn't done any yet.'

'Er . . . no. But he's got something planned. A whole series, apparently. Mary said he said he wanted to discuss the idea with someone in the business.'

'Why didn't he leave me a note?' Rachel said.

'I think he intended to get back by this evening. Perhaps he wanted to surprise you.' Jessica faltered. 'I don't know. Of course he should have left you a note.'

'So where is he, exactly? What did he say to Mary?'

'Oh, there's been some kind of bomb-scare. Trains are being cancelled, so his friend suggested he stay over.'

At last. 'Oh, I see. Well, thank you for telling me. Will he be back tomorrow?'

'Oh yes. First thing. I mean, as soon as he can get a train.' Jessica smiled. 'You know he can't bear to be away from you for very long.'

Rachel appreciated the remark. 'Yes. Thank you for coming to tell me.'

'You'll be all right here on your own, won't you?'

'Of course, yes.'

Jessica felt a lightness in her step on the way back to the house. She was relieved that Rachel had believed her story.

Rachel went to bed and cried.

And, of course, that night, for the first time since he was a baby, Jessica slept in bed with her son.

·4·

THE CONFERENCE WAS a bore.

In Edward's experience, all church conferences were a bore. The truth was, Edward reflected, that none of those who attended church conferences had any interest whatever in the subject-matter. They all came to get away from something or someone and to forget themselves and their routines for a day or two. The church was, Edward reflected, a profession like any other, with all the same vices and probably not as many virtues.

It had been a long time since Edward had seriously attended to the business of spreading the word of God throughout the world. This is what he had imagined he was doing in his younger days. As he yawned his way through the opening, late-afternoon session on 'The Role of Communion in the Modern Church Community' – a subject that would have thrilled him when he had just 'graduated' – Edward took a few moments to reflect on the nature of the changes that had, imperceptibly, taken place in his life and indeed in his heart over the years.

In the early days of his work and of his marriage to Jessica, when the flame of passion still burned in both,

Edward had himself been full of fire. He had drawn notice to himself as a progressive at a time when such ideas were highly thought of in the church, as in the rest of society. His energy, enthusiasm, even his controversy-seeking zeal, had contributed to his rapid rise within the diocese and had brought him to the attention of the central organising body of the church. He was the youngest bishop to have been appointed in the last hundred years.

With the responsibility had come a greater acceptance of the church as it actually was rather than as he wanted it to be. His work-load had increased and his responsibilities had become administrative as much as spiritual. His children had come and Jessica had been preoccupied with them and his energies had dwindled and his ideals modified ever earthwards. But even this had gone in his favour, because with the change in the times came a change in the church and Edward was again promoted. Again his responsibilities were increased and his work further removed from the everyday spiritual life of the parish.

As Edward reflected, he felt sorry for the young priests like Simon whose progressive energies were destined to cause only frustration while their careers were usurped by well-trained bookworms and Bible-lizards whose ideals – or lack of ideals – suited the times. It occurred to Edward, then, that, ironically, in the long run Simon might benefit from the lack of a responsible position within the church hierarchy which would distract him from immediate engagement with the spiritual life.

It was only over years that real change took place in one's life. Like the hands of a clock, movement was discernible only if your attention was elsewhere for a time; when you looked back the hands had moved to a different position, life had changed, gone, the movement was impossible to detect until it was too late. Here he was, a fifty-year-old bishop, attending a conference that held no interest other than that of escape from his routine. He was bored. His religious work now consisted of simple, everyday tasks performed with dutiful attention to detail, rather than with love. Keeping the spirit of the parish alive now consisted of saying mass twice a week to a half-empty church, writing endless memos and circulars about matters that affected few people and interested even fewer, and the odd visit to an ailing parishioner. It was this last activity that Edward considered to be his most honestly Christian these days. Even though he was often not very attentive or sympathetic when he actually conducted a visit – the sufferers were often in no fit state to notice Edward stifling a yawn or nodding distractedly at their remarks – once he had performed his duty and was driving home, Edward felt good about himself, closer to God. He would resolve at times like these to take on more work of the compassionate kind, but then, as the daily routine settled him back into his ways, he forgot all about his resolution until the next time.

The lecture finished at last, but the questions session dragged on interminably. Just as one subject became exhausted so another, equally uninspiring, came up for discussion. Edward was amazed by the interest some people were showing and infuriated by the length of time the discussions took. But then not everyone at the conference had the same interest in post-discussion activities that he had.

Even after the questions session Edward was intercepted and detained by a couple of young priests who remembered him from another conference. The two young men seemed determined to prevent him from getting back to his hotel. To get away Edward had to twice lie, which irritated him greatly. Then he realised he was hungry and that was why he was so irritated. Being away from home it was easy to forget things like eating on time.

Then, at long last, and with a lightness of step he felt only at such times of release, Edward was free to return to his room and hide away from the world. The hotel was one of the better ones and Edward had been delighted when he arrived to drop off his bag that morning.

The key was not at reception, which made Edward smile.

He took the stairs to the third floor and let himself into the room, which wasn't locked.

He could hear Anne in the bathroom, in the bath.

That was the great pleasure of conferences. Furtive sex on sofas, in offices, had its appeal, but Edward preferred to take his time these days, and the hotel room with its *en suite* bathroom seemed to him the ideal venue for long, luxurious, passionate excursions into the realm of the human comforts, which is what he and Anne had planned.

Anne had heard him.

'Come in, the water's lovely,' she called.

He did so.

Gabriel was aware of a severe pain in his head.

He was in his mother's bed. She had just opened the curtains.

'Oh, my God. What time is it?'

Jessica sounded as bright as the light. 'Half past eight. It occurred to me that your train might be leaving about now. Say it takes an hour and ten minutes. Then you jump into a taxi. Another ten minutes. You've got about an hour and a half before you should be getting back to the Lodge.'

Gabriel stared at her blankly and sat up.

Jessica nodded. 'You don't remember.'

He grimaced and shook his head. 'I'm catching a train?'

'No, but Rachel thinks you are. I had to tell her

53

something to explain why you weren't tucked up beside her in bed last night.'

Gabriel remembered now. 'Ah.'

Jessica explained the story without a word of admonition.

At the end of it Gabriel said, 'Thanks, mum.'

Jessica said, 'You behaved very badly.'

Gabriel hung his head. 'I'm so sorry.'

'I'm not saying worse than other occasions, but on those occasions you weren't married.'

Despite his apparent calm, there was nothing Gabriel could do to stop the tears that welled up and choked him. Jessica immediately stopped scolding and put her arm around him while he sobbed and apologised over and over, saying he was utterly hopeless and he'd definitely get himself together, he owed it to Jessica and Edward and Rachel and just about everyone else he could think of.

'You owe it to yourself, Gabriel,' Jessica said.

When he was calmer, Gabriel said, 'Why don't I tell Rachel the truth? Tell her I got ridiculously drunk, and then tell her that that's not the worst of it. Say I'm also a registered drug addict. It used to be heroin, but now it's methadone and my mother has to ...' He looked at Jessica. 'What do you think she'd say?'

'What do *you* think she'd say?' Jessica said, simply.

Gabriel shook his head. 'I've no idea.'

Jessica got up and started to tidy up the room briskly. 'Well, until you have, I think it would be madness to tell her anything.'

'Mary, imagine you're my wife, welcoming me home. How do I look?' Gabriel was trying his best to eat breakfast.

Mary was the housekeeper Gabriel and Charlie had

laughed about the previous afternoon. She looked at Gabriel. 'You look better than you have a right to, from what I hear.'

Gabriel grimaced. 'I think I'll take that as a compliment.'

Charlie came in and Gabriel was able to console himself that his little sister looked ten times worse than he did.

Mary laughed. 'Oh and here's the other one.'

Charlie ignored Mary, as she always did unless she was trying to get Mary to do something for her.

'What are you doing here?' Charlie croaked in Gabriel's direction.

'I stayed the night. But Rachel thinks I'm in London.'

Charlie grunted. 'Then she must be even stupider than I thought.'

Mary tutted. 'That's no way to speak of your sister-in-law.'

'I'm more concerned about how she speaks *to* her sister-in-law,' said Gabriel. 'Please don't forget, Charlie. I was in London. All right? You didn't see me.'

'God, I hate all this lying,' said Charlie, without the slightest irony.

Mary laughed freely. 'Well, of all the nerve!'

Charlie showed Mary her teeth.

That was when Jessica came in and showed Charlie none of the understanding she had shown Gabriel, giving her a serious dressing-down in front of the others that made the girl threaten to tell *poor little Rachel* everything at the first opportunity.

Gabriel escaped into the drawing room to pretend to read the newspaper. When he had gone, Jessica tried another tack with Charlie.

'Let me ask you a question. Do you like Rachel?'

Charlie shrugged. 'Not particularly.'

Jessica's eyes narrowed. 'So, would you like to see her marriage to Gabriel ended? Is that what you're aiming at?'

'He got drunk all by himself, mum!'

'You encouraged him. Selfishly. And now you're planning to stir things up for him.'

Charlie hung her head as Gabriel had done earlier.

Jessica was on a roll. 'Do you want Rachel to divorce him? Huh? And have all the reasons spelled out in court so that everybody will know about his family's private affairs? Is that what you want? How will that make Gabriel feel? What's likely to happen then? Is that what you want, Charlie?'

'Course it isn't,' Charlie muttered. 'I didn't mean it. I won't say a word. I wouldn't.'

Jessica hadn't quite finished. 'Well, that's where we'll end up if we have any more performances like yesterday's.' She let her voice go quieter. 'We must all *help* Gabriel. He's in danger. Serious danger. And so is the family.'

Charlie sat very still, utterly defeated by Jessica's words.

Rachel was reading the newspaper when Gabriel arrived.

'Darling, I'm so sorry.'

Rachel kissed him. 'I'll let you off, because I just *know* you've bought me a superb present all the way from London.'

Gabriel's face fell into a picture of guilt.

She nudged him. 'Come on, I know you haven't got me one. I know you're far too busy with your career to think of me.'

'Oh, God. I'm double sorry now. I'm a monster.'

Rachel was determined not to play the nagging wife. She smiled. 'Tell me how it went. Did they agree to buy anything, or whatever it is they agree to do?'

'Er . . . he was seriously interested. And he's back in a

couple of weeks, so that's when he might, er, come and have a look at what I've done so far.'

'You haven't done anything so far!'

'Yes. I mean, I know. I mean, I'm going to have to now, aren't I? I work better when the pressure's on, I always have.'

Rachel smiled. 'Marvellous. Darling, well done.'

She clung to him and he felt like the biggest liar ever to have trodden the earth.

'Thanks. And it won't happen again,' he said. 'I mean, going away like that.'

'What, without even a bag?'

'Um.'

'Well, I'm sure you wouldn't have done it unless you had to, would you?'

'No. No. Of course not.'

One thing Jessica could guarantee about family life was that the expected never happened.

Jessica dropped Charlie off in town, probably so that she could hang around in the shopping centre smoking cigarettes with her friends. When Jessica arrived back at the house the unexpected had happened – she should have expected it. Her elder daughter, Lenny, had come home, babe in arms. She was sitting at the kitchen table with strands of her fine golden hair stringing down over her face. Like a true distressed daughter, she did not stand on ceremony.

'Mum, I've left Mark.'

Jessica digested the information, realising that they would have a baby in the house for the foreseeable future. 'Oh, darling, you haven't.' She tried to sound sympathetic but succeeded only in sounding disappointed.

Lenny nodded. 'Yes, look. Bags, baby. I've left him and,' she burst into tears, 'and I'm not going back.'

Sensing her distress, Ben, her little son, began crying too and the kitchen was filled with sobs and yells. At that moment, thank goodness, Mary came in.

Jessica was highly relieved. 'Ah, Mary. Please take hold of Ben. Helena's left Mark. She'll be staying with us.'

With a simple 'Poor dear', Mary went into action. She took the crying infant and at the same time put the kettle on and brought out some cups. No sooner was Ben in Mary's arms than he was quiet again. It was Mary with whom he felt comfortable, rather than Jessica, his grandmother. When Lenny and Mark came to stay, it was Mary who spent the most time with the child. Jessica loved Ben – he was family – but so far it had been a love restricted to the realm of admiration, rather than one committed to the field of action. Ben was too young, as yet, for Jessica; she preferred children who were old enough to follow conversations sensibly.

'Are you all right there, Mary?' Lenny managed to say as she pulled herself together.

Jessica sat down, put her arm around her daughter and answered for Mary, who was in raptures. 'Of course she is. She's been waiting for another baby in the house since Charlie grew up.'

Lenny smiled. Mary, in a state of gurgling bliss, took Ben away from his mother to enable her to have the necessary conversation with her own mother.

When Mary had gone, Jessica asked what had happened.

Lenny was obviously very angry. 'Oh, nothing new. Nothing original. Just that boring old story you think happens to everybody else but is never going to happen to you.' Jessica nodded. 'He's been having it off with another woman. A secretary at his firm. Not *his* secretary, but somebody else's. She's called Sarah.' Lenny began to cry again. 'I just can't believe how he's lied to me. Just looked me in the face and lied and lied!'

Jessica was gentle. 'But he has now admitted it, this affair?'

'Only when he'd no choice. Because I had proof. I had the bills from the hotel room and, on top of that, a friend of mine had seen them. So he admitted it when he had to, yes.'

'Did he say anything else?'

'Like what?'

'Well, I mean, is he in love with this woman, or what?'

'What does it matter what he says,' Lenny said bitterly. 'I couldn't believe it anyway, since everything he's said so far has turned out to be a pack of lies.'

Jessica could see that further questioning would be useless for the time being. 'Well, of course you can stay here until we get this all sorted out.'

Even that had been a mistake.

Lenny almost growled. 'Its never going to be sorted out!' Then she blew her nose and asked, 'Who's that friend of daddy's that specialises in divorces?'

Jessica thought this was premature, but Lenny wouldn't be stopped.

'That's what I want! And you can say what you like. And I'm sorry if it doesn't look good when your father's a bishop. But that's what I want.'

Jessica judged it best not to interfere and gave Lenny the name of Edward's friend, reminding herself always to expect the unexpected.

·5·

Saturday aft.

I feel so depressed.

One minute Gabriel is elated and full of himself and his work. The next minute he's down in the dumps.

He got back from London this morning having disappeared without trace yesterday – without even leaving me a note – so that I had to find out last night from Jessica that he'd gone to London on business and got stuck there because of a bomb-scare. So we had a really nice morning because I didn't get cross with him when I think he was expecting me to go mad at him. He sat there being all lovey-dovey, asking me if I wanted to move back to London, how did I feel about Jessica and giving me all the attention a girl could need. He was so sweet about my job and told me that if I was going to be working then he would make an extra-special effort to get down to it. Then we had a gorgeous romp all round the downstairs of the house.

Then this afternoon I said something simple to him about his work and he got all shirty with me, saying he couldn't just turn it on you know!!! And he called my job a poxy, part-time job and asked how I could bear to live with him in this boring, tedious place with such an appalling family breathing down our necks all the time, and why *don't* we go back to London, we could go this week, couldn't we!! And now he's gone up to the house again which only a few minutes before he was cursing because it was so near.

If he was a girl I'd say he had his period coming!!!

But he's not, is he?

And here's another thing. I can admit it now I've had a good rant. I didn't believe Gabriel's story about going to London. I mean, he didn't even have a bag with him. I asked him the details of the story twice and he told it to me in exactly the same way both times, but something doesn't add up. The only thing that convinces me is that Jessica came here and told me about it herself and why would she lie for him? Yet at the same time something about that makes me suspicious too!!!

It's niggling me, but it's probably just because he was horrible to me before he stormed off to the house. And that's irritating me too. He goes up there at least twice a day. I just wish we could spend some time together here without the bloody family hanging over us. Every time he goes up there he's gone for ages and I'm sure he's running away from things we should be sorting out between us.

But at least I'm getting on well with Jessica. Even though she annoyed me last night. I went for coffee in Market Cross with her yesterday, can you believe, and we even had a bit of a giggle in Laura Ashley.

Oh God! Why do I feel that I'm in a mess when everything's going fine? I've got nothing to worry about. That's probably all it is. I'm a natural-born worrier. I'm going to be nice to Gabriel when he gets back even though I want to shout at him for being a stupid idiot and even though I don't really believe him – Oh, I *do* believe him, but I'm just suspicious and I don't know why.

I'm going to shut up now.

Lenny was sitting alone in the drawing room of her mother's house.

How she wished that she owned her own home instead of this phoney joint ownership where Mark paid the mortgage and made her feel guilty about it. Luckily she'd insisted she had her name put on the mortgage agreement. She bitterly envied her mother whose own family's wealth had bought the mansion where they lived – and that was what it was, a mansion. How much easier it would have been if she could have ordered Mark to leave the house, or if she could have changed the locks and told him to get out. How much power that would have given her.

For a few moments she pictured Mark, unable to gain access to the house, having to crawl home to his own parents and confessing his vile secret to them, that he had been sniffing about like a dog, that he'd . . . Well, anyway, confessing that he was no better than an animal in season and having to beg them to put him up for the night until he could get his wife to forgive him and let him crawl back into his kennel. Lenny pictured Mark at her own front door, apologetic, no, begging her to forgive him, making all kinds of promises, of fidelity, that he would work hard at home, that he would never sit in front of the television all weekend again, that he would never watch football again, that he would never see that vile friend of his from the office, fat John.

She became aware that she was grinding her teeth.

As she played around with her fantasy, she realised that it was not a very likely scenario. If she did lock Mark out, the chances were he'd go straight round to Sarah the floozie's house and spend the night there. He'd probably not have to beg for access there. Lenny pictured her husband in the arms of another woman and suffered a piercing pang of jealousy. She almost growled aloud with the pain and the rage. What was Sarah like? A picture of large, firm breasts with no baby suckling at them sprang to mind, and a flat belly, a youthful smile, an easy-going, non-nagging, do-anything-you-want-darling attitude. Oh God. She felt sick. She wanted to scream. She wanted to beat Mark and make him feel the pain she was going through.

Instead she burst into tears and at the same moment heard a noise in the kitchen. It was her mother, talking to someone.

Mark.

With haste she found a handkerchief and wiped her eyes, determined to remove all traces of suffering from her face. She checked herself in the mirror and turned on an expression of indifference. Or did her best.

Jessica showed Mark into the room.

Lenny prepared herself to receive Mark's cringing apology.

He looked straight at her. 'Oh, great,' he said, with foul sarcasm.

Lenny was staggered. 'What?'

'You've had me running around after you. I might have known you'd have come here.'

She was almost too shocked to be angry. 'I didn't ask you to follow me.'

'You didn't have to ask,' Mark scowled. 'You knew I would.'

Lenny began to collect her wits. 'No. If you were running after anybody, I didn't think it'd be me.'

Jessica was probably as shocked as Lenny at Mark's

defiant attitude. 'Er. Well, I think I'd better leave you two to it,' she managed to say before doing so.

Lenny said, 'How's Sarah?'

Mark ignored her. 'I suppose you've gone and told everyone all about it, have you?'

'Oh! Should I not have? Was it meant to be a secret?'

Mark sighed impatiently. 'We've been through all this. I mean, most of last night.'

'Oh, I'm sorry if it's boring you.'

The thing that was really annoying Lenny at this moment, apart from Mark's total self-absorption, was the fact that, standing there in front of her, dressed as smartly as usual, he seemed so powerful and attractive, when really he should have seemed ugly and pathetic.

He was really huffing now. 'I am not denying that I had a relationship – a brief, silly relationship – with Sarah.'

Lenny felt her stomach turn over at the very mention of the woman's name. 'No, you're not denying it *now*. Not now you've got no choice.'

Mark ploughed on. 'But that was just . . . it wasn't anything to do with our marriage.'

Lenny's eyes flashed. 'Well it is now.'

Mark conceded the point and calmed down a little, or, as Lenny saw it, changed his tune. 'It is now. Yes, of course, it is now. I realise that.'

'You do? Oh, then we have made some progress.'

Mark's shoulders dropped a little. A fact which didn't escape Lenny's notice. 'Lenny . . . do you want a divorce?'

Lenny looked at him. Her husband. Not only her husband, but the man she had loved for as long as she could remember, the only man she had ever loved. Not the only man she had ever had sex with, but the only one with whom it had ever mattered. The only man with whom sex had ever been enjoyable. She wondered if she could ever really leave him and doubted it, shuddering at the very thought.

'Do *you* want a divorce?' she said at last.

Mark was firm. 'No.' He even became passionate. 'No! Lenny, I want you. I want Ben, our son. Our *son*, Lenny. A divorce is the last thing I want! *Sarah* is the last thing I want, for God's sake!'

'What *would* Sarah say if she heard you say that?'

'I don't care what she thinks, either about that or anything else. All I care about is you. You and our child and our life together.'

As she gave vent to her frustration in the form of sarcasm, Lenny felt a very unwelcome surge of lust for the man in front of her, a proper throb. It annoyed her and at the same time its intensity reminded her how long it had been since they'd made love in that special way of theirs. Before Ben had come along. She swallowed down her longing and tried to swallow the rest of her pride. 'If you thought that much about us, why did you try and spoil it?'

'I didn't . . . I promise. It was just stupid.'

'You had me, you had Ben, but you chose Sarah.'

'It wasn't like that.'

'So what *was* it like?'

Mark looked very grey and worried. Now he was practically on his knees. 'Look,' he said, 'I'll go to Sarah this afternoon. Well, not to her. I'll go to the firm – on Monday – and I'll explain what's happened. Oh, I'll talk to her as well and tell her we're never going to see each other again. Then I'll get the firm to transfer her to another office. In another area. She won't want that so she'll leave. We'll never see one another again. I promise.'

Lenny nodded, thinking how ruthless Mark could be when it suited him. 'Then you'll expect me to have you back and everything'll be just as it was?'

Mark shook his head. 'I don't *expect* it. But it's what I'd like more than anything in this world.'

Lenny enjoyed that last reply. It felt as if Mark meant it.

Neither of them spoke. They just looked at each other and Lenny could not help but smile.

Within the hour Lenny and Mark's car was shrinking into the distance as Jessica and Mary waved them off from outside the family mansion.

With a heavy heart, Rachel was preparing a meal for Gabriel. She hadn't seen him since she had written her last melancholy diary entry.

She heard him come in the front door and go into the living room. A few moments later Gabriel wandered in with two glasses of whisky, placing them on the draining board and nuzzling up behind Rachel, sheepishly catching her ear with his nose.

'I owe you an apology,' he said.

Rachel was light. 'For what?'

'For the way I was earlier. All that moody performance.'

'Oh that. I didn't think anything of it.'

'Well, I'm sorry. I want to say that. You deserve better.'

Rachel shrugged. 'I was just worried that you didn't seem very well.'

Gabriel picked up his glass and began to pace about the kitchen. 'I sometimes get a bit claustrophobic. I don't know what it is. It's not you. It's . . . I dunno. Acute claustrophobia. Huh. I suppose I should just get on with work – then I'd be outside . . . part of the landscape.'

Rachel turned to him. 'You would tell me if it was something else?'

Gabriel looked at her. 'Of course I would. I tell you everything, don't I?'

Rachel nodded. 'Because you know what I thought?'

'What?'

'I thought what I said about your family being near had upset you, or that I'd hurt you and you wanted to run away.' She hung her head sadly. 'I don't know what I thought.'

Gabriel took her in his arms and rocked her. 'It's nothing you said. And you can say whatever you like about my family – wait, I'll say it for you. They're snobs, they're conceited, Charlotte's a nympho – an immature one at that. Dad's got about as much religion in him as . . . as my glass of whisky. Slightly less, probably.'

Rachel laughed. 'You don't have to run them down for my benefit.'

'It's all true. And what's more, I love you because you're nothing like them. You're better than they are. More honest.'

'No, Gabriel . . .'

'Yes. And the thing that matters more than anything else is that we don't change you. If anything, you must change us.'

Rachel smiled happily, as she usually did when Gabriel took her in his arms. 'Well at least don't include yourself in with them. At least you're honest. And beautiful.' She looked up at his blushing face. 'And totally forgiven.'

Charlie was in her bedroom amid a scene that resembled backstage after a fashion show. There were clothes, shoes and underwear strewn about the place, as well as hair bobbles, slides, makeup, lipstick, scarves, jewellery, sunglasses, badges, in short, everything she possessed that could possibly enhance her appearance in any way. Standing naked in the middle of it all, gazing at her reflection and no nearer to a decision about what to wear than she had been an hour ago, Charlie took a long hard look at herself.

Her figure was her strong point, she reckoned. Her face was more characterful than pretty, but, she reassured herself, she had recently seen a survey in one of her magazines that guys preferred girls with unusual faces to those with pretty, nondescript good looks. Yeah, and with makeup she looked pretty damn hot anyhow. But the best was below the neck. Great breasts, gorgeous shape. She turned sideways and checked her breasts again and liked what she saw. That was the chief advantage of her age. What she lacked in experience, she made up for in sheer gravity-defying bounce, in tautness. She was thinking here of her older sister Lenny who always talked to Charlie as if she had no idea about sex, while Lenny's breasts drooped ever earthwards and her hips spread like butter – especially since she'd had the sprog. She turned back and examined the contours of her waist and thighs, and liked what she saw there, too. She even fancied herself, she was so hot. It's a pity I can't go out like this, she thought. Put all those condescending older bitches to shame.

Tonight she needed all her assets.

As she again tried on bits of underwear and various pieces of her finest clothing, she thought that impossibly delicious thought: Thomas Hunt had agreed to go out with her tonight. As she did so, her belly jumped back up to her chest and her legs filled with hot water. She wanted to jump up and down like a girl.

'Calm yourself, girl,' she said aloud. Then she replayed the earlier scene. She had come back from town, where she had been bored all day, to find Thomas in the kitchen. Oh, my God, what if she'd turned up a few minutes later – she'd have missed him!

Charlie had paid almost no attention to the fact that her older sister had left her husband and then gone back to him in the space of a few hours, an event which, on a normal day, would have been the most interesting thing to have happened in a month of Sundays, and which would have kept her in sarcasm for months.

In his official capacity as best man, Thomas had come to check upon Gabriel. Gabriel had confessed that he had been a bastard to Rachel that very afternoon and Thomas instructed him to go and make amends immediately, telling Gabriel that he would call again on Monday.

Charlie knew that here was her opportunity. She wondered as she approached him whether her eyes were shining like the Hood's, the eastern baddie in *Thunderbirds*. 'Hi, Thomas,' she said casually.

'Oh, hi, Charlie, how are you?'

Charlie sighed. 'Bored. And don't say, "How can someone as beautiful as you be bored?"'

Thomas laughed. 'Hey, you took the words right out of my mouth.'

'And *please* don't say, "You must have so many young men queuing up to take you out."'

'Hey, mind-reader!' He laughed easily with her, as though they were already familiar. Which they were.

She threw herself on to his arm in a display of mock despair. 'Oh, Thomas. Help me. I'm a woman in great distress.'

'You in distress? From what I hear you can look after yourself all right, Charlie.'

'I need help disposing of someone.'

Thomas laughed. 'You want Murder Incorporated.'

Charlie laughed more than the joke warranted.

Thomas said, 'You want to get rid of your boyfriend?'

'Good guess, star. Help me, *please*. I've tried everything but he won't take the hint.'

'Have you tried telling him directly?'

69

'You sound like Gabriel. Of course I haven't! Men never take you seriously if you ask them something direct.'

'I would.'

She looked at him. 'Thomas. Help me ditch Nick?'

He shrugged and smiled that infinitely gorgeously brilliant smile. 'See – direct.'

Charlie nodded. 'So? What are you saying – tonight? You'll have to play my boyfriend at a club.'

He shrugged easily, in a *why not* sort of way. 'He's not a rugby player is he?'

Charlie ignored the unpleasant feeling that Thomas was behaving as if she were his younger sister and decided to get very excited about it. Thomas was taking her out. Tonight. Which was mega-double-groovy. Like her underwear.

Charlie thought Thomas's car was the coolest thing on earth – it was an old Mercedes. Even the rust seemed groovy to her, as if he just didn't care about things like that. As they pulled up outside the bar she put her elbow on the window and tried her best to look nonchalant.

As they walked into the bright, loud, Saturday-night throng of the downstairs area, Charlie felt as good as she imagined everyone thought she looked. Thomas had complimented her on the length of her short skirt and Charlie was certain he hadn't been taking the mickey. Out of the corner of her eye she clocked Nick immediately, and at the same time waved ostentatiously to someone on the other side of the room who she knew wasn't looking in their direction. She saw Nick's head turn to see who she was greeting.

'Don't look round, but he's at that table over there,' she hissed to Thomas.

Thomas shook his head as they arrived at the bar. 'I'm really not sure if this is in good taste, you know,' he said.

Charlie grinned. 'It's in extremely bad taste, that's why I'm going to enjoy it.'

Thomas ordered the drinks. Charlie tried to look as intimate as possible with him. 'Try to look as though you're madly in love with me and at the same time as though you'd kill someone if they looked at you the wrong way.'

Thomas pulled a stupid face and said, 'How's this?'

Charlie burst out laughing and took the opportunity to press right up against him, putting her head on his shoulder. 'Absolutely awful,' she giggled, 'but it makes you look cute anyway.'

When the drinks arrived, Charlie said, 'OK. Wait here. I'll be back.' Then she went straight over to Nick.

Nick looked as though he'd been sucking a lemon.

'Hi,' Charlie said, and checked over her shoulder to make sure that Thomas was looking at them.

'Hi, Charlie . . .'

'Don't touch me!' Charlie hissed.

Nick frowned. 'What?'

Charlie waved at Thomas who waved back. 'I had to tell him you're my cousin. We're at school together and you just want to talk about some homework.'

Nick blinked. 'Tell who?'

'Oh dear, this is *soo* difficult,' said Charlie.

'What's going on, Charlie? I thought you wanted to meet me for a drink.'

'No. I wanted you to be here so you'd see it for yourself, so you'd understand and wouldn't do anything stupid.'

'What? See what?'

'OK. See Thomas over there, the big guy?'

Nick looked at her as if she'd gone mad. 'You mean Thomas? Yes. He was best man at Gabriel's wedding.'

'Right. Yeah. So we were, like, thrown together, right?

71

And what's happened? We've become lovers. Only he's very jealous and possessive. And you see the size of him. He used to be a boxer ... that is ... before he was a professional pianist, right. So it's more than your life's worth to be seen near me after today.'

'You mean you're going out with him?'

'You really are an intelligent guy, Nick. Got it in one.'

Nick was gutted, but managed to hide it apart from the way his mouth curled up a little at the corner. 'You're joking?'

'Its more than *my* life's worth to be seen near *you*,' she added.

'How old is he?'

'Yeah, exactly. And don't say anything about his age because that's the one thing that's guaranteed to drive him crazy.'

Nick couldn't find anything else to say.

Charlie's straightened up. 'Right. See ya,' she said and walked away.

'What did he say?' Thomas asked, as Charlie waltzed back up to him.

'Oh, just that I'm the most gorgeous creature he's ever met or is ever likely to meet in the whole of his life.' She turned to look back on her prey. 'Oh, look,' she squealed, 'he's going, he's going!' She had to stop herself jumping up and down in glee. *Calm yourself, girl.* Thomas won't be impressed by infantile behaviour. 'He's going,' she repeated, more sedately.

Thomas said, 'Yes. Well, so are we.'

Charlie looked at him. 'Er, you want to go?'

'Yes. We've played your little game, haven't we?'

'Um, yes.'

'Right. Well, I'm taking you back to mummy, then.'

Charlie was thunderstruck. She searched his face for

clues. Did Thomas think she was a pathetic little child who had embarrassed him. Or herself? Oh, God! She was seized by panic. She wanted to ask him directly if he thought she was a git for what she'd done, or what. But of course that was out of the question.

'So, you don't want to stay for even one more drink, then?' she asked, in a voice far smaller and stupider.

'No thanks.'

'Oh.'

They stood there for a few moments finishing their drinks while Charlie racked her brains for something to say. Inside she was blushing right down to the bone; she could only hope the colour in her cheeks enhanced her looks.

Then they were back in the car and it was even harder to talk.

'What are you going to do for the rest of the night?' Charlie asked.

'I'm practising. My piano. I've got a concert next week.'

'Would you like someone to turn the pages for you?' Charlie managed to get out.

Thomas didn't even answer that one. He dropped her off and went home, or perhaps he went out somewhere without her.

Shit Mega-death.

On Sunday morning Jessica went for a pleasant walk in the woods and, although it rained a little on the way back, she felt something almost resembling peace in her heart. For a few moments, half an hour even, she allowed herself to entertain the notion that things would work themselves out in a tolerably manageable way. With her help and with the help of Rachel, with whom relations would gradually improve as she become more responsible and adult, Gabriel would gradually settle down, stop using drugs, develop his talent and his considerable imaginative skills and earn some decent money. Eventually it was even possible that the young couple would have children of their own.

Charlie and Lenny, her two daughters, occupied less space in Jessica's thinking and their respective problems were sooner dealt with in her mind's eye. Charlie's antics of late, especially that ridiculous incident with Gabriel, would be forgotten. Lenny's marriage would get back on to a sensible footing.

Even her husband, Edward, would find some outlet for his energies that would take him closer to God, or at least to the church. And then, when all those problems were solved . . . hum.

What came next was uncertain, but in Jessica's heart that afternoon the space was occupied by a feeling as fresh and peaceful as the light rain that fell, by the smell of the wet afternoon and the light beams of sunshine peeping out from behind the clouds and shining across the meadows.

Yes. This afternoon she was almost content and could see a picture of life as she wanted it to be. This was a blessing after the previous weeks of anxiety.

On Sunday evening Edward returned from his conference.

They had a tolerable family supper, spent the evening watching television, Jessica described Lenny's storm in a teacup and then the two of them went to bed. As they sat in bed reading, Jessica asked Edward, 'How's Anne?'

Edward hummed. 'Oh, fine.'

Jessica didn't look up from her book. 'I hope you treat her well on those little excursions of yours.'

Edward looked up from his own book. 'Of course I do.'

Jessica nodded vaguely. 'I don't want to pry,' she said. 'I mean, it's your business, but . . . does she know that I know. About you two?'

Edward frowned. 'No, Jessica. You know she doesn't know that you know. We agreed.'

Jessica looked at him. 'Oh, I know we agreed. But I just wondered whether, in a moment of — let's call it passion — you might have let it slip.'

'No,' Edward said, 'and I don't think it's fair we should be talking like this.'

'Not fair, Edward?' Jessica raised her eyebrows.

'To Anne.'

Jessica was amused more than anything. 'Not fair to Anne?' Then she was less amused. 'I think I'm very fair towards the pair of you. The way I've turned a blind eye all these years.'

Edward realised his error. 'Yes. Yes, I'm sorry. I didn't mean . . .'

'I think most people would call that more than fair. I should think most people would call that extremely generous.'

'Yes, yes. Of course.'

As she went back to her book, Jessica added, 'Some might even call it foolish.'

Edward didn't have anything to add, so he went back to his book.

·6·

FIRST THING MONDAY morning, Lenny returned. She marched into the kitchen having deposited Ben in the drawing room with a delighted Mary. It was hard to distinguish the baby's gurgling from that of Mary.

'Hello, mum. Hello, dad.'

Edward stopped eating his breakfast.

Jessica said, 'You've left him again.'

'Yes, mummy. Or rather, no, Mummy, if when you say *again* you mean like last time. Because I haven't left him like last time. This time I *have* left him and I'm *not* going back.'

Edward looked puzzled to the point of pain. 'I thought your problem with Mark had been resolved?'

'So, did I, daddy.'

Jessica noticed that Lenny looked less tearful this time. She's probably all cried out, she thought. 'Edward, weren't you about to leave for work?' she said.

'Well, yes, I was but . . .' Edward stopped as he recognised the look on his wife's face.

'I can deal with our daughter.'

'Yes, yes, of course.'

Edward made the required exit. 'Helena, dear, I'm sure you'll sort this out,' he said as he went. 'Mark's a good man at heart.'

'Is he?' Lenny said.

Edward nodded reassuringly. 'Yes, I believe he is.'

Jessica glared. 'Edward. You're making yourself late. And then you'll be driving too fast . . .'

He left.

Jessica made tea and settled down to hear the full story.

'He went to see her,' Lenny said. 'Supposedly to tell her it was all over. And he never came back.'

Jessica could not hide her amazement. 'Not at all?'

'Not at all. All I got was a triumphant phone call from *her* at about one o'clock this morning.'

'Oh, darling, that *is* awful.' Jessica could hardly believe her ears and silently cursed all men to hell.

Lenny nodded staunchly. 'I thought either I leave, or I kill him when he gets back. And it wasn't that the idea of killing him didn't appeal. Just, I didn't know how long I'd have to wait.' Lenny let her anger show at last. 'Well that's it! This time he's gone too far for apologies or explanations! This time we're finished.'

That was when Charlie came down. She took one look at Lenny and grinned. 'I wondered when you'd be back.'

Lenny looked at her. 'Get lost, Charlie.'

Jessica didn't say a word.

By late morning the sisters were chatting amiably, school ignored, while Jessica nipped to the village shop for some stamps.

Charlie said, 'Listen, you know Thomas Hunt?'

'Gabriel's best man?'

'What d'you think? Do you think he's sexy?'

'Yes. But he's too old for you, Charlie.'

'Oh? Is that why he took me out for a drink? And why I'm going to see him today at the Lodge?'

'He's going to see Gabriel.'

'Uh-huh. Wanna come? If you do, you're leaving Thomas to me, right? I don't want you taking revenge on Mark at my expense.'

Lenny shook her head. 'Actually, what I'd like ... Oh, God, this is pathetic. Oh no, forget it!'

'What? Tell me.'

Lenny sighed. 'If you go to the Lodge, don't tell Gabriel I'm here, OK.'

'Why not?'

'I always used to give him a hard time 'cause he always came running home whenever things went wrong for him.'

Charlie said, 'Yeah, so now you look pretty pathetic yourself.'

Lenny flinched. 'Yeah. Yeah.' She shook her head. 'You're so tactful, Charlie.'

Charlie smiled. 'I try my best to tell the truth at all times.'

Lenny said, 'Humm.'

Gabriel felt guilty because he hadn't seen Thomas since his wedding.

One of the things he said he was going to do when he got back from London was renew his friendship with Thomas, but so far he'd been so wrapped up in himself that he hadn't bothered. He was irritated too because he'd lied to Rachel about it. Rachel had gone off to work, her first day, and he'd told her he was going to spend the day working, knowing full well he was going to spend the day with Thomas. He felt guilty about her going to work while he lazed about; he felt guilty because he still wasn't painting, and somehow he felt guilty about his friendship with Thomas, as though he were being unfaithful to Rachel, which was ridiculous.

It was funny, though. When he was with Thomas he always wanted to run away with him and behave like the adolescents they had once been, in the days when things were still fun, when trouble wasn't serious, when they could do whatever they liked without worrying about the consequences. When he was with Thomas now, Gabriel smoked cigarettes, it was the only time he ever did that. They just sat and chatted and smoked and laughed.

'I'm delighted to be married,' Gabriel was saying. 'I'm just not sure I'll be very good at it.'

'Why the hell not?' Thomas said.

'You're not supposed to have secrets when you're married, are you, you're supposed to have total intimacy.'

'Of course you have secrets. Everyone does.'

Gabriel shook his head. 'I seem to spend most of my time lying to Rachel.'

'What about?'

Gabriel shrugged. 'About how much I've had to drink . . . about . . . you know . . . that sort of thing.'

Thomas laughed. 'That's not lying. That's marriage.'

Gabriel laughed, mainly to cover the fresh pangs of guilt he was feeling. Here he was, talking to his best mate about lying – and lying to him about what he lied about. He cursed himself for not being able to mention his drug problem and punished himself with a hot stream of self-loathing. 'Do you want another coffee, Tom?'

'Yeah, great.'

'You don't want a drink?'

Thomas shook his head. 'It's a bit early for me.'

Gabriel nodded. 'Yeah. And me.'

Thomas could tell Gabriel was taking the conversation about Rachel to heart. 'Anyway,' he said, raising his voice so Gabriel could hear him in the kitchen, 'you don't know what Rachel's lying to you about.'

Gabriel emerged, having put the kettle on again. 'Yes I do. She isn't lying to me about anything.'

'Well. Lucky you.'

Gabriel flopped back into his chair. 'The other problem is, we're living so near to the bloody family. It's almost as if I'm living at home again.'

That was the moment Charlie arrived, carrying a shoulder bag, dressed in her school uniform, with a few embellishments.

'Hi,' she said, walking straight in.

Gabriel said, 'See what I mean?'

Thomas nodded. 'Must be a problem,' he said.

Charlie assumed they were talking about something else.

'What do you want?' Gabriel said.

'I don't want anything,' Charlie said. 'I've come to offer you the pleasure of my company.' She turned to Thomas. 'How was your piano practice?'

'Fine, thank you.'

Charlie explained about Saturday night to Gabriel and didn't notice Thomas blush, or the slight flicker that passed across Gabriel's face as she spoke.

At the end of it Thomas said, 'I was what you might call *conscripted*.'

Charlie took the bag from her shoulder. 'Mind if I change out of this stupid uniform?' she asked.

Both guys shrugged and Charlie changed there and then, talking as she did so, making sure that Thomas caught a glimpse of her legs and her mega-sexy underwear. She was firing on all cylinders, completely oblivious to any reaction but the one she imagined.

'By the way,' she said, 'Lenny's back again. And this time she's staying.' For Thomas's benefit she added, 'Her

80

husband's screwing around.' Down with her jeans. 'Gabriel, Lenny specifically told me not to tell you she was back in case you think she's pathetic.'

Gabriel frowned. 'So why have you told me?'

'Because I knew you'd want to know. And then you won't be surprised when she tells you.'

Gabriel turned to Thomas. 'You follow that?'

Thomas shrugged. 'From a distance.'

Charlie was down to her essentials now and thought she saw Thomas take a crafty look. 'So how's Rachel, Gabriel? Where is she? She hasn't left as well has she?'

Gabriel was getting irritated enough for Charlie to catch something of it. 'She's gone to work. It's her first day.'

'Oh great,' she said, ignoring Gabriel's annoyance, 'so it's just the three of us.'

Gabriel and Thomas had been doing their best to discuss art and music.

The problem was, every time the conversation got off the ground Charlie would intervene with some comment designed to show off her ability to grasp difficult ideas as easily as the two older men.

Gabriel was talking in his usual way about his idea for a series of paintings and Thomas was comparing it to some obscure ideas he'd read about from the German Expressionists. Charlie was being a pain. She was also doing her best to bury the feeling that was making her uncomfortable. Charlie wasn't sure exactly what the feeling was, but it reminded her of their youth when she had always wanted to be with the two older lads and they had wanted her to get lost. She told herself that it was only her desire for Thomas, that she was nervous in case he got away.

After about half an hour, Charlie sighed. 'Anybody want a drink?'

Thomas said, 'No thank you, Charlie.'

Gabriel scratched his eye.

'I've got two bottles of finest champagne.'

'Where the hell did you get those?' Gabriel said.

'Where the hell do you think?'

'Charlie, if you keep taking bottles out of the cellar, dad's going to notice.'

'So what?'

Gabriel smiled despite himself. 'You know, I think you're worse than I ever was.'

Under the circumstances Gabriel's smile seemed to Charlie as great and as full of blessings as a hot spring. 'Why, thank you, bro. Shall I get a glass?'

'No. You can go and put the bottles back.'

'Gabriel . . . don't be so boring. Who wants a drink?'

'Neither of us.'

Charlie grimaced in what she thought was a comic way. 'Course you do.'

'I'll ask our guest. Thomas?'

'No thank you, Gabriel.'

Charlie looked at them both. There was no way she was going to give up. She knew that if they were all drunk things would be a lot easier, the two guys would chill out and, maybe, she would get to sit on Thomas's knee or something, maybe even snog him. She knew what guys were like when they were pissed, especially on champagne. So she just opened the bottle.

'Get the glasses, Gabriel.'

'No way, Charlie. Leave it out.'

Bang. Off came the cork, out came the fizz. Charlie grabbed one of the coffee mugs. 'Quick, get some glasses.'

Gabriel sighed and tutted and did so. He felt like a bloody drink anyhow.

Charlie looked at Thomas. 'Cheers,' she said and drank straight from the bottle.

She took Thomas's exasperated sigh to mean, 'Gosh, Charlie, you're so wild.'

Really he just wanted her to go away and leave them alone.

Jessica was on the telephone talking to Edward.

She was in the drawing room with Lenny, trying unsuccessfully to steer the conversation with Edward away from their daughter's marital problems, but Edward would not be prevented from having his say, whether Lenny was in the room or not. He had grave doubts about Lenny coming to stay indefinitely. Jessica put her hand over the mouthpiece and spoke to Lenny. 'Darling, could you give me a moment? Edward wants to talk.'

Lenny looked at her mother. 'About me? And Mark?'

Jessica admitted it with an apologetic face.

'Talk away. I'll listen.'

Jessica sighed and steeled herself.

Edward was saying, 'I mean, of course we should offer Helena all the help we can.'

'I'm glad you think so,' Jessica replied.

'She's our daughter.'

'Yes. She is. And she is also an innocent young woman. With a baby. Whose husband has been fornicating with the office tart.'

Edward said, 'Well, we don't want to judge.'

Jessica almost laughed. 'Oh, *I* do. I find *no problem* judging in this instance.'

Lenny was listening intently to her mother's side of the conversation, trying to work out what Edward was saying from what she could hear.

'I'm only saying . . . Oh,' Edward sighed. 'You make it

83

sound as though Helena is moving in with us permanently.'

'She might be.'

'And I am asking – is this wise? We should be encouraging her to talk to her husband, help them find a way of resolving this.'

'Edward, I am not one of your parishioners. And nor is your daughter. So spare us the party line.'

'It's not the party line, Jessica.'

'Well, it sounds like it.' Jessica glanced at her daughter and raised her eyes to heaven.

Edward huffed, aware that he was about to tread on thin ice. 'Look at it from Mark's point of view. What kind of message is it going to send him if Helena moves in permanently with us? He's going to conclude she doesn't need him any longer. She's back with her mum and dad.'

'Well, if that is the message, then fine, yes. Good.'

'Jessica, it isn't fine! We're only helping to make their separation permanent.'

Jessica was getting angry. 'So will you please tell me what I am supposed to do? Shall I tell her to get out? To go and sleep on the streets. With the baby?'

Edward had nothing to say to that. He sighed. 'We'll talk about it later. When I get home.'

Jessica put the phone down without a goodbye and turned to Lenny. 'I think sometimes being a bishop gets in the way of being a father.'

Lenny nodded. 'I can understand, though.'

'Understand what?'

'Why he doesn't want me moving back in here.'

Jessica's lips tightened. 'Don't be ridiculous, darling. He will want what we tell him he wants. It just takes him a little time to realise it, that's all.'

★

Edward was highly disgruntled following his conversation with Jessica.

He had very mixed feelings over the whole affair. Mark, Lenny's husband, was a fool and Edward cursed him for it without the slightest feeling of hypocrisy. Mark's marriage to Lenny was hardly at that stage when, naturally, a man's interest begins to wane. Obviously the two had known each other for a number of years, but even so. The icing had only recently dried on the wedding cake, for God's sake. It was foolish to mess around in a situation where one was going to get caught, or where getting caught would lead to complications of that kind. If only one could be patient, things had a way of working themselves out, people grew more understanding with age. Really, Mark was a bad sort, foolish and immature.

These irritations occupied Edward for a few minutes after his conversation with Jessica and served to divert him from a deeper unease. He was uncomfortable with having to act the tyrant *vis-à-vis* Lenny. He repeated to himself that it was no good trying to provide the soft alternative for their daughter, offering her permanent residence. Yes, she had a child, but she also had responsibilities, and what's more she had a husband whom she had sworn to love in front of God. The deeper unease was caused by the fact that Edward knew in his heart that really he was concerned about Lenny staying permanently because of how it would *appear* to others, having a daughter at home who had deserted her husband. It wasn't very pleasant to admit, but no matter how forward-thinking people claimed to be, Edward knew that it reflected badly on him in the diocese. No matter that Lenny might even be justified in her decision to leave, the family would still be judged harshly. It was very bad timing, especially as Bishop Harris would be retiring sooner or later and Edward was his obvious successor.

Edward was pacing about his office by now and was about to calm himself with a glass of sherry when there was a knock at the door.

'Come.'

Anne came into the office and stood before him.

Edward was very glad to have someone with whom to share his reflections on Mark's foolishness and Jessica's obstinacy and the danger of providing safe refuge for his daughter when she had made vows before God. Anne stood there, demurely umming and sympathising for nearly ten minutes before Edward finally realised that she obviously needed to talk.

'Is something the matter, Anne? You look a little, well, out of sorts.'

Anne looked down. 'You obviously have enough troubles of your own, Edward.'

Edward said he was only too glad to have someone else's troubles to worry about. 'Please. Sit down, Anne. Do you need to talk now?'

She nodded and sat. As Edward looked at her, something made him decide that he too needed to sit down.

They were silent for a few moments before Anne spoke. 'I should have told you this earlier, but I . . . didn't believe it could have happened. Then finally I thought it was absurd, I had to know one way or the other. So I went to the chemist and . . . Edward, I'm pregnant.'

They looked at each other in silence. Edward was stunned. He didn't know what to say. After a moment he managed, 'The test . . . is it . . .'

Anne nodded. 'They're very reliable. But I've made an appointment with the doctor.'

'But . . . you're fairly certain now.'

Anne nodded again. 'I'm sure he'll confirm it.'

Edward looked up and caught the eye of an ancient

bishop who seemed to be frowning darkly down on him from where he hung, framed, on the wall.

Edward had poured himself a scotch, Anne had refused to drink anything.

'I haven't done this on purpose, Edward.'

'No.'

'Or to trap you.'

'That didn't even occur to me.'

'Quite honestly, I don't know how it's happened.'

Edward hummed. 'And what do you . . . how do you feel about it?'

'I feel as though I've trapped myself,' Anne said, forlornly.

'Anne, I'll be here. I'm not going anywhere.'

Anne looked at him. 'You're also married to Jessica.'

Edward nodded. 'Yes. I am. Yes.'

'It's not as if I've ever wanted a baby,' Anne said, sounding angry with herself. 'I've never felt that. I like my life the way it is, I don't want it to change. That's what's so awful. I don't *want* a baby.'

Edward felt slightly calmer when he heard Anne say that. 'Well, of course, it's entirely your decision.'

'I've never seen myself as a mother. I can hardly imagine it.'

'It *is* an *enormous* commitment.'

'And what sort of mother would I make? What sort of life could I give a child?'

Edward gave his most reassuring expression.

'I just can't see it,' Anne went on.

'How many weeks is it, Anne?'

'Five or six. Seven at most.'

'Yes. It's still very, very early then.'

Anne nodded.

Edward thought how he'd never seen her looking so

meek before. 'There shouldn't be any, er, problems in that department, then,' he said.

It was then Anne realised that Edward was assuming that they were talking about an abortion. She looked at him as though he had just punched her in the belly. She felt tears welling up but somehow found the strength to stop them overflowing. In doing so she temporarily lost the ability to communicate.

Edward was pacing around the room now, oblivious to Anne's changed condition.

'There really is no need to worry, Anne,' he was saying. 'Really, no need at all. I mean, so long as we stay calm and keep communicating with each other, everything will work out all right. There's nothing that can't be overcome with a little understanding on all sides.'

Anne was about to say something when the door opened and Simon put his head round.

'Edward, we really ought to get moving if we're going to get there on time.'

Before Anne knew it, Edward was going out of the door with his jacket on. He turned and said quietly, 'Anne, we must talk more tomorrow. You will be all right, won't you?'

He didn't wait to see her nod.

Monday afternoon.

I feel such a frump. I know I shouldn't because it's mainly Charlie that's made me feel like that, but I bloody well do.

Today was my first day, or I should say morning at work – and I'm ashamed to say I enjoyed it thoroughly. A bloody insurance office, and to me it was the most fun I'd had in weeks!! So much for my dreams of being an international ad exec with a gold

AMEX card and my own BMW. There I was having the time of my life filing old claims and answering the telephone. No, really, it was nice – the people round here are very friendly. And I'm very lonely, I guess.

Anyway I get home all excited, dying to tell my gorgeous hubby all about it and when I get in there's a party going on. Thomas, Charlie and Gabriel all hammered and having a laugh. Charlie was actually sitting on Thomas's knee when I walked in and Gabriel was smoking a fag!! He never smokes, so it must have been quite a party.

Anyhow, the moment I walk in Thomas shoves Charlie off, Gabriel stands up looking like a boy who's been caught out misbehaving and Charlie makes some comment about me being disapproving!! All I fucking wanted was to have a drink myself, but no, the party breaks up, Thomas and Charlie get off and Old Mother Hubbard here looks like a member of the No Fun Party.

Gabriel sulked – or went very quiet and sheepish for about twenty minutes – so I went upstairs to get changed, but really it was to have a good cry. Maybe I should start smoking marijuana or something to prove that I'm not the boring little wife, or have sex with all the men in the village!! Only joking!!!

Anyway, it turns out Gabriel feels guilty because I was at work and he had invited Thomas over for a chat and Charlie had gatecrashed. Thomas and Gabriel were so pissed off with Charlie hanging around that they decided they may as well have a few drinks and so it had gone on until they were all pissed. Gabriel apparently thought I'd think he was a lazy good-for-nothing while I was out sweating for both of us.

So anyway I told him I'd forgive him if he had me over the kitchen table, which he promptly did – with considerable zest!! I must make him feel guilty more often!!!

Anyway, he's sitting there sketching now while I write this.

I spoke too soon. Now he's bloody gone up to the house to see Jessica about some charcoal sticks she promised to get him or something. And I've reported all there is to report in my exciting life, so I'm going to watch telly. On my own.

Later that evening, as Edward was preparing to go to bed he decided to nip downstairs for a nightcap. When he turned on the kitchen light he was surprised and slightly dismayed to find his elder daughter sitting there in the darkness.

'Helena! What on earth are you doing?'

It was obvious from the look on her face what Lenny was doing. She was brooding and had probably been crying.

Lenny spoke in a monotone. 'I rang the house. There was no reply. Bit of a relief really. I wasn't sure what I was going to say.' Lenny banged her fist on the table. 'How could he do it! You're a man, daddy, you tell me. How could he choose this other woman in place of his wife and his son?'

Edward blinked. He wondered whether God had perhaps sent his daughter home on this very day to torment him, to talk to him indirectly. He sighed heavily. 'I'm sure he hasn't really done that, not in the way you put it, Lenny.'

'Then where is he tonight? Where was he last night? And all those other nights? Have you any idea how much this hurts? It's like he's taken my guts and wrung them out. No, torn them out and is now burning them in front of my eyes. Doesn't he think about anyone but himself. It really hurts a woman to know that her man is . . .' Lenny shuddered at the thought. '*Sleeping* with another woman. He's a dog, daddy, no better than an animal.'

Edward wished the light wasn't so bright. 'I'm sure it wasn't something he deliberately intended. I mean, to hurt you.' Edward found that he was wringing his hands.

'So what *did* he intend?'

Edward shook his head. 'Oh, I doubt if he knew. He's obviously become involved with this woman somehow . . .' It was hard to know what to say. 'I expect he was just being selfish,' Edward said.

'You would never put mum through anything like that, would you? You would never betray mummy – *you* couldn't have done it. What makes him different?'

Edward felt despicable. 'That's what I'm saying, Helena. I'm sure Mark . . . I mean, it's not a deliberate betrayal.'

'So *what* then? Some game? Is he just playing with my feelings? That makes it worse.'

Edward nodded. 'It's the sin of wanting more than we're entitled to. And I admit, yes, the sinners are mostly men. And believe me, Helena, there will probably be a price to pay.'

'Well, if there's a price, he deserves to pay it.'

Edward looked at his daughter, at the pain written on her face and felt for a moment as if he'd caused it.

God was definitely talking to him.

·7·

FOR ONCE IN her life Charlie was smiling at breakfast.

'Mary, I'm in love.'

Mary was happily changing little Ben's nappy and cooing stupidly at him. She looked up and smiled indulgently at Charlie. 'I was only saying to Lenny this morning that it seems like ten minutes since I changed your nappy, Charlotte. And here you are telling me you're in love.'

'I'm mega-besotted. I can hardly sleep.'

'I remember when you weren't in the least interested in boys,' Mary teased. 'You used to complain that they were always trying to kiss you.'

'He's not a boy, Mary.'

Mary looked up from her wiping and wrapping. 'Not a boy?'

Charlie shook her head and grinned. 'Uh-uh.'

'It's a girl?' Mary laughed warmly, determined not to be the fuddy-duddy. 'Well, you always were one for experimenting. I expect it's a lot easier to get along with a girl. Men are so difficult to talk to sometimes.'

Charlie couldn't keep a straight face any longer. 'Mary!

– It's not a *girl*! When I said it's not a *boy* I meant it's a *man*. I've finished messing around with stupid boys who don't know what they're doing and fall in love with you and then you can't get rid of them.' Charlie laughed. 'I can't *believe* you thought I was a *lezzie*!'

Mary went back to wiping Ben's bottom. 'It's nice to know you've got an open mind, Charlie. That's what I like about your generation.'

Charlie ignored that. 'Aren't you going to warn me about the dangers of going out with an older man?'

'How old is he?'

'It's Thomas Hunt.'

'Gabriel's best man?'

'Uh-uh.'

Mary sighed. 'He's a young man to me, Charlie.'

'I'm totally in love.'

'And how does Thomas feel about that?'

'He doesn't know. Yet.'

'I see. And is he interested?'

'Oh, definitely. I know the signs.'

'Well, just be careful.'

'See, you *are* going to warn me about the dangers of older men.'

Mary looked up. 'I'd just make sure you don't turn out to be a girl who doesn't know what she's doing and who falls in love and who can't be got rid of.'

Charlie was indignant. 'No way! It's not like that.'

'How do you know?'

'I just know.'

'Well, that's the danger of older men. You might end up getting your heart broken.'

'No way,' Charlie said again, and started getting ready to go.

'It might do you some good, anyway, to know how it feels to be on the receiving end for a change.'

'Thanks, Mary. Love you too,' Charlie said, picking up her bag. 'Right. I'm going to school. See you later.' She hopped over to Mary and kissed her on the cheek.

'Be good,' said Mary, smiling to herself.

'I won't,' Charlie sang, happily.

Anne was late arriving at work because she had been to the doctor's.

Edward was nervous, even though both he and Anne knew what the result would be. By the time Anne arrived he had practically gnawed through his thumb. She came straight into his office, still in her coat, and closed the door behind her. Neither of them had mentioned the subject for days, each avoiding being alone with the other. There was nothing Edward wanted to say until he was sure; Anne sensed this and had needed time to think things out herself.

'Well?'

'There's no surprise, Edward. I'm in the sixth week of pregnancy. The doctor confirmed it.'

'I'm sorry, Anne.'

'So am I.'

'I understand how hard this must be for you,' Edward said. 'I'm so sorry.'

Anne looked at him, waited for him to continue. She wanted him to reveal his true feelings on the subject without prompting from her.

'You haven't been out of my mind for a moment since . . . since we spoke the other day. I keep thinking about what you said.' Edward looked at her with his most charming and loving face. 'You were right, Anne. I think you're very brave. And very realistic.'

Anne nodded. 'I hope I am,' she said.

'We're both sensible people. We knew what we were doing. And we enjoyed it.'

'I don't regret any of it, Edward.'

'No. No, it's been beautiful. And I'm sure it will be beautiful again.'

Anne nodded, and continued to wait.

Edward began pacing the office. 'There are so many reasons why you can't have the baby. If you were younger; if I didn't have a wife and family; if the world wasn't so quick to criticise.' He turned to look at her again. 'Nothing's going to change between us, Anne. Nothing.' Anne's expression had changed now. Edward was apparently oblivious to that. 'I've thought very carefully about what we should do next,' he went on. 'It's important that we support each other. I don't want you to face any unpleasantness on your own.' He had considered everything. 'There are things I won't be able to do. Realistically I can't go to the clinic with you, but I will take care of the medical bills. That much I *can* manage. It's the least I can do.'

Anne shook her head. 'There won't be any need, Edward, I . . .'

'We must get the very best treatment. We'll find a very good clinic – private. Very discreet.' He waved his hand generously. 'Take as much time off work as you like.'

'Edward, I *can* cope on my own.'

Edward was amazed. 'But why *should* you, Anne. This is as much my problem as it is yours. I have no intention of evading my responsibilities.'

Anne took a deep breath. 'I understood the situation I was getting myself into. I know there are limits to what I can expect from you.'

Edward was adamant. 'We'll face things together. It doesn't make any difference to how we feel about each other. It's sad, and I wish it hadn't happened, but nothing's changed. Nothing *could* change.' His own generosity was making Edward feel a lot better about the situation.

95

Anne was perfectly calm as she looked at her lover. Calm, but sad. She knew it would be hard for him to accept, she knew that it would be a burden for him. But she knew she could cope with what was required. 'Edward, I'm thirty-seven years old. You've been the only man in my life for years now, and you've got your family. Even if I started seeing someone else right away, I could be thirty-nine or forty before I became pregnant again.' Edward just looked at her. 'This could be my last chance to have a child.'

Nothing, only Edward's blank face staring at her. Perhaps he was waiting for her to put what she was saying into a single, decisive statement before commenting, before believing her.

'Edward, I'm not having an abortion. I know it's the clean and tidy solution, but I'm not taking it. I want this baby.'

Edward shook his head. 'You don't, Anne.'

'I do, Edward. I want it more than I've ever wanted anything. I'm adrift. I need something to commit myself to. It's taken this to make me realise. The baby's a chance I've been given, and I'm not going to throw it away. Nothing you say will change my mind about having this child. Now, if you'll excuse me, I have work to do.'

Edward went over to his desk and sat down.

Thomas had been practising his piano for an hour when there was a knock at the door.

Things had not been going well lately for Thomas. Respectable work had been hard to come by, so lately he'd been reduced to doing session work on radio jingles and had even played with a couple of aspiring local pop bands, all work he considered beneath himself. He was quite glad therefore that someone had called to distract him.

It was Charlie.

'Do you ever go to school?' he said, when he saw her.

'I try my best not to.'

'Come in.'

'Am I interrupting anything?'

'Yes.'

'Oh, good.'

Charlie loved Thomas's flat. It was everything a teenage girl dreams about when she fantasises about falling in love with a fashionable man, and although in Charlie's case dreams usually took place somewhere like Paris or at least London, Thomas's flat struck her as the best thing she had ever seen.

'It's like a film set!' she said.

'That's where I got the idea,' Thomas said.

Charlie felt her legs trembling slightly. 'Is it cold or is it just me?' she asked. Even her teeth felt like chattering.

'I'm fine,' Thomas said, 'but I'll turn the heating up a bit for you.'

'Put the kettle on while you're at it,' Charlie said.

When Thomas had gone Charlie nearly fainted with excitement. She knew that her trembling had nothing to do with temperature. Her plan had been to tell him to put the kettle on and, while he was in the kitchen, take all her clothes off and lie on the sofa like Kate Moss in that Obsession for Men advert. But now she was here she found herself frozen with fright. She was on the verge of doing it, yet she was suddenly too scared of him saying something dreadful like, 'Oh, come off it, Charlie, put your clothes on,' in that big-brother tone he used sometimes which filled her with dismay.

Thomas popped his head round the corner of the kitchen area and caught her dithering. 'Shall I put some fresh coffee on? Are you all right?'

'Um, yes. Er, coffee, yes.' *Jesus!* She could hardly even speak. Come on, girl, don't be pathetic.

She thought back to the day she had spent with Thomas and Gabriel, before the Bore came home and broke up the party. She'd had some serious doubts later, when she replayed scenes in her head. An alternative scenario had haunted her throughout the evening: that Gabriel and Thomas had secretly been wishing she would leave them alone. She had been slightly uncomfortable all day and it was only later that she recognised the old feeling of not being wanted, of being in the way. But then again, she told herself, as she stood poised to remove her clothes and be either rejected or taken by Thomas in anyway he saw fit, by the end of the day she had been sat there on Thomas's knee and the three of them had been laughing like old comrades.

She caught a glimpse of herself in Thomas's long, ornamental mirror.

Maybe she should just change into her casual clothes and wait to see how things developed. Thomas had seemed pleased enough to see her. He must have just wanted to spend time with Gabriel the other day. That would explain why he had seemed a bit cold to begin with, then. She blushed. Dammit. I was too bloody hasty! Now she had to make a decision: take a risk and be hasty again, or play safe. One way or the other.

She didn't like the idea of playing safe, it went against her philosophy, but then again the stakes were high. Charlie felt herself trembling even more and pondered that if she was trembling now, what would it be like if Thomas were to take her to bed!

'Do you mind if I get changed out of my school uniform?' she called.

'Of course not,' came the reply from the kitchen.

★

After what Anne considered to be a long time, Edward emerged from his office.

'Anne, I wonder if I could have a word, please.'

'Yes, Edward, certainly. Simon, would you answer the phone, please?'

'Yes, of course.'

As soon as the door closed behind her, Edward said, 'Sit down, Anne. We must talk.'

'Thank you, Edward. Yes, we must.'

He looked at her for a long time before he spoke, weighing his words carefully, as though reading from a prepared script. 'Anne. Everything has changed. We knew where we were before. We knew what we were doing. This was not a part of the plan. We've both got too much to lose.' Getting no reaction from Anne, Edward went on: 'We've always played by the rules. You shouldn't be pregnant. It just shouldn't have happened.'

'It has happened, Edward.'

'Yes, well, it shouldn't have.'

Anne knew what Edward was thinking. 'Edward, I won't tell Jessica. Ever.'

His response was far too quick. 'I'm not thinking about Jessica.'

'You must be. It's only reasonable . . .'

'I'm worried about you, Anne.'

'Don't be, there's no need. Honestly.'

'You're not thinking straight, Anne. You're on your own.'

'I always have been.'

'A secretary's salary won't take you very far. I know how much children cost. It's time as well as money. You won't be able to manage by yourself.'

'Other people do.'

'I don't want you to struggle.'

'I've got savings.'

'How much? How long will they last?'

'Long enough.'

Edward sighed and shook his head. He knew he was not going to change Anne's mind and he suddenly felt uncomfortable trying. The poor woman had little enough in her life and he could understand her wanting to bring up a child, even with the stigma of being an unmarried mother. He opened his hands in a gesture of surrender. He had thought it would come to this. 'OK. OK. I can see you want to keep the child.'

Anne smiled, very warmly.

Edward sighed, very deeply. 'I'll give you financial support. It'll have to be on an informal basis, but I can set something up.'

Anne said, 'I don't want you to be compromised, Edward. I love you.'

Edward nearly flinched at this last remark, but managed to contain himself. 'You should move away,' he said. 'You need a new home, a new job. Start your life again.'

Anne felt this as a blow. 'Move away? Why?' She shook her head.

'It makes sense, Anne.'

'Not to me, it doesn't.'

'I'll buy a house, or a flat, whatever you need. I'll give you money for a new car, clothes, a holiday maybe. And when the baby comes . . .'

Anne didn't want to hear any more. 'This is my home. My friends are here.'

'You'll make new friends.'

Anne was getting angry now. 'You're trying to get rid of me!'

'I'm doing what's best.'

Anne was staggered. 'You're doing what's best for you, not for me.'

Edward was oblivious to her distress. 'Have you any

100

idea what it'd be like for you in this town? It's a small community. Church people aren't as forgiving as they make out. An unmarried mother working in my office? There'd be gossip. There'd be fingers pointed.'

Anne set her face. 'I don't care.'

'They'd make your life a misery.'

'Who would? Small-minded bigots don't worry me. Inside or outside the church.'

Edward was getting angry himself now. 'We've got to think of the future.'

'That is exactly what I am thinking of, Edward.'

Edward banged his fist on his desk. 'Be sensible, Anne!'

Both of them were shocked at Edward's gesture, though Anne was better able to hide it. 'What is sensible about going away, leaving everything, my friends, my . . . my lover? Being stuck by myself in a new part of the country? Nothing.'

'You'd be the cause of great scandal here, Anne, you've no idea.'

'I'd be a nine-day wonder.'

'It's you I'm thinking of, Anne.'

Anne stood up. 'Is it?'

Edward stood up and came around his desk to her. 'I don't want you to suffer, Anne.'

'It sounds like it!'

He took hold of her arm. Firmly. 'I'm not making a good job of this, I know. I know how you must feel. But you have to understand. I don't want to lose you. That's the last thing . . . If I arrange for you to live in a town, I can visit in the course of my work. It'll be easier to carry on seeing you. No matter where you decide to go, I'll make sure there are reasons for me to travel there.'

Anne was shaking her head. She spoke lightly, sarcastically. 'There are only so many conferences a bishop can attend, Edward.'

'I'm in a position of authority. Meetings can be rescheduled to suit my busy timetable.'

Anne's face hadn't changed. Edward would have given anything at that moment to have control over her face, to make it look on him in that friendly, that *compliant* way of hers. 'Nothing's impossible, Anne, you know that. It would be easier if you had your own place, away from prying eyes.'

Anne seemed at last to give way, slightly. Edward felt her arm go limp in his grip. 'I don't know,' she whispered.

It was enough to give Edward some hope. 'Think about it. I'm begging you. Just go away and think things through.'

Anne looked distinctly uncertain.

'I'll stand by anything you decide,' he said, and immediately realised that that wasn't necessarily true. He reassured himself, though, that she was emotional, that she was overcome with the shock of it all. 'I want what's best for us both.'

'And for the baby?' Anne said.

'Yes. Yes. And for the baby.'

For the first time in her life, Charlie had opted for the middle way, somewhere between safety and haste. She decided to wait until the coffee was ready before changing in front of Thomas – this time Gabriel was not there to restrain them. When Thomas appeared Charlie pretended to have been distracted by his record collection, and when the coffee was poured and Thomas seated comfortably on the sofa, she went for it.

Right down to her bra and pants she went even before she opened her bag to produce the clothes she had brought with her. As she stripped off she chatted about the records in his collection, calling Thomas an old hippie and questioning his knowledge of bands that were around now. She was, however, quite impressed by his familiarity with the current scene, and when he told her that he was trying to get work with one of her favourite bands, which was a bit of an exaggeration, Charlie abandoned all pretence at wanting to put on the clothes she'd brought and hopped excitedly over to the sofa in her underwear, demanding to know more as if in her excitement she had forgotten she was undressed.

After a while Thomas said, 'Are you warmer now, then?'

Charlie just laughed. 'It's nice to be able to sit around like this,' she said. 'If I had my way I'd go round naked the whole time.'

Thomas looked at her. 'It would be nice, wouldn't it.'

Charlie nearly had an orgasm on the spot, or so she told herself later when she replayed the scene. Haste at this stage would have been in extremely bad taste, she was enjoying the tense, sexy atmosphere which felt as if it were nearly choking her. She stretched back on the sofa and let her body present itself like a cat's belly.

'Sometimes I wish I had my own place just so I could spend whole days naked,' Charlie said.

Thomas said, 'Oh, I often do that here,' which actually wasn't true.

'Do you?'

- 'Sometimes.'

Charlie wanted to purr and squirm about. 'I'd invite people round and we could all be naked together.'

'Yeah?'

Charlie nodded. She could hardly believe the way she was feeling. It was quite unlike any of the sexual feelings she'd experienced so far. It was nicer sitting there in her bra and pants than it had been screwing other guys. She let the feeling spread and as she did so her teeth chattered.

'You *are* cold,' he said.

Charlie shook her head. 'No. Actually, I'm feeling pretty hot.'

Thomas smiled. 'You're very attractive, Charlie. Do you know that?'

Charlie laughed. 'You don't just see me as an annoying little git you want to get rid of, then?'

'Hardly,' said Thomas. 'You look very like Gabriel, you know. I've often thought that.' He laughed. 'Especially with no clothes on!'

Charlie laughed, too. 'It's just as well I happen to think Gabriel's one of the nicest-looking girls I've ever known.'

Thomas continued the theme. 'You definitely have nicer breasts than him.'

Charlie was about to say, 'Oh, thanks' to that, when she had a better idea. She stood up and undid her bra. 'Are you sure about that now?' she giggled, and stood there while Thomas double-checked.

Thomas said, 'Come here.'

Charlie felt as if she might pass out on the way.

Gabriel was sketching and Rachel was pretending to write in her diary; really she was watching Gabriel.

Lenny knocked at the door and came in. She'd visited several times that week already and knew she was welcome, despite, as she put it, the fact that she was family.

'Let me in. I can't take another minute.'

'Mother?' Gabriel asked.

'How did you guess? Hi, Rachel.'

Rachel said, 'Hiya, you look exhausted.'

'Her voice penetrates every nook and cranny of the house!' Lenny said. 'I never noticed it before.'

Gabriel said, 'Every bugger else did.'

Rachel smiled. 'She's a *wonderful* woman.'

'I told her to say that,' Gabriel quipped.

'No, actually, I'm having to Be Fair to Jessica week,' Rachel laughed.

Lenny tried to smile, but didn't quite make it. 'You should have seen her in Market Cross today. Mrs Rattigan in full credit-card regalia. Ben has enough baby-grows now to last till he goes to university. That's if she doesn't decide to make him study for his degree from home on a correspondence course!'

Rachel and Gabriel roared with laughter at the heresy of Lenny's words.

Rachel said, 'She brought us some wonderful items to furnish the Lodge.'

'Where have you hidden them?' Lenny said.

Rachel said, 'You could stay here with us, Lenny. We wouldn't mind, would we Gabriel?'

Rachel had grown very fond of Lenny over the last few days; she felt very sorry for her too.

'We'd be delighted,' Gabriel said.

Lenny knew as well as they did that it was impossible. 'If I didn't have Ben, I would,' she said.

'If you didn't have Ben, you wouldn't need to be here at all,' Rachel said.

Lenny nodded. 'True.'

'Coffee?' Gabriel asked her.

'How about Mother's Ruin?' Lenny grinned. 'No, coffee's fine.'

When Gabriel was out of earshot, Lenny said, 'I feel about fifteen again. I only intended to stay a few days, but already it feels like I never left home in the first place and I'm gunna be stuck here for ever.'

Rachel put her arm round her.

Lenny went on, 'This family's a wild animal, Rachel. Once it gets hold of you it won't let go until . . .' She stopped. 'I'm being over-dramatic.'

'Are you?' asked Rachel.

'I bloody well hope so,' Lenny laughed.

Late evening.

I swore I'd write this:

Having a nice time.

There. For a few days now nothing much has happened. Poor Lenny seems to be getting all the trouble, but – touch wood – everything's going OK for me and Gabriel. I'm looking around expecting the roof to fall in now I've written it, but no.

Gabriel keeps coming up to me and telling me he loves me. What more could a girl want?

Sighs, takes a sip from her glass of whisky, looks over at her gorgeous husband and looks forward to the sex she's going to have at bedtime.

The time had come for Edward to talk to Jessica.

To do so, he had manoeuvred her into the bedroom. Jessica was suspicious in case Edward wanted sex for once, which would have been out of the question; sex was not something they had had for a long time, or which Jessica ever wanted them to have again, so she had been reluctant to go upstairs at that time of the evening.

There was no way he could be subtle about it. 'Anne's pregnant,' he said and braced himself.

Jessica's voice was ten degrees colder than death. 'You don't mean that.'

'I'm afraid I do.'

'How could she be pregnant? How could you allow her to be?'

'It was an accident, of course.'

Jessica's head twitched rather than moved. 'There is no such thing.'

106

'It happened.'

'Is that all you can say?' Jessica hissed.

Edward sighed. 'She suspected she might be and the doctor confirmed it yesterday. I thought she wanted an abortion, but now she says she wants to keep it.'

Jessica looked puzzled. 'Why keep it?'

'It could be her last chance.'

Jessica was still puzzled. 'So what?'

'She seems determined.'

'And what are *you*, Edward?'

Edward waved a hand. 'I offered to find her a new job. I said I'd put in a word with the right people.'

'Did you say you'd give her money?'

'Yes.'

'How much?'

'She turned it down.'

Jessica's lips tightened. 'She'll want more. She knows you can get it.'

'Darling, she's not like that.'

'Nonsense!'

'Jessica, she wants a child.'

'Yours?'

'She feels that she needs something else in her life.'

Jessica made a noise through her nose. 'She's got you where she wants you and you're too blind to see it. You mustn't allow it, Edward.'

'I can't force her to have an abortion.'

'Can you force her to move house?'

Edward shook his head. 'No.'

'I thought not.' Jessica laughed coldly. 'What are you going to tell your flock? Will you introduce them as your second family? Will they be welcomed into the Christian community?'

Edward had expected this. He had to let Jessica have her say.

'Because churchgoers count, you know. You may not hold them in high esteem, Edward, but they have faith in you. You are their leader, their shepherd. To them you can do no wrong.'

Again Edward waved a hand. 'I'll try again. I'll persuade her to move away.'

Jessica was adamant. 'If a whisper of this gets out, your career's finished. You'll find yourself on the street. Bishops don't spawn bastards, Edward, however liberal they may be.'

'I'll do all I can,' was all Edward could say.

She looked straight at him. 'Think of me. Knowing another woman has your child. Think of the family, what they'd be exposed to.' Jessica no longer looked cold. Now she looked hurt. 'You're not *any* man, Edward. You hold a position. You offer moral leadership. People come to you for guidance. You've written books; you've made broadcasts.'

'I know I have, Jessica, I know.' Edward wanted to go down before her and ask forgiveness. It was out of the question.

'It threatens everything. *You* threaten everything, Edward. You're a fool who can't get the basics right. You always have been.'

'I'll talk to her.'

Jessica was unbending. 'That's not enough. She's not going to get the chance to announce the name of her child's father. She could hold that over us for years. Ten. Twenty. Whatever she felt like. If she has the baby, we live with the threat. And I'm not going to, Edward. There's no choice about it. She has an abortion. Simple as that.'

·8·

CHARLIE FELT HALF an inch of air between the soles of her feet and the ground.

Mary noticed it and Charlie loved her for it.

'Do I detect a little success on the love front?' Mary asked the following morning.

Charlie ran up and gave her a hug.

'I thought so.'

'Oh, Mary, he's just so brill!'

Charlie talked non-stop about Thomas's flat, calling it his *pad*, and about all the things he'd done recently, especially about the band he was going to join, which according to the way Charlie told it, included a record deal and a single that was definitely going to be a smash. She desperately wanted to tell Mary about the sex they'd had, too, but it would have been impossible, partly because she could hardly describe it to herself. She would have to wait until she got to school and collared her best friend, Melissa. It was the only day in the term when Charlie had been looking forward to going to school.

On the way there she thought back over the events of the previous day as a prelude to describing them to Melissa. It had been both mega-fantastic and a bit weird at the same time. She'd had a bet with Melissa that if you went with an older man it was guaranteed that they would go down on you. The idea of this activity had held the two friends in suspense for a number of years now since they had first discovered its existence in a Jackie Collins novel that Melissa had stolen from her mother. It was, according to Charlie, the highest compliment a man could pay a woman and would automatically bring a rush of the deepest sexual ecstasy the very moment it was performed. Melissa thought that no one would ever do it to you and if they did you'd be too worried in case you smelled bad. Both, however, were equally fascinated by the idea and Melissa would be very glad that it had happened to Charlie first.

For happened it had.

As soon as Thomas took her in his arms on the sofa Charlie just knew he was going to want to do it to her. She had once persuaded Nick to do it to her, but when Nick got down into the area all he could do was sort of poke her in the wrong place with his tongue and then come straight back up expecting to be considered Casanova. With Thomas it was entirely different. Thomas had kissed her as they lay on the sofa and then picked her up and carried her to his bed, or at least to the bottom of the ladder leading up to his bed, which was a double-groovy cave in the top corner of the gallery-like living room, full of hanging curtains and velvet covers. She couldn't believe how turned on she was by then and actually felt dizzy by the time Thomas had taken his own clothes off and laid himself down beside her.

She nearly tingled to death as he gently kissed her and stroked her all over. She wasn't used to it, so far she had only been with guys who wanted to jump straight on top of her and roll off again three minutes after. Then he started working his way *down there*. Charlie moaned with delight as soon as she realised what was happening. Unfortunately, though, it wasn't quite the deepest sexual ecstasy the very moment he started touching her with his tongue. Thomas, despite his willingness, was a little clumsy and she jumped when he caught her awkwardly. But then a *really amazing* thing happened. Thomas *asked* her how to do it and where he should do it exactly, where it felt nicest and how hard he should do it. Apart from being a little shy at first, Charlie was staggered that Thomas wasn't the world's leading expert on the subject. But then she was glad because when she did tell him which part felt nicest and he got down to it, sexual ecstasy did come, especially as she felt less intimidated by him because he'd asked her advice.

It was the first time she had come with another person and afterwards she felt so excited and so *honoured* that she wanted to climb up on to the roof and tell the world that Thomas Hunt had gone down on her and made her come. It was definitely worth going to school the next day just to tell Melissa about it.

The peculiar thing, though, and this gave Charlie some considerable food for thought, was that Thomas had been content to leave it at that. He didn't want to do it to her afterwards and when she had gone to do what she had practised on Nick, he told her not to bother, he was happy for now. Although this disturbed Charlie, she said nothing about it. It was obvious that older men were a different kettle of fish altogether.

When she told Melissa all about what happened, she missed out this last episode. When Melissa asked Charlie what it had been like when they had had *proper* sex, she just said, 'Great.'

Jessica was a stone wall that morning. She saw Edward to the door like a military attaché.

'You'll need your coat. It's quite chilly.'

Edward nodded. 'Yes.'

'Here's your briefcase.'

'Thank you.'

'Edward?'

'Yes, Jessica?'

'She has to get rid of it.'

'Yes.'

'I won't accept the risk of humiliation.'

'I would be humiliated, too.'

'You've had the pleasure, Edward.'

Edward looked at his wife. 'Do you think I intended this to happen?'

Jessica looked at him. '*She* may have done.'

'I doubt it.'

Jessica smiled up at him. 'In that case, persuading her will be easy. Talk to her straight away.'

'I may not be able to, Jessica. Simon is in the office.'

'Get to her before the notion of keeping the child really takes hold. Tomorrow may be too late.'

'I'll speak to her as soon as possible.'

'Telephone me,' Jessica insisted. 'I'll be here. I'll wait for the call.'

As soon as the office door closed behind Anne, Edward took her in his arms and kissed her.

The kiss lasted for nearly a minute and a half and, by the end of it, both of them wanted to make love there and then, on the great leather *chaise longue*.

As he pulled back, Edward said, 'I've been longing to do that.'

Anne seemed surprised. 'Have you?'

'The last thing I ever wanted was to hurt you.'

'You haven't hurt me.'

'Yesterday I upset you.'

Anne pressed herself to his chest. 'It's all right, Edward.'

'I said things off the top of my head. I panicked.'

'So did I. I thought you were trying to get rid of me. I thought you didn't want to know me any more.'

Edward held her even more tightly, partly out of a feeling of profound guilt. 'That's not it, Anne. I was worried about what might happen to you, and I still am.'

'I'll be fine. Really.'

Edward took hold of Anne's shoulders and held her at arm's length, looking earnestly into her eyes. 'Anne, listen to me carefully. I think it would be the wisest choice not to continue this pregnancy.' Anne held his gaze, steadily. Encouraged, Edward went on, 'It's hard, but you have to put yourself first. The child isn't here yet. Think of the consequences, and the difficulties the child would face. It's not easy. It could never be easy . . .'

Anne pulled away, unable to listen any longer. 'Don't put pressure on me, Edward.'

'I'm trying to help! I want you to look at every possibility.'

'No. You want me to look at one possibility. Not the possibility that things might work out OK, that I might be *happy* with my baby, with *our* baby. Abortion is a horrible thing. It's ending life . . . life born out of love . . .' Anne shuddered at the thought. 'Horrible.'

Edward tried to stay calm. 'There are reasons for every action we take. No one could accuse you of being hardhearted. You're not selfish.'

Edward stopped. He could see his words were having no effect.

Anne looked at the floor. 'I couldn't do it.'

The intimacy that had come from their embrace was dissipated. Edward knew that without intimacy, all hope of sensible conversation was lost.

'I'm sorry, Anne. We can't talk here.'

She looked at him. 'No. I don't want to talk here. This is horrible.'

'We should meet.'

'Yes.'

'Why don't we eat out somewhere, tonight?'

'Not tonight, Edward.'

'Tomorrow, then. Somewhere nice.'

'You don't want to come to my house.'

Edward could feel Anne's pain. He shut down on it. 'No. I don't think it's a good idea.'

'Why not? In case I get hysterical?'

'No.'

'Come then.'

'Anne, please. Let's meet somewhere where we won't make matters worse.'

Anne nodded coldly. 'All right. You decide somewhere and let me know. There's no reason why we should change our habits now.'

Lenny had two surprises that morning.

She had concocted what she considered to be a master plan. She was going to Oxford, to the house, to take her belongings while Mark was out at work. Her first surprise was at Mary's reaction. All she said to Mary was that she was thinking of going to Oxford.

Mary said, 'You're going to raid the house,' and, 'Can I come?'

Lenny laughed and Mary agreed to look after Ben in the car, to keep a look-out while Lenny went in and got everything she wanted.

'I'd love to give that husband of yours a bloody nose.'

The second, even bigger, surprise had come when Lenny told her mother what she and Mary were planning.

Jessica said, 'I'm glad you're coming to your senses at last.'

Lenny nearly did a double-take. 'You don't mind?'

'Certainly not. Why should I?'

'I thought you'd want me to be cautious.'

Jessica was putting on her coat ready to go out. 'He's cheated on you,' she said. 'He's lied. He's brought you down. You're entitled to whatever's there. You've got the car. Fill it with anything you can move. I don't advise caution. Quite the opposite, Lenny. Take the bugger for everything he's got.' So saying, Jessica marched to the door.

'Where are you going?' Lenny asked, her mouth open in awe.

'I'm going to see your father,' she said, and slammed the door behind her.

Charlie nipped out of school at lunchtime to phone Thomas from the phone box over the road.

He didn't sound that pleased to hear from her.

'Hello, Charlie. Where are you?'

'I'm in a phone box. Can I come and see you after school?'

'I'm busy.'

'I'll soon put a stop to that.'

'I'm going out.'

'I'll come over later.'

'I'm out all night.'

'All night . . . over night?'

'No, just till late.'

'I'll come over late, then.'

'No, Charlie, not tonight.'

'Tomorrow night.'

'Leave it till next week, OK?'

'How about the weekend?'

'I'm busy.'

She had to try another tack. 'Gabriel said why don't we go over to the Lodge Friday evening,' she lied.

There was a pause at Thomas's end. 'You've told him?'

'Yes,' she lied again.

'What did he say?'

'He was cool.'

'You mean he was cold.'

'No, I mean he said it was cool.'

'Humm. Friday night?'

Charlie felt a little stab of excitement. Thomas had changed his tune. 'Yes,' she said. 'Friday night.'

'It would be nice to see Gabriel.'

'The Bore will be there, too, probably.'

'I like Rachel.'

'Well, good. Friday night, then?'

'OK.'

Yes! 'Shall I come round to yours first?'

'No. I'll make my own way and see you there. Did Gabriel say a time?'

'Er . . . seven-thirty.'

'OK. See you there.'

'OK. Er, Thomas?'

'What?'

'Thanks for the other day.'

He softened. At last. 'It was nice, wasn't it.'

'Yeah. See ya.'

'See you Friday.'

She waited for the dialling tone before she put the phone down.

Yes!!! *It was nice wasn't it!* Those had been his words. They rang in Charlie's head for some minutes before she finally sobered up enough to realise that she'd better get down to Gabriel's double-quick – as soon as she got home – and wangle an invitation for Thomas and herself on Friday night.

★

116

'Good morning, Simon. Good morning, Anne.'

The sound of Jessica's voice, as she strode into the office made Anne's blood run cold.

'Morning, Mrs Rattigan,' she managed. 'It's nice to see you.'

Simon was on the telephone and nodded to Jessica.

'It's nice to see you,' Jessica said to Anne. 'Is my husband in his office?'

'Yes. I'll tell him you're here,' Anne said, getting up. 'He didn't mention you'd be dropping in.'

Jessica said, 'He didn't know,' gesturing that she would see herself into Edward's office. 'There's no need for formalities,' she said. 'We're all friends here, aren't we?'

Anne watched as Jessica disappeared into the inner office, thinking how dreadful it would be if Jessica found out.

'Why haven't you telephoned?' Jessica hissed as soon as the inner office door was closed behind her.

Edward looked decidedly dejected. 'I haven't had the chance. I can't just . . .'

'Have you spoken to her?' Jessica snapped.

'Of course I have, but . . .'

'Has she agreed?'

'It's very difficult . . .'

'Edward, is she getting rid of it?'

'Jessica, please, not so loud.'

Jessica nodded. 'She wants more money.'

'No, no.'

'What then?'

Edward was highly agitated. 'We're talking about an *abortion*.'

'Edward, I'm not worried about the niceties of Anne's feelings.'

'Shhh. If I try to force her she'll become difficult,'

Edward said, doing his best to whisper what he wanted to shout.

'You have to insist.'

'I have.'

'In the strongest possible terms.'

Edward sighed. 'I've arranged to meet her tomorrow night.'

'*Tomorrow* night?'

'It's no use rushing her. She wants to think things over.'

'Where are you meeting her.'

'A restaurant in town.'

'Oh. A candle-lit dinner for two? Very romantic. I'm sure you'll have a very cosy chat.'

'I'll try and talk her round. But to be honest, Jessica, I doubt if she'll agree. She keeps saying she wants the child. It matters to her.'

Jessica stiffened with suppressed rage. 'And what matters to *you*, Edward? Is it Anne? Perhaps it's her child? Or is it your *family*? The Rattigan family.'

Edward looked at her. 'There's no question. The family.'

'Then start acting as though the family matters.'

'Yes. You're right.'

Jessica could see her message had got through. 'Talk to her again before you meet her tomorrow. If she won't change her mind, we'll think of something else.'

Early evening.

OK, maybe I am a bit of a fuddy-duddy after all. I can't help it, but I find myself judging Charlie pretty harshly and I think the main reason is because she actually does shock me.

Really she's nothing but a spoilt little posh girl. When he first discovered sex, my brother always used to say, 'The posh girls are the worst', meaning the dirtiest in bed – which to him was the highest compliment you could possibly pay someone. I think he must have been right. Although I don't mean it as a compliment.

Charlie came round after school to announce she is sleeping with Thomas. Although he denied it, poor Gabriel was more shocked than I was. Apparently she went round to see Thomas yesterday, walked into his flat and just took her clothes off. Poor Thomas. I just can't imagine it. Thomas being one of the sweetest, most sensitive guys you can ever imagine and Charlie . . . well Charlie is Charlie. I don't think Gabriel wanted to hear all the details of the encounter – far too pornographic to repeat in writing – but Charlie stands there and tells us both all about it. Suffice to say that if we are to believe Charlie, Thomas, despite appearances, is a raving stud who likes to do it all day long and isn't afraid to – what was the term she used? – 'Go down on a girl.' I'll leave it to your imagination to make sense of that!!

Anyway. It's one thing taking your clothes off in front of a guy and him taking you to bed – I mean, what guy is going to refuse an offer like that!! But quite another thing for him to want to take you out. When I pointed this out to Charlie, which I'm afraid I couldn't resist doing, she got all shirty and announced that she and Thomas had invited themselves round to have dinner with Gabriel and me on Friday evening and that it had been Thomas's idea. You should have seen Gabriel's face. Poor thing – I had to laugh. I'm sure he was jealous. I mean it *is* quite something – your best friend who you spent your whole youth with suddenly starts going out with your little sister – the one you always had to get rid of because she was always hanging around and getting in the way. Of course he pretended to be pleased and said yes he would be delighted to see them both on Friday night, but really he was gutted. He's sitting there now, sketching – or rather, scribbling frantically away – while I write this. And of course because he's miserable he looks absolutely ravishing and I'm dying to rip his clothes off.

Giggling themselves giddy around the house in Oxford, Lenny and Mary behaved like a couple of children.

Lenny had the idea of phoning Mark's work to see if he was there. She was put straight through and put the phone down before saying anything. He was definitely at work so she knew she and Mary would be safe to go into the house and take their time. Lenny was determined to discover that Sarah had moved into the house so that divorce proceedings could take place without any hitch. The two women conducted a search of the premises that would have put the CID to shame.

At the end of it Lenny said, '*Bastard!* The crafty bastard must go over to her house for his orgies.' She had found nothing incriminating.

Mary said, 'Let's just take what we can and get out.'

All they'd found was a lipstick. The trouble was, it was the same make that Lenny used and she had to admit that it might even have been one of her own. 'I'm sure I had none of that left,' she said. 'When the bloody hell did I ever get to wear it? He never took me anywhere. Not after I had Ben.'

Lenny looked at her son's face – Mary had been holding him while they conducted their search – and felt a deep pang of something like regret, as if she blamed Ben for her predicament. Ben must have sensed something because as Lenny looked at him he threw himself shyly against Mary's shoulder and gave Lenny an irresistibly cute look. Lenny's heart nearly burst with love and guilt in equal measure. The child had merely been responding to the mention of his name, but to the poor suffering mother the timing was all too poignant. She rushed over, took him in her arms, and poured a heartful of love into him.

As she did so her resentment forcused itself once again on to the legitimate target, Mark. Scorn for her husband bit into her all the more viciously. She handed Ben back to Mary and said, 'Right,' in such a way that Mary wanted to stand to attention and take orders. They filled up the car with everything Lenny would need and a lot of things she only wanted. When the vehicle was full and Ben was strapped into his car-seat, Lenny said she was going back for one last check.

She went up to their bedroom – or what had been their bedroom – and looked about with rage. She was going for good, but she wanted to do something to mark the occasion. She momentarily considered urinating on the bed, but quickly rejected the notion. There was no way she would stoop to that level. She wanted above all to keep her dignity. Lenny opened the wardrobe door. And there they were. His clothes. The blue suits and the grey suits and the blazers and the sports shirts. And all his nice, smart ties hanging on their stupid tie-rack. And there were his shoes at the bottom of the wardrobe: two by two, Italian most of them, shiny, expensive and well-loved. Oh yes, there were all his clothes, unsuspecting and innocent, like she had been.

She ripped off the left arm of every jacket and every shirt. Those that wouldn't tear, she cut with the carving knife from the kitchen. Then she folded all the shirts and put all the suits back on their hangers. She took all the left shoes from the bottom of the wardrobe and put them in a bin-liner, slung the bin-liner over her shoulder and left the house for good.

When she told Mary what she had done, the old housekeeper squealed with delight and Ben, hearing the merriment, kicked his feet and gurgled happily. On the motorway they sang 'My Way' several times.

When Jessica saw Anne sitting at her table in the corner of the restaurant she thought how vulnerable and alone the woman looked, and very nearly felt sorry for her.

Anne was looking at the menu and was very shocked to find Jessica standing there over her.

'Mrs Rattigan!'

'Yes. My husband isn't coming.'

Anne was stunned. How did Jessica know? How *much* did Jessica know? Her head spinning, Anne decided not to say anything.

Jessica sat down at the table and picked up a menu. 'Edward told me everything. I know about you and him. I know about your condition. We have no need to tread softly with each other.'

Anne wanted to leave, but surprise had got the better of her. She held on to her seat and tried to stay calm.

Jessica went on, 'I suggested to Edward that I meet you tonight and we sort the whole thing out. I hope you'll agree that's a good idea.'

Anne shrugged her shoulders.

Jessica raised her eyebrows. 'You *don't* think it's a good idea?'

'It's an idea. I don't know whether it's good or bad,' Anne said. She didn't know what else to say.

Jessica nodded. 'Good. Right. Well, it's a start. Now, I'd like to order, if I may.'

When they had ordered, Anne decided to try and talk

reasonably to Jessica, despite her annoyance that Edward had gone behind her back.

'Mrs Rattigan, I know you must hate me, but please try to understand that I never meant to hurt you. I worked with Edward and we fell in love. There was a time when I could have stopped it, but I didn't. I know I'm in the wrong.'

Jessica's face was giving nothing away. She wanted to scoff at the words 'fell in love', but she was not, she told herself, there to score points. 'I haven't come to extract apologies. I'd prefer to be civilised and discuss the problem rationally.'

Anne was relieved to hear this. 'You're very kind, but I feel responsible,' she said. 'I thought we could keep it a secret . . . I didn't think we'd hurt you.'

'If you hadn't become pregnant, you wouldn't have hurt me,' Jessica said, simply.

Anne looked at the tablecloth. 'I know.'

Jessica pursued her advantage. 'Have you wondered how *I* feel?' she asked. 'Have you thought about *me* at all?'

All Anne could do was shake her head.

'I've thought of you,' Jessica continued. 'It's a very difficult decision you have to make. A single woman, with no support. No real career.'

Anne nodded. She knew now what was coming.

Jessica went on, 'When I had my children I was many years younger than you. And pregnancy is never easy.'

'No.'

'You'd have no one to share the difficulties and, frankly, no one to share the joys.'

'I know. It's very hard, I'm sure.'

Jessica nodded, cautiously optimistic about the conversation so far. 'It needn't be,' she said.

Anne looked at her. 'You're suggesting an abortion?'

'I'm suggesting that you give it a great deal of thought.'

It was Anne's turn now. 'Mrs Rattigan, you've been very good to come here. I would have expected you to be bitter. I couldn't honestly do what you're doing, I'm sure.' Anne paused. 'May I speak honestly?'

'Of course.'

'I don't want to upset you.' Jessica dismissed the possibility with a wave of her hand. 'Mrs Rattigan, I love Edward. I hardly realised it until . . . I began to suspect I was pregnant. Until then part of me thought it was the secrecy that thrilled me, going out with someone in such a powerful position. But now I know it's more than that. It's the man himself.'

Despite herself, Jessica felt a sharp stab of jealousy, which she told herself was simple anger at Anne's arrogance. She wanted to slap the stupid woman. 'What are you saying?'

Anne began to sound almost chatty. 'Oh, I know it's a hopeless love. I know he'll never leave you. He wouldn't consider it. I can never be more to him than second best. But he's more to me. He's everything. He's the only man I've ever loved. That's why I want his baby. Not because it's a baby. But because it's his.'

Jessica was dumbfounded. It took her a few moments to summon the breath to speak. 'You want Edward's baby.'

Anne nodded. 'More than anything.'

Jessica took a deep breath. 'In that case, perhaps it's my turn to speak candidly to you. And believe me, I don't want to hurt you either.'

'Please, go on.'

Jessica did so. 'I have a list of Edward's past mistresses. I must show it to you some time. It reaches double figures. My husband has an appetite for women of a certain type. The type Anglican bishops frequently meet in the course of their work. Slightly faded. Slightly lonely. But with no history to encumber them. He's not the sort of man to chase a mother with three children. I knew what was going to happen the first time I saw you. I put your name on the list then. And when Edward told me about it, as he always does, I showed him the list, with your name on it and we laughed. That's the man whose baby you want. The love of your life.'

The two women fell silent. Jessica, with perfect control, ate her meal and glanced occasionally at Anne. Anne sat as if in a trance.

'Edward used me,' Anne said, at last.

Jessica nodded and then spoke without the malice sounding in her voice, as if chatting to one of the parish ladies about the Easter whist-drive. 'We enjoyed aspects of your relationship together, Edward and I. I'm sure there were things that he didn't tell me, but I know what you like for breakfast and I can describe some of the trinkets in your bedroom.'

Anne snapped out of her trance and into a profound rage. 'I don't have to listen to this.' She could have been shouting, she had no idea.

'Oh yes you do,' Jessica said.

'There are things I could say,' Anne threatened.

'But you won't say them,' Jessica countered.

'Oh, don't count on it,' Anne said, feeling as if her face were steaming hot. 'I've got a memory for detail. You Rattigans deserve everything I could give you.'

'Really? And what will that be?' Jessica still seemed in control of her temper, even though she was very angry too.

'Well, I won't wait for people to ask me who the baby's father is. I'll tell them. Loud and long.'

'No, you won't,' Jessica said calmly.

'I'll make damn sure everyone knows my side of it. How I was taken advantage of by a man of the cloth.'

'No one'll feel sorry for you. They'll think you're a fool.'

As she spoke, Anne's eyes flashed in such a way that Jessica was forced to admit to herself that Anne was obviously not the quiet little bird she'd assumed she was.

'I only care what people think about you, Mrs Rattigan. You forget: in my office we deal with the press. We know what they're interested in, and it isn't the Mothers' Union, or the toddlers' group. They don't really care what we're doing for famine victims or war orphans. They want one thing: scandal. They want vicar and choirboy. Or an archdeacon and a parishioner's wife. Or better still, they want a bishop, his wife and his secretary.' Anne stood up. 'And, Mrs Rattigan, you've handed it to them on a plate. By coming here thinking you'd humiliate me into having an abortion. Oh, they'll love you. And I'll enjoy every minute of it.'

Anne left Jessica cringing in her seat. She had been speaking far too loudly before she stormed off, so that everyone in the restaurant would know that they had been arguing. Jessica's only hope was that not too many people had heard what she was saying. She didn't dare look up in case any parishioners were there. If only she could have left immediately herself. But no, she had to stay and pay both her own bill and Anne's.

Edward spent a vastly unpleasant evening listening to Lenny and Mary describe what had happened at Mark's house in Oxford the previous day.

The two women had talked of nothing else since they got back, and Edward found himself worrying about the lengths to which a woman would go if provoked. He couldn't help thinking, as he listened to his daughter

126

delight in her revenge, that Jessica's visit to the restaurant to see Anne – which was taking place as he nodded and tried to look as if he wasn't judging Lenny while she told the story for the nth time – would have exactly that effect: provocation. He had been against the idea, but had been powerless in the face of Jessica's determination.

He was relieved that Jessica seemed to be taking all evening, both because he thought the two women must have had a sensible, lengthy conversation, and because by the time Jessica arrived home everyone else would have gone to bed. He was sitting up in bed himself, drinking a tot of whisky, when Jessica came in looking pale and worried.

'She's everything I said she was.'

Edward frowned. 'What happened? Why did you take so long?'

'It didn't take long. I've been driving around, thinking.'

Edward found himself tensing up with anxiety.

'She going to drag your name through the mud,' Jessica went on. 'She won't just tell the church authorities whose baby she's carrying. She's going to tell the newspapers too!'

'No. Not Anne.'

'Oh yes, Edward. Allow me to know.'

Edward shook his head. 'You must have said something to upset her.'

'I said nothing. I was polite. And firm. I insisted she have a termination. That was her response – total war. She caused a terrible scene in the restaurant. I was so embarrassed.'

'It can't be true. Not Anne.'

Jessica's look could have frozen the whisky in Edward's glass. 'Yes. Anne. Silly little Anne who only wanted a good time and no strings. Silly little Anne that you could twist round your little finger.'

Edward was still shaking his head, as if he was lost. 'She couldn't have said that.'

'She wasn't mistress material after all, was she? She hasn't stuck to her side of the bargain at all, has she?'

'What bargain?'

'The bargain every woman makes when they start something with a married man: it's great while it lasts and it's over when it's over.'

Edward put his head in his hands, which, to Jessica, made him seem utterly pathetic. 'I'm sorry. I swear I didn't mean this to happen. What are we going to do?'

With all the scorn of a woman who's been betrayed a thousand times, Jessica wanted to crush him. 'This won't pass us by, Edward. We're not going to be able to turn the other cheek. She'll call you every name under the sun. The press'll love it. Your career will be the first to go. You'll be a laughing stock.'

Edward looked up. His teeth were chattering. 'It won't happen!' He almost shouted it.

Jessica went on, 'Who's going to employ a de-frocked bishop? What are you qualified for, Edward?'

'She's bluffing, Jessica. She . . . she . . .'

'She what?' Edward shook his head. 'Say it, Edward: "She loves me." Make yourself seem utterly vile, go on.' Edward looked down. 'What will you tell the family? Helena? You've given her shelter from a cheating husband, and now your little affair is going to be common knowledge.'

'Don't, please . . .'

'And Charlotte? I'm sure she'll be delighted. And so will her friends.'

'It won't happen,' Edward said again, which was what Jessica wanted to hear him say.

'I'll tell you something else, that won't happen,' Jessica said. 'I won't stand by you. I won't support you. You can leave my house if it gets out. You haven't forgotten whose house this is, I hope?'

Edward went pale. 'You wouldn't throw away thirty years of marriage . . .'

Jessica laughed a hollow laugh, then said, 'You've thrown that away, Edward. What I'll throw away is you.'

Edward sat up. 'We can get through this. We've got to work together.'

Jessica said, 'I'm not going to have everything blow up in my face. If you can't make her have an abortion, I'll go to the papers myself, first. I'll tell them I found out about your affairs. I'll be the distressed wife. I'll give them the sordid details. And more in sorrow than in anger. There'll be no sympathy left for her. Nor for you.'

'You wouldn't, Jessica.'

'Oh, I would, Edward. I would.'

Edward's face was white with fright now.

'Make her get rid of the child,' Jessica said. '*Make* her!'

·9·

ANNE HADN'T BEEN at work the previous day. Edward had been relieved and at the same time found it unbearably frustrating. He had toyed with the idea of going to see her but, frankly, he had been too scared to face her. Instead, he'd had to contend with Jessica's wrath, which since her meeting with Anne, had been expressed as total silence. To Edward, this was as menacing as her fully-vented rage.

It was Friday. If he didn't contact her today it would be the weekend and that would mean he would have to go and see her at home with none of the protection from raised voices and awful scenes that work might still provide. He decided to telephone.

He got her answer-phone, but he had the feeling that Anne was there, sitting listening.

'Anne? It's Edward. Are you there? Can you hear this?' It was obvious that if she was there she wasn't going to answer. 'Anne, I have to talk to you. I'm so sorry. I'm so sorry it's come to this. I should never have let Jessica see you. Please just give me the chance to explain.'

Edward waited to see if his words would have any effect.

'Anne, are you there?'

Nothing.

Edward replaced the receiver and for the first time since he had been a student used the word 'fuck'.

The whole family were aware of the fact that Edward and Jessica had had a disagreement.

These things normally had a pattern. For a time Jessica would say nothing whatsoever to Edward unless it was completely unavoidable, and when she had to speak to him in public would use a tone of voice that brought a chill to the air. Then, somehow, behind the scenes, a settlement would be achieved, Jessica's tone would assume a polite impersonality and the house would be able to breathe freely again. Sometimes the transition from one state to the other was so smooth that it was registered only unconsciously by other family members. They felt nothing but a vague sense of unease which, as imperceptibly as it had grown, disappeared the next day or, occasionally, in serious instances, after two days, giving rise to an inexplicable sense of lightness and relief.

The cycle was in its early stage when Charlie got home from school feeling excited and nervous about her meal with Thomas and Gabriel and Rachel that night.

Lenny was looking through the newspapers; Jessica was cleaning inside kitchen cupboards that hadn't been cleaned for years, not even by Mary.

Charlie and Lenny talked about including Jessica in their conversation.

'Job-hunting, Lenny?'

Lenny tutted. 'Well, I can't sit around here for the rest of my life, and I wouldn't go to Mark if I was bleeding from the eyes.' Charlie laughed. 'Not that they're crying out for graduates in Market Cross,' Lenny lamented.

'Listen to this: "Grain silo night-watchman required." Here's another: "Vet's receptionist".'

'Shit-shovellers only round here, Lenny,' Charlie giggled.

'You know the first question they're bound to ask? "Why did you decide to move back to the area?" I'll probably end up punching them or bursting into tears.'

'You'll get over it,' Charlie said, gaily.

Lenny doubted that. 'It still feels like an open wound. I was walking round town today. I felt like I had this great cut on my face and two black eyes and everyone was pointing at me going, "Look at her! She's the one whose husband did the dirty on her. You know, the bishop's daughter."'

Jessica stopped her scrubbing when she heard that. Neither of her daughters noticed.

Charlie said, 'Rubbish. They'll all be pointing all right, but they'll be saying, "Her husband's the dirty bastard . . ."'

'Yes, and feeling sorry for me!' Lenny pointed to the back of her throat with two fingers as if to say, 'It makes me sick.' 'Anyway. It doesn't work like that,' Lenny said. 'When a man sleeps around they look at the wife. They wonder what she did wrong.'

Jessica tried to go back to her work.

Charlie said, 'Ignore them. Just stay here and leech off mum and dad. Like I do.'

It was no good. Jessica stood up and took off her rubber gloves. 'You're assuming Edward and I will always be here,' she said. 'We might not always be. What will you do then, all of you?'

'Make sure you've made a will,' Charlie laughed.

'Anything could happen,' Jessica said. 'I could leave your father. Maybe the both of us could decide we've had enough, pack our bags and disappear overnight.'

Charlie was enjoying this. 'Oh, yeah. What would happen to Gabriel, then? Proper junkie he'd end up.'

Jessica was not smiling. 'He's got Rachel now.'

'Quite,' said Charlie.

Lenny looked at Jessica. 'Are you all right, mum?'

'Oh, fine.'

'You don't look it.'

Jessica sighed. 'Don't worry. It only old age casting its shadow ahead.' She attempted to smile. 'I expect we'll be here some time yet, your father and I.' She fell silent again and fished vaguely around in the sink for something else to occupy her.

Charlie begged Lenny to come down to the Lodge that night for the meal. 'You could keep Rachel talking while I occupy Thomas,' she laughed.

Lenny sneered. 'No thanks. I couldn't stand a night out with two happy couples.'

That was when Jessica realised Charlie was seeing Thomas. 'Is that what you and Thomas are,' she said, 'a couple?'

Lenny laughed. 'Where have you been, mum! Charlie's talked about nothing else for days.'

You may well ask, Jessica thought before she quickly put on her coat and went out, leaving the two younger women exchanging glances, wondering at Jessica's distraction.

'What's the matter with her?' Charlie said.

'Haven't you noticed?' Lenny said.

Charlie said she hadn't noticed.

'Don't say anything,' Lenny was nearly whispering, 'I think she may be going through the change.'

Edward, at home, on the bedroom extension, was going to try again. And again he got the answer-phone.

'Anne, this is ridiculous. I know you're there. You

133

can't bury yourself away for ever. I know I've hurt you, but it hurts me too, and the longer you lock yourself away the longer we're both going to go on hurting.'

Bingo!

At last Anne answered, but the anger in her voice shocked him. In two years he had never heard Anne speak in such a tone. 'Oh, I *bet* it hurts, Edward,' she spat. 'I bet you both really hurt yourself laughing, you and your lovely wife, in your lovely house. Laughing at your stupid tart of a secretary!'

From this speech Edward was able to ascertain that Jessica had done more than simply talk to Anne as she had claimed. Jessica had obviously told her that he had taken other lovers whom Jessica also knew about. He wondered what on earth else his wife had said.

Jessica sat listening intently to Edward's side of the conversation. Edward went to put his hand over the mouthpiece and say something to her, but decided against it. If Anne were to discover that Jessica was listening, all would surely be lost.

'Anne, my darling,' he said, in his most sympathetic voice, 'I just want to talk to you.'

Anne was having none of it. 'Edward, you made a joke out of me – the Bishop's Mistress. And isn't that a great gag? And the baby, isn't that the best punchline of all?'

Edward could tell Anne was crying tears of anger as she spoke, or rather shouted. 'Don't do this to me,' he begged. 'You know that's not how I saw it.' Edward was angry with Jessica for having interfered, angry with himself for having let her interfere.

'You told her,' Anne sobbed. 'She knew all along.'

'Isn't it better that I was honest with my wife?' Edward said, feeling like the most monstrous hypocrite ever to have poisoned God's earth.

'Where are you, Edward?'

'Er . . . I'm in my office at the church.'

'Good. Then go into your church and pray to your God. Look him in the face and pray that he forgives liars and cheats. Because I don't!'

Edward was left with only the dialling tone. He held the phone away and looked at his wife before replacing the receiver, as if to say: You see what you've done?

'Jessica, you've made matters worse. If only you hadn't got to the restaurant. I counselled against it, I said it was a mistake.'

Jessica's face was as cold as the moon in winter. 'You're right, Edward. It's all my fault. I shouldn't have slept with her. I shouldn't have made her pregnant. I don't know what possessed me.' She laughed sardonically, determined to crush this line of reasoning. 'I don't know what possessed me. I suppose it was lust.' Edward had realised his mistake. 'Don't start this, Edward. It's a game you can't possibly win. And if we start tearing each other apart, then nothing's left.' Jessica sounded sad and tired and empty.

Edward looked at her. 'You said . . . you said you'd abandon me, Jessica.'

She looked at him for a few moments before answering. 'It's very easy to say that, Edward. Perhaps I should have left you a long time ago. The first time.' She laughed, coldly. 'But I didn't.'

'You'll stand by me?'

'I'll stay with you, Edward, if you can get us out of this mess. If not, then I can't say.'

Teatime was a laugh a minute for Jessica.

First she had to witness Edward arguing with Charlie. It was an old antagonism between the two of them. Edward had tried in vain to become accustomed to the fact that Charlie was no longer a gangly girl doting on her father, but a fashionable, over-sensitive young woman who would rather die than be seen out with him or proved wrong by him, and who prided herself on the fact that she was different from him in every respect.

As usual, the gloom emanating from the parents had affected everyone but Charlie, who, typically, seemed high-spirited. It seemed to Edward as if she were annoying everyone on purpose with her girlish teenage sarcasm. When she said she wasn't eating, Edward foolishly suggested she do her homework instead.

'Oh, dad's home early from work. Sure sign he's in a bad mood,' she quipped.

'Must we have our meal accompanied by a barrage of childish sarcasm?' Edward boomed.

'Salt and pepper's better for your digestion,' Charlie taunted.

Jessica thought Edward was spoiling for a fight. If he wanted peace he would have allowed Charlie to become bored and leave the table of her own accord.

Things came to a head when Charlie let slip that she wasn't coming home that night. Jessica thought she might have said it deliberately to antagonise Edward. Jessica thought Edward deserved it.

'I'm not having you staying out nights at your age, Charlie. I forbid it.'

'Oh? And how are you going to stop me?' Charlie seemed to take delight in saying it.

Mary, Lenny and Jessica quietly ate their tea while the wave broke.

'Don't you answer me back, young woman!' Edward said, in his most severe tone. 'If I say you're staying in tonight, you're staying in. I won't have you out after midnight. And I think that's a very fair time for a woman of your age.'

Why on earth Edward insisted on referring to Charlie's age, Jessica did not know.

'Oh, yeah? So, what, lock me in my room? Hey, why not lock me *out* – that'd really get me. Or even better, chuck me out altogether. Do you want me to go and pack my bags now?'

'I can only assume that you are doing your best to annoy me, Charlie. I advise against it. I can make life very unpleasant for you, if needs be.'

And so it went on until Charlie was sitting there as gloomy as the rest of them, remaining in her seat only to make Edward the more uncomfortable.

As she watched the duel, Jessica felt sorry for Charlie. It was the sorrow she felt for herself turned outwards, but she was powerless to speak in Charlie's defence for fear of antagonising Edward still further. Whatever power she had over Edward in private was limited in public, even in the domain of the family. Publicly, Jessica dared not cross him. She would say something to Charlie later when they were out of earshot, perhaps that she'd cover for her in the morning by telling Edward that she'd seen her go out very early. That would keep tomorrow's trouble to a minimum.

Jessica's second unpleasant surprise was Mark's appearance.

Mary went to answer the door. Lenny could hear Mark's voice in the passage. In a flash she was up. She'd taken Ben out of his highchair, where he was gurgling peacefully and smearing what was left of his dinner all over his head, and was poised to escape into the drawing room.

'Get rid of him,' Lenny said to Jessica. 'I don't want to see him.'

Jessica nodded staunchly.

Edward said, 'He's your husband, Lenny. He's driven all this way . . .'

'I don't care!' Lenny glared at Edward. 'I don't give a shit.'

Lenny disappeared just as Mary showed Mark into the kitchen.

Edward was still shaking his head when Mark said, 'Well, here we are then. Having a nice family tea.' This did not go down well.

Mark changed tack. 'I'm sorry,' he said. 'I have to talk to Lenny. I know you can't stand the sight of me at the moment – and I'm none too keen on myself these days – but it's Lenny I should be apologising to. Where is she?'

No one spoke. Edward knew that it was Jessica's place to open the communication channels with Mark.

Jessica drew her daggers. 'My daughter does not like unpleasant surprises,' she said, 'and neither do I. No doubt you think turning up on the doorstep is a disarming tactic. I do not.'

Mark was not fazed by Jessica. 'Can we cut this?' he said. 'I'm here to see my wife.'

'I'm afraid she doesn't want to see you,' Jessica said.

'I can wait,' Mark said. 'Go on, Mary, put the kettle on.'

Jessica glanced at Edward, and Edward knew that authority had passed to him.

'Now look here, young man. You can't walk in here and simply demand your rights.'

Mark looked at him. 'I have every right to see my son.'

Charlie had cheered up now and was itching to say something, but she was so impressed by Mark's arrogance that she felt there was nothing scornful she could contribute. She wanted to say, 'Go on, Mark!' as if cheering on a football team.

'You set this game in motion, Mark,' Edward said. 'You can't complain now that the rules aren't fair.' At last Mark had no reply. 'I always rather liked you,' Edward said, diplomatic with Mark where he had failed with Charlie. 'You have an edge that appeals – an arrogance I suppose you could call it – but it's a hard edge and it can hurt. It has done Lenny great harm.'

Mark's attitude softened in front of Edward. 'I know. And I want to apologise to Lenny. But how can I, if I don't see her,' he appealed. 'I miss her. And Ben.'

'I've counselled enough men in your position to know how you feel,' Edward said. 'But I've talked to women as well. Betrayal's an awful thing. I think we all underestimate its strength.' Edward looked at Jessica to see if his words were resonating there.

Jessica may as well have been a wall of rock.

Mark's attitude had changed. 'I've never hurt her on purpose. Do you believe that, Edward?'

Jessica wanted to slap Mark for that.

Edward appeared perfectly calm. 'I understand you very well, Mark. It terrifies me, how a man can give a woman so little consideration.' Now Edward felt Jessica looking at him, but he couldn't look at her.

'Edward, please ask Lenny to speak to me.'

'I'll tell her what you have said. I'm afraid the rest is up to her.'

Mark nodded. Edward's reasonable tone was impossible to attack. It was clear he had lost. 'I'll get out of your way, then.'

'Yes.' Edward nodded too.

As he left, Mark turned and grinned at Charlie. 'I don't suppose you've found a pile of left shoes anywhere. Or sleeves?'

But for once Charlie couldn't say anything. She was thinking how disappointed she was that Mark hadn't been able to defeat Edward's arguments. Men are so pathetic, she thought.

*

When Anne opened the front door, Edward was sure a glimmer of warmth momentarily flickered in the poor woman's eyes.

That was before she turned away angrily and walked into the house, leaving the door open behind her. If she had been truly determined to ruin him, she would have slammed the door shut in his face, Edward reflected. His task was, then, to withstand her wrath and reason with her, perhaps to give in to her in some way and then reach an agreement. Not that Edward's plan was calculated quite so clearly, but in his heart he instinctively knew what had to be done.

The front door opened on to Anne's living room. The furnishings were as modest as the house, which in turn was as modest as the woman herself. Anne stood facing him, silently, expectantly. As he wondered what to say first, it suddenly occurred to Edward that Anne was inviting him to come to her, to take her in his arms, perhaps to prove that, despite everything, he still loved her – not that he had ever declared love for her. He stepped towards her, hesitantly, and when he met with no resistance, he put his arms about her.

It was then that Anne stepped back, her eyes flashing. She removed his arms with some violence. Edward felt as if he had been tricked.

'Is that what you came for?' she hissed.

Edward protested. 'No, Anne, I . . .'

'Is that all you ever came for? It is, isn't it? And you didn't even have the guts to come alone. You always brought your wife with you . . .' She looked as if she wanted to slap him.

Edward hung his head in silence.

'Every hotel, every weekend, every night we were together, *she* was there! There we were, just the three of us!' Anne patted her belly. 'And now there's four.' She

140

raised her voice. 'How can one man tell so many lies? Lying to me! To your children! To your faith! I've been with you all this time and you're a stranger. *Who are you, Edward?*'

Edward sighed. 'I'm an ignorant man, Anne,' he said. 'I'm a liar. I'm everything you say, and more. Really, I have been a bad man. But, Anne,' he looked at her sadly, 'really and truly, I never meant to do you any harm.'

Edward found himself in tears.

Anne blinked. The sight was shocking and changed her mood at once. She wanted to cry herself. She fought back her emotion and held her ground while Edward spluttered and sobbed like a boy.

'Anne, you're the only person who has shown me any real kindness. The rest of my life has been so . . . so cold and lonely . . . you've been the thing that has made the past' (he waved his hand) 'bearable . . . you're the person who has made it beautiful. It's *you* who I long to see . . . it's your smile . . . and your kindness that I love.' Edward stopped. It was a long time since he had been able to cry tears. He looked at Anne and let her see his tears, and then said, 'I love you, Anne. Help me, I don't know where to turn. You're all I have in the world. You are the only thing I care about, really and truly.'

It was impossible now for Anne to hold back her own tears. For over two years she had loved Edward. During that whole time she had known in her heart that she had deeper feelings for the man than he would ever have for her. She had kept this secret, she had accepted it. She had also done everything in her power to make Edward smile at her, to hold her, to kiss her, make love to her – even just to notice her. Every present that Edward bought her she had treasured, every kind word he had spoken to her had warmed her, but before their current difficulties had arisen, she had never once told him the true extent of her feelings for him. The discovery that she was carrying Edward's child had brought her feelings to a head. Before that the romance had seemed beautiful and sweet, indeed her life had revolved round her love, but since her discovery she had fallen for him all over again, at the same time becoming sharply aware of the gulf between their respective feelings. Now as he confessed to what seemed to be an equal, or at least a more profound love for her than she would ever have dared to imagine, she felt that she would implode with joy. All the bitterness of the past few sleepless nights was blown away on a warm breeze of fine feeling and she wanted nothing but to fall at his feet.

She walked over to him and let his arms enfold her, laid her head against his chest and sobbed her pitiful tears: tears of pain, of relief, of love and joy. Edward tenderly stroked her hair and rocked her back and forth, comforting her with his beautiful voice and stroking her with his precious hands. Then she felt him guiding her upstairs.

The next thing she knew she was making love to Edward and all was forgotten, all was passion and love, kisses and caresses. Strangely, she continued to cry and afterwards she thought her heart might break with the sobs.

For Charlie, the evening with Thomas at the Lodge as guests of Gabriel and Rachel was a flop.

It got off to a bad start when Thomas thanked Rachel and Gabriel for inviting him and Charlie over. Neither Rachel nor Gabriel said a word, but each of them had looked at Charlie in such a way as to let her know that they had sussed out her little game. Charlie wasn't bothered in the sense that she felt guilty, but she knew that her status for the evening had dropped to zero. On a gut level she knew there was no way she could take liberties or get away with her usual cheek that night.

From the moment Thomas let the cat out of the bag, Rachel or Gabriel could put her in her place with a simple withering look.

Her punishment was severe indeed. She was condemned to talk to Rachel while Gabriel and Thomas spent the evening talking intensely *tête-à-tête*, completely ignoring the women. Even more infuriating to Charlie was the fact that Rachel seemed to enjoy this turn of events and kept saying how nice it was to hear Gabriel and Thomas talking like that, how she loved to see her darling hubby so happy, and going on about how much she liked him, and what else she liked about him, and what did Charlie like about him and on and on until Charlie wanted to scream, 'You pathetic, petty little froggy boring princess!' But tonight was not the night. Rachel even had the nerve to offer her, Charlie, advice about men!

'You don't want to bug Thomas, you know, Charlie. I'd say your best chance of keeping him is to let him make the running.'

As if Charlie needed the advice of a pathetic, petty, boring little princess who did nothing but work in a stupid insurance office and worship her wild and dangerous husband while trying to tame him, when really she should just piss off and leave him to the people who really appreciated his mega-brilliant talents.

So Charlie kept her sarcasm down to a minimum and tried not to disrupt Thomas and Gabriel as they ignored both her and Rachel, and tried not to pour scorn on everything Rachel said. In the end Charlie actually had quite a nice conversation with Rachel about how boring it can be at school, during which she discovered, to her great surprise, that Rachel had once been suspended from school for skiving off.

143

'I went off the rails for a few years, after mum died,' Rachel said.

'You got back on to them OK, then?' Charlie said blandly.

'Oh, yes. I've been a model of domestic and professional respectability ever since,' Rachel replied, knowing that Charlie would miss her own sarcasm.

Charlie contented herself with a plan she had concocted earlier. Every ten minutes or so she hopped up and filled everyone's glass to the brim. She knew that if Gabriel and Thomas carried on the way they were going, toasting this or that memory and taking great nostalgic gulps from their drinks, Thomas would be far too drunk to drive home.

Edward and Anne were lying in Anne's bed.

Exhausted after days of stress and the passionate love-making, Anne had fallen asleep with her head on Edward's chest. Edward lay awake, staring into the darkness.

When she stirred and realised Edward was awake, Anne reached out and put on the light. Both of them squinted in the glare.

'Does Jessica know where you are?' Anne said after a few moments of silence.

Edward nodded. 'Yes.'

Anne laughed without amusement. 'Then she's with us now.'

Edward turned to her. 'She always knew where I was, she knew when I was with you. But she never knew what we said, or what we shared. What our feelings were.'

'You told her about the baby?'

Edward nodded again. 'Yes.'

Anne laughed a little more merrily. 'I've never done that before, lost my temper in public. I think I caused a scene in the restaurant. Did she tell you what I said?'

'She said you were very angry. She said you'd tell the papers.'

Anne laughed again. 'Then she left out the most important thing. I said I loved you.' Edward looked at her and took her in his arms again. 'It took all this to really bring that home to me, Edward. How much I love you. How much I've always loved you. I've always known I could never have you, but I always thought you might want to keep me safe. And happy.'

Edward said nothing.

'Did you . . . love me, Edward? *Do* you love me?'

'I said I did.'

Anne considered this for a moment. 'I shouldn't ask you,' she said.

Without feeling, Edward said, 'I said I loved you. I meant it.'

They both sat there in bed, naked, silent, listening to the sounds of the house, the sounds of the countryside. Edward was the one who usually did most of the talking after they had made love, talking for hours about matters of interest to him that Jessica paid no attention to, even about his family life, his disagreements with Jessica, about Jessica's moods and her tantrums, such as they were. Edward sometimes joked that Anne was his confessor. Now that Edward was quiet, silence consumed them.

After what seemed to Anne like a lifetime, Edward said, 'What happens now, Anne?'

Anne said, 'Whatever you want.'

After which they made love for a second time.

Anne said, 'She'll be expecting you back.'

Edward had fallen asleep. His relief had been such that once his tension had eased with the news that Anne had come round to his way of thinking, he found it impossible not to relax completely.

'What time is it? Oh no, I really must dash. Jessica will be anxious.'

When Edward had dressed, he said, 'Anne, I never thanked you.'

Anne's laugh was bleak. 'What for, the sex?'

'You could have ruined me.'

'I still could.'

Edward laughed wryly. 'Thank you, Anne,' he said, sincerely. 'Thank you for everything.'

'Perhaps you should bless me,' Anne said.

'Don't, please.' Edward was in high spirits now, free again, post-coital and rested. 'I'll help you all I can,' he said. 'I've no idea how much these things cost, of course, but you must have the best, Anne, the very best.'

Anne's face fell. 'What do you mean?'

Edward was putting on his jacket. 'The operation. You can have it done privately, you must. As I said, I think it's right that I should pay in full.'

'Then you'd better write me a cheque,' Anne said with a coldness Edward failed to recognise.

He fished in his pocket for his chequebook. 'Yes, that would be a good idea, and if you need more just call me. What do you think would cover it? A hundred? Two?'

Anne said, 'A thousand.'

Edward blinked. 'A thousand? Er, yes, of course.' Edward could not afford to balk at figures at this delicate stage. He put his chequebook on the dresser and wrote out a cheque, signing it with a flourish.

'What's this for, exactly, Edward?'

'The operation.'

'The abortion?'

Edward looked up, at last aware that her tone was not all sweetness and light. 'Yes. The abortion.'

'What abortion?' Anne's eyes flashed as they had in the restaurant. She felt that same anger rising again. 'When did we agree to that, Edward? Maybe you had a conversation with a different mistress.'

Edward stood and faced her. 'But you agreed. You said you'd do whatever I want.'

Anne felt as if she might split in two with her rage. 'I meant I'd go. I'd get out of your way. I'd leave you to your precious wife. Not chuck the only thing I've got left in the world in the incinerator! God almighty! Is that the only reason you came here this evening? Screw her into silence and pay her off. Write her a cheque. Buy her an ice cream and hope she'll lick her lips!'

Edward wanted to throw himself at her feet. 'But, Anne! You must! You've got to get rid of it. It doesn't mean anything . . .'

Anne grabbed hold of his wrists and pushed him out of the bedroom. 'Get out! Get out of my house.' She was screaming. She ground her teeth and slapped him, pushing him again. 'Get out! If you don't get out, I'll call the police! Yes, I'll call the police.'

Edward managed to grab Anne's wrists. They were on the tiny landing; Edward felt he might bang his head on the low-beamed ceiling. 'Anne, you're being ridiculous! I'm not going,' Edward roared, his own temper flaring. 'I'm not leaving this house until I can make you see reason.'

Anne stopped struggling and stared at Edward, her eyes wide. She had never heard this tone before. Edward had summoned it from deep inside. It was a booming, intolerant voice that expected to be obeyed. It frightened her. In a flash it transformed her impression of the man before her, the man who had come into her house, into her bed, to deceive her with false words and promises, to make love to her without feeling, in order to bend her to his will.

'I'm not leaving,' Edward was saying, 'until I make you understand you cannot have this wretched child!'

147

He still had hold of her.

Anne screamed it into his face with all her might: 'Because Jessica says so!'

Edward was not deterred, he shouted back: 'No! Because *I* say so. Because it puts *me* at risk. Because I refuse to let the world see this sordid little mess.'

Anne was crying and shouting and spitting all at the same time. 'That's all you've ever thought about. You kid yourself you're thinking about your family, but the truth is coming out now. Your family don't count for any more than I do. You're pathetic, Edward, and I won't let you walk over me. You *cannot* control me, you *will not* control me, I have passed out of your hands. I will do whatever *I* want to do and you and Jessica can go to hell where you deserve to go. Only I've a good mind to make that hell here on earth. That's what you've done, Edward, you've made yourself a hell on earth and the only person who can stop the burning flames from consuming you is me. Little me. Who you think you can bully, and . . . and . . . screw and . . .'

Edward was shaking her. He had hold of her and all he wanted was for her to be quiet. 'Shut up!' he screamed at her again and again. He wanted to put his hand over her mouth and block off the noise, he wanted to crush the life out of her; he would have done anything to stop her doing what she was going to do. It was his child as much as it was hers, he had as much say over what should be done. She wasn't being rational, she was being stupid, and spiteful and revolting, utterly revolting. How could he ever had found this spitting, kicking little . . . slut attractive? He was utterly disgusted. 'You'll do as *I* say, Anne,' he shouted into the noise.

Anne was laughing at him now. 'I'll tell them, Edward. I'll tell the world what you're really like. I'll show them all. And then all you'll have left is God. You'll have to make your peace with God then . . .'

That was the last thing Edward could remember Anne saying. What right the little slut had to talk to him about God he didn't know. He was disgusted at her, by her. He was disgusted with himself; he felt an enormous loathing rise up in him, a callousness that told him he could walk away from it all, from Anne and her baby, from Jessica, from the church – from himself. With violent disdain he threw Anne down. He wanted to push her on to the floor and be done with the whole affair. He wanted to step over her and be gone.

Anne fell down the stairs. He was shocked and yet he was pleased too. She didn't cry out as she fell, but she made a noise which sounded like 'Ooof'. As he watched, Edward wanted to say, 'There, now, see what you've done with your stupid noise.' But that was stupid. He was shocked, too, and horrified and worried for Anne. He knew he should rush to her assistance. Perhaps he could apologise and she would come to her senses, perhaps she would see now how seriously he felt about the whole thing.

Such were Edward's feelings as he watched Anne fall. The whole thing took only a few seconds, and yet seemed to take a long time as well. Edward was as shocked at his own calculating callousness as he was at the pain Anne would no doubt suffer. She might break her arm. She might even lose the baby. She might do something to her back and the doctors would tell her she couldn't risk a pregnancy. All this occurred to him at some deeper level in the course of those few seconds.

One thing was certain, Edward thought, as he came down the stairs: he would never make love to Anne again. And he would have to look for another secretary.

'Anne. Anne are you all right? I'm so sorry,' he was saying.

She looked to be in some pain. She was twitching violently. Her robe was open and her legs parted. It was not a sight Edward wanted to see.

'Anne? Have you broken something,' he said, as he crouched down. 'Anne, I'm sorry, I didn't mean . . .'

He noticed that her head was at an odd angle. There was blood coming from her mouth. Those awful unnatural twitches stopped. She lay still, her eyes open. She wasn't breathing. Edward looked at her, at the angle of her head, and he knew Anne was dead. He had killed her.

Perhaps she was unconscious. He felt his insides surge. He felt for her pulse. Nothing. Perhaps he couldn't find it. He searched frantically. Nothing. No breath. Nothing. Perhaps he should try to revive her. He stared at her. It wasn't real. It was impossible. He was calm, yet he was panicking. Should he give her mouth-to-mouth? Give her heart massage? He wasn't sure how it was done. He went to the phone and dialled 999, but before the call got through he put the receiver down.

Anne was dead, which meant there would be no baby. But if he revived her? No. How could he think such a thing? He should try to revive her, give her the kiss of life. He had to do that before she had been dead for three minutes, that was it, wasn't it? He looked down at Anne. He felt revolted by her nakedness. He covered her up and took her head in his hands, but felt so repulsed by the strangeness of the angle that he was afraid to turn the head back. If she had broken her neck there would be no point in trying to revive her. He stood back, looked down at her again. There was nothing he could do.

No one except Jessica knew he had been there. He should go, leaving Anne here. There was nothing to suggest that she had not been alone. He looked around the living room. There was a bottle of vodka on the side and a glass. Anne had been drinking! He had smelled it on her when he first came in. He had smelled it on her when they made love. It was no wonder she had fallen down the stairs.

He would go. Now. Quickly.

He looked at her again. Her eyes were open. Was everything as it should have been?

The robe. He must open the robe and leave it as it was. If anybody found her the way she was now, it would be obvious someone had covered her up.

Thank goodness he hadn't panicked and tried to revive her. They would have been able to tell that her head had been moved.

What if she hadn't broken her neck, what if he later discovered that she might have been revived?

What if she weren't dead?

Edward checked again.

She was dead.

He opened up the robe to reveal her in all her indignity and left the house.

·10·

I T WAS NEARLY midnight and Lenny was sitting on her own in the kitchen drinking whisky when there was a brief tattoo on the outside door.

The door opened. 'I'm not a burglar. The light was on, I thought it might have been you.'

It was her old friend, Jimmy.

Lenny felt a stab of guilt that she hadn't called on him. Years ago, Lenny had been going out with Jimmy and Mark had been his best friend. It had been obvious to both Mark and Lenny that they were attracted to each other the first time they met. That Jimmy's heart should have been broken was as natural as the weather.

These ancient wounds were long healed now. Jimmy had stayed in Market Cross, Mark and Lenny had moved away. Lenny felt a heel for not having been to see their old friend. It was obvious that Mark would have called there when he was ejected from the Rattigans' house.

'Jimmy, hello. I'm sorry I've not been over . . .'

Jimmy held up his great spade of a hand. 'No need. I saw Mark. I understand.'

Jimmy was handsome, Lenny remembered as she looked at his great figure standing shyly before her,

152

hopping self-consciously from one foot to the other. He was one of those *nice* men: big, dependable, loyal, doesn't drink too much, loves children, doesn't womanise, speaks kindly of people, enjoys simple things – such as his job, landscape gardening – wears corduroy jackets, has a clear face with nice blue eyes. But really and truly, he seemed too nice to go out with, too much like other people's dads. In those youthful days Mark had been the dangerous and exciting alternative, with vices and sex appeal.

Lenny smiled at Jimmy; she got up and hugged him. As she did so, her emotions got the better of her; perhaps it was the sound of Jimmy's kindly, concerned voice, his lovely caring smile. Lenny sobbed and Jimmy held her, rocking her gently.

'I've been so upset, Jimmy. I didn't want you to see me in this state. I thought you'd think I was pathetic . . . I mean, after all this time, coming back to Market Cross with my tail between my legs . . . and my baby under my arm,' she managed to say between sobs.

'Hey, it's not the end of the world living in Market Cross as far as I'm concerned.'

'You're not staying with your bloody mother!' Lenny said, with a smile.

'True,' Jimmy conceded. 'That *is* a bummer.'

Lenny laughed a little at Jimmy's candour, said she was sorry for crying a few more times and then they sat down for a talk.

'Fancy an after-timer?' Lenny said, and poured Jimmy a drink. 'Look at me. Hard, whisky-drinking woman!' she joked.

'Cheers,' Jimmy laughed.

After a moment, and a clink of glasses, Lenny said, 'I really am sorry I haven't been over.'

'And I really understand,' said Jimmy. 'You've got a

child to look after. And I'm sure you're in a lot of pain, I understand that.'

Lenny nodded. 'You and Mark have been friends so long, I suppose I kind of lump you two together as well,' she admitted.

Jimmy grinned. 'You and I were friends before you and he were friends, don't forget.'

Despite herself, Lenny blushed at the allusion. 'Cheers,' she giggled. 'Here's to the rich tapestry of life!'

Charlie's plan both worked and backfired at the same time.

Thomas was too drunk to get home, but she was too drunk to take advantage of it.

She had manipulated the situation well enough. Thomas and Gabriel had finally disentangled themselves from their pathetic discussions about art and their endless reminiscences: the Great Holidays the two of them had spent together, travelling all over Europe when they were eighteen and to India the following year.

As soon as Thomas stood up he realised that he was too drunk to drive. Charlie immediately suggested that he stay the night and Thomas immediately accepted the offer which hadn't even been made yet. With merry exaggerated irony, Rachel and Gabriel then made the offer themselves and Thomas apologised for his insensitivity, accepted the offer all over again and glared at Charlie. Rachel and Gabriel looked thrilled anyway. Charlie thought to herself how bored with each other's company Gabriel and Rachel must be to look so pleased to have guests.

Charlie then invited *herself* to stay the night and Gabriel looked pretty peeved. Charlie couldn't tell whether or not Thomas wanted her to stay. Thomas just looked embarrassed but then – miracle of miracles – Rachel came to her rescue and said to Gabriel that it was too late to send Charlie out into the night and why didn't they let her stay on the sofa downstairs. Gabriel said, 'OK.' Thomas blushed even more deeply, bless his sensitive soul, and Charlie said: 'Thanks, guys. I'll stay with Thomas in the guest room.'

Everyone stood round looking embarrassed for a moment, then Gabriel muttered that he was going to bed and he and Rachel disappeared upstairs.

Then Charlie and Thomas were in bed – the single bed in the spare room – with Charlie poised, ready and determined to practise her technique for sending older men straight to heaven, so far tested only on the unfortunate Nick. But then Thomas started talking about Gabriel, about the things they'd been talking about all evening, about their holidays together. Charlie did her best to sound interested while wrapping her leg irresistibly around his and pressing her perfect parts against him, pressing her lips to his shoulder. To no avail.

Next thing, the rolling of her eyes got the better of her and she was fast asleep.

Edward managed to hold his humanity in check until he was back in his own house.

All the way home from Anne's he kept the image of her ungainly corpse from his mind: her open eyes, the way her robe had fallen open. He concentrated instead on what he should tell Jessica, on how they should pretend to know nothing, how they should be surprised when the news broke. He would tell her how there was nothing he could have done, how it was an unfortunate accident – very unfortunate – but that it had not been his fault, how Anne had been fighting against him, being very silly, being wild, being downright irresponsible . . .

The moment the great wave of his own responsibility

155

in the affair threatened to break – his foolishness, callousness, his doubts and fears, his nausea, the terrifying image of Anne's body, the very fact of death itself – Edward, with an enormous effort of will, crushed down his feelings and concentrated instead on the minutiae of the event, the immediate dangers of discovery, the details of the plot he would have to weave.

It was hard, but somehow he knew he had to keep himself in one piece until he could get home and speak to Jessica.

There was a light on in the kitchen when he arrived back. He listened at the door and heard Lenny's voice and someone he didn't recognise. For a terrible moment it occurred to him that it might be a policeman's voice, but then he heard them laughing in a familiar kind of way and deduced that it was a friend of hers. He moved silently back down the passage to the stairs and crept up to the bedroom where Jessica was sitting up in bed waiting for him.

Edward froze with fright. He realised how difficult it was going to be to explain what had happened to Jessica, to anyone. It seemed so unreal in the cold light of the bedroom. Edward felt he needed darkness to make what he had to say explicable. He was not able to turn the light off, however, for the very action would reveal his desire for concealment. So he stood there, back to the door, frozen like a rabbit in the beam of an on-coming headlight.

'Edward. What's happened? Talk to me.'

Edward was not sure how many times Jessica had asked him to explain himself.

'Edward! Tell me. What has she said? She's refusing to change her mind, isn't she?'

Edward said, 'She's dead.'

Jessica laughed. 'I wish,' she said. Then she realised that

Edward was perfectly serious. She frowned. How could Anne be dead? Surely Edward hadn't killed her? Jessica became angry. He was being ridiculous. Why was nothing ever straightforward? 'Tell me, Edward! Tell me what happened. What do you mean, she's dead? For God's sake, talk to me!'

'It was an accident,' Edward said, in an empty voice. 'We'd talked and it was fine, then — it wasn't my fault, Jessica, it was an accident. It was . . . an act of God . . .' He broke off.

'What was an accident? Edward, tell me what *happened*.'

'She fell.'

'What do you mean she fell?'

'She was at the top of the stairs. She must have been. All I heard was the noise. And she'd fallen. When I looked, she'd fallen. Her eyes were still open. Staring . . .'

'Oh, my God, Edward, how awful. She . . . died . . . while you were there?' Edward nodded. 'I can't believe it. How awful. My God, what did you tell them? I can't believe you were there when it happened.' Jessica shook her head. 'It's typical. I mean, if you hadn't been there . . . Oh, Edward, I'm sorry. I'm thinking selfishly. I'm thinking how convenient it is . . . and if you hadn't been there . . . Forgive me.'

Edward nodded and shook his head at the same time.

Jessica shook her head too, at their bad luck, at the horror. 'What *did* you tell them?' she asked. Edward hadn't moved. 'They must have wondered what you were doing there. You should have called me.' Jessica's mind was racing. 'But it makes sense. She was ill. You're her employer, not only her employer, but her . . . bishop, you're a bishop. It's perfectly natural, you'd be there to see how she . . . was. Did you tell them why you were there, did you have to?'

Edward's face was ashen.

Jessica took in the picture as she waited for his reply. It gradually became obvious that there wasn't going to be a reply. Slowly, Jessica began to form another picture in her mind's eye. After a moment she said, 'No one knows.' Edward moved his head to confirm this. 'Dear God, Edward, what have you done?'

'It wasn't my fault,' Edward said again. 'It was an accident.' He looked at Jessica. 'No one saw me. No one knows I was in the house. And she just fell. She would have fallen whether I had been there or not. I was nowhere near her. She'd be lying there now and we wouldn't know. We'd still be here, doing nothing. Do you see? We don't know she's dead.'

Jessica sat for a time looking at her husband, who held her gaze for as long as he could before looking down at the floor.

'Yes, Edward.'

'I was here with you. We were together.'

Jessica nodded and spoke slowly. 'You were here. With me. We were together.'

'All night.'

'She would have fallen anyway,' Jessica said. 'She would have died alone. She . . . did . . . die alone. She fell down the stairs.'

'She'd been drinking.'

Jessica nodded and then frowned. '*Had* she been drinking?'

'Yes. Quite heavily.'

'She'd been drinking. Poor . . . foolish . . . woman.'

'She turned and fell,' Edward said again. 'She just did.'

'You *saw* her?'

Edward looked at her. 'I *heard* her. Then found her.'

'From where you were?'

'From where I was. Downstairs.'

'Yes?'

'Yes.'

'God rest her soul.'

Edward nodded. 'God bless her. And her child.'

Jessica nodded. 'We were here all evening.'

'Yes. You were reading.'

'Yes. You were reading too. We were both reading.'

'Yes.' Edward hung his head. Some of his real feelings began to surface. 'And she'll stay where she is.'

'Yes.'

'No one to tend to her body.'

'Yes, Edward, that's the way you left her.'

Edward began to look more upset. 'No one to tend to her soul.' He put his hands to his head. 'Jessica, I never even prayed for her.'

Jessica could see Edward was beginning to deteriorate. 'Then pray for her, Edward. Pray for her now if you think it'll help. I'll join you. We'll pray for Anne and the baby together.'

Edward stepped away from the door for the first time. He suddenly felt very lost. 'How can I do that?' he said fearfully. 'I wanted the baby dead! We both wanted rid of it. And now you're suggesting we pray for it.'

'Calm yourself, Edward. We might not have wanted the child to come into the world under those circumstances, but that was because of the life it would have had to have led. All those damaged children, Edward, it's not right.'

Edward was staring at her with an expression Jessica had never seen before.

'Pray with me, Edward,' she said.

Edward tore off his collar. 'I can't pray,' he said angrily. 'I don't know what that means now! I haven't known for a long time. God seems a very long way off, Jessica. I can't . . . I couldn't reach him, I couldn't look him in the eye, if he *were* there.'

159

'Sit down, Edward. Listen to me. Perhaps it was God that made events in this pattern. Perhaps he has saved you. Perhaps he brought you home, perhaps he put the idea in your mind to leave her there.'

'It wasn't God who put that idea there, Jessica.'

'Edward. Look at me. You're safe. God will protect you. It's over now. You mustn't blame yourself.'

'I ran away. I looked at her, I . . . saw her . . . I ran away, leaving her there like that. Her eyes staring like that . . . her . . . Oh, Jesus, no . . .' He buried his head in his hands again and wept.

Jessica put an arm around his shoulders. 'It's all right, you're safe, my love. Let go of her, let go of it all. It's over. Anne's gone. Her suffering is over.'

Edward wept like a child. He felt vile. Here he was taking comfort from his wife, having told her a pack of lies. He felt like an impostor, even his tears were phoney. He was not crying for Anne, he was crying for himself, for the despicable liar he had become, for the cruel turn his life had taken, because he knew he would, one day, have to face God. And he knew in his heart that God, who now felt as small as an atom, would return as bright and terrible as the sun. He was crying tears of fear and remorse, while his wife was comforting him as if he was a sensitive man, weeping tears of pity for the soul of another. That was the worst of it: he absorbed the warmth of human trust from his wife as a burglar enjoys the fruits of his plunder, as if they were his due.

As he wept and cursed himself, he realised, too, that he was, in fact, safe for now. His conscience could and would make amends with God when the time came for true remorse. His immediate concern, he told himself, was to protect himself and his family from the consequences of this desperate predicament, this situation which had at each stage been beyond his power to control.

He calmed himself and looked at his wife. 'Thank you, Jessica.' Jessica nodded. 'Let us pray,' he said, 'for Anne and the child.'

So they did. Down on their bended knees, they both closed their eyes and Edward recited words that seemed to him utterly meaningless and Jessica repeated them as if her life depended upon it.

When they had finished, Jessica said, 'So, no one saw you?'

Edward said, 'No.'

'The house? It stands on its own? No one nearby?'

'That's right.'

Jessica blinked. 'Edward. Did you check the answer-phone?'

Edward froze.

Jessica felt a stab of fear. 'Your message today? Will it still be on there?'

'I don't know . . .'

'And what else did you leave behind you?'

'Nothing . . . I don't know . . . nothing.'

'Christ, Edward, you're still on the answer-machine.'

Edward was speechless with horror.

Jessica began pacing. 'You've been phoning her all bloody day. What did you say?'

'I don't know.'

Jessica spun round and laughed bitterly. 'Ha! She'll get what she wanted even in death. You'll be condemned by your own voice.'

'They still won't know I was actually there.' He knew he was clutching at straws.

'You even mentioned me. They'll know. They'll know everything. Edward, you bloody fool! You must go back. Take the tape out of the machine.'

'No.'

'You must!'

'Jessica, no. I can't.'

'Go back, destroy the evidence, phone the police, tell them you found her there.'

'Jessica, I couldn't do that. I'd have to tell them the truth. I couldn't stand there and tell the police a pack of lies.'

'Why not? You've told me enough lies over the years.'

'You knew everything. That was the point. It was the only way.' Edward took a deep breath. Could he do it? Could he go round, take the tape, phone the police? What if they suspected something, there might be things they would find if they were suspicious. They would know she had been making love, from the autopsy. If he were there, they would know it had been him, it would be the obvious thing. They would know the child was his. Edward shook his head. 'No. It's impossible.'

'For the sake of your family, Edward.'

He looked at her. She had invoked the ultimate authority. He looked into his heart afresh. Could he, *for the sake of his family*, go back to the house? Could he remove the tape and come straight back? What if the body had already been discovered? What if he were discovered there with the body? His heart froze. He knew there was no way it could be done.

'No, Jessica,' he said.

Jessica looked down at him contemptuously. At that moment he had never looked so repugnant. The words he had spoken – that he had only told her of his mistresses because he was not even man enough to lie to her – seemed suddenly to sum up the man. He had given her a burden, the burden of his infidelity, which she had carried all these years, because he was incapable of deceit. Even that speck of honesty had been nothing more than cowardice. And now, here he sat before her, a wretched coward who would endanger his whole family for the

162

same reason. 'Stay in here, don't talk to anyone, just stay in here. Give me the keys.'

'Jessica, I can't ask you to do this.'

'On the contrary, Edward, you are forcing me to do it for you.'

Edward looked at her. He wanted to go down on his knees, to fall at her feet and say, 'Yes, please save me. I can't do it, you must do it for me.' Instead, he said, 'I can't ask you to go.'

Jessica said, 'Give me the keys, Edward.'

There was no way Edward could acknowledge what he was asking his wife to do, yet there was no way he could refuse her. He sat, motionless.

Jessica took the keys from his pocket.

Edward did not resist.

She did not look back as she left the room.

In the kitchen, both Jimmy and Lenny were a little drunk now, unaware of the comings and goings elsewhere in the house.

'Do you remember sitting here when we were young, when we were in school?' Jimmy said. 'After parties, when we'd been on the cider? We used to love coming here, because you had the biggest house. And you were the vicar's daughter.'

'I used to love that,' Lenny said. 'People expected me to be outrageous, so I was. I even bought wedges. Remember them?'

Jimmy didn't remember the wedges. Fashion had never really been his thing. 'My dad was proud of me being friends with you, you know. Especially when we started going out. He used to say he liked me going out with someone related to God.'

Lenny laughed. She felt a little sad, suddenly. 'I should

have stuck with you,' she said. 'You would never have done this to me.'

Jimmy laughed good-humouredly. 'Well, you've only got yourself to blame,' he scolded. 'That Christmas party, when I caught you snogging Mark!'

Again Lenny blushed at the memory. 'I can't believe I treated you like that. What a monster. Maybe I deserve this now, after all.'

Jimmy frowned. 'Don't be daft, Lenny. That was not the same thing. You two are married with a child. We were young. I should have seen it coming. Mark had been asking me about you for months. You two were always together. It was destined to be. You and Mark – the Golden Couple.'

'Huh. Tin-pot couple, you mean.'

Jimmy put his hand on Lenny's arm. 'Don't be so hard on yourself.'

Lenny huffed. 'Jesus, here we are, we're still here, sitting at the same table.'

'Yeah, but we're not on the cider,' Jimmy joked. 'And we haven't been to a party.'

Lenny sighed. 'I wonder if I'll ever grow up.'

'You? Lenny, you've got a child.'

'Yeah, but I'm stuck here. With mum and dad.'

'You won't be for long.'

Lenny was getting morose. 'Mum and dad make me feel so inferior. I mean, they don't say anything, but ... well, look at them. The perfect couple.'

'I'm sure they've been through plenty of shit in their time.'

'Cheers,' Lenny said, and they drank in silence for a couple of minutes, Jimmy smiling at her. Lenny took a large gulp and slammed her glass down on the table. 'Go on then, you bastard!' she laughed.

Jimmy was taken aback. 'What?'

'You're gunna make me ask you, aren't you?'

'Ask me what?'

'What bloody Mark said, when you saw him today. I've been waiting for you to bring the subject up. But you're not going to are you?'

'Nope.'

'You're so bloody good, aren't you? You know, I sometimes think you're too bloody good for your own good – if you can follow that.'

Jimmy grinned bashfully.

'So?' Lenny said.

'So what?'

'So what did he say?'

Jimmy shrugged. 'He's upset.'

'Well, good. Very upset?'

'Yeah. Very upset.'

'How very upset?'

'Huh, what do you want to hear?'

'I want to hear blood.'

'He's very upset.'

'Is he staying at your place?'

'No, he had to go back to Oxford.'

Lenny groaned. 'Oh, life must go on.'

'He had work.'

'It's the weekend.'

'Well, I don't know. He thought you didn't want to see him. He thought if he stayed around he'd make matters worse. I think he thinks you need space. I don't know.'

'I'm sorry, Jimmy. I know it's not your business. I . . .' she shrugged.

'I love you both,' Jimmy said. 'I didn't come over to give you a message. I only found out you were back today. I came to see you.'

'Yeah, yeah. And I appreciate it. Thanks.'

'But if you want my opinion, that's a different matter.'

Lenny brightened. 'Oh, now we're getting somewhere!'

Jimmy laughed, blushing again slightly.

'Yeah?' Lenny prompted.

'Well, I think you should phone him.'

Lenny waited.

'Yeah? . . . And? . . .'

Jimmy laughed. 'That's it, I'm afraid. That's the sum total of my wisdom on the subject.'

'Phone the bastard?'

'Yeah, phone the bastard.'

Lenny examined the contents of her whisky glass. 'That's what I thought you might say.'

Jessica was appalled to see Anne's near naked body.

It was as if God was reminding her of her husband's infidelity, perhaps God was punishing her for the part she was about to play in the drama. It was then that it occurred to Jessica that Edward had probably slept with Anne, and that was why she was dressed only in her robe.

It also occurred to her that if Edward *had* made love to Anne – if making love were the appropriate term, which she doubted – then she had better check the upstairs of the house for evidence too. And when she got upstairs she found Edward's chequebook open with a cheque payable to Anne for a thousand pounds, written but not torn out. Again Jessica felt a stab of anger. Careless man! Careless fool! Not only was his voice on the answerphone, but his chequebook was there, by the unmade bed – *upstairs*. For the sake of his shame, Edward had not told her that he had been upstairs! For the sake of his shame, he would have ruined the family! With deep untrammelled rage, Jessica made the bed, pocketed Edward's chequebook, inspected the bathroom and went back downstairs.

And now, in her rage, Jessica could stand the sight of Anne's semi-naked and strangely distorted body crumpled there at the bottom of the stairs. Jessica stood over her and forced herself to look at Anne's terrible death, took in the obscenity of the vision that was Anne's final communication with the world: drunken, naked, broken, carrying within her the child of someone else's husband. She made herself look at it; she wanted to ensure that she would have the strength to go forward. It was as if she was looking at an alternative ending to her own life, of what might become of her if she allowed Edward to destroy her, or the family. This was the price one had to pay for failure, these were the stakes.

She took the tape from the answer-phone and left the house.

Thomas left Charlie in bed and went downstairs.

He hated sleeping in single beds with another person and he wasn't tired. He was just drunk and it didn't always make him sleepy. He put the television on quietly and settled into the sofa, still thinking over his conversation with Gabriel, still lost in the recollections of those happy days.

Ten minutes later Gabriel came down.

'Shit, sorry, did I wake you up?' Thomas said.

'Na. Couldn't sleep, mate. I never sleep well when I've had a few drinks.'

'You've changed. You were always the one who could sleep over a washing line – no matter what we'd been doing.'

'A few more things have changed, since then.'

'Huh, yeah. You've got married for one.'

'And the rest.'

Gabriel sat himself down on the sofa next to Thomas. They stared at the TV for a while, happy in each other's company, Gabriel's leg resting lightly against Thomas's.

'Thanks for tonight, mate,' Thomas said. 'It was lovely.'

'Thanks for inviting yourself,' Gabriel laughed.

Thomas grinned. 'Charlie's a bugger,' he said. 'But I'm glad of it.'

'Are you?' Gabriel asked.

'Yes. I'm glad of it.' Thomas knew they would have to talk about it sooner or later. He knew, too, that this was his cue. 'She's very like you, really.'

'She's also a lot younger.'

'OK,' Thomas smiled, 'concerned brother.' Gabriel didn't say anything. '*Are* you concerned about us?' Thomas asked. Nothing. 'She knows what she's doing.'

'Are you sure?' Gabriel said.

'Yeah, yeah. I'm sure.'

'She's only seventeen.'

'She's nearly eighteen, Gabriel.'

Gabriel shrugged.

'Gabriel, you and I went to India when were eighteen!'

Gabriel looked at his friend. It was unreasonable to be peeved. He didn't even know why he was. 'You're right.'

'Remember what *we* got up to at that age?'

It was a moment before Gabriel replied, 'Umm.'

It was a moment, too, before Thomas said, 'Or would you rather forget that?'

Gabriel looked at Thomas. 'I'll never forget it.'

'Neither will I,' Thomas said. 'Do you regret any of it?'

Slowly Gabriel shook his head.

Thomas smiled. 'Do you ever still think about it?'

Gabriel looked down. 'Yeah, I still think about it.'

They sat in silence for a long time, staring at the television, comfortable in the glow from the screen, conscious now of their legs touching. Thomas gradually increased the pressure on his friend's leg, until Gabriel said, 'I'd better get back to bed.'

Thomas said nothing.

Gabriel didn't move.

They sat there for a while longer. Then Gabriel yawned and said again, 'Well, I'd best be off. Rachel'll start to wonder where I am.'

Thomas said, 'Goodnight.'

Their heads were leaning back against the sofa. They looked at each other. Thomas moved towards Gabriel a fraction and Gabriel continued to look directly at him. It would only take the slightest hint now from either of them. They both knew it and they were both afraid to do it.

'It's been a long time,' Thomas said.

'Yes.'

'A very long time.'

Gabriel nodded. 'Ages,' he whispered.

'You can kiss me if you want,' Thomas said.

Gabriel smiled.

'Do you want to?' Thomas asked gently.

Gabriel nodded. 'I want to. I'm just not sure I can.'

'Try, then you'll know.'

Gabriel laughed, gently. 'OK.'

He managed it quite well.

It was a good half-hour before they returned to their beds and to their women.

When Jessica arrived back at the house, all was quiet.

The only light was the faint, guilty-seeming glow from under her own bedroom door. When she entered the room, now an active accomplice to Edward's sin, Edward was on his knees leaning on the bed, apparently in prayer.

Edward looked round at a face he barely recognised,

cold-hewn, stressful and angry, yet unmoving and placid, too.

'It's over,' she said simply.

Edward was captivated by his wife's image. In her absence he had remembered the frightful picture of Anne's final undignified posture and felt a stab of bitter shame that his own wife would now be forced to witness that obscenity. It made him feel so despicable, made his marriage seem so repulsive and phoney, that his breath had nearly choked him and he had finally caught a glimpse of God, or perhaps a shadow of God's displeasure had fallen on him, but, whichever, he had felt the need to fall on his knees and pray, to beg for mercy, not for forgiveness, but only that he be spared God's wrath. The more he prayed, the more he felt deserving of punishment, the more repugnant he seemed to himself. When he saw the look on Jessica's face he could not help but think of how she had looked on the twisted remains of a sacrifice his rotting and profane heart had made to the demon of lust. His victim. Anne. Poor, vulnerable Anne. Sweet Anne. It made Jessica seem like God looking down on him in judgement.

When she saw Edward's face, Jessica's wrath was indeed provoked. 'It's funny,' she said without humour, 'how you can hear things and not really listen, how they only click into place afterwards. Like, "She fell downstairs." It didn't occur to me to think, What was she doing upstairs? And of course: you were both upstairs, because that's where the bedroom is, that's where you had sex. You left that bit out, Edward, the sex, or did you call it making love? Which was it?' The casual tone made her question all the more chilling to Edward.

'Please, Jessica, don't . . .'

'Is that what she said? "Please. One last time, Edward, darling"?' Edward could not reply. 'And what if there's an

170

autopsy? It's likely there *will* be an autopsy. And what will they find? Oh, yes. You, Edward. As if a foetus isn't enough. No, you had to go one better. You had to . . . to . . .' It was too revolting for Jessica to name.

'Do you think they will . . . examine her?'

'Oh, yes, of course they'll examine her. Oh, yes, they'll know she had just had intercourse. And they'll wonder who it was who had had intercourse with her.'

Edward was immobilised by fright. Now that Jessica was saying it, it seemed as if he had already been discovered.

Jessica took his chequebook from the pocket of her jacket. 'And they'd have *known* who'd had intercourse with her if I hadn't removed this little piece of evidence.' She threw the book on to the dressing table. 'And now I think you're safe,' she said casually. 'Not that I think you deserve to be, but they'll have no idea whose the baby is, or whose is . . .'

Edward put his head in his hands, not to pray this time but to think. Would there be any way he could be associated with the scene? Would there be any signs of struggle that Jessica had not detected? He wanted to ask if she'd noticed anything like that, but it was impossible. That was a burden he would have to carry alone. It was bad enough, Jessica's knowledge of what had happened, dreadful enough that she had seen the mess he had made of . . . of Anne, of another human being, without her knowing the full extent of his culpability. That was a matter for him alone, for him and God.

Edward was again overwhelmed by his guilt. Then it occurred to him that he could begin to make amends immediately. It would be simple. He could telephone the police and tell them the truth, and accept the consequences like a man. He blinked. It was that simple. Of course it was. He had been distracted by the horror of the scene, by the shock, by his guilt and shame.

171

He looked at Jessica for the first time without horror.
'I can't do this. *We* can't do this. It's not right for me to
ask you to do this for me. I'll telephone. This is madness.
I'm so sorry . . .'

Jessica's eyes flashed. 'No.'

'I should tell the truth. It's the only way. I mean, I
won't tell them you were there.'

Jessica suddenly became very frightened. She realised
she had scared Edward more than had been necessary. She
had been angry with him – she had needed to be angry
with him, to release her feelings of disgust. But it had
been a mistake. She needed to comfort Edward, like a
child, or else he would begin to behave like a child. He
was in shock, she must be careful not to upset him further,
not to push him over the edge.

'No, Edward, not now,' Jessica said softly. 'If you are
to tell the truth, I would have to tell the truth and they
would come for me too. It makes no sense.'

Edward was shaking his head. 'I can't live like this.'
Was he crying? 'I can't live with you, I can't live with
myself, like this.'

'Don't say that, Edward. You're in shock. You've done
no wrong. Not any real wrong.'

'Oh, but I have, Jessica.'

'No, Edward, you have to think of your family. It's the
natural thing, the *good* thing. It's the *only* thing you can
do.' Jessica began to pace about. 'It's what *Anne* would
have wanted, Edward. Would Anne have wanted you to
suffer, because of a *mistake*?'

Edward looked at her. He wondered what Anne would
have wanted. Revenge? Perhaps not. She had only wanted
to keep the child because she was in love with him,
surely.

Jessica saw her advantage. 'Edward, Anne told me she
loved you. She told me that she would never want any

172

harm to come to you. She said that a few times. She wanted me to tell you that, I could tell.'

Edward sighed. 'She was a very caring person.'

'She would never have wanted you ruined, not over an accident.'

'Yes.'

'A stupid accident.'

Edward was silent for a while. Jessica sat down on the bed next to him and began to stroke his head, comforting him, telling him he had had a shock, that the police might not investigate an accident after all, and even if they did that they would not be able to tell who had been there, and anyway if it was an accident there would be no reason for them to be suspicious of anyone who *had* been there.

Eventually Edward calmed himself with the thought that he had to do what was right for his family and that Anne would have fallen anyway and that there had been nothing he nor anybody else could have done for her. It was obviously going to be treated as an accident, a dreadful, unfortunate accident.

'There was nothing anyone could have done.'

Jessica said, 'That's right, Edward, nothing.'

Edward said, 'For either of them.'

They eventually went to bed, rigidly clinging to their own sides, not touching, nor speaking, nor sleeping.

·11·

GABRIEL AWOKE IN hell.

He always felt bad when he woke up, but this morning the flames were hot. He was, of course, withdrawing from methadone and in need of his injection. The pain was compounded by a hangover and by the awful feeling that not only had he been unfaithful to his wife, but he had done it with the man who was his best friend.

The tenderness of the night before – not to mention the pleasure – was forgotten. Gabriel cursed his friend for having seduced him while he was drunk and vulnerable because of his drug problem, a problem about which Thomas knew nothing because Gabriel was too ashamed to talk about it.

He looked over at Rachel was still sleeping, as serene and beautiful as ever, and cursed her too. She made him feel wretched sometimes, with her perfectly balanced thinking and her organised simplicity. Sometimes even her very generosity was unbearable, reminding him of his own pathetic condition.

He looked about the room. The femininity of the place infuriated him; the decorations were bland and not at all what he would have liked had he lived alone. Sometimes he wanted to run away, back to London, back to his old life, his old flat, his old friends who didn't give a shit, who wouldn't look at him as if he were some kind of monster if he were drunk, or if he filled up a syringe with heroin and stuck it in his arm and sat there dribbling all day . . .

There *was* no escape. He knew he couldn't go back to that hell, there was nothing there for him but ruin. But today, staying here, in this mess, in these chains, seemed vile too. Quietly, without disturbing Rachel, he got out of bed and went downstairs. He would go up to the house for his injection, then he would face the day. Or not face it as the case may be.

Charlie woke up in heaven.

Thomas was running his hands over her before she even opened her eyes. The moment she was awake they were kissing. She hadn't even brushed her teeth! But Thomas didn't seem to mind.

This time she wasn't going to let him get away. This time he didn't seem to want to get away. What Nick had received ungratefully, or at least without any grace, that day in the woods, Thomas responded to with the utmost style and gratitude. Whereas Nick had expressed his pleasure with an instantaneous and unwelcome spurt, Thomas moaned and writhed and touched her head and told her how to do it best and showed her how to help her mouth with her hands so as to give him the greatest and most satisfying time he must surely have ever had in his life, by the sound of him.

As she performed her role, and Thomas his, Charlie felt like the most sophisticated, sexy, daring and exciting girl in the history of sex. When Thomas asked her if she minded if he came, she told him she insisted, and even though she gagged when he did so, she was utterly

175

determined to make a breakfast of every last drop of him. She felt so grand afterwards that she didn't even mind him getting straight up and going downstairs to look for Gabriel without returning the compliment, or even kissing her by way of a thank you.

She was going straight to the house and to telephone Melissa.

Gabriel couldn't look at Thomas when he came downstairs.

Thomas noticed it but told himself it was because Gabriel had a hangover. Gabriel told *himself* it was because he had a hangover. He would rather have gone straight to the house without having to face his friend but it was too late, he had just poured half a glass of milk down his throat to try and calm his stomach when Thomas appeared, followed shortly by Charlie.

Charlie said she was going up to the house and Gabriel asked Thomas if he'd mind waiting to tell Rachel that he'd gone there himself, to see if his mother was . . . going into town . . . where she could . . . er . . . get him some things he needed.

When Charlie and Gabriel got outside, Charlie linked her arm through Gabriel's and said, 'God, I'm so in love.'

Gabriel said, 'No, Charlie, you're not in love, you're obsessed. Being in love takes time.'

'Oh! Mr Wisdom! Sorry for feeling anything so childish!' Charlie scoffed.

'Come on,' Gabriel said, 'Thomas isn't interested . . . not really.'

'Not interested in *what*?'

'I don't know,' Gabriel shrugged. 'He's not interested in relationships. Especially not with . . . younger women.'

'Well, you could have fooled me, Gabriel, especially a

few minutes ago when your old man there was writhing round in a fit of sexual ecstasy.'

Gabriel looked at her. 'You had sex? Just now?'

'Can't you tell from the colour of my cheeks and the way my feet aren't actually touching the ground?' Charlie laughed.

Gabriel seemed to scowl.

'Oh, for God's sake, the great bohemian is all moralistic now his little sister's getting a decent shag.'

'It's not that . . .'

'Gabriel, I know you're only jealous.'

'Don't be stupid,' Gabriel said, with a little too much scorn.

Charlie squeezed his arm. 'Don't worry, I'm not going to take your precious friend off you. I'll make sure he gives you enough attention.'

'Charlie, I'm not bothered about that. I'm just trying to tell you you're going to get hurt, that's all.'

'What, are you saying he only wants to use me for sex?' Charlie said.

Gabriel hesitated. 'Possibly.'

'How do you know that's not all I want him for?'

'You'll get hurt,' Gabriel said again.

'So everyone says.'

'So be careful.'

'God, you're so miserable before you get your morning fix,' Charlie said.

Gabriel tried not to show how much that hurt him.

By the time Gabriel reached the back door of the house he was feeling pretty sick.

The neat, extended lawns and ornamental borders that stretched from the Lodge to the family mansion, like something from a gentle pastoral novel of eighteenth-century England, were as unremarkable to Gabriel as the

177

kind summer sun that touched down on his rigid shoulders.

There was an unbearable lightness about Jessica that morning that cut into him, like a light suddenly turned on in the dark. She was all breeze and efficiency. She whisked Gabriel upstairs and gave him his medicine, told him that he and Rachel were to come to tea that evening without fail, and dismissed him before he could even shake off the initial effects of his dose.

Jessica was just as brusque with Charlie, demanding that she stay out of Edward's way and telling her that she, too, was to come to tea that evening. When Charlie insisted on inviting Thomas, Jessica immediately gave way, insisting only that they be there by five o'clock. When Charlie told Gabriel he reluctantly agreed to pass on the invitation to Thomas.

Edward was, apparently, upstairs, not feeling well.

Gabriel stumbled back down to the Lodge, trying to get his head together as he went. He had to stop and be sick behind the rhododendrons. When he got back Thomas was waiting for him, Rachel was still in bed.

'Shall we go for a walk?' Thomas asked.

'That'd be nice,' Gabriel said, doing his best impression of sobriety.

'You sure you feel like it? You look a bit rough.'

Gabriel waved a hand. 'I'll be fine in a minute, I'm always like this first thing in the morning.'

Suddenly Gabriel felt OK again; that is, he no longer wanted to be sick.

It always took about half an hour to get over the initial rush from the drug.

The two young men were down by the old lake now. Gabriel was talking away about nothing very much – not even about work, or old times, just any old rubbish. He was beginning to annoy Thomas.

'Gabriel, if you're going to talk shit, I'd rather you just said nothing. You don't have to get defensive because of last night. Just relax, OK.'

Gabriel looked at him, feeling a sudden anger that Thomas should mention what he was finding so hard to deal with in the cold light of day. 'I'm not being defensive. I'm not even thinking about it, if you must know.'

Thomas shrugged casually.

Gabriel was even more annoyed by that and fell silent.

Ten minutes further along the lakeside path, Thomas said, 'If you're going to sulk, Gabriel, I'm going back.'

Gabriel, much to his own embarrassment, continued to stare painfully at the ground as he walked, unable to raise his head.

Thomas went on, 'All right. We kissed. We had a bit of sexy fun. Where's the crime? We're friends, aren't we?'

Gabriel stopped. 'That's what's worrying me. I don't know.'

Thomas said, 'Oh, thanks.'

Gabriel felt exasperated. 'I mean, I know you're a friend to me. But what am *I* to *you*?'

'Oh, I see.' Thomas seemed annoyed. 'You think I'm out to wreck your marriage, do you?'

'Course I don't. I'm just worried you . . . you're . . .'

'In love with you?'

Gabriel nodded.

Thomas tutted. 'Don't be stupid. You're just ashamed. And paranoid. You feel like you've been unfaithful to your wife after a couple of weeks of marriage – which you have – and you're worried I'll start causing trouble. Which I won't. We were pissed. It was fun. Don't worry about it.'

This speech didn't seem to have much effect on Gabriel who was still slouching and looking miserable.

'For God's sake,' Thomas went on, 'are you worried because of the past, is that it?' Gabriel shrugged. 'Gabriel, just because we . . . had sex when we were younger, had an affair, doesn't mean anything now. Forget about that.'

'It's difficult to forget about it when . . .' Gabriel shook his head. 'What was that about, last night, then?' Gabriel said.

Thomas laughed. 'Remembrance.'

Gabriel looked as if he was taking that the wrong way.

Thomas shook his head. 'It was sex, for God's sake, between friends.'

'And what about Charlie?'

Thomas stopped and looked at him. 'She's my girl-friend. Same as she was last night. She's not the love of my life, but I like her. She's sexy. And good company.'

Gabriel still looked troubled. Thomas wanted him to smile.

'What, Gabriel? For God's sake, speak your mind.'

Gabriel obliged. 'Are you fucking gay or what?'

Thomas looked at him. 'Are you?'

'I'm fucking married.'

Thomas looked angry. 'Well, I'm fucking your sister.'

That did it. Gabriel's face cracked into a grin. He realised he was being daft. 'I'm sorry,' he said. 'I think you were right. Paranoid and guilty. That's what comes of being a bishop's son with a guilty secret.'

'You don't need to feel guilty.'

'I was unfaithful to my wife, with another man!' Gabriel laughed.

'Not *very* unfaithful.'

Gabriel looked at Thomas. 'True.'

'Just let it go,' Thomas said. 'And don't worry about me. If I was still in love with you, wouldn't I say?'

Gabriel stopped smiling again. '*Still* in love. Then you *were*? In love with me?'

Thomas looked down. He felt as if he had been caught out. It was a moment before he could reply. 'Yes. At the time, yes. But it's long gone, Gabriel. Now it's like . . . remembering your first love. It's just a sentimental memory, even a bit funny. But it means no more than looking at an old photograph.'

Gabriel looked at him. 'Do you find that sad?' he asked.

'No,' Thomas said, a little awkwardly. 'Do you?'

'No,' Gabriel said firmly. 'Not at all.'

'Then there's no problem,' Thomas said and started walking again.

After that Thomas let Gabriel get on with talking rubbish for the rest of the walk.

Edward and Jessica were outside the church office.

Simon was there. He had a wedding that morning and they knew the young priest liked to work Saturday afternoons to get through the paper-work that he never had time for during the chaos of the week.

Edward and Jessica both felt scorched by their experience and their sleepless night, but Jessica had insisted they come in to the office. She had an idea of how to get over their biggest hurdle. The family invitations to an early tea had been the first part of her plan, now was the time for part two.

'I can't do this, Jessica,' Edward hissed, as they prepared to face the world for the first time since Anne's death.

'It won't seem so bad after we've made this important first step, Edward. The longer we leave it, the harder it will become. We have nothing to fear. We know something that the rest of the world doesn't know – that is our crime, that is all. Very soon that will no longer be the case. Now, pull yourself together.'

Edward sighed a deep sigh that sounded as dull and as grey as he looked. 'Very well.'

Simon was obviously disappointed to see them. He liked the peace of the office on Saturday and felt their presence as an intrusion. He covered his disappointment with a bright hallo.

Edward said, 'Morning, Simon. Jessica and I . . . er . . . that is, I had one or two things to attend to left over from the week. Jessica was going into town to do a bit of shopping and being as we were both coming in she decided it would be best if . . .'

Jessica cut him off. 'Morning, Simon, are you well?'

'Yes, very well, thank you.'

'We won't be long,' Jessica said, and shoved Edward into the inner office, closing the door behind her. 'Simon doesn't need an explanation of our every move, Edward. He doesn't suspect us of anything.'

'Yes, I know,' Edward said. 'I'm sorry.' He shook his head. 'I feel so . . . so guilty.'

'Well, don't, Edward.'

'I can't help it.'

'Well, if you must, then don't let everyone else in the world know it. Just feel it. For God's sake keep your feelings to yourself for once.' Edward nodded. 'Now, we sit here for five minutes and then you can go and have a little word with Simon about Anne.'

Mary was the only member of the household who had consciously noticed that Edward and Jessica were suffering from something more than a simple disagreement.

That morning she had been shocked to see Edward looking so drawn and ill. Jessica told Mary that Edward had a migraine, but took Edward off to work and invited half the world to tea that evening.

Mary wasn't in the least suspicious; she was simply

worried and a little shocked, too. Edward looked *old*. It was the first time she had ever really seen him looking that way. That morning it occurred to Mary what Edward would look like as an old man; the lines were there, his skin seemed puffy and wrinkled, his expression that of a man who had stopped wondering about tomorrow and the next day, but whose only concern was with living through the day at hand. It made Mary sad, too, to see Edward like that. It made her anxious for her own tender mortality. She too felt old, but not tired; she wasn't feeling her age, as it were, but rather felt the shrinking of years, the shortening of the future.

Mary was glad to see Charlie that morning and chatted to her warmly. Charlie was full of life and love and Mary was pleased for her. It was one of those mornings when the sunshine seemed brighter but gentler than on other days, and life seemed short and precious, the sort of day when God seemed gentle and serene and people were his shadows.

It nearly broke Mary's heart when she came upon Lenny sitting at the kitchen table, struggling with Ben and looking lost and miserable. Lenny smiled bravely at Mary and was very glad when Mary took the child from her. Ben loved Mary and gave her a smile as bright as the morning's light.

'Mary, what do you think I should do?'

'Mark-wise?'

Lenny nodded. 'Shall I phone the bastard?'

Mary was twiddling Ben's nose as she spoke. 'It might be an idea. If only to arrange for him to see Ben.'

'Jimmy came round last night and talked me into it.'

'Jimmy's a good man,' Mary said. 'He's a friend of Mark's, isn't he?'

'He's my friend too.'

'He's always had a soft spot for you.'

183

'Yeah, I've got one for him,' Lenny said. 'He's just too nice to go out with.'

Mary didn't agree with that, but she wasn't one for judging.

Lenny remembered when she was a little girl she had always told Mary all those things she was too scared to talk to Jessica about. Mary had always been there, part of the family and yet not part of the family too.

'I do think it's a good idea to phone him,' Mary said. 'Even if I hate his guts. Even if he doesn't deserve it. Even if you deserve better.'

Lenny grinned. 'That's what I love about you, Mary, you're so loyal.'

Mary smiled and thought to herself that she'd do anything to protect the family she had lived with all these years, the family she thought of as her own, the family that she sometimes felt she was the heart of.

Gabriel and Thomas had walked a full circle.

They were sitting on the wall by the Lodge, looking in the direction of the Rattigan family home at the end of the drive. Rachel was still in bed, having a rare Saturday lie-in.

'It's funny,' Thomas said. 'When we were little, we used to do everything we could to escape that house. It's only now you realise it's magnificent.'

Gabriel nodded. 'Rachel's not keen on living so close.'

Thomas grinned. 'Ah — I warned you. You can take the girl out of the city, but you can't take the city out of the girl.'

'There's no need to criticise her,' Gabriel said.

Thomas tutted. 'Gabriel, I *wasn't*. Look, I'd best be off. We'll go out again some time. The four of us.' Thomas jumped down off the wall and shrugged. 'Last night was fun.'

Gabriel jumped down, too. 'Yeah. And thanks for coming over.'

Thomas said, 'Yeah' and went to give Gabriel a kiss on the cheek. Gabriel lurched backwards as if Thomas was about to hit him.

Thomas looked hurt. 'Oh, for God's sake.'

'Don't . . .'

'I was saying goodbye, Gabriel. Can't I even do that without you treating me as some kind of leper? What's the point of all we've said this morning, if it hasn't cleared things up?'

'We talked. We can talk for ever,' Gabriel said, coldly. 'I'm still not sure what you want.'

'You still think I'm in love with you?'

'I said, I'm not sure what you want.'

'Why would I lie to you, Gabriel?'

Gabriel wouldn't look at his friend. 'You can lie to the person that means everything to you if you think it'll keep them close. It's not cunning. It's just an instinct. To keep someone close by.'

'That's *your* problem,' Thomas said, struggling to hold his temper. 'If you're obsessed by what happened years ago, ten years ago, then maybe it's you who doesn't know what he wants. It's *you* who is lying to someone close to you, not me.' Thomas walked to his car. 'Get it into your head, Gabriel, I don't want you like that. Don't flatter yourself.'

As Gabriel watched Thomas drive off, Rachel came out of the Lodge.

'What was all that about?' she asked.

Gabriel sighed. 'Oh, nothing. I challenged him about Charlie, he took the hump.'

'Don't you think he wants her?'

'I've got no idea,' Gabriel said, and went inside.

★

'I don't suppose you've heard anything from Anne, have you, Simon?'

'No, Edward. I actually phoned her this morning, to see if there was anything I could get her, but she wasn't in.'

'Oh, I'm sure she's in,' Edward said, casually leaning on Simon's desk. 'She was poorly yesterday, wasn't she?'

'Yes, but she didn't answer the phone. I tried three times and I kept getting the answer-phone.'

'Oh, dear. Perhaps she's so poorly she can't get out of bed.'

'Well, yes, it's possible,' Simon said. 'Maybe she's gone to her mother's to be looked after.'

Edward shook his head. 'Oh. I don't think that's like Anne, do you?'

'I don't know, Edward, she's been a little unpredictable lately, I must say.'

'I wonder if you could pay her a visit on your way home tonight. You live out that way, don't you? I mean "ish".'

'Yes. Yes, all right.'

'Er, maybe take her some flowers or something.'

'Good idea, Edward.' Simon grinned and nodded towards the church. 'Maybe pinch a few from the altar, eh?'

Edward said, 'Yes, yes, if you like,' which shocked Simon a little.

'I was only joking, Edward. I'll stop and buy some on the way – if there's anywhere still open.' Simon looked at his watch. 'I'll be stuck here until five.'

'Yes. You've got that service. For Mrs Cavendish's niece.'

'What a good memory you have, Edward.'

Edward nodded. 'It was Jessica who remembered, actually.'

Simon was still arranging the papers on his desk. Edward dithered for a few moments longer.

'So, you'll call in at Anne's. On your way home.'

Simon looked up. 'Yes, Edward. That's what I said.'

'Yes, yes. Good.'

Jessica appeared at the door to the inner office, from where she'd been monitoring the conversation. 'Right, let's go, then, shall we, Edward.'

Edward said, 'Right,' then he said, 'I'll hear from you later, then, shall I?' to Simon.

Simon looked puzzled. 'Will you?'

'Er, yes, about Anne.'

Simon looked surprised. 'Oh, right. Er, yes. I'll phone you and let you know how she is.'

Jessica took Edward by the arm. 'Don't be so worried, Edward. I'm sure Simon will only phone you if Anne needs anything. Won't you, Simon?'

Simon was very puzzled by now. 'Erm, yes, yes, of course. Erm, right. Goodbye.'

Jessica pushed Edward out of the office before he could say anything more.

Saturday afternoon

Had a lovely lie-in this morning. Thomas stayed last night and he and Gabriel went for a walk, so I had the bed to myself for a change.

I think Gabriel and Thomas had a row about Charlie. Thomas went driving off at a hundred miles an hour and Gabriel was in a mood all morning. I think they were up half the night together. Gabriel got up again after I'd gone to sleep and I could hear him and Thomas laughing and giggling away like a couple of girls. Gabriel's paying for it now with a hangover. Honestly, you should have heard them last night, like a couple of old women going back over their long-lost memories. Of course I loved it. Gabriel looked so happy and free – it was almost as if the pair of them were back in India and wherever else they went. I wish I'd known them both then and gone away with them. Not even as Gabriel's girlfriend, but just as a friend. Sometimes I think you get to know more about your friends than you do about your lovers.

Gabriel is so beautiful, but somehow I think he's unhappy. His moods are still all over the place. He's still off up to the Lodge every five minutes, which depresses me. It's not that I mind him leaving me down here on my own, but it just gives me the feeling that he's not happy with our life together. It makes me feel like clinging to him and begging him to stay just one whole day with me, all day, just him and me and nobody else, no outside world. You'd think that would happen automatically, wouldn't you, stuck out here in the country. I sometimes wonder if I really know him at all, or if I've been blinded by his looks, his charm and his sheer brilliance! Oh, blinded by love!! I know I know him really, but I tell you there's hidden depths to the boy that I'm determined to get to the bottom of. No one escapes the Spanish Inquisition!! – especially not the bishop's son!!!

Jessica came over this morning. Edward was in the car, they were on their way out somewhere. She wanted to ask me herself, to tea, this evening. She'd already practically ordered Gabriel to come over – five o'clock prompt – but she said she wanted to make sure that he'd mentioned it to me. Nothing special, she said, but it would be nice, wouldn't it, to get everyone together for once? As if we're not altogether every ten minutes as it is! It's as if there is no door to the house and the Rattigan army can march in at any moment and order you around.

Anyway, we're going, of course, like good children.

'Lenny. Hallo.'

Mark's voice was as cold as the Atlantic. Lenny felt sick. She had expected him to be pleased to hear from her and highly apologetic.

She froze.

'What do you want, Lenny? I presume you must want something.'

'Erm. I wondered . . . I was just thinking . . .'

Her voice sounded so fragile and pathetic she couldn't bear to hear it, so she shut up and waited for him to say something.

Mark didn't say a word.

'Oh . . . nothing,' Lenny said, and slammed the phone down.

She waited for him to ring her back, cursing herself again for expecting him to be eager and apologetic. She stared at the phone for three whole minutes before she finally admitted with a surge of anger that he was not going to phone her back. As soon as she realised this for certain, she boiled with shame and embarrassment.

'Bastard!' she shouted to no one. 'Bastard!' She felt so small and pathetic that she could have crawled out of the door and jumped through the grating into the drain. She'd given it all back to him, all the power.

As she sat there she gradually became aware of how murders could be committed and why they often happened within the family.

When Mary came into the kitchen and asked her how it had gone, she cried so much she thought she might float away. Mary held her as if she were the little girl she had once been.

Teatime was a very grim affair.

Charlie was upset with Gabriel because he said he'd forgotten to invite Thomas.

'You never forgot!' she shouted, in front of everyone, when Gabriel confessed his guilt. 'You're just jealous of me and Thomas, aren't you?'

Gabriel looked as if he wished the ground would open and swallow him up. 'Don't be stupid! I'm sick of you, Charlie. Just piss off and mind your own business.'

Everyone went very quiet for a moment. People were surprised to hear Gabriel so vehement. Rachel went crimson because she assumed everyone would think they were in a bad mood with each other, then she cursed herself for worrying *what* the Rattigans thought of her or her marriage. But she still blushed. Then Gabriel sat at the table, making no effort whatsoever to look as if he were enjoying himself.

Lenny was steaming. As the meal started she declared her support for all those women who wanted to murder their husbands and then fell into gloomy silence herself, occasionally throwing sullen looks in Rachel and Gabriel's direction as if thinking how sorry she felt for them in their miserable marriage.

Charlie contented herself with guerrilla warfare. Anything anyone said, she shot down in flames. Her every word was a challenge: Come on, then, start something and see what you get. No one did her the favour.

Mary, who served up the meal as usual, was worried about Jessica and Edward. Edward not only looked old, but he looked seriously ill. It crossed Mary's mind when she saw the couple returning from the church that afternoon, that Edward had been diagnosed with something very serious and that Jessica and he were waiting to break the news to her.

Edward really did look pitiful. He was obviously trying to appear involved in the few conversations that did take place – he smiled a hollow smile and ummed a half-hearted um when he needed to – but clearly he wasn't taking in a thing.

The only two people attempting to make conversation were Rachel and Jessica.

Rachel was appalled by the atmosphere and felt as if it were her own fault. Every moment of silence was agony to her and she soon realised that Jessica was her only ally against the dread of quiet.

'I suppose you heard we had Thomas to stay at the Lodge, last night, Jessica?' she said, and cringed at the sound of her voice and the inadequacy of her conver-sational gambit.

'What did he think of the place?' Jessica said, and Rachel was sure she detected a sympathetic glint in Jessica's eye, as if she were trying to communicate her gratitude to Rachel for her effort.

'Oh, he seemed quite taken with it, didn't he, Gabriel?'

(Gabriel said, 'Huh? Oh, um . . .')

'He and Gabriel went for a walk down by the lake this morning while I had a nice lie-in.' Even Jessica couldn't think of anything to reply to this, so Rachel struggled on. 'I think I must have been tired after my hectic week in the rip-roaring world of insurance broking!' she tried.

Charlie was there for that one. 'Oh, I'm sure you were *absolutely exhausted*!' she said, as if Rachel had been serious.

'Life in Market Cross can be more exhausting than you think,' Jessica said, giving Rachel a kind smile and stealing a look at Edward.

And so it went on. Rachel felt as if her cheeks were going to burn up with the embarrassment she felt.

After half an hour the phone rang.

Nobody except Jessica noticed that Edward flinched.

Mary answered and came back to fetch Edward.

Jessica put down her knife and fork and waited for Edward to return.

Poor Rachel was completely stranded then, even Jessica was unable to come to her aid. Finally Rachel gave up and sat in angry silence with the rest of them.

Then Edward reappeared, looking very pale.

Everyone looked at him.

It was a dreadful moment for Edward. It had been Simon on the phone, as he knew it would be. Simon had told Edward what he already knew – that Anne had died, probably the result of falling down the stairs. Simon had been terribly upset: Anne had lain there all day, possibly more, undiscovered. Edward was as sympathetic as he could be. He was very relieved to be able to express his regret to someone and did so at some length until he found that Simon was comforting him. Then he thanked Simon and came to break the news to the family.

As Edward stood poised to do that, looking at the people who were gathered there in the dining room, just as Jessica had planned, so that they could all witness Edward hearing the news, so that they could hear the news from him, he felt as if he might collapse on to the floor and cry out his pain and his misery, confess everything to them. He wanted to cry now for Anne.

Jessica sensed something was going to go wrong and stood up. As he saw her do so, Edward raised a hand to stop her.

'Are you all right, Edward?' Jessica said.

'Yes. Yes,' he said. 'I'm afraid I've got some bad news. Anne – my secretary . . . Anne . . . is dead. I . . . I . . . She fell down the stairs and broke her neck.'

Then he cried. Standing there in front of them all, he

cried like a baby. He let his wife comfort him and lead him from the room, leaving everyone thinking that he was a fine human being for showing his feelings, for caring so much for one of his employees.

When they got upstairs to the bedroom, Edward threw himself on to the bed and wept uninhibitedly while Jessica looked on. There was no holding the man back as he sobbed wildly and begged Anne aloud for forgiveness and cursed himself to hell for being an irredeemably devious man, incapable of the slightest feeling of humanity.

Jessica said, 'Shhh! Edward, not so loud.'

·12·

A T THE FUNERAL the whole parish agreed that Anne's death was tragic.

Everyone in the parish attended the service and the vast old church, seeming in the drizzle even more sombre and grey than usual, was full to overflowing. The floral tributes stretched from the arch of the graveyard gate to the huge mock-gothic entrance hall of the church itself. Nearly everyone cried, including many of the men who could not for the life of them recall who Anne was, but who were none the less overcome by the grief expressed, *en masse*, by the women. Poor Anne had not been a great personality within the parish, but she had been kind and efficient and all the ladies claimed to have loved her; a love no doubt enhanced by Anne's position as secretary to the bishop, a role that she had held for a long time compared with some of her predecessors.

People were moved, too, because the bishop himself seemed so upset. Twice during the service he paused to collect himself and once he stopped to blow his nose.

The event was something of a public tragedy. It was as if an accident had happened to the community itself and part of its body had been broken, or lost for ever. The fact that Anne was such a lonely figure increased the sense of loss. It was well known that Anne's mother had travelled from Skegness for the occasion, and that the two women had been in less than frequent contact. If Anne had no family locally, it followed therefore that in effect the parishioners themselves had been her family.

Shortly before the ceremony began there was a knock on the office door.

'Come,' said Edward, his voice sounding as flat as the medieval earth.

It was Dr Kenyon.

'Gerald. Come in, sit down.'

'Morning, Edward. All right if I close the door?'

'Yes, of course.'

The doctor sat down. 'Sorry, Edward. Just wanted a quick word. Tragic. She was a lovely person. You must all be feeling pretty shell-shocked.'

Edward blinked. 'You knew Anne?'

The doctor nodded. 'She was a patient.'

'I didn't know. I . . .' Edward braced himself for some alarming relevation.

The doctor looked uncomfortable. 'This probably isn't the best time to tell you this, but I'm afraid I have to. I want you to tell me that I'm doing the right thing.' He took a breath. 'A couple of days before Anne died, she came to see me. She wanted a pregnancy test. She'd already done one herself and she needed it confirmed.' The doctor looked embarrassed. 'I confirmed it. She was pregnant.'

'No!' Edward said, doing his best to look surprised. His job was made easier because of the surprise he felt that his friend had been Anne's doctor.

'The thing is,' the doctor went on, 'her mother is here today and . . . I've decided not to tell her. The autopsy

195

was straightforward. Her neck was broken. That's all anyone really needs to know.'

Edward nodded to indicate that he understood how delicate the situation was.

'I don't think there's any point upsetting anyone further, but I wanted to ask your opinion, Edward.' Edward said, 'Humm.'

'If you *do* think I should tell her, I'll try to have a word with her – poor woman – before she goes back to Skegness.'

The doctor waited for Edward to speak, but Edward could not yet formulate any kind of reply.

'I'm sorry to tell you now, Edward, just before the funeral. But you see the point.'

Edward could see the point only too well. 'I . . . I'd . . . just leave it. You're quite right. Leave it. She'll have quite enough on her mind for one day.'

The doctor nodded. 'That's just what I thought. One could argue that she has a right to know, that's all. I suppose the father has even more right to know – that is assuming he didn't know already. Do you know who the father might be? I know she had a regular boyfriend, but . . .'

Edward tensed. 'Er? Did she? I mean, I don't know – I have no idea. I thought she was single . . . and unattached. That's why I was a little shocked. I . . . Did she say anything to you? Anything at all? Anything that might give you a clue as to . . . as to who he might be?'

'No idea at all, I'm afraid.'

'None at all? There must have been some indication?'

The doctor sighed a little heavily. 'Between you and me, Edward – and I'm only telling you because you are a man of integrity – it's nothing she told me directly so I'm not breaking confidentiality . . .' Again he sighed. 'I think it may have been a married man.'

Edward nodded. 'What makes you think that?' he managed to ask calmly.

'As I say, it's no more than a hunch.' He shrugged. 'It's the impression I got when I was asking her about the pregnancy. She was very discreet, I should say *secretive*, about the man. I got the distinct impression that she was hiding something – giving me the signs – *don't intrude*. I didn't, of course. If it is – or rather was – a married man, I understand her need for discretion.'

'Umm, quite.'

'This is a small town, Edward.'

'Indeed.'

'So you've no idea who the father might have been?'

Edward shook his head and tried to look as if he were doing it sadly.

The doctor nodded. 'Causes you a bit of a dilemma, I suppose?'

Edward looked puzzled.

'The funeral. I mean, do you have to . . . say prayers for the unborn child?'

'Um. Yes. That is a dilemma.'

Never before had Edward felt such a hypocrite as during the service.

There he stood in front of the whole parish, speaking kindly of the woman he had killed, asking God to have mercy on her soul and on the souls of all sinners. The only way he could cope with the feeling was temporarily to shut down his own humanity. He spoke the words of the service with feeling, only because he was speaking the words for the benefit of others, because he wanted to comfort others around him, not because the words were sacred, or because he expected them to reach God.

Never had the words of the Bible, the rituals of the service, the liturgy seemed so empty and meaningless.

Never before had he seemed so empty himself. Occasionally a vision of Anne as she had been, the little lovable, faithful and loving woman with whom he had shared many warm and joyful nights, would seem to materialise before him.

At the graveside he was determined to remain impassive. He longed to cry for her, but he knew that if he allowed himself any feeling, it would overwhelm him and he would fall down upon the coffin and howl his suffering aloud, begging to be taken with her to peace and tranquillity.

As he paid lip-service to the obsequies, he realised too that he had been paying nothing but lip-service to his faith for many years. He had stood complacently before his parish, allowing them to see him as a spiritual leader and yet all the while he had been fornicating, betraying his wife and his family, denying reality. How many times had he mouthed these and similar words without feeling? Without looking inwards to his heart? Without looking at God?

When the service was over Edward avoided Anne's mother and went straight back to the house. He resolved to write her instead, explaining that she was pregnant when she died.

Rachel was alone in the Lodge when Thomas appeared.

'Hi, Rachel. Have you been to the funeral too?'

'Yes. Gabriel's not here, he's up at the house as usual.'

'Is he? I was just there seeing Charlie. I must have missed him. Damn. I wanted to invite you and him to dinner at my flat tonight.'

Rachel hesitated. 'Tonight.'

Thomas nodded. 'Go on. Let me cook for you. You put me up last week, let me return the compliment.'

'I don't know if Gabriel's got anything planned.'

'Well, if he has, get him to cancel it.'

Thomas obviously wasn't going to take no for an answer.

'I . . . thought you two had argued.'

'Oh, that's nothing. We're always rowing. In fact, if you get him to come you're doing us a favour. That's how we make up. By pretending nothing's happened and just getting on with it.'

Rachel sighed. 'OK, but you know me and Charlie don't exactly see eye-to-eye. In fact, I've got a feeling she hates me.'

Thomas nodded. 'I know what you mean. She doesn't exactly jump all over you. She can be very abrasive.' He shrugged. 'Since I've been seeing her I've seen a different side to her. She's very different when she's not surrounded by the family. By the parents, I mean.'

'Is she?' Rachel didn't sound convinced.

'You know what they're like. They can't stand Charlie having a mind of her own. In fact, she's much more like Gabriel when you get her on her own stomping ground. You'd actually get to like her if you saw her like that, I'm sure.'

'Maybe I should make more of an effort. She is my sister-in-law.'

Thomas grinned widely. 'So I'll see you there?'

Rachel nodded. 'Gabriel permitting.'

'Don't take no for an answer!'

Rachel grinned too, even though she felt a little uncomfortable with Thomas's presumption. 'OK. See you there.'

Gabriel was peeved that Rachel had accepted Thomas's invitation without consulting him, but accepted it anyway.

Rachel thought that Thomas must have been right about their way of resolving their differences. Gabriel was moaning about Thomas and Charlie again as he was getting ready. Rachel assumed it was his way of moaning about Thomas as a prelude to making up, and laughed to herself about the funny way in which men behaved towards each other.

Gabriel seemed convinced that Thomas and Charlie wouldn't last. It was almost as if he wanted to see it finished.

'Well, he seemed very fond of her the way he was talking about her this morning. He said she reminded him of you.'

Gabriel scowled into the bathroom mirror. 'I'm sure he is *fond* of her. But it won't go any further than that. He'll hurt her. I've seen it happen before. I feel very uncomfortable sitting round a table with them, pretending that I think they're an item, when I know it just won't happen. Not properly.'

Rachel laughed. 'Mr Serious. She's having fun now, so what can you do? If you said anything to her you wouldn't change anything. *You* should know that.'

Gabriel sighed heavily. 'I know.'

'I think he might actually fall in love with her. She's very pretty. And she's probably quite daring in bed. And if she *is* like you when she's not at home, then . . . wow!'

No matter what Rachel said, Gabriel wasn't going to take this lightly. 'There's no way he'll fall in love with her,' he said. 'I know him. He's only ever been in love once. When we were younger. Someone he couldn't have. Someone he never got over.'

'Oh, now, this is getting interesting. Thomas: a man of dark obsessions! Was it anyone we know?

'Oh, just a friend of ours. Someone we used to know.'

'What was she like?'

Again Gabriel gave his sigh. Rachel was enjoying this. It was as if Gabriel was some kind of concerned parent, or something; it was a new side to him, or at least one that Rachel hadn't seen much of, and she liked what she saw.

'It wasn't a she,' Gabriel said at last.

Rachel looked at him as he continued to check out his shaving in the mirror. It took a moment for the words to sink in.

'Thomas is *gay*?'

Gabriel shook his head. '*Was* gay. At one time.' Then he shrugged. 'Oh, I don't know. He says he's not.'

'Gosh. How interesting,' Rachel said, and began to put on her makeup.

Edward had just finished his letter to Anne's mother when Jessica came into the bedroom.

'What are you doing, Edward?'

'I'm writing a letter to Anne's mother.'

'I see. And what does it say?'

Edward put down his pen and looked at his wife. 'I was all right this morning, Jessica. I thought: I can get through this. But then Dr Kenyon came to see me a few minutes before the service.'

'Gerald? What did he want?'

'He was her doctor – *Anne's* doctor. He told me that Anne went to see him a couple of weeks before she died, for a pregnancy test. He told me that he had no idea who the father was, other than he suspected he was a married man.'

'Did she tell him that?'

'No. Everything is safe, Jessica. Anne was very discreet, Gerald said. The post mortem showed she had broken her neck. There were no questions about the pregnancy – at least it wasn't thought necessary to mention that at all. Everything was perfectly in order.'

Jessica shrugged. 'And why shouldn't it have been?'

It was a moment before Edward said, 'Quite.'

'So, Edward, what's the problem?'

'Gerald was in a dilemma.'

'Oh?'

'He didn't know whether he ought, or ought not to tell Anne's mother that she was pregnant. He wanted my opinion.'

'And what did you say?'

'What do you think I said?'

'I'm *asking*, Edward.'

Edward explained that the doctor had decided not to say anything and that he'd agreed with him.

'I think that was very wise, Edward,' Jessica said, pointedly.

'Gerald pointed out, however, that she had a right to know.'

'Right? What sort of right?'

Edward glared at Jessica. 'She was her *child*. Her flesh. Of course she has the right to know.'

'No!' Jessica almost shouted it, before calming herself. 'Gerald's right. It can only cause more pain. To her. And to you, Edward.'

Edward was becoming emotional now. 'I've decided that I'm going to tell her myself.'

'No, Edward, there's no point.'

'The point is my sanity. I can't go on like this. Jessica, it's been a week now. All week I have felt like a stone, like an unfeeling, uncaring monster. Then today I had to stand there in front of the parish and read from the Bible, to speak to God in front of the world. I felt despicable. I *have* to write this letter.'

Jessica felt herself clench like a fist. 'You're using this as an excuse. You're doing it for yourself, not because of any right Anne's mother may have!'

'I only want her to know the truth.'

'What? You want her to know that her daughter died

shouting at her married lover? About the bastard that she had inside her? You want her mother to know all the sordid details? So that *you* can feel better? Anne's mother would spend the rest of her life in torment if you tell her the truth, Edward. Anne wouldn't want that, now would she?'

Edward put his head in his hands. 'I can't go on like this.'

'And when she receives the letter, she'll ring the police.'

'Perhaps.'

'Make no mistake, Edward. She'll go running to the police. You'll be humiliated! We ... You ... you'll lose your job. Edward, it's possible you'd go to prison – I don't know.'

'Anne's mother must do as she thinks fit.'

'No! Edward, you cannot send that letter.' Jessica snatched it from him.

'Jessica, I told you. I can't go on like this.'

'You must, Edward. You've got to go on. It'll get easier. It will. It's bound to. There's no way anyone can discover what happened now unless you tell them. And if you do, the pain you'll unleash will be enormous. For all of us. You have to be strong. It will get easier, but, Edward, for the first time in your life you must be strong.'

They looked at each other for a long while.

Edward again had the feeling that Jessica was standing in judgement over him, and Jessica had the feeling that she would like to bind Edward hand and foot and throw him into a dungeon under the house where no one would ever see him or hear him again.

'Are you going to be strong?' Jessica asked at last.

Edward nodded guiltily, feeling like a scolded child. 'Yes,' he said, and Jessica crossed the room to embrace him.

·13·

Dear Caroline

Fasten your seat-belt and prepare for some amazing
revelations. This deserves a special letter all of its own.
I think you probably got the rest of it only a day or so
ago, but there's more to this life of excitement I live.

If I sound light-hearted, don't be deceived. I'm in
bits – I'm writing this at work. They've stuck me in
reception this morning so I've got a bit of time. I'll try
and get it all in the right order both for dramatic effect
and so that you'll know what happened and how it
happened. Forgive me if I sound confused. That's
because I am!!

We went to dinner with Thomas and Charlie last
night.

Thomas came round and invited me – that is *us*. At
the time I thought Thomas was being a bit too
insistent, he said he hadn't seen Gabriel up at the
house so he'd come to ask me to bring Gabriel round.
He was dead pushy, but very charming. He told me
how Charlie was just like Gabriel and if I got to know
her I'd get to like her too, so why not make an effort?

I thought nothing of it. Gabriel and Thomas had a row last week and hadn't seen each other since. Thomas said if we went over they would forget their differences. I thought nothing of that either and persuaded Gabriel to go, which didn't take much doing.

Anyway, just before we went Gabriel dropped a bombshell. He's always going on about how Thomas has never got over this lover he'd had when he was young. When I asked who it was, Gabriel told me it was someone they'd known – but *it wasn't a girl!!!*

So is Thomas queer? Gabriel said he didn't know. But what about Charlie, I thought. Huh, must have been a phase Thomas was going through. Know-wot-I-mean?

So, anyhow, there we all were in Thomas's trendy flat – which was a bit grubby actually, although if you cleaned it up it would be fab – and I was looking at Thomas trying to see if there was anything gay about him. You know – all gay men are as camp as frilly knickers. Only joking!!! And Charlie was being Charlie – just the same as she always is – sticking the knife into me as often as she could as if she's the most witty and sophisticated person in the world, when mostly she's too stupid to know when I'm joking and when I'm being serious. Bloody bitch (excuse me!!).

Oh, God. Let me get to the point.

Gabriel and Thomas did their usual thing – that is, talking away, totally ignoring me and Charlie – when the subject of their holiday in Greece came up. I can't remember exactly how it came about but there was something about the way Thomas was talking. He was going on about how he and Gabriel were totally inseparable – about how they'd had the time of their lives – they were always in each other's pockets – how

fantastic it all was. And something about the way
Gabriel suddenly looked over at me, looking dead
guilty and tried to change the subject – it suddenly
clicked. *Gabriel was the love that Thomas has never got
over!!* They had been lovers!!!

I couldn't believe it. I wanted to go over and slap
Thomas for being a devious manipulative little bastard.
All that talk about how Charlie looks like Gabriel!
About how they always argue – *like a couple*, no doubt!
I felt so stupid.

Anyhow, Gabriel noticed something – probably
because I sulked all night after that. Not that Thomas
or Charlie noticed of course – I'm invisible to them.
Jesus, what was I supposed to do?!!?!! It was as if I had
to sit there and watch as Thomas fawned all over my
husband while he lapped it up!! Not that he *was*
lapping it up. Not after he saw the look on my face.

Anyhow, so when we get back to the Lodge I
sulked for about half an hour until Gabriel was
begging me to tell him what he already knew – that
I'd sussed out his little secret.

I said, 'You must think I'm really stupid!!'

Gabriel looks all wide-eyed and innocent. 'What are
you talking about?'

So then I hit him with it – after keeping him
guessing for a while longer. 'It's you, you bastard. It's
you who Thomas never got over!' I think I felt
revolted by him for the first time ever. Not
completely, but I felt as if he'd been lying to me. I
didn't trust him suddenly. 'That's why you don't want
Charlie going out with him, isn't it?'

'It's only because he'll hurt her,' Gabriel said, trying
to wriggle out of it.

I told him that I thought it was disgusting that he'd
been friends with Thomas all this time when he knew

206

Thomas was in love with him. Then he admits it! He said, 'Look *I* wasn't in love with *him*, OK?' As if that makes it OK?!!

'Most men would run a mile if they knew another man was in love with them,' I said.

'He's my friend,' Gabriel said.

Jesus!! I can't believe I'm writing this. I think I said, 'So what? Did he screw you, or did you screw him?'

Then Gabriel went out – just like that. Got up and left the house. Maybe he went up to see mummy, though I doubt it because it was after midnight.

So I went to bed and Gabriel came in at about two or three and climbed into bed. I pretended to be asleep. What the hell's going on? He didn't talk to me when he got up this morning and when I came to work he was still up at the house. So I'm dreading going home.

I'll send this off. I'll probably have phoned you by the time you get it, but I feel like I needed to write straight away.

I love you. (Oh God, what does it mean when Gabriel says that to Thomas?!!! *Does* he say that to Thomas??!!)

Rachel.

Gabriel was waiting for Rachel when she got home from work.

He looked pale and worried. 'We've got to talk,' he said.

Rachel ignored him and went to put her shopping in the kitchen. This slight was too much for Gabriel and he grabbed her arm.

'Rachel, please!'

'Get off me!' she scowled.

Gabriel began to look scared. 'You've got it all wrong.'

She stopped and looked straight at him. 'You slept with him.'

'Years ago.'

'Your best man.'

'He's my friend, Rachel.'

'And what am I?'

'You know what you are. You're my wife, for God's sake.'

Rachel pulled away and continued into the kitchen. 'I don't even know why you married me. You should've married Thomas.'

'Don't be ridiculous!'

'You want him, you don't want me.'

'It was years ago.'

'You were together for the whole holidays, two years running!'

'It meant nothing.'

'Liar!'

Gabriel was practically begging now. 'I swear it was nothing.'

'You made vows to me. With him standing by your side. How could you do that?'

Gabriel shook his head. 'I married you because . . .'

'You couldn't marry him?'

'Oh, Rachel. Don't be stupid. It's over. What more can I say?'

Rachel made to push past him. 'I'm getting out of here.'

Gabriel grabbed her again. 'I won't let you.'

'You make me sick. I lay awake all night wondering what was wrong with me.' She was close to tears now.

'There's nothing wrong with you.'

'There must be. Look at what I married. Look what I

fell in love with.' Now she did cry. 'You're right. I am stupid. You don't want a woman. You used me . . .'

'I never said you were stupid. Of course I want a woman.' Gabriel was aching to hold her. 'I never used you.'

Rachel wiped her face and looked hard at him. 'Are you gay?' she demanded.

'No.'

Rachel called him a liar again.

'I love you,' Gabriel insisted.

Rachel wasn't listening. 'Did you tell him about us? Did you say it wasn't as good as with him? Did you laugh about me?'

'Of course not.'

'Did you think it was a great joke?'

All Gabriel could do was to continue to deny everything and hope that Rachel was venting an anger that would soon be exhausted.

As soon as Rachel left the house, without having given Gabriel any indication that he was forgiven, or that he was about to be understood, Thomas telephoned as if by magic.

'Hi, Gabriel. How goes it?'

Gabriel did his best to sound unfriendly, but didn't do a very good job. 'Oh. Hi. Er, what do you want?'

'Not a lot. I wondered how you were, that's all.'

'I'm fine,' Gabriel muttered. 'But I've got to go.'

'Is everything all right, Gabriel? You sound strange.'

'I'm fine. I'm . . . er . . . thanks for last night. We had a nice time.'

'Nice?'

'Er, yeah. I mean it was lovely. Thanks.'

'My pleasure. I love cooking.'

'Yes.'

There was an awkward silence, which Thomas filled. 'Rachel seemed a bit ... *strained* last night. Was she all right when you got home?'

'She was fine.'

'She didn't have much to say.'

'She said she enjoyed the meal.'

Thomas wasn't convinced. 'Isn't she normally more sociable?'

'You know she is.'

'Did she feel left out of the conversation?'

'No. Look, I've got to go.'

'I know what you and I can be like when we get together. Charlie told me off afterwards.'

'Um.'

Thomas wasn't going to be got rid of easily. 'There's so much we have in common, she must have felt excluded.'

Gabriel couldn't hold back any longer. 'Stop it, Thomas. I know what you're trying to do and I don't want any of it.'

Thomas's voice was suddenly cold. 'What do you mean?'

'I'm not interested. Get it? It's finished with. On my part, it was a mistake. Forget it, *please*.'

There was silence on the line. Gabriel resisted the temptation to break it.

'I can't forget it, Gabriel,' Thomas said at last.

'Well, I can,' Gabriel said, and put the phone down.

There was only one person Rachel felt she could talk to in the absence of Caroline, her friend from home, and that was Edward.

When she arrived at the church she found only Simon, who told her that Edward was around somewhere. She found him, or rather saw him, in the graveyard, standing over Anne's grave, apparently in prayer. She noticed that he looked very upset and wasn't sure whether or not to approach.

The way he looked decided her. Rachel felt she had an affinity with Edward; he looked so sad, she thought she might comfort him. When he saw her, Edward looked a little worried, scared even.

'Are you all right, Edward?'

Edward mumbled something Rachel didn't catch. She thought he'd said he was praying for the child.

'You're praying for Anne?' she asked.

Edward shook his head forlornly. 'I'm praying for her baby. She . . . she was pregnant. She . . . No one knew at the funeral. No one prayed for the baby.'

'Edward, how awful. Why not?'

'No one was supposed to know. I mean, her mother . . . she was a single woman.'

'I see.'

'I was told in confidence.'

Rachel looked down. 'How sad.'

'She was in the very early stages. But I . . . thought . . . I'd offer prayers.'

Rachel nodded sympathetically. 'That's very good of you, Edward,' she said, not really knowing what she should say. 'I'm sure Anne would be grateful.'

Edward sneered a little cynically at that, Rachel thought.

'She had nothing,' he said. 'An ordinary job. Small house. No one to care for her.'

'I'm sure she had friends, Edward. There were a lot of people at the funeral.'

'She was lonely.'

'You don't know that, do you? Didn't she have a relationship with someone?'

'No one who really cared for her.'

'Gosh. Then that really is sad, Edward.'

Edward nodded. 'I feel . . . very sad about it,' he said.

'It sounds to me like you cared for her, Edward. She must have felt that?'

Edward somehow nodded and shook his head at the same time, but said nothing. After a few moments, he said, 'The baby? Please, don't mention that to anyone, will you? I feel I can confide in you, Rachel. Anne's . . . secrets died with her.'

'Of course.'

'Jessica knows, but no one else.'

'Yes.'

As they stood, Edward became aware that Rachel was waiting to talk to him. He realised for the first time that she had come to look for him.

'You look tired,' he said, to prompt her.

The sudden turn in his attention confused her slightly.

'What's wrong?' he asked, glad to forget his own troubles for a moment.

'Oh, I don't know.'

'Is there anything your – what was it? – fabulous father-in-law can do for you?'

Rachel smiled at his reference to her previous compliment and then lapsed into gloom. 'I don't . . . think I know myself any more,' she said.

Edward *ummed* very deeply at that.

'I feel like I don't know Gabriel either,' she went on. 'There's a barrier between us.'

Edward longed to comfort her. She seemed so vulnerable, especially in the light of what he himself knew of his son. 'You haven't been married long,' he said. 'These things take time.'

Rachel nodded. She loved the sound of Edward's voice, that deep, sincere, fatherly tone that warmed her when she heard it. 'I don't understand him. He seems to be . . .

keeping things from me.' She stopped. She wanted to explain, but felt it wasn't fair.

Edward nodded. 'Gabriel is kind, talented, intelligent – and very self-indulgent.'

'Maybe I'm too harsh. Maybe I expect too much, too soon.'

'It takes years to get to know someone. Many years to get to know one's self. If you can, enjoy the journey. In the end, it's all a journey.' Edward cringed slightly at his own words. Who was he to sound so wise, he thought.

Rachel looked at him with what Edward took to be a womanly yearning. 'Do people change, Edward? Do you think they do? I mean, truly.'

He looked at her for a long time, feeling a deep sadness. 'I really hope so, Rachel. I really and truly hope they do.'

She looked down at Anne's grave.

Edward said, 'If we can't, or don't, or won't change, what is it all for? We *must* change,' he said, and they both stood for a time, in silence.

Lenny had been having good times with Jimmy lately.

Since her conversation with Mark on the phone, or rather since the conversation she didn't have with Mark on the phone, she had been determined not to think about him. Instead, she and Jimmy had gone out together to the pub a few times and had gone driving late at night, and she had done her best to enjoy her life as it was. Let's face it, she thought, for the first time since Ben was born I've had some support with my child so, sod it, have a good time.

Her determination had been in vain. The more she remained silent on the subject of Mark, the more she thought about him and the more miserable she became. The pain seemed to be getting worse. Jimmy had been kind. He must have sensed that she didn't want to talk about Mark and had maintained his own news blackout.

Once or twice when they were together, Lenny had felt genuinely happy. Not for very long, but long enough to feel a surge of loving gratitude towards Jimmy. Once when they were walking down by the lake she had taken his hand in hers and they had exchanged a lovers' smile. One or twice Lenny had entertained the notion of kissing Jimmy. But it would be foolish, she told herself, and the best thing would be to leave their relationship as it was: old friends, glad of each other's company. The best kind of company.

Then one day Jimmy turned up with flowers. Lenny was sitting in the kitchen with Jessica, who had also been doing her best not to mention Mark.

'Jimmy, thank you. You're so sweet,' Lenny said, when she saw him and the huge bunch.

'I know I'm sweet, but the flowers are not from me.'

'Ah.'

Both women's faces suddenly hardened.

'Mark's here. He's staying at my flat. He . . . sent these.'

Jessica remained impassive.

Lenny flushed with anger. 'These are not what I've been waiting for.'

'He said he was sorry.'

Lenny stood up. 'He might have told *you* that. He hasn't said anything to *me*.'

'Lenny, he wants to see you. He's sorry for everything he's done. He wants you back.'

Lenny felt annoyed with Jimmy. She knew it wasn't his fault and he was only doing what his friend had asked, but for a few moments she resented Jimmy for being associated with her husband. At the same time she felt a prick of joy at the words, 'He wants you back.' She cursed

214

herself for it. 'Ha! He wants me back!' she sneered. 'Has Sarah taken up with another man, then?'

Jimmy shrugged, but spoke earnestly. 'He hasn't seen her. He's been at home doing some straight thinking.'

'Yeah. So have I.'

'He wants you to give him a chance. That's all he's asking.'

'I've already done that!'

'Give him one more, Lenny,' Jimmy said, suddenly arguing directly for Mark. 'Otherwise you've got no future together.'

'Maybe we haven't anyway.'

'You have to find that out, Lenny. Even if you only talk to him.'

'Talk? What's the use of talk. Last time I phoned him, he treated me like a stranger.'

Jimmy didn't know what to say. 'I haven't talked about you and Mark, Lenny. I thought it was the last thing you needed to hear. I mean, I'm his friend, and you needed me as your friend. But right now, as your friend, I'm saying talk to him. Think of your son.'

Jimmy stood there a little self-consciously, aware that Jessica was looking at him in a less than friendly way. He wasn't used to an audience; he spent a lot of time alone, a fact which, Lenny felt, added weight to what he was saying.

Lenny suddenly felt less certain. She shook her head. 'I don't know, Jimmy. You said speak to him on the phone and that back-fired.' She shrugged. 'I just don't know.'

At last Jessica broke her own silence. 'Why *should* my daughter go and speak to him?' she said. 'Mark is like a lot of men. He's gone off and had his fun while his wife was having his baby. It will happen again. Since his son was born, Mark has spent more time with his mistress than with his own child . . .'

'She's not his mistress.'

Jessica dismissed this with a wave of the hand. 'Twice he's messed my daughter around. Why should he expect anything from her at all?'

Lenny's own anger was rekindled by her mother's outburst. 'He went off with a tramp, while I was having his child,' she said.

Jimmy looked at her. 'Lenny, please. Talk to him.'

Lenny's bottom lip curled. 'Where is he?'

'He's at my flat, now, waiting for you.'

Lenny stood up and grabbed the flowers from Jimmy. 'Right!' she spat, and made for the door. She turned to Jimmy, who was a little surprised. 'Well, come on, then, follow me down if you want to see me talk to the bastard.'

Mark was sitting watching television in Jimmy's flat when Lenny marched in, a little ahead of Jimmy.

Without looking round, Mark said, 'So, how did she take it?'

Lenny threw the flowers at him and shouted, 'I don't want your bloody flowers!'

'Lenny, you came, how nice,' Mark said, in his usual insolent style.

Lenny waited a moment, allowing her anger to take shape, rather than overwhelm her. 'I don't want you, Mark. I want a lawyer. And you should get hold of one as well, because that's the only way you'll ever get to see your son again. Through an intermediary at a predetermined time and place. You can fit him in like you fitted in Sarah. You can arrange it. You're good at that. And sort out what you're going to pay me at the same time.' Lenny was talking now, not shouting. She felt proud of herself. 'So you'd better warn Sarah that you'll have less to spend on her now. And believe me, Mark, when it comes to your precious money, I'll take your needs into

216

account as much as you took mine into account when I was having our son. All right?'

Mark and Jimmy looked at one another, but before Mark could say anything, Lenny was off again.

'And if you *do* want to see me again, don't send a messenger. It shows me what a genuine, hundred per cent coward I married. And I don't like being reminded of that little mistake.' She turned to go. 'OK,' she said, nicely, 'bye.'

Then she was gone.

Jimmy was about to explain what had happened at the house, when Mark said, 'Terrific, wasn't she?'

Jimmy was aghast. 'Terrific? She was desperate. I've never seen her so unhappy.'

'She was passionate.' Mark punched the air eagerly. 'That was the woman I married.'

'She'll be crying her eyes out now,' Jimmy said.

'She was on fire.'

'Only because you're upsetting her, because you've hurt her.'

'She can take it,' Mark sneered. 'She gives as good as she gets, that's what you can't accept.' Jimmy shook his head. Mark went on, 'Did you see her face? I thought she was going to attack me with more than the flowers.'

'She bloody well should have done.'

'That's the sort of woman I want. Admit it, Jimmy, she was marvellous.'

'Jesus, Mark, if you love her, for God's sake, chase her now, beg her to forgive you. Show her you're a bloody human being.'

'Jimmy, Jimmy, I wouldn't do that because she wouldn't want me too. She didn't marry a wimp.'

Jimmy felt like hitting Mark himself. 'It takes guts to admit you're in the wrong.'

Mark tutted. 'I know I'm in the wrong. But she came

round here anyway. To see someone who played fast and loose with the first available office girl. Now, what does that tell me?'

'Probably not what it would tell anyone else.'

'Jimmy, my boy. It tells me she loves me. It tells me I've won. Already. It might not be immediate. But can't you see? I'm going to get her back. No matter what she says to herself, she's going to come back.'

All Jimmy could do was wish that it was him that Lenny loved, because, if she did love him, there was no way she'd have to put up with stuff like this ever again.

When Rachel returned to the Lodge, she found Gabriel utterly despondent.

He looked at her apprehensively. She sat next to him on the sofa, careful not to touch him, but at least giving him a friendly smile as she approached.

Gabriel said, 'I was scared you wouldn't come back.'

'I'm angry with you. But that's not going to get us anywhere. I'm sorry, I don't know what I'm supposed to do. I want to resolve this, but I don't know how.'

'We will resolve it,' Gabriel said, keenly.

Rachel looked at him. 'You want me to accept that you had a sexual relationship with Thomas. You want me to be OK about it, but I can't.'

Gabriel sighed. 'It was a long time ago. We were kids.'

'I hate the thought of you two together. I've tried to convince myself that I don't, but it doesn't work.'

Gabriel sounded as if he were begging again. 'We were never . . . it was nothing, nothing at all.'

'Then why does he still want you?'

'He doesn't.'

'Oh, Gabriel! He was all over you! I don't know how Charlie didn't see it!'

218

'There is nothing for her to see. We were talking over old times.'

'Don't talk crap, Gabriel! Thomas is infatuated with you. If you're going to keep denying it, I may as well leave. Right now.'

'I mean . . . I mean, he *might* want me. I'm not denying that. But *I* don't want *him*. He knows that. There's no way.'

'How does he know you don't want him?'

'I telephoned him this morning, and I told him.'

'Told him what? What did you say exactly?'

'To stay away from me. Not to come near me again.'

'Why only now, why have you left it till now to say that?'

'Well, because it upsets you.'

'I see. And did you tell him that was why?'

'Of course not. I told him I thought he might have got the wrong idea, and that I'd only just realised it, and I wasn't interested in him or in any other man. And I never would be.' Rachel was starting to look a little more as if she wanted to believe him. 'It's the truth, Rachel. I couldn't have made it any clearer.'

There was a knock on the door.

Rachel said, 'Who's that?'

Gabriel shrugged. 'Who is it?' he called.

The door opened. In walked Charlie and Thomas.

Thomas said, 'Hi. We should have telephoned. We're just going out for a drink. Fancy joining us?'

Rachel stood up and went upstairs without a word.

Charlie said, 'Hi, Rachel,' in a sarcastic voice as she went past. Then to Gabriel, 'She's obviously gone to get her coat, she looks like she's dead pleased to see us.'

Gabriel said nothing.

Thomas said, 'So? Fancy it?'

'What do you think?' Gabriel said, coldly.

Charlie said, 'Great, then I can have you all to myself. Come on, Thomas, let's leave the happy couple to their thrilling marriage.'

But Thomas resisted. 'Please, Gabriel, just come out for a quick one.'

'No, Tom, leave it. For God's sake.'

Thomas tutted and stormed out, leaving Charlie and Gabriel stranded.

'Thanks, bro,' Charlie said, smiling and following Thomas. 'Leave him to me.'

That evening Jessica overheard Edward talking to Mary in the kitchen.

Edward was telling Mary about his day and that he'd spoken to Rachel who'd noticed him looking off-colour. Mary said she'd noticed it herself. Edward said he'd been upset over Anne and hadn't felt quite the same since he'd heard about her death.

Later that evening, Jessica spoke to Edward about his relationship with Rachel. There was something in the way he'd spoken of her to Mary that had made Jessica feel uneasy.

'What did you tell Rachel today when she noticed you were upset?' she asked as soon as they were alone.

'Nothing.'

'Edward, you must have said something.'

'I said I was upset over Anne. It's natural to feel sad when someone you work with dies.'

'She was only your secretary, Edward. An employee.'

'She was a close colleague, Jessica.'

'You must be careful what you say.'

'Anne and I had worked together for a long time,' Edward said, beginning to get annoyed.

'You're over it now, Edward.'

'I'm not an automaton. I can't turn off my feelings.'

Jessica was becoming angry herself. 'You have no right to talk to anyone, Edward! If you must talk, talk to me.'

'I'm not stupid, I know how much I can say.'

'Why talk to Rachel?'

'I like the girl. She's my daughter-in-law.'

'I see. And are you planning on sleeping with her?'

'Of course not, don't be ridiculous.'

'It's not ridiculous to suppose you might sleep with her if you could, Edward. That *is* why you usually take an interest in women.'

'Well, not in this instance,' said Edward, very much ashamed now, as well as angry. 'She came to me with her troubles.'

'What troubles?' said Jessica, her worries suddenly compounded.

'Nothing in particular. She needed to talk.'

'Hum. So she confides in you, does she?'

'Yes, as a matter of fact.'

'And you thought you'd return the compliment.'

'I suppose. In a way. Yes.'

Jessica's eyes flashed. 'Well, don't! Of all the people *not* to talk to, Rachel is the first. She's not one of us, Edward. She's an outsider.'

'What are you talking about, Jessica?'

'Tell her one thing, and you risk telling her another.'

'I know when to stop.'

Jessica found that remark very amusing, except that it didn't make her want to laugh. 'You know nothing. You're a fool. Keep your secrets to yourself. And keep *everything* from Rachel,' she said, and left the room.

After Thomas left, it took Gabriel an hour even to get a word out of Rachel, let alone start any kind of conversation.

After some fairly turgid begging and coaxing on

221

Gabriel's part, Rachel finally admitted that she wanted to believe he loved her.

'I've told you that over and over,' he said.

'You told me you had spoken to Thomas.'

'I did . . .'

'You said you'd been clear, that there was no way he could have misunderstood.'

'I did, I swear.'

'Then he just walks in and casually asks us out for a drink?'

There was another long silence after that, until Rachel said, 'Which of us matters to you?' The question gave Gabriel some hope, because the answer was so obvious.

'You know the answer to that,' he said, gently.

'Thomas doesn't.'

'Who cares what Thomas thinks? What matters is you and me,' Gabriel pleaded. 'I love you,' he said.

'You loved him first.'

'No, I *never* loved him. *Never!*'

'He's even using Charlie to get near you.'

'That's between those two, I'm not responsible for that. I tried to stop it, I couldn't. They have to work that out.'

'You're avoiding your responsibility.'

'No. I know Thomas. He'll ditch Charlie, he'll be off again. He'll just move away. He never stays anywhere very long.'

'He's carried a torch for you long enough.'

'Only because he couldn't have me.'

'Oh, so what? Give him a taste, perhaps that'll solve the problem.'

It went on like that for a long time, until Gabriel began to despair of getting Rachel to believe him after all. He thought how awful it would be if she knew what had really happened that night he and Thomas had got drunk.

'I thought I knew you,' Rachel was saying. 'It turns out

that I don't. Maybe I'm artistic after all. I created a man I wanted to marry, but he only existed in my imagination and I mistook you for him. Yeah. And so what am I left with? Who am I supposed to spend the rest of my life with?'

This image of Rachel's – that Gabriel was a stranger, a phantom she had never known – scared him. He felt the truth of her words as they gutted him. Suddenly he was able to cry. As soon as he did so, Rachel took him in her arms and held him, feeling that at last she had found a little truth to hold on to.

·14·

CHARLIE WAS BEGINNING to feel distinctly
uneasy about Thomas.

It had been bad that morning. When they
woke up in Thomas's mega-cave-bed, Charlie
wrapped her legs round him and tried to kiss him. He'd
been very distant the night before, especially after Gabriel
and Rachel said they weren't coming out for a drink, but
she thought she might be able to cheer him up, if only
he'd let her.

'Thomas, I really want you to fuck me,' she said. 'Like
I'm *aching* for it.'

'No, Charlie.'

'I don't mind how you do it, you can tie me up,
blindfold me, anything you like.' He shook his head. 'I'm
offering you the chance to try out anything you like,
anything at all, on a nice young woman. And I mean
anything. I've got a very open mind, Tom.'

'You know I don't like fucking. I told you.'

'Yeah, but I thought you might have some special way
of doing it that you like . . . that you wouldn't ask for
unless . . . unless someone told you they didn't mind
anything.'

Thomas disentangled himself and got out of bed. Straight down the ladder and into his jeans. Charlie watched him from the bed.

'You're absolutely gorgeous,' she teased. 'I even love watching you put your knickers on!'

It didn't work. Thomas didn't laugh, or even look friendly. He didn't even look as if he *knew* Charlie. 'I've got stuff to do,' he said.

'Do it then,' Charlie said, meaning: I'll stay in bed while you do it then.

'I mean, I've got to go out.'

'Do you want me to tidy your flat while you're out?'

'Charlie, I want you to go home and leave me alone.'

Charlie couldn't hide her disappointment that he'd go so far as actually to tell her to go home. It showed in her tone of voice. 'OK, OK. I'll go when you leave. Are you going into town? You could give me a lift.'

Thomas looked pained. 'Just go, will you? Now. I'll call you a taxi.'

That was when Charlie's spirits had collapsed. She couldn't win. When he was cold she wanted to eat him, and yet if she moved towards him he became cruel and all the more distant. She wanted to scream with the pain and frustration. She fell back on to the bed out of his sight and lay looking at the ceiling, which she could reach up and touch. What could she do? Was there anything that would make him come up the ladder and take her there on the bed? What was wrong with him? Ever since she'd grown breasts she'd spent her life fighting guys off, usually she just had to give them a little flash of her eyes and she couldn't get rid of them for months.

She put on her clothes and went out of the door without waiting for the taxi, slamming the door behind her. She didn't say goodbye, she couldn't even look at him for fear of bursting into tears which would have been mega-death.

As soon as she had slammed the door behind her, Thomas opened it again.

'Charlie,' he called softly.

Her world span round as she did. 'Yes?' she said, or tried to say.

'See ya,' he said.

'See ya,' she said, and turned to go, hoping he'd say something else.

She heard the door close behind her and kept walking.

At about the same time, Gabriel and Rachel were talking about Charlie. Rachel was getting ready to go to work.

'You should tell her, Gabriel.'

'No. I'm staying out of it. She has to find out some things for herself.'

'If you don't tell her, I will.'

Gabriel said, 'You don't understand. You'll hurt her.'

Rachel laughed. 'I think I understand that better than anyone.'

'Well then.'

'The longer you leave it, the worse it will be when she finds out.'

'Why are you so worried about Charlie all of a sudden?'

'I just want to get this thing out into the open where it can't do any more harm. Gabriel, if you don't speak to her I will.'

'All right. You win.'

'And if you don't speak to *him* – and I mean make him understand – I will. *I'll* make him understand all right.'

'OK, OK. You've made your point.'

Rachel smiled. 'Well, good.'

Gabriel smiled back. It was the first time she'd smiled

at him for a couple of days; it seemed like a couple of lifetimes. 'I'll sort it all out.'

'Right.' Rachel was going.

'And, Rachel . . .'

'What?'

'I love you.'

She stopped and looked at him. He looked so vulnerable, scared even. It would have taken a heart of stone not to want to kiss him, but she had to go to work.

As soon as she'd gone, Gabriel rushed up to the house for his injection.

Some time later, when Gabriel had finally recovered from his shot, he floated down to the kitchen to make coffee.

Charlie was there.

'Aren't you supposed to be at school?' he said, jokingly.

'Piss off,' was all Charlie could say.

Gabriel could see she meant that. She was supposed to be at school, but she seemed to choose when she went according to how was feeling these days. Gabriel wondered why Jessica hadn't said anything to her. 'Charlie, what's the matter?'

'Nothing's the matter,' Charlie said. It sounded as if she was saying, 'I'm about to die.'

'Has Thomas finished with you?'

'No. It's nothing to do with Thomas.'

'Charlie . . .'

'All right! It's fucking Thomas. Or more like it's *not* fucking Thomas.'

Gabriel's ears pricked up. 'He's turned you down? Is that it?'

'Course he hasn't turned me down!'

Gabriel volunteered to make her a coffee.

'Make it a treble whisky,' Charlie said.

Having made the coffee, Gabriel decided to press on with his cross-examination.

'Isn't he interested in you?' he said.

'Who?'

'Thomas. Does he, I mean, do you have it off?'

'Hey! Do I ask you the positions you and Rachel like to do it in?'

'No. I . . .'

'Or doesn't she like to do it in any positions? I can't imagine it somehow.'

Gabriel was annoyed by that. 'Oh, and what positions does Thomas like, then, eh?'

Charlie looked at him. 'Has he said something to you?' she asked, anxiously.

'No.'

'Well, how do you know?'

'What's going on, Charlie? Talk to me about it.'

'It's none of your business.'

'Yes it bloody is, Charlie. I'm worried about you. Last week you were walking on air, now you're miserable as . . .'

'As what? You and Rachel?'

Gabriel smiled. 'Yeah, only we're entitled to be miserable because we're married.'

That did it. Charlie suddenly let it all out. About how she couldn't get Thomas to do it any more, how they had been great, well, at first, then he'd gone cold, or at least gone cold when they were in bed. She even admitted that she couldn't do anything about the way she behaved in front of him, how she knew she shouldn't phone and go round, but still did.

Gabriel nodded sympathetically and told Charlie he understood.

She made him promise not to tell anyone, especially not Jessica and mega-definitely not Rachel. Gabriel told her to leave Thomas, and Charlie repeated that she *couldn't* and Gabriel repeated that she *should*. Charlie said she would, knowing that she wouldn't, just to shut him up.

Then Charlie said she was going up to her room and went to phone Thomas. Gabriel sat as if in a trance for about half an hour before returning to the Lodge. He telephoned Rachel and told her about the conversation, only he exaggerated how upset Charlie had been and how difficult it was to make her see sense. He made it sound as if it had been impossible to tell her the truth about Thomas, but his real reason for not telling her was that he didn't want Charlie to think he was queer too. There was an easier option: Gabriel believed Thomas would dump Charlie when he finally understood that Gabriel had no interest in him.

Later that day he told Jessica some of Charlie's woes, and even some of his own.

The knot in Jessica's stomach was getting tighter.

Edward was worrying her, Gabriel was worrying her, Lenny was worrying her, Charlie was worrying her. And unless she was very much mistaken, that was the entire family.

There was something she could do for Charlie, however. Jessica didn't like the way her younger daughter had suddenly been included in Gabriel's little circle. She had wanted to intervene straight away, but had judged it unwise. She'd had more pressing matters to attend to at the time, and she knew that while Charlie was in the seventh heaven of earthly love with Thomas, there was nothing she could do. Indeed, to support and listen to Charlie, and to win her confidence, had been the best course. Jessica knew, as surely as she knew her body would one day turn to dust, that Thomas would cool off before too long. So she had bided her time, waiting for the signs. There had been a gradual but unmistakable dimming of her daughter's spirit, and the poor girl's ecstatic smile had become a sufferer's pained sneer. Jessica waited until the point of no return before making her intervention. She let Charlie miss school and mope about the house for two days before finally confronting her.

'Has he stopped making love to you, darling?' she asked, on the second morning of Charlie's agony.

To Charlie this was a strange question coming from her mother, for the two women had never before had any kind of conversation concerning sex. Sure, Charlie had made girlish remarks to let her mother know that she had lost her virginity, that she knew more about sex than her mother had ever known, and that she 'knew' what she was doing' contraception-wise. But these comments and remarks had been intended to signal that she didn't want to talk about sex, not to invite intimate, direct discussion that would reveal her actual doubts and fears.

Charlie opened her mouth to say something, but nothing came out. For the first time ever Charlie saw her mother as another woman with whom she could have a conversation about something which actually meant something to her.

'Has he gone cold on you?' Jessica said, by way of enabling Charlie to pretend that she wasn't completely dumbfounded.

Charlie nodded. Suddenly she wanted to tell Jessica the whole story, but quickly realised that that would be impossible. 'He ... I think I've been getting on his nerves.'

Jessica nodded.

'And you're right. He won't make love to me. He did at first ...'

'But now he's stopped?'

'Yeah.' Charlie was clearly embarrassed, but Jessica knew she wasn't being told to get lost.

'He was only interested for a short while?'

'Yeah, and he's dead moody. I mean, one minute he's all over me, the next – nothing.'

Jessica sighed deeply. 'Men are like that,' she said. 'Some are a lot worse than others. They'll just play with you. They like you for a time and then that's it. It stops. It goes away as quickly as it came.'

Charlie wondered how her mother could use the word 'men'. As far as Charlie knew, her mother had only ever had the one guy, whom she'd married – and he was a bloody bishop! *And* they'd been together for over thirty years. Charlie nodded knowingly, though.

'You should get out while you still have your dignity,' Jessica advised. 'Don't put yourself through it. If things are like this now, they'll only get worse and you'll get hurt even worse than you're already hurting.'

Charlie looked at her mother sadly. The poor woman had no idea. It was impossible for Charlie to leave Thomas. It felt as if he could subject her to any torture and she would simply have to take it. It would be easier for Charlie to cut off her own foot with a rusty fork than to leave.

'He'll change,' Charlie said, with the voice of ages. 'I know he'll change. I just have to let him do what he wants. I have to be careful not to get in his way. I know he likes me. It can be really great when it's going well.'

'He'll never change,' Jessica said, with a certainty that Charlie resented.

'I love him, mum. I've never felt like this before. Ever.'

Jessica took hold of Charlie's hand and held it as she would a sick parishioner's. She sighed. 'You poor dear,' she said.

'I know,' said Charlie. 'Sick, isn't it?'

★

On the strength of her conversation with Charlie, Jessica decided it was time to take unilateral action.

She was thinking over her plan in the garden when the source of another of her worries drove up in his car. Mark seemed very disappointed to see her. He looked at her as if she were an Alsatian guard dog loose in the compound.

Jessica blocked his way. 'What do you want?' she growled as Mark approached.

'I've come to see my son. Not that it's any of your business.'

Jessica looked as if she might bite at that remark. 'You've come to see my grandson. It *is* my business.'

Mark was going to be his usual brisk self. 'Lenny can refuse to speak to me if she wants, that's up to her. But I've got rights, and one of them is to spend time with Ben.'

'He's better off without you,' Jessica declared. 'They both are.'

'This is between me and Lenny, Jessica.'

'You're wasting your time. You might as well hurry home to Sarah.'

'She's not *at* my home. She never has been. Now, if you'll excuse me . . .' Mark went to push past his mother-in-law.

Jessica didn't move. She felt a cold rage rising up from the stone path, giving her strength. 'I thought we'd all made it very clear. You're not welcome on our property – on *my* property. I suggest you get back into your car, go home, and phone to make an appointment.'

'That's what I did.'

'What?'

'I phoned and made an appointment. I'm having a *supervised visit* – I think that's the term Lenny used.'

At that moment Lenny leaned out of an upstairs

window. 'It's OK, mum. Let him in. Mary is going to watch him.'

Jessica enjoyed the look on Mark's face as he took in what Lenny had said. Perhaps Lenny was learning after all.

'Please,' Jessica said, 'be my guest.'

Mark went in without a further word.

Mary sat with Mark and Ben for an hour.

Mark looked a little lost with his son, and when it was time to change his nappy Mary had to come to his assistance. She would have enjoyed watching Mark struggle through the whole process alone but she thought that it would upset Ben. When she took over the operation she took care to show Mark her contempt for his inadequacy. She was very pleased when Mark felt the need to point out that he was a little out of practice.

After an hour, Lenny appeared.

'Time's up,' she said, and took Ben from him. 'Mary'll show you out.'

Mark said, 'Where are you going?'

'Upstairs. Why?'

'Er. Well, I came to see you both.'

Lenny shrugged. 'You've seen us. Goodbye.'

'Lenny . . .' Mark wanted to say 'be reasonable', but it stuck in his throat. He looked at Mary, willing her to leave the room. He was afraid to ask. That's a first, he thought.

'What is it, Mark?' Lenny asked with great innocence.

'Goodbye,' Mark said. 'I'll phone, soon.'

'You do that.'

Mark was slumped in the armchair at Jimmy's place, staring at a can of beer.

'It was like a prison visit. Mary sat there, eyeing me like

233

a guard. Lenny didn't even show up! Other than to tell me my time was up.'

Jimmy tried not to smile. 'What did you expect?'

'Bloody Jessica was patrolling outside.'

'So what are you going to do about it?'

Mark shrugged and sank even deeper into the armchair. 'Hire a decent solicitor, I suppose, with experience in family law.'

'You're jumping the gun,' Jimmy said.

'You weren't there.'

'Not long ago you were jumping for joy at her forcefulness.'

'I was a fool.'

'So what's changed?'

'I now realise she doesn't want me.'

'I thought you said she told you to phone.'

'That was to arrange another prison visit.'

Jimmy shook his head. 'You're pathetic. If you want Lenny back, get her back. You expect it to be easy. For God's sake, you've hurt her. Badly. She had to ask her parents to take her in.'

'They've taken her *over*.'

'She wants out of there, Mark. She feels humiliated. Like a total failure. And you did that to her.'

'I know, I know. Don't rub it in.'

'Well, if you want her you'll have to bloody fight for her. And if you don't, I'll fight *you* for her.'

Mark looked at him and grinned. 'You?'

'Yeah. Me.'

Mark laughed. 'Well good luck. There's nothing I can do. I've got to go back to work in the morning.'

Jimmy was getting angry. 'Forget work!'

'I can't, they'll sack me.'

'You didn't seem to have any trouble sneaking off work to shag Sarah.'

Mark looked at him. 'True.'

'So find an excuse and take the risk. I warn you, if you go back Lenny'll think you've gone back to Sarah. I might even tell her that myself.'

Mark shook his head. 'You bastard,' he grinned. 'You're as keen to get us back together as I am.'

Jimmy raised his own can of beer. 'Cheers,' he laughed.

Mark said, 'God, I'm a fool.'

Jimmy said, 'Actually, I think you're about to stop being one.'

Thomas wasn't pleased to see Jessica when he let himself into his flat and found her waiting there for him.

'How did you get in?' he asked, coolly.

'I used the key you gave Charlotte.'

'Well, you'd better leave it on the side on your way out,' Thomas said, and went into the kitchen.

'Just exactly what are you doing with my daughter?' Jessica asked.

Thomas was already very angry. It was almost unbelievable that Jessica had the nerve to let herself into his flat, let alone expect him to talk to her about Charlie. He turned to look at her. 'It has absolutely nothing whatsoever to do with you. You have no right to ask. Just as you have no right to be here. Now, please leave before I ring the police.'

Jessica returned Thomas's stare. 'You won't get to *him* through her,' she hissed.

Despite himself, Thomas felt himself blush. 'Get to who?' he said with disdain.

'She's his sister. He turned you down years ago.'

'I don't know what you're talking about,' Thomas said, turning away.

Jessica moved to put herself back in Thomas's field of

vision. 'If it had been what he wanted, I can tell you I wouldn't have cared.'

'What the hell do *you* know about him?'

'I know he forgot you quickly enough.'

'Well, for your information, he didn't. There's more to mine and Gabriel's relationship than you could possibly understand.'

'That's where you're wrong, Thomas. I've spoken to Gabriel and he's told me all about it.'

'Just who the hell do you think you are?' Thomas shouted, suddenly feeling as if he wanted to strike her.

Jessica was going to have her say. 'I saw you that summer,' she said. 'You made a fool of yourself. I watched you do it. It wasn't romantic. It wasn't innocent. It was sad. I watched it all happen.'

'And was I alone?'

'You might as well have been.'

'Is that what you've come to tell me?'

'I've come to tell you that I can see you doing it again. Only I won't stand by this time. I thought it had all run its course, and it had. Gabriel walked away. But Charlie's different. She's a lot younger than you are, which means she's vulnerable . . .'

Thomas had had enough. 'Did Gabriel send you here?'

'No.'

'So you're interfering. Like Gabriel always said you did. You could never leave him alone, could you? Always manipulating him, trying to get him to do what you wanted, trying to keep him all to yourself. And now you've started on your daughter as well, have you?'

'You're poisoning my family,' Jessica said.

'No wonder Gabriel ended up trying to get as far away as possible.'

'I want you out of our lives for ever!'

'You're pathetic,' Thomas said. 'I never forced Gabriel

to do anything, nor Charlie. Actually it was quite the other way round.'

Jessica's eyes burned with hatred. 'You're not a man, Thomas. You're nothing like one and you never will be. Stay away from us!'

'Or else? Come on, what's the threat? Maybe you'll tell them all about me.'

'Maybe,' Jessica said.

'Well, I think you'll find Gabriel already knows. And Charlie would never believe you.'

'I'm warning you,' Jessica said. 'Stay away.'

As Jessica left the flat, Thomas shouted after her, 'I'll do whatever I like, Jessica. As I always have. It might be with your son or it might be with your daughter. But one thing is for certain: you are completely and utterly powerless to stop me.'

The door banged.

·15·

EDWARD HAD DONE nothing for days.

It seemed as if he'd done nothing for years. His work routine had completely fallen apart, his office was a mess and he was badly neglecting his ordinary duties. It was only now that he realised just how essential Anne had been, not only to his personal well-being and his happiness generally, but to the smooth turning of the wheels of daily parish life. Only that morning Simon had been saying the same thing.

The young priest had come to see Edward in tears, telling him how he had found a bag of Anne's personal effects in her desk, containing ordinary items such as makeup, tissues, an eye-pencil, and how the discovery had upset him dreadfully. Simon confessed to Edward that he had not been working properly and had come to realise how dependent he had been on Anne, and how much he had liked the woman. Then, when he had calmed down, with a guilty shuffle Simon pointed out that they had also been neglecting the task of replacing her, which would have to be done before the two of them were buried for ever in a pile of papers and dust.

When Simon left Edward to his meditations, an

uncomfortable truth hit home. Edward found himself contemplating the task of selecting a replacement for Anne with something of his old relish for life. He had no idea who his new secretary would be, but he already knew what kind of woman he wanted for the job. Before he knew it, in his mind, Edward had hired another young woman who was attractive and practical and who suited his needs . . .

As soon as he caught himself daydreaming like this, he felt ashamed and resolved to hire an older woman who was married and past child-bearing age, as he put it to himself. Nevertheless, he telephoned the usual agency and asked them to send him a selection of women they considered fit for the job, as he always did under the circumstances. He could select an appropriate person when the time came, he told himself, sincerely.

As he put down the phone there was a knock on the door and Simon, shamefacedly, announced Bishop Harris. Edward and Simon exchanged a glance as the most senior diocesan bishop came in. It was very unusual, indeed unheard of, for Bishop Harris to pay them a visit unannounced, and both hosts were embarrassed by the scene of disorder and neglect that greeted the man.

'Patrick! Er, please come in. Take a seat. We really must apologise for the state of the place. We've been a little disorganised since the . . . accident.'

The kindly-looking older man held up a hand. 'Edward, don't. I understand. You must have been very shocked. Please. Sit yourself down. I've instructed Simon to put the kettle on; that's all the hospitality I require.'

Edward made an effort to pull himself together. Thank goodness Jessica had made him shave that morning. If she hadn't insisted, he simply wouldn't have bothered.

Bishop Harris had made himself comfortable. 'Well, Edward, my wife and I are staying in the area with her mother for a couple of days, so I thought I'd pop in. I wanted to speak to you personally . . .' Edward nodded, a little nervously. 'It's nothing official, don't worry. I suppose I'm sounding you out, really.'

Edward really didn't know what to say. It was only now, as he faced a person to whom he was answerable in his work, that he realised how far from society he had drifted, or rather veered, in recent weeks. He felt unable at that moment to formulate a sentence without saying too much, or incriminating himself in some way, or at least making a fool of himself. He restricted himself to 'Humm', for now.

'Edward, I'll be retiring shortly. I've decided not to stay past the end of the year . . .'

'Humm.' A cough.

'I've had a good long run at the head of the diocese. It's been a good, rewarding time, but in the end one has to move over and make room for the younger man.'

'You've always been held in the highest regard, Patrick,' Edward managed to say.

'Yes, well, it hasn't been easy. Often I've had to struggle to keep my head above water.'

'Oh, I find that hard to believe, Patrick.'

'It can be a tricky job, Edward. You need a strong woman behind you. Like Ellen.' Edward nodded at the reference to the senior bishop's wife. 'Or like Jessica. Someone who can help take the strain.'

'Umm. Jessica has always been a great help to me,' Edward said. He could hardly believe his ears. It was obvious what was coming. Edward had thought his old friend good for at least another five or six years. Such a position was a glittering prize for a relatively young man which, in terms of the job, Edward was. There was something about the timing, however, which struck a chord of warning, doom even, in the younger bishop's heart; as if it were a test, a trial he knew he could not withstand at this time.

'You have a lovely family,' the old bishop was saying. 'Two of them married already, and a grandson. You have the respect of the whole diocese. A very impressive record for a man of your age, Edward.'

'It would be nice to think so,' Edward mumbled.

'It's true. And I wanted to let you know that your name is being mentioned as my successor. Edward, it's a foregone conclusion. As near as dammit.'

This last remark was a joke. Edward did his best to respond.

'You are a man whose reputation is beyond reproach,' the older man went on. 'There's never been even a whisper against you in all your years – and believe you me, Edward, that is an increasingly rare phenomenon in the church hierarchy these days.'

'Umm.'

'Don't doubt it, Edward, you don't hear of most of it. Though unfortunately you will.' The old bishop looked very serious for a moment. 'It's one of the great drawbacks of a senior position in the church, Edward, clearing up after a scandal. There is no more pathetic figure than that of a shamed clergyman. There is no more *broken* figure, Edward, believe me.'

Edward sighed and said he did believe him.

The older man sat up. 'So you see, good men like yourself are in shorter supply than you imagine.'

'I'm quite sure it seems worse than it is when you have to clear up after people, Patrick.'

The old bishop smiled. 'You always did see the good in humanity, Edward. I hope you'll be able to stay that way when you move up again.'

As he was going, Bishop Harris said, 'Now, Edward, we haven't had this conversation. There are many candidates for the position. There are procedures, as you know. But as you also know, there are some men who are bound to succeed.'

Alone again, Edward had to fight back tears of bitter remorse as he contemplated his ruined life.

There was another knock on the door.

It was Rachel.

'Are you free?' she asked, but when she saw the look on his face, she went to retreat. 'I'm sorry, Edward, you're busy.'

'No. Please,' Edward said, rising to his feet. 'Come in. Sit down.'

'Thanks,' Rachel said, smiling at him.

Edward was very pleased to see her. She was the only ray of sunshine in his life right now, the only thing that could take him away from peering over the edge of the abyss.

Indeed, Rachel sat there beaming at him as if she was waiting for him to say something. It was Rachel, however, who had something to say. 'Edward, I've left my job.'

'Oh, er, is that a good thing?'

'Yes, Edward, I'm very relieved. It was a nothing of a job and it was doing nothing for me, but boring me. And besides, I have something else in mind. Something altogether more meaningful. Working with someone I respect, doing a job that is very worthwhile.'

'Really? Splendid. And what is that?'

'I'm going to be your secretary, Edward. And I won't take no for an answer. I'll do the job without pay if I have to, until you realise that my services are indispensable, when I'll charge you the going rate for the job.'

They both smiled at this speech.

'I need you as much as you need me, Edward.'

★

Gabriel was doubly pleased.

Rachel had walked out of her job and was going to work for his dad. This made him feel good because it smacked of permanence. If she was about to walk out on him, she would hardly have marched into Edward's office and told him he was going to take her on like that. He had laughed heartily when she told him about her 'interview'. Gabriel was extra-glad because Rachel had been at home all afternoon and hadn't once mentioned Charlie or Thomas.

It was teatime before she said a word on the subject.

'So,' she said, 'what happened in the great soap opera? What about Thomas?'

'Uh, I haven't heard a thing.'

'I thought you were going to speak to him?'

'Was I?'

Rachel sighed. 'Yes.' She tutted. 'What have you been doing all day?'

'Er . . . painting.'

'Don't lie. You've been hanging around up at the house, haven't you?'

'I was up there for a bit.'

'What the hell do you find to do up there?'

Gabriel looked down. 'I think it's more a question of avoiding doing things, actually.'

'I thought you were going to start work.' Rachel sighed.

'I am . . . I'm sorry. I've . . . been upset.'

It was Rachel's turn to look down. 'I know. I'm sorry. It's been a lot for me to take in,' she said.

'I know,' Gabriel muttered. 'And I'm sorry too.'

They ate in silence for a while, glad they were able to talk to each other again, or at least to breathe more easily. Gabriel asked her to tell him the story of walking out of the insurance office again and then to repeat what she'd said to his father, laughing generously at both anecdotes.

243

Then there was a knock on the door and Rachel went to answer it with a sigh.

Thomas was standing there.

'Come in,' Rachel said, calmly. 'Sit down.'

Thomas did both.

Rachel called to Gabriel. 'It's Thomas. Make him a coffee.' Then she turned to the new arrival. 'Right then. Let's talk about it.'

Thomas looked surprised.

Both Rachel and Thomas noticed that Gabriel was taking a long time making the coffee.

'I'm sorry. I've disturbed you?' Thomas said, a little nervous suddenly. He wasn't used to seeing Rachel so confident-looking.

'You've disturbed me far more than this, Thomas.'

Thomas laughed and pretended not to realise that Rachel was deadly serious.

The two competitors for Gabriel's affections faced one another in silence. They could hear Gabriel tinkering about in the kitchen.

Rachel spoke first. 'So. What about Charlie?'

'What about her?' Thomas said, feigning innocence.

Rachel shrugged. 'Have you told her yet?'

'Told her what?'

'Come on, Thomas, you can drop the games.'

Gabriel had stopped making any noise at all now. Thomas knew that something had spilled out somewhere, but he wasn't sure what or how.

'I just wondered,' Rachel went on, 'whether you'd told Charlie that you used her to get to Gabriel.'

Thomas laughed a cynical laugh, largely out of surprise.

'I don't think it's funny, Thomas. In fact, I think it's pretty bloody nasty of you.'

'Hold on,' Thomas said. 'What are you talking about,

Rachel? Have you been reading cheap psychology books, or something? I happen to like Charlie. I've known her for a long time.'

'So that's why you've been messing her around and making her utterly miserable, is it?'

'Oh, I see. The whole of the Rattigan family have been discussing my affairs, have they?'

Rachel was furious now. 'I am not a part of the Rattigan family. And I wouldn't have to be to see what a mess you've made of Charlie.'

Gabriel had appeared now, coffeeless, listening sadly to the argument. Thomas saw him and changed his attitude.

'Rachel, I'm sorry. You are right – I have been messing Charlie around. I . . . I just didn't know how much hard work she would be. I don't like her enough. I don't know how to end it. It's very bad of me, and I intend to put it right. But you're wrong to say . . . what you said just now.'

'So you deny being in love with Gabriel?' Rachel said.

Thomas sighed, pretending to be exasperated when really he was angry.

Gabriel said, 'Rachel, don't . . .'

Rachel pointed at Thomas. 'He's not denying it.'

Gabriel and Rachel both stared at Thomas. Gabriel looked as if he wanted Thomas to deny it, but Thomas still wasn't saying anything.

'You're a fool, Thomas,' Rachel said, 'if you think anything can come of this. All right, you had some juvenile crush on Gabriel years ago, but, for God's sake, that was nearly *ten years* ago. Can't you just, oh, grow up or something! Gabriel and I are married!'

Again Thomas sighed. It was time to start getting real. 'I can't change the way I feel,' he said.

'Well, it's tough,' Rachel said. 'Gabriel doesn't love you.'

245

'What do *you* know?' Thomas said, disdainfully.

'Damn you, Thomas,' Rachel spat.

'Let him speak for himself,' Thomas insisted.

'I wish he bloody would!'

All eyes turned to Gabriel, who was almost concealed in the shadows by the kitchen door. He spoke slowly and softly. 'I'm sorry, Tom. I've loved you as a friend, nothing more.'

Thomas laughed his cynical laugh again. 'It isn't an easy thing to admit, Gabriel. But it's harder to live a lie,' he said, in what Rachel thought was a pathetic, pleading tone.

'I've told you how I feel,' Gabriel said simply.

'You love me, Gabriel,' Thomas said. 'You know you do.'

'Not like that,' Gabriel replied.

Thomas was obviously getting angrier. 'That's not true, Gabriel!'

Gabriel rose to Thomas's challenge. Suddenly his face curled up cruelly. He wanted to stop this charade. 'It's true,' he said, nearly shouting. 'It's . . . I'm not . . . I'm not fucking *twisted* like you, Thomas!'

Thomas smiled coldly, when he should perhaps have yelped with the pain. 'Yeah?' he said, coolly. 'Well, you wouldn't have known from the way you kissed me the other night.'

It was a moment before Rachel could scream, '*What's been going on?*'

Gabriel said, 'Nothing. Thomas, I'm warning you!'

'*What does he mean?*' Rachel was still shouting.

Thomas obliged where Gabriel couldn't. 'The other night, Gabriel. You can't have forgotten it so quickly. We were right there . . .' He pointed at the sofa.

'Shut up!' Gabriel shouted.

'It was special, you know it was!'

'It didn't mean anything. Now be quiet!'

Rachel realised it was true and felt herself go hot and dizzy.

Thomas and Gabriel were shouting at each other, face to face now.

'Don't kid yourself, Gabriel, you know you . . .'

'Fuck off, Thomas. Out of the house, now!'

Gabriel had punched Thomas in the face before anyone knew what was happening, including Gabriel. Thomas's nose exploded with blood and Gabriel punched him again, viciously, on the side of the head and kicked wildly at him.

Thomas burst into tears at the same time as Rachel.

'Get out of this house,' Gabriel was screaming. 'Get out! I never want to see you again!'

Edward made the mistake of telling Jessica about his interview with the diocesan bishop.

He had done so only to soften the blow of his announcement that Rachel was taking over as his secretary, which he knew would cause a scene. Despite the news of Edward's impending promotion, Jessica was outraged and railed at Edward for being irresponsible. Edward protested that his intentions were entirely honourable. 'She's my daughter-in-law, for goodness' sake.'

'Nothing would surprise me about you, now, Edward!' Jessica replied.

'Rachel insisted.'

'Yes, I see,' was Jessica's reply to that. 'And so now – and for the first time in your life – miraculously, you are able to make decisions on the basis of not wanting to hurt people's feelings.'

Edward replied that the office was his domain, and that he would run it the way he saw fit, which he realised was not a sensible line of argument for it gave Jessica another twenty minutes' worth of speechifying.

Eventually his wife went away and left him alone for as long as it took her to track down the visiting bishop's wife and invite the important couple over for a meal during the week. Edward was aghast when Jessica told him.

'Why on earth did you do that?'

'Why do you think? It won't do your prospects any harm to entertain them.'

Edward conceded the point with a sigh. 'Nevertheless, I think it's a little soon. It's not cut and dry . . .'

'All the more reason to act decisively.'

'Jessica, you're jumping the gun.'

'No time like the present. It's what you've always wanted.'

That was the point. Edward shook his head wearily. 'I'm . . . not sure. I don't know whether I want it now.'

Jessica froze. 'Oh, no. Edward, what are you talking about?'

'I don't think I deserve it.'

Jessica was genuinely shocked. 'After all these years of work? After everything I've done alongside you? This is precisely the time to be bold and grab the opportunity.'

Again Edward shook his head. 'I don't know,' he mumbled.

'Well I do, Edward! And I intend to make damn sure you get this position, even if you are temporarily insane. What if they offer you the position? Will you turn it down? What reason will you give?'

Edward shrugged. 'I don't know. I don't know what I *could* say,' he admitted.

'Well then, don't be ridiculous.'

'Leave me alone, please, Jessica,' Edward said.

Jessica shook her head. 'You mustn't let this position slip away from you,' she said, angrily.

Edward looked at her. 'From you, you mean.'

Jessica's eyes flashed. 'Do you think it was easy what I did? Going into that house? Covering up after your . . . after you.' Her voice was cold now. 'Edward, you know the lengths I've gone to for you. The very least you can do now is make an effort to give me something back.'

Edward sat and listened and, when Jessica had finished, he said, 'Please leave me alone now. Thank you.'

The door slammed as Jessica left the room.

It was raining outside in the churchyard.

Jessica stood under the old arch and glared up at the blackish-grey clouds as if they were sent by God specially to soak her clothes and chill her heart. On her cheek, raindrops mingled with her tears of frustration and anger. In the vastness of the overcast and moody sky, Jessica found only a mirror of her own dejection. God and nature were absent from the scene and everything was Jessica and Edward – the bitter turn their lives had taken, failure.

The grit and granite of old gravestones, glistening black and lichen green, the spatter of a million raindrops on the tangled, untended foliage that grew in this ancient quarter of the churchyard, even the gloomy splendour of the church rising squarely up before her, aptly reflected the landscape within. Jessica could imagine her name on one of the flagstones, long forgotten, and that of Gabhriel on the next.

How could her life have come to this? She had done her duty as best she could. She had done more than her duty. She had kept her family in more comfort than they would have otherwise experienced had she not had an independent fortune. She had been a faithful wife, even to the extent of allowing her husband to take mistresses.

Perhaps that had been the point. Had she spoiled Edward? She understood from her study of history that many of the great religious figures of previous centuries had taken mistresses – that, indeed, until recently this had been the norm for men of influence. It was only our own, small-minded times that took exception to such things. It had seemed natural to Jessica, too. She had, like all the other married women she knew intimately, lost interest in her husband after the first few years of marriage and the birth of her children. Perhaps she had even taken a mild, vicarious interest in her husband's affairs over the years. She had certainly, as she truthfully told Anne, laughed about them on occasion with Edward himself.

As she thought of this indulgence, Jessica felt a stab of bitter remorse. It was difficult not to feel the weight of religious superstition in a place like this. She had been rotten. She had gone against God and good. She had laughed at Edward's sins and now she was suffering the consequences. She had helped Edward to commit a sin to protect herself and his career. No! It had not been to protect herself and Edward; it had been to protect her family. This was not a sin. She had to protect Edward so as to protect her family. She thought again of Gabriel and his dependence on her. She thought of Charlie and her suffering, her waywardness. What would happen to them without her, if disaster struck?

Then she pictured Edward and his intended refusal of the bishopric. What of the bishopric? Did it matter? Did they – yes, *they* – even deserve the bishopric? After all, it would be as much Jessica's achievement as his own if he were appointed.

She decided that she could not let things slide. Edward could not be trusted. If he had his own way in the matter of refusing the promotion, it would be the beginning of the end, she thought. The click of her heels sounded on the path as she marched, now oblivious to the rain, to her car.

★

Night

I'm sorry about all those tears on the telephone, Caroline.

Thank God you were in when I phoned. If I'd had to write all that I think I might have set fire to the paper!

Gabriel's very subdued now. I've never seen him cry like that. Thomas was crying his eyes out after Gabriel hit him – I know I was crying when I spoke to you, but this was total breakdown. And I was glad, too, because he's hurt me so badly.

By the way, I think Gabriel broke Thomas's nose (serves the bastard right!!! – ooops, I don't mean that!). Actually, Thomas was very sweet in the end. I felt really sorry for him. After all, who can blame him for falling in love with my own sweet bastard of a hubby!! Thomas said Jessica had been to see him last night at his flat and he'd realised how horrible he was being to Charlie and he wanted to sort it out with Gabriel once and for all. The poor guy's obsessed. He said he had to know one way or the other and that he now knew he was being stupid and that there was no hope of him ever having Gabriel. He said it was his fault Gabriel had kissed him and he'd put Gabriel under pressure when he was drunk. They both said they'd not done anything else, and I believed them. Though I gave Gabriel a hard time later, just in case he was going to admit to anything more. But I really believe it was just a drunken kiss and that Thomas was being a bitch – yuk!

Anyhow. I'm officially sulking now. There's no way I feel like kissing Gabriel tonight, not after that – I mean two men kissing!! OK, so it's sexy to think of really, but if I let him know I'm going to forgive him too soon he'll think he can walk all over me. And anyway, I am *really* angry with him. The truth is I'm jealous of him kissing Thomas. For God's sake, we've only been married five minutes and he's doing that!!!

What can I do?

Well, what I can do is make him suffer for a few days. Every time I go to talk to him I want to shout at him anyway, or hit him, and tell him he's a lying bastard and how dare he, and what the hell else is he hiding from me, and if I find out that he's hiding anything else I'm off. And when I do say it all, he looks incredibly hurt and I feel guilty and that makes me angry again. So even if I tried to be nice I couldn't. So watch out, world!!! I'm quite proud that I can be a bitch myself when I need to be!!

I'm sleeping in the spare room for a couple of days while I cool down.

Sensible, eh?

Well, this is the new me. I'm not going to take any more shit. I mean it, if I find out anything else I'm on the first train back to London. I've had enough. So I hope you didn't get off with that guy you were chasing because I might need a couple of nights in your bed. (Oh, my God, don't tell Gabriel I said that, he'll think I'm up to his tricks!!)

Anyway, my hand's dropping off now with writer's cramp. Don't worry about me. I think I can survive this one – just about. I'm feeling calmer already. Or maybe I'm just all cried out.

Who knows?

See ya.

One morning, when she and Mary were together in the kitchen Jessica said, 'Mary, please sit down, let me make you a coffee.'

Mary had suspected for some time that something was wrong, but now that Jessica was going to talk to her about it, she experienced a pang of fear. Edward still looked unwell and she was convinced he had been diagnosed as seriously ill.

When the coffee was ready, Mary asked, 'Is it Edward?'

Jessica's nod was hardly perceptible.

'Is he ill?' Mary asked.

Jessica's laugh was cavalier. 'No more than he has always been.'

Mary felt a great surge of relief. 'Ah. So it's another woman,' she said. And then suddenly she knew. 'His secretary. Anne Fraser.'

Jessica nodded.

So did Mary. 'I see.'

The two women sat for a long time lost in thought. Long ago, Mary too had been in love with Edward. They had made love, but only once, when Jessica was pregnant for the first time. They both agreed it had been a mistake, but still Mary felt a fresh pang at every new lover of Edward's. She had long ago accepted that Jessica was the right woman for him, but somehow Mary felt she could share Edward with Jessica. In her way, Mary had remained faithful to Edward through the family, in the same way that Jessica had. A part of Mary felt proud of herself for standing by Edward and the family all these years. Neither of the two women had ever been able to possess Edward, and in many ways Mary felt that, of the two of them, it was she who had survived better. After all, it was Jessica whom Edward betrayed every time he stepped outside his marriage. Yet Mary still felt a twinge of her old hurt at the news that Edward was mourning Anne as a lover. She had suspected, of course; perhaps she had known.

'Was he in love with her?' Mary said.

'She was carrying his child.'

While Mary listened, impassive, Jessica told her the story of the night Anne had died. How Edward had been to see her, how she, Jessica, had been to the house to destroy all traces of his visit, how she had discovered that they had made love that night, and how Anne had threatened to ruin Edward and the family.

At the end of it Mary raised her eyebrows and said, 'Quite a story.'

Jessica nodded. 'I'm worried about Rachel,' she confessed.

Mary stiffened. 'Rachel?'

'Rachel has volunteered to act as his new secretary.'

Mary laughed coldly. 'Will she be expected to perform the usual duties?'

Jessica shook her head. 'I can't see it,' she said. 'She doesn't seem the usual type.'

'That's what I thought,' Mary said.

'I'm worried because he seems to want to confide in her.'

'Perhaps he's trying to soften her up.'

'It's possible,' Jessica conceded. 'But I have the feeling there's something else. Something Edward isn't telling me.' Mary nodded. 'The other day he said he didn't feel worthy of promotion – just when Patrick Harris announces he's going to retire. I mean, we've been waiting years.' Jessica shook her head sadly. 'He was even going to write to Anne's mother telling her she was pregnant.'

'Oh, sweet Jesus!'

'I think he feels responsible for Anne's death.'

'Sounds like he wants to tell someone so as to get it off his chest,' Mary agreed.

'I'm worried in case he chooses Rachel.'

Mary nodded. 'I'll talk to him.'

'No. If you talk to him, he'll know I've spoken to you, which might make him feel as if everyone knows already.'

'What shall I do?' Mary asked.

'What you've always done,' Jessica said. 'Stand by us.'

Mary nodded.

'Help me,' Jessica said. 'Help me keep an eye on Rachel.'

'Yes,' Mary said. 'We must be vigilant.'

Charlie woke up next to Thomas.

She was in her underwear, but she had no idea how she had got there. Thomas explained that he had found her asleep on his doorstep last night and he had carried her in and undressed her.

'Didn't you ravish me?' Charlie joked.

'No, Charlie,' Thomas said, adding the fatal words that Charlie was both dreading and waiting for: 'We've got to talk.'

He hadn't been in touch for days. Somehow Charlie had resisted the temptation to telephone, only to get drunk and, in her delirium, call on him. She was so drunk when she arrived that she lay down and fell asleep on his doorstep. 'You want to tell me it's over, don't you?' she said.

Now that the words had been said, Thomas kept quiet. He wouldn't even look at her.

'I'm making things easy for you, Thomas. You can talk to me.'

Thomas nodded slowly. 'It's not your fault, Charlie.'

Charlie felt a stab in the guts. 'It doesn't matter,' she said.

255

Thomas looked puzzled. 'What doesn't?'

'My age. Your age. Nine years. Doesn't matter.'

'It's not your age, Charlie.'

'Good. Because there isn't much I can do about that.' Charlie was determined that this was her opportunity to sort it all out. 'I know I've been a pain,' she said, 'but I can change.'

Thomas shook his head sadly. 'It's me. It's me that can't change.'

'I know what it is,' Charlie went on, not listening, 'I come on too strong. That's only because I like you so much, but I won't be one of those girls who suffocate a man, I promise.'

Thomas just looked at her, so she began to think that her words were having some effect.

'I haven't phoned and hassled you this week, have I?' Charlie said. 'I know you like to have your own life, but I do, too. I understand if you feel suffocated, but I won't let it happen like that again. I know it's because you're a sensitive guy and all that –'

'Stop it!' Thomas almost shouted. 'You don't understand at all. It's all got to end, otherwise you'll get hurt, Charlie, and that's the last thing I want.'

'I don't care if you hurt me a bit,' Charlie begged.

'For God's sake, Charlie! Have some self-respect.'

'Thomas, I *have* got self-respect. The most important thing in my life right now is that I love you. In order to respect myself I have to do what you want,' Charlie said.

Thomas cut her off with a cold laugh. 'I don't feel the same way.'

'I know that, Tom. People don't always fall in love at the same time. You can do what you want. I'm not trying to dictate things, I don't care what you do; you can even

256

have other women. All I want is to be a part of your life. I don't care if it's only a small part.'

Thomas shook his head. 'Oh, God, I don't want to have to tell you.'

Charlie brightened. If there was some explanation, she could come up with a proper argument. 'Tell me, Thomas. I can handle anything. Whatever it is, it won't change the way I feel about you.'

'Charlie, I'm gay.'

Charlie roared with laughter.

'Don't be stupid. Just because you couldn't do it a few times, doesn't mean you're gay, Thomas!'

'It's not a joke, Charlie. I thought I could, but I can't. I could never love a woman.'

Charlie's expression changed suddenly. If this was true, there really was no hope.

Thomas was still talking. 'I wasn't sure at first, but now I am. I didn't mean to hurt you like this. I do care for you. But just not in that way. It wasn't deliberate. Please believe that much.'

Charlie said, 'You're serious, aren't you?'

Thomas nodded sheepishly.

'Well, it's a good job I wasn't serious, then,' Charlie said, sitting up and hurriedly pulling on her clothes. 'You didn't think I was, did you? I mean, I play these games to stop me getting bored. Like, you were a project. Yeah, you were fun at first, but really you're not my type, no point in me pretending any more.'

'Charlie, you don't have to . . .'

'You know your problem, Thomas? I mean, one of them? You think too much of yourself. You've been lucky to have me around. You think it was *me* who was lucky, don't you? Well, you're fucking-well wrong, Thomas.'

By this time Charlie was dressed. She hurried down the ladder from Thomas's cave-bed in the corner and ran for the door. Before her tears came, she had slammed the door behind her and made off down the stairs.

·16·

JESSICA DECIDED TO spend some time in the office to help Rachel settle in, or so she said to Edward.

Almost as soon as Jessica arrived, Rachel was in Edward's office talking about Anne.

'I found these,' Rachel said, holding up a pair of gloves and an umbrella. 'Do they . . . I mean, did they belong to Anne?'

Edward looked very disturbed to see more of Anne's belongings. 'Yes. Yes, they were Anne's,' he said, and Jessica thought he might actually cry.

Rachel nodded. 'Shouldn't we send them to Anne's family? I know there's nothing of importance but –'

Edward cut her off. 'Ask Simon to deal with it, would you?'

Jessica intervened. 'I'm not sure that's a good idea, Rachel. I'm sure her mother would get a shock to receive something like that.'

Rachel realised that Jessica was right. 'Yes,' she said. 'How silly of me. That poor woman. She looked so confused at the funeral. You're right, Jessica, it'd be unbearable for her.' Rachel was shaking head now, sadly.

'It's just so sad, the whole thing. To think that her mother will never know about the baby, too.'

Jessica stiffened. 'Yes, yes, it was tragic, wasn't it.'

As soon as the door was closed behind Rachel, Jessica turned a look of scorn upon her husband. 'Are you mad!' she hissed. 'What *were* you thinking of! You told her about the baby. Have you told her anything else?'

'No, Jessica, of course not.'

'Don't *of course not* me! Edward, you are a bigger fool than I suspected. I knew there was something you weren't telling me. I've a good mind to keep you off work until you . . . sober up.'

Edward looked as if he were about to say something, but then closed his mouth and hung his head miserably.

'You fool!' Jessica went on. 'How could you be so stupid? Don't you know the risks you're running? You're risking *everything*! Now, you're not to speak to her again, do you hear me? You'd better be very, very careful.' She saw his blank expression. 'Edward, I'm talking to you.'

Edward was crying.

Jessica stopped, shocked and revolted. She realised that she was pushing him too far, endangering her own safety and that of the family. She immediately softened her tone and put her arms about him. 'Edward, I'm only trying to help you. I want only what's best for us, for us all. Just be careful, that's all I'm asking. And if you are careful and can keep calm, I'll carry you. I'll do everything.'

Edward let himself go and sobbed on Jessica's breast while she comforted him.

After a few moments and in a soft voice she said, 'Oh, Edward, when did you get to be so weak?'

Mary was the first person to encounter Charlie's wrath.

Mary came into the drawing room to find Charlie guzzling whisky from the drinks cabinet. The old housekeeper tried to discover the cause of Charlie's distress, only to receive an 'Oh, leave me alone, will you,' for her trouble.

'If you tell me what's happened, Charlie, I may be able to help,' Mary tried.

'You don't understand about the things that really matter, Mary, you're too bloody old!'

Mary could see that Charlie was quite drunk already; it was still only early afternoon. 'Why don't you go and have a lie down, Charlie?' she suggested.

It was a mistake. 'Keep out of everyone's way, you mean!' Charlie sneered. 'Be a good girl! Well not any bloody more, Mary, you won't see any more of that!'

'Since when have you ever been a good girl?' Mary said with a smile, trying to lighten things up.

Charlie was inconsolable. 'You unfeeling cow!' she screamed. 'Bloody well piss off, will you!'

Even Mary, who had witnessed a lifetime of Charlie's tantrums, was shocked at the sheer ferocity of this outburst. She decided to leave well alone.

'Who's done this to you, Charlie?' she asked, as she backed off.

'Why do you always try and interfere! You're not my mother – you're nothing to me!' Charlie screamed.

Mary left her to it.

Gabriel was next.

'What's wrong, dying for a fix?' Charlie sneered when Gabriel found her in the drawing room, still guzzling the whisky.

'What's happened, Charlie? Is it Thomas?'

'Don't come the sensitive dick with me. Yes, he's bloody finished with me. Yes, I'm upset. Yes, he's a bloody bastard. Yes, I should have bloody listened to you. OK? No further questions, please.'

'What did he say to you?'

Charlie screamed her reply to that one. 'I said, in case you're fucking deaf, *No further questions, please!*'

'I'm sorry, Charlie,' Gabriel said tenderly, putting his hand on her shoulder.

'I know you think I deserve it, after what I did to Nick, but I swear I've never hurt anyone like this,' Charlie sobbed.

Gabriel thought this was bullshit, but he nodded and said, 'I know,' sympathetically.

Charlie wondered whether she should tell Gabriel about Thomas, but she felt too stupid, as if it would show her up as a naïve little kid who hadn't got a clue. She wondered whether Gabriel knew, but concluded that he definitely didn't because he would have said something. Thomas had said he wasn't sure himself, hadn't he? Huh. Not until he met Charlie . . .

A part of her felt as if it were all her fault, as if Thomas had decided he was gay *because* she was inadequate. She felt utterly unattractive and loathsome; she hated herself and her body and wanted to block out all feeling.

'He's a bastard,' Charlie said.

Gabriel said she was right.

He sat with her until Jessica showed up with Edward and Rachel.

Jessica came into the drawing room first and signalled with her eyes that Gabriel should take the door that led upstairs.

At the same moment he heard Rachel's voice in the next room asking Mary if he was there. He darted out of the room. Gabriel knew that Mary would deny his presence. He didn't want to have to make awkward excuses to Rachel about why he was going upstairs to the bedroom with Jessica, and neither did Jessica.

Jessica saw at once that Charlie's crisis had hit, but there was nothing she could do for now. Gabriel's needs had to come first.

As they went up the stairs, Gabriel and Jessica heard Edward discover that Charlie was drunk.

Edward was already in a bad mood.

The last thing he wanted was to spend the evening with the bishop of the diocese and his wife, and of course that was exactly what Jessica had arranged. When Edward begged her to cancel the visit, Jessica had refused, telling him that she would carry the evening, that all he had to do was smile and nod and generally behave himself. This reply had angered Edward who felt more and more as if Jessica was treating him like a child, which indeed she was. The more Jessica treated him this way, the more hopeless and depressed he felt, and the more he was tempted to take some action to relieve his miserable condition. This was not the ideal occasion for Charlie to be drunk in the middle of the afternoon, talking with a foul mouth in front of her father.

Edward was instantly furious, all his own troubles focused on the teenage aberration before him. 'You're drunk again,' he boomed.

'You don't know,' Charlie slurred. 'Something awful's happened to me.'

'You've had too much freedom and look what it's done to you,' Edward shouted. 'You're a damn mess and I'll have no more of it!'

'Didn't you hear what I said?' Charlie shouted.

'I'm not listening to your silly schoolgirl rubbish. Whatever it is, nothing gives you the right to behave this badly.'

'Oh, stupid man,' Charlie spat.

Edward grabbed hold of Charlie with a violence she

had never known before, pulled her out of her chair and manhandled her across the room, shouting with anger as he did so. 'You are a disgrace. You are a selfish, spoiled young woman who is wilful and stupid. Now get up to your room like the ten-year-old you act like and don't come down again today.'

Unfortunately for Edward, though, Charlie was no longer the ten-year-old she was acting like and she tore herself away.

'Why don't you piss off!' she screamed, leaving Edward utterly dumbfounded.

The two stared angrily at each other. It seemed as if Charlie was willing Edward to strike her across the face, which he felt very much like doing. 'You're pathetic, all of you, and I hate you all!' she announced as she stumbled, heartbroken, for the door and made off across the lawns.

Edward turned to Rachel whose eyes were wide with wonder, at least in part at having witnessed a previously undreamed of side of Edward – his roaring temper.

'I'm sorry,' he said. 'I'm sorry you had to witness that.'

'I'll go after her,' Rachel said, and hurried after her young sister-in-law.

From the upstairs bedroom window Gabriel and Jessica watched them go and then got on with their business.

Rachel caught up with Charlie by the old greenhouse.

Charlie always used to come there was she was a little girl and needed to get away from the world. She loved the old red brick of the broken wall and the rickety, tumble-down old building; it made a pleasant change from the order and grandeur of the rest of the house and grounds.

Charlie was sitting on an ancient up-turned barrel when Rachel approached. For once, Charlie gave her a smile.

'I'm puffed out,' Rachel said, smiling back. 'Are you all right? I've never seen Edward like that before.'

'He's a prick,' Charlie said bitterly.

'I know it's Thomas,' Rachel said kindly.

'Oh, do you? Everybody seems to know. It's none of your business.' Charlie's pleasant front was abandoned as quickly as it had risen.

'Do you want me to go? I'll leave you alone if you like.' Rachel maintained her friendly tone.

'Yes,' Charlie said.

'All right. Just don't fall in a ditch and drown, OK?'

As Rachel turned, Charlie said, 'Why did you come after me?'

Rachel shrugged. 'I thought somebody should, that's all.'

'They all think I'm drunk – and I am – but I can't get drunk enough to block it out.'

'Block what out? What did Thomas do?'

'*Do*? Darling, Thomas doesn't do very much.'

Rachel knew he'd told her now and nodded.

Charlie smiled a crooked grin. 'Do you really want to know, Rachel? You might not like it.'

'You don't have to tell me.'

'I know I don't have to,' Charlie's girlish sarcasm surfaced. 'I don't have to do anything. But I like to do things I shouldn't do, don't I?' Charlie looked down. She wanted to tell someone, but her ego was getting in the way. 'Like falling in love with a man who couldn't love me.'

'Umm,' Rachel said, encouragingly. 'I'm sorry.'

'I knew he didn't love me as much as I loved him. But I thought if he liked me a bit . . . I thought he might . . . Oh, fuck . . . can you believe it! I could have any man I wanted, but I have to go and chose a man who wouldn't want me in a thousand years.'

'He probably loves you in his own way,' Rachel said.

'Oh, great.'

'He's a nice person.'

'Don't say that. I hate him.'

'You don't hate him, really,' Rachel said, 'Do you?'

'No. I just wish I'd chosen someone I stood a chance with.'

'I know,' Rachel said. 'It was a shock to me too.'

Charlie looked at Rachel. 'A shock?'

'Well, that's an understatement actually. I mean, when I realised that it was really Gabriel he wanted, I mean, well . . .' As she spoke, Rachel disliked herself for being a bitch, but somehow she felt compelled to go on, as if she was angry at Charlie suddenly. Perhaps she was. 'I could see then that he was using you to get close to Gabriel. It can't be very nice to find out you've been used like that.'

It was clear by the look on Charlie's face that her remarks had hit home, hard. Rachel instantly regretted her words; she had again mistaken Charlie's front for Charlie.

'You mean, he used me . . . like a bloody stepping stone!'

'Er, well, I don't think he meant it to happen exactly like that.'

'Then he never cared for me at all!' Charlie almost wailed.

Rachel felt the pain in the cry. She hated herself, for having been cruel and vindictive. 'He *does* care for you,' she said.

Charlie looked at Rachel anew when she heard that. 'How do you know?' she demanded.

'He told me and Gabriel.'

'When?'

'When he came round to the Lodge a couple of days

266

ago.' As soon as she'd said it, Rachel knew this was the wrong thing to say.

Charlie howled again. 'You knew! You *all* knew! Why didn't you tell me?'

'I couldn't,' Rachel said weakly.

Charlie went quiet. 'Huh. It all makes sense now.'

Rachel wanted to make amends. 'There was nothing I could do. He said he'd tell you . . .'

'Yeah, so you just sat back and waited.'

'It wasn't like that.'

'Don't bother. I hope you got a kick out of it.'

'No, Charlie.'

Charlie looked at Rachel with new eyes then. 'You can certainly dish it out, can't you, Rachel. Act the friendly sister-in-law, then twist the knife.'

Rachel felt disgusted with herself.

Charlie had a wicked glint in her eye now. 'But can you take it as well as you give it out? I'd like to see you try.'

Rachel caught something she didn't like in Charlie's tone. 'Take what? What are you on about?'

'Home truths, Rachel. There's enough for everyone round here.'

Rachel was stern. 'What home truths, Charlie?'

Charlie laughed harshly. 'Do you really want to know, dear sweet Rachel?'

'Yes. Tell me.'

'If you really want to know the truth about your dear sweet hubby, darling, take a look in Jessica's bedroom now. Don't knock, just walk in. See the kind of medicine he's getting.'

Rachel felt a cold fear seize her. Something told her that Charlie was being serious. She didn't know what she was expecting, but she knew that she would discover something that would explain why Gabriel was tied to the house. She ran until her lungs were bursting. She went straight through the kitchen, down the passage, up the stairs and stood poised outside Jessica's bedroom. All she had to do was open the door. She could hear Jessica talking and Gabriel muttering. She couldn't make out what was being said.

When she opened the door all she could do was stare in horror at the macabre spectacle of Jessica injecting Gabriel with a syringe.

'What on earth are you doing?' Rachel managed to ask, at last.

Gabriel and Jessica were every bit as shocked as Rachel.

Jessica spoke first, to Gabriel. 'Let me finish.'

'What is *that*?' Rachel stammered.

Again Jessica spoke. 'It's making him better. *I'm* making him better. For you, Rachel.'

'It's nothing,' Gabriel said, 'I don't need it . . .'

'*What is it, Gabriel?*'

'It's not important what it is,' Gabriel said. 'I've finished with it, there was no point in telling you. I . . .'

'*Tell me what it is!*' Rachel shouted.

'It's methadone,' Gabriel said, and hung his head.

'Keep still, Gabriel. Nearly there,' Jessica said, calmly finishing her work.

'Heroin,' Rachel said. 'You're a heroin addict! That's a substitute for heroin, isn't it?' Her voice sounded hollow, her eyes looked it.

Gabriel shook his head. 'I'm off the heroin now. Another month or so and I'll be off this stuff. I've beaten it. You didn't need to know.'

That woke Rachel up a bit. 'I didn't need to know!' she shouted. 'Only your mother and father and Charlie and . . . anyone! Anyone but me!'

Jessica had finished. Gabriel went to stand up, but then

thought better of it. 'I've beaten it,' he said again. 'I got myself off it. I met you and I said, no more. I decided right there and then . . .'

Rachel felt dizzy. Again she felt the unreality of the world about her. 'You were using heroin when we first met?'

Before Gabriel could say anything Jessica snapped the clasp of the little leather case in which she stored everything and said, 'Excuse me.' She left the young couple to their misery.

Downstairs, Edward was waiting.

'Jessica, we *must* cancel this evening.'

'Impossible, Edward.'

Edward was beside himself. 'Charlie is drunk as a lord, goodness knows what's happening upstairs. Jessica, I can't . . . I can't sit here and hold a polite conversation. Not this evening. Cancel it.'

Jessica walked away. 'Charlie will be asleep by the time they arrive, Edward, and there is nothing going on upstairs that a little love and understanding won't smooth over.'

Edward stomped off and for the first time in many weeks got down on his knees and prayed.

Jessica put the oven on to 275 degrees.

Gabriel was again begging Rachel to understand him.

Rachel was sitting on the bed next to him now, angry, depressed and indignant all at the same time.

Gabriel's voice whined, irritatingly. 'What if I'd told you straight away, when we met? How would you have reacted?'

'Like this,' Rachel said.

'You'd have run a thousand miles . . .'

'I would have been right to run a thousand miles!'

'No, Rachel. You love me. I know you do.'

Rachel gasped. 'I don't know you!'

'You do! I know you do. You're hurt. But now you know everything.' Rachel shook her head. 'As soon as we met I wanted to fight it. For the first time I felt I could win. But it was hard ... sometimes I'd fuck up ... and shoot up again.'

'Your lost weekends. You said you'd been off getting drunk.' Rachel nodded. 'Another lie.'

'That's what heroin does to you. Turns you into a liar, and a thief. You'd do anything for the money. *I'd* do anything for the money. I was bang at it, and then you came along. Of course I lied to you. And there was never a right moment to tell you.'

'Huh. And I helped. Being blind.'

Gabriel wouldn't have that. 'No. It was all my fault, you can't blame yourself.'

Rachel laughed at that. 'Don't worry – I'm not blaming myself! Not for a second. With this level of deceit, I didn't stand a chance.' She looked at him. 'Just tell me why.'

'So you wouldn't leave me.'

'I know why you *lied*!' she said bitterly. 'I mean, why the heroin?'

Gabriel laughed bitterly now. 'You don't know what it's like, to feel utterly useless. Everything you do, everything you touch. Useless.'

'Gabriel, that's no big deal. We all feel like that sometimes. But most of us don't go out and stick a needle in our arm. What is it like?'

'I don't want to talk about that ...'

Rachel was angry. 'I'm trying to understand this ... and I'm barely holding on. I have to know. Tell me what it is like.'

Gabriel snorted. 'Like having the sun in your face. Like

270

watching yourself from above, in the sunlight, and finding it all funny. All your problems gone.'

'Your problems ignored. And all alone, Gabriel, no room for others.'

Gabriel nodded. 'Yes. And then you came. And I needed you more than I needed a fix.'

'But you turned to your parents! And Charlie – she's only seventeen, but you trusted her. Oh, why didn't you tell me? Why didn't you trust me? I mean, maybe at first . . . but now? We're married. Oh, God!' She stopped. 'You must have been stoned at the wedding.'

'Rachel, don't . . .'

She was in tears now. 'And I believed it all. Coming back here so you could get back to the land. The great artist. When all the time what you really needed was a fix, off your mother.'

It seemed as if the room had gone dark.

'There was a night,' Rachel went on, calmer now, sounding more depressed than angry, 'we'd been going out for a month or so. You were fast asleep and you said my name in your sleep. And it made me feel so happy. God, I can't believe I was so stupid! So young! Like a little girl, poor little orphan girl. I just sat there and hugged my legs and thought it was all so wonderful.' She turned on him angrily. 'You probably only said it because you felt guilty or something!'

'No. I always adored you.'

Without knocking, Jessica came back into the room. 'I'm sorry, I came to see if I could help,' she said.

'I think you've done enough,' Rachel said, with heavy sarcasm.

Gabriel piped up in Jessica's defence. 'Rachel, that's not fair. I forced it on my mother and made her promise to keep quiet.'

It was Jessica's turn to make a speech. 'That's true,' she

271

said, in that calm tone of hers that annoyed Rachel so much. 'He forced it on me. But I'm also old enough to make my own decisions. I could have told you, Rachel, but I didn't. I'm truly sorry for that. It's easy to say in hindsight, I know, but what's happened has happened. Now you've found out, I feel bad, but we must get on with it.'

'What? So it's only now you feel guilty about it, is it?' Rachel wasn't going to let Jessica get away with anything ever again. Not now.

Jessica protested. 'No.'

'Then you felt guilty all along?'

Jessica shrugged. 'Of course I did.'

Rachel stood and faced her old adversary. 'Jessica. When I feel guilty, I avoid people. I can't look at them. I'll do anything to keep away from them, anything to avoid their company . . .' There was a glint of anger in Jessica's eye as she held Rachel's gaze and listened. 'But did you? No, Jessica, you had me at your table as often as possible, with that secret binding you all together and leaving me out. There you were, presiding over us, enjoying your secret! Enjoying it!'

Jessica's eyes narrowed. 'I resent this. Do you think I enjoyed injecting my own son with . . . with that stuff?'

Rachel stood her ground. 'Didn't you love nursing him? Keeping him close?'

Gabriel felt obliged to object again. 'You can't blame my mother. She did what I asked.'

Rachel still looked at Jessica, burning with anger and resentment. 'Isn't that the problem? Whenever he cries, you cradle him, spoil him like the child he has always remained. You've made everything worse.'

'With what alternative?' Jessica asked with great indignation. 'If I push him away, where will he turn? To heroin.'

Rachel laughed bitterly again. 'Not to me? His wife?' Rachel stopped. She'd had enough of Jessica now. 'Now, if you'll excuse us, we have to go.'

When Charlie finally returned to the house, Jessica gripped her by the arm.

'I hope you're proud of yourself, young lady!'

'Let go of me!' Charlie spat. 'You're hurting me!' Jessica had grabbed the same spot as Edward had earlier.

'Do you realise you might have endangered Gabriel's life?'

'Don't be so stupid, mother. Gabriel's a big boy now.'

'You may well have broken up his marriage for him. If Rachel leaves, he may follow her, and then what's going to happen to him, out there on his own?'

'Oh, poor little Gabriel. Should learn to stand on his own two feet like me.'

'You are a wretched, stupid, arrogant little girl, who's been spoiled rotten. What do *you* know about standing on your own two feet?'

Charlie said she'd show Jessica what she knew about standing on her two feet, but the force of pulling herself away from her mother sent her flying on to her backside. As she hit the floor she jerked backwards awkwardly and banged her head on the wall. She laughed with her first breath and then cried tears of pain. She was drunk, hurt and angry.

At that moment Edward came to see what all the noise was about, as did Mary. The three adults then had to witness the spectacle of a seventeen-year-old woman stiffening with rage and screaming at the top of her voice. For a moment all three of them thought Charlie was having a fit, but they soon realised that it was nothing more than a wild, childish tantrum, which actually made the sight more unsettling. Charlie writhed in an agony of frustration, cursing and kicking, pulling her hair and tearing her tights on the polished wooden floor.

Edward imagined some demon sneering at them, damning them all to hell.

Rachel and Gabriel didn't speak on the way back to the Lodge.

They sat together on the sofa in silence as the evening darkened around them.

It was Rachel who spoke first. 'I had this picture-book idea of marriage,' she said. 'Me at the altar in a white dress, our little cottage in the country, my husband the artist. All beautiful, all unreal. Huh! Such a childish notion of happiness. And now I have this other picture of our wedding. You, drugged up, Thomas standing there, Jessica watching over us . . . God, think of the lies! Add them up!'

Rachel had made up her mind to leave. It was the only way. If she stayed after what she had seen, now that she knew the whole thing had been based on lies, how could she claim to respect herself?

'I'll go and stay with Caroline for a while,' she said. 'I'll get the train – I'll phone for a taxi. I can't breathe here, I need time to think. I'll phone you in a week or so, let you know what I'm thinking, how I'm feeling when I've had some space to myself. You can go back to the house. They'll look after you. Jessica will be delighted, I'm sure.'

She turned to see Gabriel's reaction.

Overcome by the effects of the drug, Gabriel had fallen asleep.

Rachel sighed, phoned for a taxi, packed her bags, wrote a note which ended with the words 'Don't smoke in bed', and left.

As the taxi pulled away, Gabriel stirred. When he found the note he screamed angrily and burst into tears. Then he turned off the lights, saying over and over, 'I love you Rachel,' until the darkness entirely enveloped him.

The meal that evening was the low point of Edward's life so far.

As he watched Jessica perform the role of bishop's wife, as she had a thousand times before, he felt as if something must surely give. He thought of his younger daughter, asleep in a drunken stupor upstairs, crazed and tormented; of his son and his drug habit; of his elder daughter's failed marriage; of his own ruined life and faith; of Anne; of Mary – he had even soiled his relationship with Mary in the past. His lust had destroyed everything. He had allowed himself to drift far away from his faith, from God, from the church, from even the most basic human decency and consideration.

The spectacle of Jessica bubbling away despite what she knew – although even she didn't know how low Edward had really sunk – performing her role in order to impress the diocesan bishop and his wife so that she and Edward, with their guilty secrets, might step into their trusted and respected positions, seemed an act of hubris that must surely cause some reaction, if not from God, then from nature herself.

But no, there they sat, with Mary serving them as if they were worthy of grace and privilege. Edward wanted to stand up and declare himself a sinner and denounce Jessica as a fraud. He could see Jessica looking at him in that way of hers, eyes veiled, scolding him as if he was a child incapable of moral or logical action. And, Edward felt, she was right to do so. Her looks denounced him, just as his own soul denounced him.

Edward wondered for a moment whether he might be about to suffer some kind of breakdown. Perhaps this feeling of anxiety was what preceded a heart attack;

certainly his chest felt as if it might explode. Did he have pain in his arms? That was supposed to be a symptom. There was certainly a tingling in his fingers. He was becoming so preoccupied by this that when Mary came and announced that Gabriel had arrived looking as if he needed someone to talk to, Edward was only too pleased to turn his attention elsewhere. He made his apologies and followed Mary from the room.

It took a moment for Edward to understand what Mary was saying. Gabriel had locked himself in their bedroom upstairs; he had looked very distraught and had muttered something that made her think that Rachel had left him.

Edward stood, looking bemused.

'Edward. Please. Do something.' Mary was very anxious.

At that moment Jessica, having made her own apologies, came into the kitchen. Mary repeated herself. In a flash Jessica realised what was going on. Rachel had left; Gabriel was going to kill himself.

'Don't be ridiculous,' Edward heard himself say. Then he followed Jessica and Mary upstairs.

At the same time, a small figure was arriving at the Lodge.

At the station in Market Cross, Rachel had found herself incapable of leaving Gabriel in his pitiful condition. She decided then and there to stay and give their love a chance. Perhaps it was true that she didn't know Gabriel, but she didn't know any other man either, and didn't care to. Surely now, if she stayed, they might find that love came to them with truth and hard work. And if it didn't, then she would be no worse off than she was now.

As soon as she had made her decision she felt a strong pang of guilt and panic. It occurred to her that Jessica had engineered their separation. Hadn't she tried to make their life difficult from the first? Perhaps Jessica was in love with her own son and was slowly poisoning him so that no one else could have him. She convinced herself then that she *did* know Gabriel, but that he was slowly being stolen away from her.

Breathless and excited, she had run to the taxi stand and got back into the same cab that had just dropped her off. She calmed down on the journey and went back to her original sober assessment of the situation, telling herself that Jessica was simply a very dominant character who was in panic herself because of the danger her son faced.

The Lodge was deserted. When she switched on the lights she discovered that their wedding photograph had fallen victim to Gabriel's temper, leaving a dent where it had been smashed against the wall. There were shards of glass on the floor.

Rachel swept up the glass and decided to wait for Gabriel to return.

Jessica knocked on the bedroom door, begging Gabriel to open up, but received no response.

The enormity of what was happening suddenly struck Edward and his mind cleared. He brushed Jessica aside and sternly demanded that Gabriel open the door. When he too received no answer, he immediately determined to break down the door.

The operation was far more difficult to perform than he imagined.

Five great crashes resounded through the house, scaring the guests and causing Edward to cry out in pain and frustration, before the lock finally tore through the wooden frame and the door flew open to reveal Gabriel, prostrate on the bed, needle in his arm, dying.

·17·

CHARLIE CAME DOWNSTAIRS to find Mary and Lenny sitting at the kitchen table.

She'd been woken by the commotion and eventually staggered out of bed to find the place deserted. Her head ached like thunder.

'Is the party over?' she croaked. 'Where the hell is everyone?'

Lenny looked at her. 'Gabriel's in hospital. He took too much methadone. He was unconscious. The ambulance men gave him something, but he didn't wake up.'

'You mean he took an overdose?' Charlie said.

'I don't know. They found him upstairs.'

Charlie didn't seem impressed by the news. 'What, on purpose?'

Lenny shrugged.

Mary said, 'We don't know. We're waiting to hear.'

Charlie went to the cupboard and took out a bottle of sherry that was used for cooking. 'Typical Gabriel. He tries to kill himself and doesn't even get that right.'

Lenny shouted at her. 'He could be *dead*, Charlie!'

'Is he?'

'*We don't know.*'

'Well, there's no point in speculating,' Charlie said, and poured herself a drink.

In great confusion, bordering on despair, Rachel rushed to the hospital.

Mary had phoned the Lodge as Gabriel was taken away, unconscious, by ambulance, Edward and Jessica with him.

As she ran along the antiseptic-smelling corridors to the emergency ward, Rachel cursed herself and Jessica and the family and everything that had happened since she had arrived in the quiet little town of Market Cross. She begged God to spare Gabriel. It was the first time in her life she had ever prayed sincerely.

She found Edward and Jessica, both white with fear, agitated and despairing. Strangely, Jessica seemed younger, full of nervous energy. Rachel hardly recognised her.

'How is he?' Rachel gasped. 'Mary didn't know.'

Edward replied, 'We don't know.'

'Surely they can treat methadone?' Rachel said. 'It can't be lethal. He's used to it, that must help.' She was clutching at straws.

'I keep asking, but they won't say yet.'

Rachel looked at Jessica. 'What happened?'

Still it was Edward who spoke. 'I found him. He locked himself in our room. He was white as death. He must have wanted to escape, with the drugs.' Edward shrugged. 'They're an escape . . .'

Now Jessica spoke, and bitterly. 'Gabriel *knew* a second dose could kill him.'

'He can't have,' Edward insisted.

'We can't deny it, Edward. It would be dangerous to do so.'

Edward shook his head. 'How could Gabriel feel so alone?'

'That's what we need to find out,' Jessica said, 'so we

can make sure it never happens again.' At last she spoke to Rachel, lowering her head humbly as she did so. 'This is where our lying has brought us,' she acknowledged. 'I think it's time we all changed.'

Rachel felt a great surge of warmth for Jessica. The tension of the moment gave way to a feeling that perhaps this crisis, if resolved, could bring new life to them all. She sighed deeply and smiled, shaking her own head sadly. 'Five minutes more and I think I'd have been back in time,' she said. 'I got as far as the station in Market Cross, but I couldn't get on the train. I couldn't leave him.'

Jessica had stiffened, her expression changed. 'Leave him?'

Rachel nodded. 'I was going to leave him.'

'Tonight? You were going to leave him tonight?'

'Yes,' she said.

Jessica shook her head, thin-lipped and contemptuous. 'You tore him apart and then left him on his own.'

Despite herself, Rachel was flabbergasted. 'I came back,' she said, but even as she said it her words sounded weak in the face of Jessica's indignation.

'And you wonder that we kept his problems secret!' Jessica hissed. 'When you act like this? He needed you and you discarded him like a broken toy!'

'That's not fair,' Rachel said.

Even Edward said, 'Jessica, please,' at that.

But Jessica was not going to be stopped. 'Is it fair that I have to stand in this corridor waiting for a stranger to tell me whether my son is alive or dead?' she asked with incredulity. 'You took him away from the house, down to the Lodge and then left him there. You didn't even let me know you'd gone. And doing so you brought us here, to this. If Gabriel dies, Rachel,' she shrieked, 'it'll be *your fault*!'

★

280

Charlie was still in the kitchen drinking sherry.

Lenny and Mary were doing their best to ignore her.

'Why should I care?' Charlie was saying. 'No one cares about me.'

'Oh, shut up, Charlie,' Lenny said. 'Gabriel's . . . Oh, for God's sake!'

'Since when have *you* been Gabriel's best friend, Lenny?' Charlie asked, with a sarcastic sneer.

Lenny looked at Charlie, but couldn't think of a reply.

'How many times have you been down to see him since you arrived, eh?' Charlie went on. 'How many times have you discussed his problems with him? You're his older sister. He looks up to you. All you've done is go out with Jimmy every bloody night, boring old Jimmy, just because he gives you a bit of attention!'

Lenny was hurt by this. All she could think to do was to defend Jimmy. 'Jimmy's not boring . . . he cares about me.'

At that moment Mary banged her fist on the table, making both women jump with fright. 'I am sick and tired of listening to this!'

'Well, sod off, then,' Charlie said.

Mary glared at her, angrier than either of the young women had ever seen her before. 'Gabriel is very seriously ill – he may be dying – and I have to listen to you two sniping and bickering! You make me ashamed! I've never heard such selfishness!'

Lenny was amazed. 'Hold on a minute! Don't tar me with the same brush as her!'

'I'm sorry, Lenny, but you're no better.'

'What have *I* done?' Lenny asked, horrified.

'Since you came home,' Mary replied, coldly, 'I get asked to look after Ben practically every day, whenever the whim takes you. Never mind that I might have other plans . . .'

Charlie cut in, 'What? Like an exciting afternoon at the shops?'

'Shut up, Charlie!' Lenny said, looking at Mary, deeply ashamed of herself.

Mary was determined to have her say. 'I pity your mother. She looks at her children and all she can see is your indulgence and . . .' Her look of disdain subdued even Charlie. 'When you were little, I'd take you out, one by one, over the years, and we used to go to that playground in the village. There'd be, what, a dozen or so children running around. But you could always spot the Rattigan in the crowd. They'd be the one shouting the loudest, demanding all the attention, picking on the others, being downright nasty. They'd smile at me, those other women. I think they pitied me.'

Lenny and Charlie sat with their heads bowed. Mary gave it a moment before continuing with a deep, sad, sigh.

'So perhaps some of it is my fault. I knew you were selfish, but didn't ask you to change. If I'd been stricter with you, if I'd made you respect yourselves and others, perhaps Gabriel wouldn't have done what he did.' She sighed again. 'And let's face it, suicide is the ultimate selfish act.'

By the time Mary had finished, Lenny was crying, quietly. Charlie let Mary take the sherry glass from her.

'Mr and Mrs Rattigan?'

The doctor had appeared suddenly.

'Yes?' Jessica, Edward and Rachel said as one.

The doctor smiled. 'He's going to be all right . . .'

The rest of his speech was lost in the wave of relief that washed over them. They all knew that Gabriel was lucky that the ambulance had arrived so speedily that he had suffered no brain damage. Under different circumstances, he might have died. None of them could recall later how they had learned that information.

Rachel and Jessica wept. Edward comforted Jessica.

'Can we see him?' Rachel asked.

'I don't see why not,' the doctor said.

But before Rachel could move, Jessica intervened. 'You have no right to see him!' she hissed viciously.

Rachel was astounded. 'He's my husband!'

Jessica's eyes flashed angrily. 'Evidently you decided not, when you walked out on him. You've pushed him to the edge once tonight, now leave him in peace.'

With a look, Rachel appealed to Edward to intervene, but the doctor beat him to it. 'I'd rather any family arguments weren't carried to the bedside. He's still in a delicate state.'

Rachel squared up to Jessica. 'Fine by me!' she said, and then to the doctor, 'Is he in there?'

The doctor nodded and Rachel led them in.

The gloomy kitchen vigil was broken up by the good news.

Lenny and Mary hugged and cried. Charlie muttered something about Gabriel being a stupid bastard and went back to bed.

Just as Mary went to bed, Jimmy called. He'd been out seeing an old school friend. He'd seen all the lights on, so here he was. Lenny was delighted to see him and burst into tears.

Before long they were drinking her father's whisky again and chatting warmly. Lenny explained what had happened to Gabriel.

'Jesus!' Jimmy said. 'That was a well-kept secret. Didn't Mark know about it?'

'Uh-uh.' Lenny shook her head. 'We seem to have been quite good at keeping secrets from one another.'

'I don't think he was very good at keeping his,' Jimmy joked, daringly for him.

'Jimmy?' Lenny asked, a few drinks later, after they had discussed all the ins and outs of Gabriel's addiction. 'Do *you* think I'm selfish?'

'Why,' he laughed, 'who said you were?'

'Mary,' Lenny said. 'She said I'm always asking her to look after Ben and going out whenever I feel like it.'

Jimmy smiled. 'And is it true?'

Embarrassed, Lenny smiled. 'Yes, it's true,' she admitted.

'Then maybe you have been acting a bit selfishly lately,' Jimmy said.

Lenny was seriously embarrassed now. 'God,' she said. 'Even *you* think I'm a selfish bastard.'

'Excuse me!' Jimmy said. 'I don't think I said that. I said, *maybe* you were being a bit selfish lately, for God's sake. How long have you been struggling away unselfishly with Ben all on your own while Mark was out shagging! Oh!' Jimmy blushed. 'I'm sorry, I mean ... Oh, you know what I mean.'

Lenny laughed, glad of Jimmy's slip-up because it made him seem a bit more human. 'You're right. On both counts. I needed a bit of a release,' she said.

'Yeah, but to be honest I think Mark probably wasn't out shagging that much, you know.'

'Oh, sod Mark,' Lenny laughed. 'Sod the bastard for once.' She looked at Jimmy. 'I sometimes think you and me are better friends now than me aned Mark ever were,' she said.

Jimmy blushed again, but for once he didn't object.

They sat drinking in silence. The atmosphere seemed to have grown very intimate, even sexual. Lenny wondered whether she did actually find Jimmy attractive and discovered that she could no longer tell what was and what was not sexually attractive about a man. Neither of them knew how to proceed with the conversation.

Then Lenny came to a decision. 'Jimmy, would you stay the night with me?' she asked. 'I mean, as friends.'

Jimmy didn't know how to reply.

Ten minutes later they sneaked up to Lenny's bedroom giggling like a couple of teenagers.

Gabriel did his best to smile, especially at Rachel.

'They said you can have some water if you want,' Jessica said, fussing around the room.

Rachel held his hand and sat gazing at him.

Edward stood over the bed looking at Gabriel until he said, 'Dad, please. Don't look at me like that.'

'Gabriel,' Edward said, 'I have to know. Did you know what you were doing?' Both Rachel and Jessica tried to interrupt him, but Edward persisted. 'Did you intend to take your own life?'

Gabriel looked away, unable to return his father's intense stare.

'This isn't over,' Edward said, 'until you answer my question.'

The women tutted impatiently to register their disapproval of Edward's inquisition, but it made no difference.

Gabriel sighed painfully. 'I don't know what I was thinking,' he said, and then huffed again. 'That's not true. Yes. In that moment, I wanted to die.'

Both Rachel and Jessica started to cry again.

Edward continued. 'But why? I was outside the room. You must have heard me calling. Did that mean nothing?'

Rachel reached over and touched Edward's arm. 'Edward, I know we have to talk about this, but now's not the right time . . .'

But Jessica joined in. 'You could have come to see me, Gabriel.'

285

All went quiet.

Gabriel said to Rachel, 'I thought I'd lost you. I couldn't see anything beyond that.'

Rachel squeezed his hand. 'That's exactly how I felt. We were both insane. Completely.'

Jessica said it again. 'You could have come to see me.'

Gabriel turned to her. 'You couldn't bring Rachel back.'

Jessica looked at him. 'No.'

'I got to the station and changed my mind,' Rachel said, adding, 'Woman's prerogative,' to lighten it.

'But Gabriel wasn't to know that,' Jessica said bitterly.

Gabriel ignored her. 'Why *did* you come back?'

Rachel was still trying to make light of it all. 'I thought, What are my options? Living with a madman, or a typing pool in Balham? Huh – it was close, but you won.'

Jessica felt the need to retreat. She was hurt and tired. She could start again tomorrow. For once Gabriel was in safe hands. She told Rachel they would wait for her outside and left them alone to say their goodnights.

'So you're staying?' Gabriel said.

Rachel nodded. Then they kissed.

As she went, Rachel said, 'Oh, there was one other reason why I came back.'

'Uh-huh?'

Rachel nodded. 'I love you.'

Gabriel sobbed his heart out then.

At first Lenny and Jimmy lay close, but not in each other's arms.

Lenny's bed was not small, but it was not a grand double bed, either. They giggled for a while over how ridiculous it was having to sneak around at their age, then they both undressed as far as their underwear.

Jimmy tried not to look at Lenny as she dived modestly

286

under the covers, but he did manage to see her out of the corner of his eye. As he tiptoed across the room from the light switch, he thought what a bad idea it had been to pretend to himself that he would be able to handle a platonic night with his old friend.

It was a long time since Jimmy had spent the night with a woman. The last few times he had done so, it had hardly been worth the effort, so he had sworn he would not do so again until it was someone he was in love with. Obviously he didn't intend to have sex with Lenny, but lying there next to her he felt that if she turned to face him, or if she reached out to touch him, he would surely be unable to resist a bursting forth of his old love for her, no matter how much of a betrayal that would be to Mark who was at that moment asleep in Jimmy's flat.

In short, he was very turned on.

Lenny was very pleased to have Jimmy with her that night. During the last months that she and Mark had spent together, she had not felt this sort of closeness with him. Now, talking and giggling with her old friend, she felt something of her youthful freedom returning. She was warm and safe, and the more they talked, the more she felt like reaching out and touching him. She found herself fantasising about what it would be like to have a relationship with Jimmy. How nice he would be and how considerate, how good he was with children and how Mark would feel, how it would bloody well serve him right . . .

The two of them fell silent and curled up, Jimmy with his back to Lenny who snuggled in behind him.

Some time later, Lenny said, 'Mark's a bastard.'

Jimmy said, 'Yeah, he's a stupid bastard.'

This was the first time Lenny had heard Jimmy really sound disloyal to Mark. 'I don't know why I bother with him,' she said.

'You don't at the moment.'

Lenny laughed.

Jimmy sighed. 'But you should. I think he's learned his lesson. I think he's changed.'

Lenny slept more peacefully that night than she had for weeks. Jimmy stayed awake most of the night, sighing and tingling, feeling guilty and ecstatic by turns.

·18·

Wednesday evening

Gosh I'm so tired.

Thank God you were in again this morning. I'm so
sorry I got you out of bed early, but you were lucky I
didn't get you up at four o'clock when we got back
from the hospital and kept you up all night!!! And you
know, the lovely thing is, I know I could have done
that if I needed to. Come to think of it, I don't know
why I didn't, I couldn't sleep as it was, with
everything running round in my head.

I'm so angry and confused. Not by Gabriel – now
I've got to the bottom of things I feel a bit more safe.
I mean, I know my husband's a fucking heroin addict,
but at least I know that now and I feel that I can help.
So what's annoying me – yes, you guessed it.
Jessicaaaarrgghh!!!!!!!

If you ask me, she's having a field-day. Of course
she blames the whole thing on me!! The moment she
heard that I'd left Gabriel – after months of being
deceived by Jessica *and* everyone in the house – no
doubt at Jessica's behest – wham! the whole bloody

289

thing is my fault. It's like one of those Greek tragedies when the mother is in love with the son, or the son sleeps with the mother (she wishes!!!) or some crazy idea like that.

You know, the funny thing is, I don't know what it is she wants. Maybe she does just want them all to herself.

Anyway, let me tell you what happened today. I'd got all evening on my own – having refused Jessica's kind invitation to spend the evening up at the house with *the family from hell*.

Jessica didn't come in to the hospital till late this morning, saying she wanted me and Gabriel to have time together. She seemed perfectly at ease and was very polite, even friendly towards me, offering me a lift home for lunch. The hospital are great – they've got visiting in the morning, afternoon and evening. So anyway, as soon as we got outside the room, I decided to make my peace. 'Look,' I said, 'last night. We were both upset. We both said things we didn't mean.' (I was careful not to say sorry.)

'Did we?' Jessica says. 'I'm very much afraid my opinion hasn't changed. You let him down, Rachel. Almost fatally.'

I was totally gob-smacked. I asked her if she blamed it *all* on me.

She says, 'In twenty-seven years, Gabriel has never sunk this low.'

She reckons he's survived heroin, he's nearly off the methadone (which is bullshit, according to the doctor I spoke to) and the moment I come along – wham! He tries to kill himself.

So I have to restrain myself from killing her!! And from asking her how much of it is *her* fault, does she think.

Oh, she's done it all for him, she's always wanted the best for him, always tried to protect him, what could she do? Blah blah blah . . .

I said, 'Well, actually, he could have had treatment from a treatment centre or you could have got him some professional help.'

'Oh, Gabriel would never have agreed to that. You know Gabriel and his will . . .'

'Did you ask him?' I say.

'Oh, he's like a child, he enjoys the danger. There's no one can tell Gabriel what to do!'

Then comes the crunch. I said (I think), 'What about telling me, then – did you ever think of that?' I could see from her face that the answer was no. 'No,' I said, 'all you wanted to do was *mother* him.'

That did it. You should have seen her face. 'That's *terrifying*, Rachel,' she says, 'that you can use the word "mother" as an insult.' Then she launches into this speech about how the family is all a person ever needs, how the family is the most important thing on earth (or words to that effect). Then she attacks me for being an orphan. 'I feel sorry for you, Rachel, who'll never know what it is like to have a family that loves you.'

So it went on. As she talked, or rather spouted, her head started to jerk angrily and she went red and blinked as if she had a nervous twitch. Honestly, I thought then, we've got to get away from this madness!!! It suddenly felt as if I was in a bad dream where you're running along through treacle and you can't move quickly enough to get away. And we really must. I've spoken to Gabriel and he says as soon as he's back on his feet we're going to leave. We don't know where, but we're just going to get away, as far away as possible.

Anyhow. After lunch and wondering if I hadn't imagined it all, I went up to the house for my lift back to the hospital and Mary is there, as if she'd been waiting for me. Jessica won't be long, would I like a cup of tea?

Then it really does get spooky.

Right out of the blue, Mary says, 'If you don't fight us, Rachel, if you don't kick at us, you'll find this family can provide you with all the support you'll ever need.'

I said, 'What do you mean, *fight* you?'

Mary looked at me, just like Jessica had earlier, and said, 'If you see this as a battle, then you're on very dangerous ground. Because Gabriel will be caught in the middle.'

I don't know what I said, but I said something. Probably a sort of paranoid babbling.

Then she said, 'Don't set yourself up as an enemy.'

I said, 'So what are you saying Mary, "Either I'm for you or against you"? Is that how you see it?'

And she says, 'Yes.'

I couldn't bear to look at her any more, so I turned back to my cup of tea. She was pottering around. 'And what if I decide I'm against you?' I said, half joking.

She says, 'Then it'll be Gabriel who suffers the consequences,' in this really threatening voice.

That got me. I was so cross. I said, 'You sound just like Jessica . . .' and turned round – and guess who was standing there next to her. Yes, you guessed it. Jessicaaarggh!! The two of them were like something out of the *Stepford Wives*. They had the same look on their faces and they were standing there in exactly the same pose. No kidding, I wanted to scream and run out of the house and run away from them!!!

I have to kidnap my husband from these people

before they destroy him, literally. Meanwhile, I'm going to be the Good Little Wife.

You must think I've gone completely and utterly off my rocker. I think you're right!

What the hell is going on here???

Jessica found Edward in the bedroom, on his knees again, tormenting himself, blaming himself for Gabriel's attempt at suicide, and talking of Anne in the most ridiculous terms.

'Edward, if it's anybody's fault it is mine — and Rachel's,' she said. 'Mine for keeping it secret from her, but really and truly mostly hers for behaving like a spoilt child and taking him to the Lodge and abandoning him there like that.'

Edward looked up at her and she noticed for the first time the black rings under his eyes, the loose puffy skin around his jowls.

'Jessica, I know you believe that, but really it is me who is to blame.'

'Nonsense. They argued. She left him. It is as simple as that, Edward.'

Edward shook his head slowly. 'It started before then. It is not as simple as . . . scientific cause and effect. Not even as simple as the psychology of a young marriage.' Jessica sighed and sat down heavily on the bed. 'Sometimes, Jessica, a man is punished for his sins in a way that he would not have anticipated . . .'

'Edward.' Jessica took a deep breath. 'You're a good man, a good father and a good husband.' Edward was already shaking his head again. 'You've done nothing that could possibly warrant such . . . such a punishment. You're being ridiculous.'

Edward had tears in his eyes. Jessica couldn't bear the

sight, but she reached out and brushed the hair from his brow in a comforting way.

'I understand how you feel, Edward, but you mustn't, you *can't*, hold yourself responsible.'

'You were right, Jessica, I'm weak. And I don't understand how it happened.'

Jessica shook her head and spoke insincerely. 'You're not weak, Edward, you're ... wounded. But you'll heal ... like Gabriel.'

Edward shook his head again and sighed. 'I can't live with this guilt,' he said. 'It's killing me.'

The last thing Jessica wanted at this time of night was a long discussion with Edward. She felt angry with him for not being able to deal with things in the way that she could, but she knew that if she showed her true feelings she would make matters worse, perhaps even push him over the edge. 'Edward, we can't always blame ourselves for the mistakes of our children.'

Edward looked up at her. 'That's not what I'm talking about.'

Jessica sighed again. 'Oh, Edward, you're still talking about Anne. You have to let her go, there's nothing we can do for Anne, or her child.'

'You don't understand ...'

'I understand perfectly. You're grieving for Anne. For God's sake, Edward, you counsel people yourself. Guilt is part of the grieving process.'

'Jessica, I killed Anne.'

Jessica tutted. 'You're just being silly. Anne fell down the stairs and broke her neck. She was drunk. She was a fool.'

'I pushed her.'

'Oh, stop it, Edward. I haven't got the energy for this now.'

'I pushed her.'

'You put pressure on her to have an abortion. She fell. She didn't cut her wrists, or take drugs, she fell.'

Edward was determined to tell the truth at last, no matter what the consequences. 'I murdered her.'

'Oh, for God's sake, grow up, Edward.' Jessica stood up. She had heard enough, she had had enough. 'I can't help you. Not tonight. We'll talk some more in the morning. I'm tired. I'm going to sleep in one of the spare rooms, perhaps for a few nights. You must pray, or something. I need my energies to help Gabriel.' She hesitated at the door, looked for some clue as to whether he might do something stupid himself that night. She decided that she was right to leave him. She had to look after herself for once.

'Goodnight, Edward.'

Edward watched her go, feeling powerless either to stop her or to make himself understood.

Conversation between Rachel and Jessica had been polite, if distant, for days.

Neither had acknowledged the state of war that existed between them, knowing that nothing further would be achieved until Gabriel returned from the hospital.

Rachel turned up at the house for her lift one morning to find Gabriel sitting in the drawing room, talking to Jessica.

When he saw his wife, Gabriel said, 'Oh, hi, I was just going to phone you.'

Rachel was aghast. 'Why didn't anyone tell me you were back? I was just coming for my lift!' She looked at Jessica.

'I didn't want to worry you unduly,' Jessica said, simply.

Rachel held out her hand to Gabriel. 'Come on,' she said, crossly, 'let's go home.'

Jessica held up a hand to stop them. 'We think Gabriel should stay at the house. For a while, at least.'

Rachel was furious. '*We?* Who's we?' She tried not to shout.

'Edward and I. We think it would be for the best.'

Rachel looked at Gabriel whose head was bowed. 'Did you know about this?'

Gabriel made no reply, only shaking his head vaguely.

Rachel went on, 'Is it unreasonable to think a grown man should go home with his wife and not with his mother?'

Jessica was almost smiling. 'Just for once, Rachel, could you put Gabriel's needs before your own?'

Rachel was white with rage. 'How dare you! You of all people say that to me?'

Gabriel opened his mouth at last. It seemed to Rachel that he only ever did so in defence of his mother. 'Rachel, please . . .'

'Gabriel, we have to sort things out between us.'

Again Jessica's faint smile. 'And Gabriel has to sort himself out.'

Rachel ignored her. 'It's what we have to do – you have to face things as they are.'

Jessica persisted. 'Have you forgotten how things were, already, Rachel? As I remember it was all screaming rows and packing bags . . .'

'*Gabriel?*'

'Do you trust yourself, Rachel?'

Rachel looked at Jessica again. 'I trust Gabriel.'

Jessica gave a disdainful snort. 'Really, you're more naïve than I thought,' she said.

'Gabriel, you don't have to listen to this,' Rachel said, and then turned to Jessica. 'What do you think this is doing to him, hearing you talk about him like this?'

Jessica's face hardened. 'Gabriel's life is at stake. You're using that to score points in an argument.'

Gabriel stood up and shouted, 'Enough!'

Jessica, however, went on, 'You've proved you couldn't cope with him.'

'How was I supposed to cope with a problem I never knew existed?' Rachel screamed.

'You didn't even notice.'

'Please, stop it, both of you.' Gabriel tried again.

The only effect Gabriel's request had was a lowering of the volume. 'If I didn't notice,' Rachel seethed, 'it was because the entire Rattigan family conspired to stop me!'

Jessica had an answer to that. 'If we conspired, it was to help *you*,' she said. 'Don't you remember? Even as far back as the wedding I warned you about Gabriel's drinking? But did it make any difference? You ignored me. Everything I've done you've thrown back in my face.'

Rachel took Gabriel's hand. 'Don't you see it now, Gabriel? Your mother thinks you've made a mistake marrying me, she's trying to *rescue* you from me.'

'Oh, don't be ridiculous,' Jessica said. 'Rachel, darling, you need a rest. You see how you distort everything. I'm only trying to help you, both of you. Why all this suspicion?'

Rachel looked at Gabriel.

Gabriel said, 'It's true. They are only trying to help.'

Rachel felt deflated. She had gone too far, she had been ridiculous. Whatever Jessica was trying to do was obviously only for Gabriel's benefit, even if she was trying to destroy their marriage. Rachel knew she had lost her cool. She felt she had made a fool of herself in the heat of argument, but she was not going to leave Gabriel behind.

'Well, if there's nothing to worry about, come with me, Gabriel,' she said. 'You can come here whenever you like, and I promise I won't leave you again without informing the rest of the world beforehand.'

Gabriel looked at her. 'So you *have* decided to stay?'

Rachel was exasperated. 'Yes, I told you. I've told you about twenty times. I'm back. To stay. To the bitter end.'

Gabriel smiled. 'I know, I'm sorry. I don't know what came over me. I think I got out of hospital and felt vulnerable . . .'

Yeah and Jessica collared you! Rachel thought. 'So will you come?' she said.

Gabriel nodded and looked automatically at his mother for approval. Jessica's face remained impassive. 'Mum, Rachel's right,' he said. 'We should face our problems together.'

Jessica nodded, smiled and said, 'Of course, darling. Whatever you think is best,' in a way that, though she sounded perfectly reasonable, left a bitter taste in the mouth.

Rachel shuddered inwardly and practically dragged Gabriel out of the house, thinking that she would take him away from there as soon as possible.

After she and Jimmy had spent the night together, Lenny began bringing Ben to Jimmy's flat.

She remained as cool as ever with Mark, but Mark told Jimmy that it was a sign that she was beginning to thaw towards him.

'Good old Ben,' Mark laughed, when the two men were sitting together after one of the visits. 'He's always so pleased to see me. Big selling point that.'

Jimmy pulled a face. 'Hey, we're patching up your marriage here, not selling some bloody after-shave.'

Mark grinned. 'The principles are very similar.'

Jimmy shook his head. 'Don't you think you should

move up a gear? She might be expecting you to make some kind of move.'

'Oh, I dunno. It's quite romantic really. In a chaste sort of a way. I quite like the way she's gradually coming towards me. I mean, I'm just sitting here, and she's the one who's moved.'

Jimmy was appalled but didn't say so. 'Well, if it's any help, I do think she's coming round. And I've spoken to her, remember.'

'Ah.' Mark sat up. 'What has she been saying?'

Jimmy shook his head. 'Uh-uh. Talk to her yourself.'

Mark sighed. 'Part of the problem is that Lenny thinks I only wanted her as a housekeeper. I mean, she's good at that, but I wanted her too. None of those other women were any threat to her.' Mark stopped.

'*None of those other women?*' Jimmy said slowly.

Mark looked embarrassed. 'Um. I'm afraid so,' he said.

'How many?'

Mark used bravado to cover his discomfort. 'Three and a half if you count a fumble in the back of a taxi.'

Jimmy scowled at him. 'You bastard. What did you tell them? My wife doesn't understand me?'

Mark nodded. 'Something like that,' he said. When he realised Jimmy was really upset he added, 'Thank you. I will now consider myself well and truly told off.'

But Jimmy had more to say. 'God almighty!' he spat. 'I'm busting a gut here, playing Cupid between you two and then you go and tell me something like this.'

'It's no big deal, like I said . . .'

'Tell that to Lenny!'

'Right, thank you again, Mr Moral Majority.'

'Mark. You seem to forget, Lenny's my mate as well.'

'So?'

Jimmy was pacing the room. 'So, I'm telling her what a great guy you are and how you've learned your lesson, you made a silly mistake, it was a one-off. Now it turns out I'm lying for you!'

Mark shook his head. 'You're getting this totally out of proportion.'

'You prick! Are you serious about her, or *do* you just want someone to iron your shirts?'

Mark's tone changed. 'Listen, mate,' he said, coldly. 'You might have been doing a bit of match-making lately, but don't overplay your hand. It's still my wife we're talking about here.'

Jimmy faced up to his friend for once. 'What are you trying to say, Mark?'

Mark wasn't fazed. 'I'm trying to say that if I get back with Lenny, that's my business. And it'll be because I'm serious – about her and Ben, my son. Right? Not because you've passed on a few poxy messages.'

Back at the Lodge now, Rachel and Gabriel were trying to talk their way back to sanity.

'Gabriel, we have to leave. We have to get away from here.'

'No, Rachel. It's not safe.'

'You can stop using drugs anywhere. If you stay here, you'll never get clean.'

'No. I can't leave.'

Rachel sighed. 'You're trapped. You see your family as more important than me.'

'No! Rachel, I nearly died for you.'

'But you won't leave for me?'

Gabriel sighed. 'Rachel, I had time to think in hospital. You've come back to me. That's the most important thing in the world. But I can't do this alone. My family might not be as important to me as you are, but I need them. And if I don't get their help – *mum's* help – I don't think there'll be anything left of me to give to you. And that's what I want, that's what I thought about in the hospital – I want to have something left to give to you.'

Rachel could see that even if *she* thought his family weren't helping, Gabriel was so dependent on them that to leave now would probably weaken him fatally. He needed to be weaned from his family as much as from the drugs.

'I know you think I'm pathetic,' Gabriel was saying, 'but just give in to me on this – even if it's only for a time. Let's try it. And then, if I'm clean we can go. And if I'm not, we'll go and try it on our own.'

'I don't want lip-service, Gabriel.'

'I swear.'

'And you'll try to be more independent?'

'Yes. I promise.'

'Really?'

Gabriel nodded, then hesitated. 'But I want mum to give me my injections still.'

Rachel's lips tightened. 'Well, for now.' Then she said, 'But I should try. I should learn.'

Gabriel said, 'No. It's too humiliating.'

'Good. Maybe you'll get fed up with it.'

They looked at each other. For the time being there was nothing more to be said on the subject.

'Can we stop fighting now?' Gabriel said.

Rachel grinned. 'I never wanted to start.'

'I promise you – in a few weeks all this will be over.'

'Don't promise,' Rachel said. 'Just try. Really try to tell me the truth.'

'Yes.'

'About everything.'

'Yes.'

Rachel grinned. 'Could you start now?'

Gabriel nodded earnestly. 'Of course. What?'

Rachel looked coyly at him. 'How much do you love me?'

A wide smile appeared on Gabriel's face. 'More than anyone can say.'

Jessica called at the office to check that Edward was coping with his work.

She knew that he wouldn't be. Since Gabriel's hospitalisation he had deteriorated, so really she was checking that he was not about to do something they would both regret.

She found him hunched over his desk like a vision of death.

'Sit down, Jessica,' he croaked.

Jessica did so with a cautious expression on her face. 'Edward, you have to stop punishing yourself . . .'

'Jessica, it is not me. *I* am not punishing myself.'

'Edward, please. I . . . I wonder if you should perhaps see someone.' She tutted. 'No, it's impossible, you can't be trusted to tell them a sensible story.'

'Jessica, God is telling me to act.'

'Don't be ridiculous.'

'It is very clear.'

'What? Act? In what way act?'

'To tell the truth.'

'Truth, you keep talking about the truth. What truth, for God's sake?'

'About Anne. That I killed her.'

Jessica sounded more tired than cross. 'Oh, Edward, not that again.'

'I pushed her.'

'Edward, she fell . . .'

'You weren't there,' Edward said with exasperation. 'I've got to make a clean breast of it. I *must*.'

'What *are* you talking about?'

'No more lies. We go to the police.'

Jessica just managed to restrain herself from shouting. 'Are you quite mad? The only person you've lied to is yourself!' She paused, to calm herself. 'And me. Over the years. Perhaps we've deceived ourselves.'

Edward looked at her. 'You could let me confess to you, Jessica.'

'Confess what?'

'That I killed Anne.'

'Edward, I will not let you live a lie, not one that will torment you and which may well come to destroy us.'

Edward shook his head. 'No, Jessica. I want to live with the truth, that's what I want, more than anything.'

Jessica collected herself. 'I've watched you,' she said, 'heading towards this hell on earth you've created. You're digging your own grave, Edward – deeper and deeper.' Edward tried to interrupt, but Jessica wouldn't allow it. 'And you haven't given a moment's consideration to the effect on me and the children. What if it leaked out to the press? *The bishop who thought he'd killed his mistress!* They'd think you were a damn madman!'

Edward buried his face in his hands. 'Jessica, the hand of God is upon me.'

'Well turn to him, Edward, pray to him,' Jessica said, standing up. 'And grow up.'

She swept from the room. Edward was left with the thought that she could no longer help him. He would do as he had planned without Jessica's blessing. There was no alternative now but to act alone.

Rachel was determined to see the thing through to the bitter end.

Jessica was instructing her on how to use the syringe. Gabriel was sitting on Jessica's bed with his sleeve rolled up, the women on either side of him. Jessica tied the tourniquet.

'Is that not too tight?' Rachel asked, trying not to let her anxiety show.

Gabriel shook his head. 'Rachel, please, don't do this to yourself.'

Jessica said, 'Shh, it's fine.' Then to Rachel, 'Now take the syringe. Yes, that's right, draw up the solution . . .'

Rachel was struggling but still determined. 'Like this?'

'Do you think that's ready?'

They'd been through the procedure twice already.

Rachel frowned. 'Erm, I think so, yes.'

Jessica said, 'Very well. What now?'

Rachel took hold of Gabriel's arm but Jessica snatched the needle from her hand. Rachel looked annoyed and worried at the same time.

'Do you realise,' Jessica said, barely able to conceal her satisfaction, 'that if you were to inject Gabriel with this now, he'd be dead within a few minutes, possibly only a few seconds? There's air in the syringe, Rachel, you cannot allow that to happen.'

Such was Rachel's revulsion at the whole process that she had nearly passed out the first time she saw the needle. Now the stress and anxiety of the situation rose up and choked her. She put her head in her hands and moaned.

'So. Start again,' Jessica commanded.

Rachel shook her head. 'I can't. I really don't think I can do this.'

Jessica's eyes flashed. 'Come on, Rachel,' she said, 'if you want to learn.'

Gabriel intervened. 'Leave her, mum. Look at the colour of her.'

'Be quiet, Gabriel!' Jessica hissed. 'This is what she wants. Do it again, Rachel.'

Rachel had to leave the room. Having challenged

Jessica so blatantly and failed, she felt so humiliated that she couldn't speak.

At breakfast Jimmy's face was as bitter as the thick-cut marmalade with ginger that Mark was spreading on his toast.

'What have I done to deserve this?' Mark asked.

Jimmy wanted to shout at his old friend, but didn't. 'You've . . . betrayed me,' he said.

Mark smiled. 'Well, can we start again?'

'You've betrayed Lenny and you've betrayed me.'

'What, and you've had a sleepless night?' Jimmy didn't reply to that. 'Come on, tell your uncle Mark all about it,' Mark teased.

'Oh, bugger off.'

'Sorry. Sorry. Go on, what?'

'I find it hard to take, that you've betrayed her that many times.'

'Jesus! I wouldn't have told you if I'd known it would upset your moral digestion.'

'How do you expect me to react? You're married to her.'

'I know, I was there . . .'

Jimmy shook his head. 'Well, I'm worried.'

'You take the worries of the world on your shoulders, Jim.'

'I'm talking specifically about Lenny.'

'Get off my back, mate. I can handle this.'

'Well I hope so, Mark.'

'My problem, mate, not yours. She'll come round.'

'Come round? Mark, it's not as simple as that. She's . . . she's hurting like hell.'

Mark nodded. 'Yeah. Well, so am I.'

Jimmy looked at him. 'Well, you couldn't bloody tell.'

Mark looked back at him with an expression on his face Jimmy had never seen before. 'Believe it,' he said.

·19·

CHARLIE WAS IN a state of utter desolation.
Since the fiasco with Thomas, when she wasn't feeling empty inside, she was angry, and when she was neither empty nor angry, she was drunk. She felt invisible around the house. Jessica and Edward hardly noticed she was there, they were so tied up with Gabriel's problems. As long as Charlie wasn't steaming drunk or arguing with them, they ignored her. Lenny was preoccupied, and even Mary was indifferent to her.

She roamed the fields and woods alone, drinking and sleeping day and night. After a week, during which she felt as if she had entirely disappeared from the normal world, like Brad Pitt in *Interview with a Vampire*, Charlie got up one morning, dressed in her scruffiest jeans, put her school uniform and all her books into her old dufflebag, stole another bottle of wine from the cellar and ran off into the woods to burn the whole useless lot. Every trace of school life was purged in the fire and Charlie felt a glow of satisfaction with the knowledge that she could announce this fire and its victims to her parents – rub their noses in it – the next time the opportunity arose. Which was shortly.

The very next morning Edward came down from another sleepless night to discover Charlie in her jeans, looking all set for a day off. 'Charlotte, why are you not ready for school?'

'I've left,' she replied, setting her face for a fight. 'I expelled myself a couple of days ago.'

Edward's temper immediately flared. 'Oh, don't be ridiculous, Charlotte. You can't just leave school.'

Jessica caught the end of this conversation.

'I've had enough,' Charlie said. 'It's boring. I'm not interested.'

Jessica spoke a little more gently than Edward. 'Have you had an argument with one of your teachers?'

'No.'

'Well, there must be something, darling,' Jessica said.

'It's boring. I hate it. That's all. Right?'

Edward was a little calmer himself, now. 'Have you talked to any of your teachers, Charlie? I . . .'

'No, I don't need to talk to them. I know what they'll say. They'll say what you're saying. They're all stupid.'

That was enough for Edward. 'Charlotte, go upstairs and get dressed this minute. You're going in.' Edward turned to Jessica. 'I'll take her.'

Charlie resorted to her most irritatingly sarcastic tone. 'I just said – I'm not going.'

'Decisions like that are not to be taken lightly.'

'Who said it was taken lightly?'

Edward's anger was on the rise again. 'Neither are they taken alone!'

'You don't know what it's like at school. Nobody likes me.'

Jessica spoke again. 'Charlie, that's not true.'

'Oh, and what would you know?'

'You should have come to talk to us, before you . . .'

Charlie cut Jessica off. 'Talked? To you?'

'Go and get ready for school.' Edward issued the command.

'No.'

Charlie walked away but Edward sprang after her, catching up with her in the kitchen. He caught hold of Charlie's arm and turned her roughly towards him. 'Don't you dare walk away from me when I'm talking to you, young lady!'

'Get off,' Charlie screamed, pulling her arm from her father's grip.

'We are going to talk like two civilised human beings,' Edward shouted.

'Get lost!'

'You will go to school until we have talked to your teachers.'

'Leave me alone!' Charlie was still screaming.

Edward stamped his foot. 'So what is your plan? Will you get a job as a checkout girl? Or a waitress? Have you got any sort of plan beyond missing school today?'

Charlie looked as if she were trying to kill him with her bare eyes.

Edward took this as a sign of victory. 'Now, go and put on your uniform.'

'I burned it.'

'You what?'

'I burned it,' Charlie repeated. 'And all my books – even my bag. I burned the lot of it. Days ago.'

'I sincerely hope you're joking, Charlotte!'

Charlie summoned all her strength for one last yell before she went. 'Piss off!'

It was over before they even knew it. Edward, blinded by a white flash of anger, slapped Charlie across the face with all his might, sending her reeling across the kitchen.

With an enormous effort of will, Charlie held in the tears until she was out of the back door, leaving her parents stunned by the violence of the attack. They both knew that this was surely some kind of turning point.

At Jimmy's flat, Mark was watching *This Morning* on television, cursing Richard and Judy for being the perfect couple and betting himself that they didn't have sex, when Jimmy burst in and told him to come downstairs immediately.

When he got outside Mark couldn't believe his eyes. Parked up was an enormous, authentic vintage car. He was mightily impressed. 'Where did you get that?'

'Mate of mine,' Jimmy said, nonchalantly. 'He's a farmer.'

'Have you bought it?'

'You're kidding. Do you know how much one of these is worth?' Mark shrugged. 'More than I could afford,' Jimmy said. 'Anyway. It's yours. For the day.'

'Wh . . . How do you mean?'

Jimmy grinned. 'Well, I thought you might like to take Lenny out in style. For lunch. There's a hamper in the back – that I *can* afford. I thought you could take her out for a proper picnic. I was going to get it yesterday, but it pissed down, didn't it?'

The look on Mark's face was reward enough for Jimmy. He could tell that his old friend was overwhelmed. For a couple of days relations between them had been strained. Mark was beginning to get depressed. He'd spoken to Lenny a couple of times but not really got anywhere, and at last he'd admitted that something else would be required if he was going to get anywhere. This was just it, they both knew it.

Mark patted Jimmy on the back and guffawed when his friend produced a pair of driving goggles.

'Does this mean I'm forgiven?' Mark said, half seriously.

'I still don't think you deserve her,' Jimmy said and smiled. 'But I want to make Lenny happy. OK?'

When she saw the car, Lenny said, 'Where the hell did you get that?'

Mark said, 'A friend of mine. He's a farmer.'

Lenny looked at him warningly. 'You haven't bought it!'

'Hardly,' Mark said. 'I thought you might come out with me for the day. And I thought we could have a picnic somewhere, there's a traditional hamper in the back.'

Lenny looked in at the hamper and then back at Mark. 'You did, did you?'

Mark nodded. Somehow he achieved a perfect combination of vulnerability and assertiveness — as if he was almost too nervous to ask, but wanted to ask so badly that he had forced himself to do so. It was quite conscious.

'Where would we put Ben?' Lenny said.

'In Mary's arms,' Mark said.

Lenny looked at him, undecided.

'We really need to talk,' Mark said. '*I* really need to talk.'

Still Lenny said nothing. Since her night with Jimmy she had felt like an ordinary woman again, independent, desirable even. Nothing had happened between them, but it had done wonders for her morale. She also felt as if she had one up on Mark, now.

She ran back to the house, only remembering half way that it looked too keen to rush. She slowed herself to a respectable pace.

Mary was waiting, having seen Mark pull up outside. Lenny didn't have to say anything. Mary winked and Lenny was on her way. She paused by the back door for a few moments before reappearing and then walked out, unable to resist a wicked grin.

Edward received a visitor at the office that morning, his old friend Bishop Harris.

They hadn't seen each other since Gabriel had tried to take his life upstairs while the Harrises sat downstairs. They had spoken on the telephone, but so far they had not met.

They talked for some time about Gabriel. It was obvious to Edward that Gabriel's condition, and especially the incident that evening, would affect the decision concerning the bishop's replacement on his retirement. Edward felt that this was for the best, and in his heart he was relieved that he would not now have to turn down the offer.

After ten minutes of conversation about drug addiction and young people and the problems faced by concerned parents everywhere, even in the country, the old man said, 'Edward, I have to tell you that none of this affects the church's thinking on my successor. I'm sure you must have been worried on that score.' Edward's face showed his surprise. 'As we were just saying, Edward, parents everywhere must be concerned; no one is immune from the problems of the day. You are, in the view of the committee, still very much the man for the job.'

'But ... but I'm not sure ... this really is most unexpected,' Edward stammered.

'The ways of God are always that, Edward,' the old man said, smiling.

'I don't know what to say,' Edward muttered.

'You don't have to say anything, Edward, not now. There will be a time for words and, of course, a time for deeds. For now, I would be glad if you could make the announcement on Sunday – I will be there – that I am

311

retiring and that you are to replace me.' The older man smiled. 'If you accept, that is. Make the announcement and leave the rest to the church.'

'Sunday?' Edward said. 'You'll be there on Sunday?'

'Yes, Edward, I wouldn't miss it.'

Edward seemed to have made up his mind and nodded. 'Sunday. Good. Yes. I was going to make Sunday a special day, as it was.'

'Jolly good. Sunday, then.'

Rachel had been waiting for the bishop to leave so that she could speak to Edward.

She found him looking as if he himself needed to talk.

'Sit down, Rachel, please,' Edward said. 'Really, it feels as if the world were about to stop turning.'

Rachel nodded. 'I hear you had an argument with Charlie,' she said.

'Yes, Charlie too.'

Rachel looked at him closely; she was sure he was about to cry.

'I'm very . . . confused at the moment,' he said, 'about several things. Charlie is just one of them. Even Gabriel's problem is not the whole of it.' He paused. 'Jessica . . . doesn't always help me. I sometimes find myself . . . taking her advice against my own judgement. Rachel, I'm very very glad you let me talk to you. Really, I should do it more.'

'Edward, the feeling is mutual . . .'

'I feel as though I blunder on, day in, day out, without taking responsibility, without any true feeling for humanity.'

Rachel began to see that Edward really was troubled by something deeper than Gabriel or Charlie. Perhaps he would tell her about it. She hoped so. She longed for

Edward to confide in her. She felt able to confide in him, and lately she had noticed the toll life was taking on him.

'What do you mean, Edward – responsibility?'

Edward looked at her as if surprised that she was actually listening to what he was saying. 'I feel very empty, Rachel. I feel . . . ineffectual.' He was struggling to say something. 'I've . . . relied on Jessica far too much. I've not been the best husband . . . and now I'm no use to anyone.'

Rachel was shocked at Edward's torpor, seeing it as a clear sign of depression. 'Edward, that's not true. People love you, people respect you,' she said, only to see Edward apparently sink further into himself. 'In what way have you relied on Jessica too much?' she asked. Perhaps there was some clue here, certainly she could imagine Jessica being a dominant force.

Edward patted his heart. 'I have been unkind to Jessica. She has been a fool to trust me.'

'No, Edward, Jessica is . . . Edward, I'm worried about her, about her influence on Gabriel.' She shuffled uncomfortably. 'I don't know how to say this, but I need to say it to someone who understands . . . understands me . . . and Jessica . . .' Edward nodded vaguely. 'Edward, I'm scared of the power she has over Gabriel. I find it . . .'

Edward helped her. 'Disturbing?'

Rachel nodded gratefully. 'Yes.'

'Me too, Rachel.'

'It's not just Gabriel, it's Charlie, too.'

Edward nodded gravely. 'It's all of us.'

Rachel was off. 'If she doesn't let go, they'll never stand on their own two feet. They're never going to stop being weak. They will never take any res . . . responsibility.' Edward nodded and smiled. 'I think it is essential for her to let go of them, or else they will never learn to fend for themselves. Edward, they won't survive.'

313

'This all makes sense,' Edward said.

'I know this sounds mad . . .'

'Please, say it.'

'When Gabriel overdosed . . .' Rachel was speaking with difficulty now. 'I just wondered whether in the back of his mind he knew Jessica would sort it all out. And that's why he went ahead and did it.'

Edward nodded. 'It is time to do something, Rachel.'

'I am doing something. Gabriel and I *are* doing something.'

'Yes. Good. I meant *I* must do something too.'

Rachel looked at his sunken, sad eyes. 'Edward, you don't look well.'

Edward said, 'My heart and soul are sick, Rachel, and I intend to heal them. To make my peace.' Rachel smiled at him. 'Will you be there at the service on Sunday?' he asked. Rachel nodded. 'Please come. Please bring Gabriel. I want everyone to be there.'

As the countryside sped by and Lenny felt the wind in her face, something of her recent life passed before her eyes.

Here she was, in a magnificent vintage car, sitting next to the man she had married, whose son she had borne, a woman in her prime of life. She felt fit, calm and in control. Mark was a bastard. He was handsome, witty, successful, dangerous, yet for weeks he had maintained a vigil in her honour, miles from his home, failing to report for work – she had learned from Jimmy that he had been forging sick notes – risking everything for her. Even that was typical.

Mark wouldn't hire just an ordinary vehicle to take her out and woo her, no, he had to go and get a vintage car and here they were, speeding dangerously through the countryside, alone together. It felt as if she had turned the tables on him.

She felt sexy again, especially after they had drunk a whole bottle of champagne with the picnic and Mark had been more charming to her than she could ever remember. She kept having a vision of them in bed together which took her breath away.

They were talking about how they had become engaged. Lenny was giggling away like a girl. 'I seem to remember you got down on one knee,' she said.

'Did I?' Mark said. 'Like this?'

'That's right. Though I think you were a bit steadier.'

'And I said, Lenny . . .'

'No, you were more formal than that.'

'Ah, yes. I said, Helena, unworthy as I am . . .'

'"Pathetic as I am," you said.'

Mark made a face. 'Are you sure?'

Lenny laughed and nodded.

'Pathetic as I am,' Mark went on, 'to venture such a bold question . . .'

'"Laughable suggestion."'

'Laughable suggestion, I would consider it an honour and a privilege . . .'

'"Consider it above me and beyond me."'

'You've got a good memory, Lenny. Above and beyond me to ask you . . .'

'"Entreat" me.'

'Er, entreat you . . .'

'"Beg" me.'

'Beg you. I'm begging you . . . to be my wife.'

They looked at each other.

'And what did I say?' Lenny asked, grinning.

'You said, OK, I think.'

'What a push-over!' Lenny screamed.

'You were, you know,' Mark laughed.

After a few moments, Lenny asked in a more serious tone, 'When did we stop having fun?'

'Did we?'

'You know we did.'

Mark heaved a sigh. 'I suppose when Ben was born, we couldn't go out so much. Not without organising baby-sitters.'

'It was while I was pregnant.'

Mark hung his head. 'Yes. Yes.' He didn't know what to say to that. So he said, 'I'm sorry.'

Lenny nodded. 'And then after Ben was born, I suppose I . . . *Did* I pay you less attention? Maybe it was my fault too.'

'No, Lenny. It was all my own work. I should have supported you, simple as that.' Lenny looked at him. He said, 'I'm sorry. I really am. That meant nothing . . . *she* meant nothing. I don't know if you can understand that. It was nothing, she was just there. I was weak. And stupid. And it was only once, really. We only . . . stayed together once.'

Lenny sighed. 'Open the other bottle, Mark.'

'I'm driving, don't forget.'

'Well, I'll drink most of it.'

'I can handle it, anyway,' Mark said and poured them a drink after popping the cork loudly. 'I'm sorry, Lenny,' Mark said again.

Lenny looked at him. 'I believe you really are,' she said.

'Nick? It's Charlie.'

There was a pause while Nick took in the information.

'Nick? Are you there?'

'Charlie. Hi.'

'Nick, I know it's been ages since I phoned but I really need to talk to you. Are you doing anything this afternoon?'

'Erm. This afternoon? Er . . .'

'I understand if you don't want to see me, Nick. I was pretty fucking rotten to you.'

'No, no, it's not that, Charlie . . . I was just trying to remember if I was doing anything. I'm supposed to be seeing my mate.'

'OK, don't worry.'

'No, it's OK. I mean, I can see him tomorrow.'

'Are you sure, Nick? I really need to talk to someone.'

'Have you fallen out with Melissa?'

'No, it's not that. I . . . I wanted to see you, that's all.'

Nick was clearly having difficulty believing his ears. 'Yeah, yeah. OK. What time? Where?'

'How about the Star in Market Cross?'

'The Star?' Nick didn't like the sound of that. The Star was the pub where all the bikers went. It had a bad reputation locally.

'What's wrong?' Charlie asked. 'Have you never been there?'

'No – yeah – no . . . I mean, it's fine. Fine. What time?'

'I'm there now.'

'What? On your own?'

'Yeah.'

Again there was a short silence while Nick took in this information. He decided she was probably safe – it *was* only lunchtime.

'OK. I'll come now.'

'Thanks, Nick. I really appreciate it.'

Jimmy came back to his flat to discover the car parked outside.

It was due back in twenty minutes. When he got upstairs he found an empty champagne bottle on the table

317

in the living room. Closer inspection revealed Lenny's shoes and then her skirt.

Then he heard them making love. Or rather, he heard Lenny crying out. It hit him hard in the gut. He stood stock still, listening intently, unable to tear himself away from the sound that was not pleasing him in the least. Jimmy was shocked at the force of his reaction. He was hotly jealous, but at the same time transfixed. He was projected back to the night he and Lenny had spent together; he cursed himself for being so nice as not to ask Lenny to make love to him. For once in their lives they could have made love, as adults, after their years of love and friendship. He cursed Mark for his infidelity, cursed the world for being a place where those that pushed and grabbed and cheated won through, took the women, gathered the spoils, while ordinary, decent men like himself went without.

Not that he would have changed his life. He loved his work, he loved a quiet life, he loved to get up late and then exert himself physically outdoors. He had enough to support himself, enough to live well, but he did not have a woman to love. Not the woman he wanted, the woman he had always wanted, the woman he could now hear vigorously making love to his best friend.

He slumped miserably into a chair and listened to her. He knew when she came, he felt it, and treasured it, knowing in his heart that he would never again hear the sound, and that he would never spend another night with her as long as he breathed.

When it was over he heard the door open in the passage and he nipped into the kitchen before whoever it was came into the living room to discover him.

It was Lenny. 'Jimmy! Hi. I didn't know you were here,' she said, blushing, wondering if Jimmy had heard anything.

'Just got in,' Jimmy said. 'Putting the kettle on.'

'Sorry,' Lenny said. 'I borrowed your dressing gown.'

Jimmy could see that. 'Did you have a nice picnic?'

'Yes, it was lovely. Really. Mark said you were out for the day.'

'I have to take the car back. It was due ten minutes ago. I guess the keys are in Mark's pocket?'

Lenny frowned. 'You organised the car?'

Jimmy realised his mistake. 'Er, it was Mark's idea.'

'And the hamper?'

Jimmy nodded. 'Same.'

Lenny smiled at him, then she came over and hugged him.

'I take it things are back on course, then?' Jimmy said.

'Possibly,' Lenny said. 'Probably.' She smiled up at him. 'I'll get the keys.'

Considering that Charlie wanted to talk, Nick thought she was being pretty uncommunicative.

He thought she had changed since the last time they had met. Her clothes seemed different, or was it her look? She looked older, really. Rougher in a way. Less like a schoolgirl. Sexier.

As soon as he arrived at the Star, Charlie ran over and gave him a hug.

'Let's get out of here,' she said, much to Nick's relief.

He followed where she wanted to go, asking a few questions – about Thomas, about friends they had in common – but, unusually, Charlie didn't say much, insisting that they spend the afternoon in the park.

When they'd walked for about half a mile and found the hut next to the old golf course, Charlie produced a little slip of paper from her pocket. She seemed nervous suddenly, as if she was trying to say something. Then she said it. 'Have you ever tried speed, Nick? I've got some here.' Nick shook his head. 'Do you want to try it?'

After a moment, Nick shook his head again.

Charlie tutted. 'You never were much fun, Nick.'

·20·

EDWARD HAD MADE a great fuss to ensure the whole family were at church on Sunday morning.

In the end, the only person who didn't turn up was Charlie who, much to Edward's annoyance, hadn't been seen for a couple of days.

'Do you think we should call the police, Edward?' Jessica said.

'No, Jessica, that will only play into her hands. She's trying to get a reaction. We must leave her to her own devices.'

Jessica would have disagreed, but she was too concerned about Edward. He had been distant for some days now and his attitude to the service today had made her both nervous and at times downright suspicious. Mary said she thought Edward was going to make an announcement, but Jessica remained sceptical.

She spoke to Edward as he was preparing for the service.

'Edward, you know that Patrick Harris and his wife are here, don't you?'

'Yes, Jessica, he came to see me the other day and told me.'

'Did he say anything about . . . his retirement?'

'Yes.'

'Yes? Edward, why didn't you tell me?'

'I've already discussed the matter with you.'

'What did he say . . . is he . . . are you to replace him?'

'Please, Jessica, leave me. I'm about to . . . I'm going to celebrate mass.'

Jessica looked at him. She was scared. 'Please, Edward, please think of me. Of *us*. Your family.'

'I shall act with your best interests at heart.'

When Jessica left him, he took off his bishop's vestments, bowed to the cross on the wall and prayed for the strength he needed.

It was only when Jessica saw Edward approaching the altar – led by the altar-servers, carrying the cross and the candles – dressed in his ordinary day wear that the fear really set in.

Instead of going to the altar as he normally would have, Edward genuflected, allowed the altar-servers to take up their usual positions and then made his way solemnly to the pulpit. When he arrived he turned to face the large congregation and with a very sad expression on his face, said, 'Will you all sit down, please.'

Perplexed, the whole congregation sat, with the exception of Jessica who, transfixed, remained on her feet, overwhelmed by a feeling of dread. Mary, who was next to her, touched Jessica's arm and she sat down. Jessica looked over at Bishop Harris who raised his eyebrows to her as if to say: I'm afraid I don't know what this is about either.

'I know this isn't the conventional way to start a service,' Edward said, in something not quite resembling his usual tone. 'You'll have to forgive me. What I have to say to you is difficult . . .'

322

Jessica felt as if her heart might leap from her chest to silence him.

'If I falter . . . I apologise. Forgive me. Many times, standing here before you, I've talked about love – the love of God. What that means. And how the love of God is different – very different – from other forms of love – from the way we love one another . . . our families . . . those close to us . . .'

Jessica felt rage welling up within her. Out of the corner of her eye she could see other members of the congregation exchanging glances, already whispering.

'Human love is often tinged with impurities. With jealousy. Selfishness. A desire . . . to hurt another . . .' Edward had begun to stammer. 'And sometimes . . . to protect . . . those we love . . . we do things that are equally wrong. Things which show a lack of faith . . . in God.'

At this point Jessica stood up. She was in the front row, directly in Edward's line of sight. When he saw her, his voice wavered even more and he began to hurry what he was saying.

'I love my family . . . in my . . . desire to protect them, I have . . . failed you. I have . . . failed God. Some of you . . . perhaps all of you will be unable to forgive me . . . for what I have done . . . but now . . . I seek only God's forgiveness.' Edward began to cry and he was shaking badly, as if he might break down and sob uncontrollably. Again he tried to speed up what he was saying. 'I feel I must tell you the truth. Anne Fraser . . . was loved by a great many people in the parish . . .'

There was a general uncomfortable shuffle among the congregation. Jessica could listen to no more. She stepped forward, briskly.

'Annie was caring . . . caring and thoughtful . . . she was a woman who shouldn't have died when she did. She

323

should be here with us now.' Great sobs bubbled up as Edward spoke. 'It is my fault ... it is because I ... because of me that she is not here with us today ...'

Jessica was by his side. Edward felt the need to shout out his guilt, but found the words had snagged somewhere inside him. Before he knew it, his wife's arms were about him and he was being led away by her and by Mary. Gabriel and Rachel were following close behind, but Mary asked them to stay in the church.

Bishop Harris was able to step in to conduct the service. On reflection, he decided that it was probably not the right time to make his announcement regarding his retirement and Edward's appointment in his stead.

As soon as she got Edward into the vestry, Jessica sat him down and spoke firmly to him.

'Edward, you must come home, to bed. You must sleep.'

Edward shook his head. 'I am not a child, Jessica.'

Jessica struggled to control herself. 'That's exactly what you are, Edward.' She watched him put his head into his hands and spoke more softly. 'Let me help you, Edward, *please.*'

Before anything more could be said, Mary came into the room, looking pale and frightened. 'What's wrong?' she asked.

Jessica gestured. 'Not now, Mary.'

'Everyone's shaken. Gabriel was going to come ...'

'They all should know,' Edward said. 'I'll go back.'

Jessica pressed Edward back into his seat. 'No! You'll come home with me.'

'People will want to know something,' Mary said. 'What shall I tell them?'

Edward cut in. 'Tell them I killed Anne Fraser.' Jessica and Mary exchanged a glance. Edward would not be stopped. 'Tell them that my wife will not accept the fact that I pushed her down the stairs, in anger, to silence her, because she was threatening to ruin me ... because she was carrying my child. Tell them I went round to her house to seduce her into submission – that I *did* seduce her into submission – or I thought I had – but when I realised that my efforts had failed, we fought, at the top of the stairs and in frustration and in anger I threw her down. And that in doing so I was glad of her pain, that I wanted to crush her into silence and afterwards I was glad, in my heart I was glad that she would not be able to betray me. And I did nothing to help her, I abandoned her there to die alone.' Both women were staring at Edward; Mary in horror, Jessica in awe. Jessica knew that she had to let Edward continue. 'Tell the good people of this world that I turned to my wife for help. I lied to her in order to obtain her support. I told her that Anne had fallen. My wife ... my own wife returned to the scene of the crime and removed all the evidence that I had been to the house. Then she too abandoned Anne Fraser to her lonely death.'

Edward stopped talking. Nobody moved.

It was a full minute before Edward went on, relieved that he had at last spoken the truth to another person. 'It was a split second, but that is no excuse. In that second, for the first time in years, I knew exactly what to do. And for the first time in years, I did it.'

Now it was Jessica's turn. 'Edward, you're unhinged. If you look to purge all your past sins with this one absurd confession, if you think for one moment that I am going to let you tell this ridiculous story to the world ...' She turned to Mary. 'You know it's madness, don't you, Mary?'

Mary nodded very slightly, not quite meeting Jessica's eye.

'You know the dangers of whispering and gossip – especially in a small parish, don't you, Mary?'

Again Mary's vague nod.

After a moment, Mary said, 'I'll go and take care of the family. You had better get Edward home to bed.'

After the service everyone was very sympathetic.

They were told that Edward was suffering a nervous breakdown and Jessica had called the doctor who had recommended rest. Bishop Harris was very understanding indeed and his wife, Ellen, said that her brother, a bishop in southern England, had experienced something similar last year, and he was now back at work and stronger for the experience. The old couple sent Edward their regards and insisted that Mary contact them if there was anything they could do.

Gabriel was convinced that everything was his fault.

'He thinks I feel nothing for him,' he said to Rachel, after the service.

'Nonsense, Gabriel,' Rachel said. 'He understands about your problem.'

'No, Rachel. Don't you remember how upset he was when I told him that I wanted to . . . that he had been outside the door . . .' Gabriel hung his head.

Rachel took his arm. 'Gabriel, you have to let all that go. Do you love Edward?'

'Of course I do.'

'Well, then. You have to make yourself better. That's the best you can do.'

'I want so much to be free of all this,' he said.

'We will be,' Rachel said. 'We will be.'

Everyone else tended to blame it on Charlie. They knew Edward was worried. They knew Edward and Charlie had fought.

They sat round the kitchen table when they returned

326

from the service and the subject of Charlie having gone missing came up. Gabriel was incensed. 'You mean Charlie hasn't been home for days and no one told me?'

'Oh, yeah,' Lenny said. 'I'm sure there's lot you can do for Charlie when you can't even look after yourself.'

Gabriel wanted to shout at Lenny for that, but he knew that what she had said was true. 'I can look for her,' Gabriel said, standing up.

'Just you look after yourself, Gabriel,' Mary said. 'You've already given us enough to worry about.'

'I'm sure she's out there somewhere – somewhere I should know. It'd be just like her. She always wanted to be like her big brother.'

Rachel laughed without humour. 'More fool her.'

Mary remembered something. 'Oh, Gabriel. Nick phoned.'

'Nick?'

'Charlie's old boyfriend.'

'Oh, Nick.'

'Said he wanted to speak to you.'

'What did he want?'

Mary shrugged. 'He didn't say.'

Gabriel thought it might have something to do with Charlie so he phoned him right away.

It *was* something to do with Charlie.

'Hi, Nick, it's Gabriel.'

'Gabriel, hi.' Nick sounded relieved to hear from him.

After a few brief and slightly awkward pleasantries, Gabriel said, 'Is it Charlie? Have you seen her?'

'Yeah, I saw her a couple of days ago.'

'Where is she? Is she all right?'

'She's . . . I don't know where she is . . . I'm not sure she's all right.'

'What makes you say that?' Nick hesitated. 'Nick, you can tell me, I'm not her dad.'

'Yeah, I know.' Still he hesitated.

'Is she using drugs?'

'Yeah . . . yeah, she is.'

'Is she using gear? I mean, heroin.'

'I don't know. I think it was speed. But . . . you know . . .'

'What?'

Nick sighed. 'Well, I don't know much about drugs, but I thought speed was supposed to make you . . . well, speed up.'

'What happened?'

'Well, she didn't inject anything, but she certainly didn't speed up. She fell asleep on me, in the park. And she was sick.'

Gabriel swore. 'How did she take it?'

'She sniffed it.'

Gabriel thanked Nick and put the phone down. 'She wants to be me,' he said.

Upstairs in their bedroom, Jessica was trying her best to reason with Edward.

'Forgive my ignorance on the subject,' she was saying, 'but if a man does something wrong and feels the compulsion, the *need* to confess his sin . . . Edward! I'm talking to you! I want you to tell me the church's position on this. If a man wants to confess to a sin and face the punishment, if he sees this atonement as the way to save his soul but the act of confession itself will create even more intense suffering for the innocents who surround him and destroy all the good works he has spent his life creating,' she looked at Edward, willing him to see sense, 'is the act of attempting to save his own soul then simply an expression of the vice of selfishness? Edward! Answer me!'

Edward was adrift, his eyes sunken. 'I do not do it to make my peace with God. I don't even know if he exists.'

'Perhaps God does exist,' she said. 'Perhaps he is talking to you, through me.'

'You the voice of God?' Edward said, disdainfully.

'I'm saying I might be the voice of love, love of family. We may have failed our children – I'm fully willing to concede that – but I don't wish to destroy them. Do you, Edward? Do your children mean nothing to you?'

'I mean nothing to them. And they . . . feel a very long way off, Jessica. It feels as if there is no one, nobody.'

'There's me, Edward. There's your wife.'

He looked at her cruelly. 'A sham. A charade. You want me to continue to play a part so that you can control them.'

Jessica was staggered. '*Control?* Protect, Edward. Love them. I have done nothing but try to love my family!'

'You've choked them. Just as you're choking me.'

Jessica's anger took hold of her. She stood up and paced as she spoke. 'How dare you, Edward! I've lived through your affairs! I've put up with all your childishness, I've stood by you! Do you think it was easy to do that? Do you think that made me feel whole? And human? I have wanted to stand up in my pew and denounce you for years, Edward, listening to you spouting your hypocrisies about Christian love and fellowship, while all the time you were torturing me!' Tears of anger shone in her eyes. 'But I held my peace, Edward, I swallowed my pride and sat there praying . . . praying to the Lord with the rest of those vile busybodies who would love the slightest chance to see me crawling through the mud. Those jealous, back-stabbing . . . Gaghh!' She broke off with a vicious curse.

Edward looked up at her and said, 'Do you believe . . . perhaps it's possible . . . we can't go back . . . but maybe

329

we just . . . lost our love. Sometimes I think that's what I've done with God. Misplaced him. Put him down somewhere.' Jessica felt a pang of relief; Edward sounded a little more optimistic, suddenly. 'I need to remember, Jessica. I need to remember how we loved.'

Jessica sat down next to him on the bed and stroked his head, held him at her breast. 'Oh, we loved, Edward,' she said with effort.

He nodded faintly. 'Yes. We loved.'

Jessica held him there, hoping that his line of reasoning was that they could honour that old bond, and move forward together, at last.

'I remember how much I needed you,' Edward was saying. 'How much I yearned for you. You have no idea.'

'I have some idea, Edward,' Jessica said, automatically.

'You remember?'

Jessica nodded. 'I remember.'

Edward raised his head and looked at his wife. Then he kissed her lightly on the lips. Jessica felt revolted by this display of affection, but rather than push him away as she felt like doing, she remained motionless, simply not responding. Edward began to kiss her cheeks, softly, saying how he longed to feel love again, how he needed it. Then he kissed her lips again, this time more forcefully.

Jessica pulled back, but still managed to speak softly so as not to upset him further. 'No, Edward, not yet, please. It will take time.'

Edward looked at her urgently now. 'No, Jessica. It takes only memory. Can't you feel it?' he said and began kissing her neck with some passion.

Jessica's heart leapt in terror. 'Edward, I can't suddenly turn from black memories into sunshine! Edward! I can't!'

Edward pushed his wife back on to the bed. 'Jessica, I love you, I have always loved you, you have to believe

330

that,' he said as he nuzzled her greedily and pushed his hand up her skirt.

Jessica struggled to protect herself from the onslaught, begging her husband to desist, but the more she struggled the more Edward fought her. He implored her to kiss him, to take off her clothes, utterly oblivious to, or worse, taking pleasure in, her humiliation.

'Jessica, let me touch you,' he said, in a commanding tone. He pulled at her skirt and when it came loose tugged at her underwear. Jessica felt herself obscenely exposed. She pulled vainly at her skirt and gripped his rough, hairy hand. Suddenly he seemed very strong.

Her voice was weaker than it had ever been before, her hissing and her imploring seemed pathetic and girlish in the face of the assault. When she summoned her most commanding tone, she found only a whimper of unconvincing complaint. Her tights and pants were round her knees and Edward was looking down on her, holding her down cruelly, painfully, and attempting to undo his trousers. Then he climbed on her, kissing her protesting mouth. Jessica pounded him ineffectually with her fists, but felt unable to raise her voice for fear of raising alarm.

Suddenly Mary was standing there, shouting Edward's name.

All at once Edward realised that Jessica was crying and hitting him, calling him a monster. It was as if he had awoken from a nightmare to find himself attacking his own wife, while her friend looked on in disgust. He rolled off and sat up, awkwardly doing up his trousers, while Jessica pulled up her pants and adjusted her clothing. As soon as she could, Jessica stood angrily over him.

'Look at him, Mary,' she gasped, with undisguised hatred. 'Look at this monster! This is the man that I once loved!' She turned on Mary and laughed viciously,

331

pointing at her. 'Ha! And that is the man you've worshipped! Did he take you like this? Was that what you liked? Did you enjoy the violence?'

Mary shook her head in horror. She was shocked enough without this attack from Jessica. Besides which, she was shocked that Jessica knew of her mistake with Edward, committed all those years ago.

'Don't play the innocent with me!' Jessica hissed. 'You might have charmed him with that! You might have thought he felt something for you, but now you see the real Edward.' Mary started to protest, but Jessica silenced her with a wave of her hand. 'Don't pretend!' Jessica went on. 'Do you think I haven't always known why you stayed all these years, allowing us to treat you like a serf? I knew exactly what you were dreaming of,' Jessica spat, grabbing hold of Mary's arm and hurling her across the room. 'Go on! Go to him, if he's what you want, you can have him!'

Mary was aghast. 'Jessica, no! I don't love Edward. That's not right! I don't want him . . .'

It was as if Edward was no longer there.

'Well, what is it? What is it you want?'

Mary looked down, timid and lost. 'A family,' she stammered. 'I wanted a family to love, a family to love me. I love you all. You're all I have,' she said, and gave herself up to the tears that shook her.

Edward had been put to bed.

Jessica knocked on Mary's bedroom door. 'He did kill her,' she said, without ceremony.

'I know he did,' Mary said. 'What matters is saving the family.'

Jessica flopped on to the bed, exhausted. 'Is there anything to save?' she said.

'Oh, yes,' Mary replied. 'Edward is calmer. I gave him

some of my tranquillisers. So long as we can keep him from telling the whole world, we're safe.'

Jessica looked at her. 'It's not the whole world we have to worry about, now, Mary,' she said. 'It's Rachel.'

'Rachel?'

Jessica nodded. 'She knows. Edward told her about Anne and the baby – not that he had slept with her, but that she was pregnant. He talks to her. I don't know what it is between them. As far as I can tell it's innocent. But Rachel uses him, to keep in with the family. She encourages him to talk to her and . . . you know Edward with young women.'

'Rachel?' Mary said.

'We've got to keep Edward quiet.'

'I'll speak to him,' Mary said.

'I'll speak to her,' Jessica said.

Edward awoke in the spare room.

Mary was sitting by the bed when he opened his eyes.

'Mary? Where am I?'

'This is the spare room, Edward.'

'My head . . .'

'Here, take some of these. Two now, two later.'

'Mary, I . . .'

'Please, Edward.'

Edward did as he was told.

'Now, Edward, dress yourself.'

Edward looked at her. 'Mary, did you spend the night here? With me?'

Mary nodded. 'We were worried about you, Edward. We're still worried about you.'

Edward's voice was very weak. 'I'm not well, Mary.'

'I know, Edward. Come. Get out of bed. Kneel here with me. Confess your sins.'

'You think I should confess?'

'To God, Edward.'

'There is no God, Mary. No God who will listen to me.'

Mary spoke very earnestly. 'Be patient, Edward. You have sinned. God is not pleased with you. But you must ask him to forgive you. Wait for the still small voice. Then let God guide you, speak to no one until you hear God's voice.'

An hour later Edward appeared downstairs, dressed for work.

He was stooping and seemed very distant.

Jessica said, 'Good morning, Edward.'

'Morning.'

'Where are you going?'

'Er, to work.'

'No, Edward. I've phoned Simon. I've explained that you will be having a few days off.'

'I'm perfectly able to work, Jessica, it is what I need to do.'

'Edward!' It was the closest Jessica had ever come to screaming at him. 'Last evening you tried to rape me. Before that you tried to condemn your whole family to ruin from the pulpit.' Edward was rocking himself back and forth. 'You are not well. Now rest!' It was an order.

'What did I say?'

Jessica frowned. 'Enough.'

Edward shook his head and muttered to himself. 'No. No. It wasn't enough.'

'You need to rest.'

'I have things to do.'

'Rest!'

Edward laughed. 'What is it, Jessica, you mean to lock me away?'

Jessica's eyes flashed. 'That's exactly what I'm trying to save you from.'

'I don't want to be saved,' Edward said.

'That's a strange statement from a man of the cloth.'

'What do you suggest, Jessica, that I grant myself absolution?'

'Only Christ can do that.'

'Do you believe that?'

'I believe in it more than I do in the police.'

'Anne believed,' Edward said.

'Oh, well, I'm glad you found time to discuss spiritual matters,' Jessica spat.

'We didn't,' Edward replied. 'But perhaps we should have.'

Jessica stood up. 'Edward, are you going to go to work?'

He looked up at her, remembering his humiliation last night. He felt his will drain away, he felt sleepy, and ruined. 'No,' he said. 'I'm going to rest.'

Rachel had a great love for the church when it was empty: the cool, dark air, the smell of polish from the old wooden pews, carved in that intricate Victorian lattice style.

She was taking a few minutes to herself in the church when Jessica approached. Rachel was surprised. 'I thought you would be spending the day with Edward,' she said.

Jessica shook her head. 'He's resting.'

Rachel nodded. 'Is there anything I can do?'

'I rather wanted to talk to you, Rachel.'

They sat together in the first pew, overlooking the great ornate altar, beneath the spires of the mock-gothic arches that seemed to stretch into an eternity of blackness above.

The two women had managed to stay out of each

335

other's way since Rachel's failed attempt to wrest Gabriel from Jessica's control, but Rachel had felt better for the separation. At least she now knew where she stood. She no longer felt threatened by Jessica's thinly disguised hostility towards her; indeed, lately Rachel had come to look upon Jessica rather as a pathetic, neurotic woman than as a tyrant. Now she had won Gabriel's confidence, she believed it was only a matter of time before they would finally get away from this ridiculous game-playing for ever. She wondered what on earth Jessica could want to talk to her about.

'How *is* Edward, Jessica?' she asked.

Jessica looked at her and said, 'I've come to ask you for help, Rachel.'

Rachel was surprised. 'As I said, if there's anything I can do . . .'

Jessica chose her words carefully. 'I'm aware how supportive you are trying to be, Rachel. And I'm afraid that's rather the problem. Edward is . . . well, you can see, the man *is* going through a deep crisis of faith. Outside the church they might even call it a nervous breakdown. And they would suggest certain remedies. But those within the church understand something of the complexities of a man searching to reaffirm his faith, to rediscover his soul. That's why I thought it better to have this conversation here, in the church. The words might seem odd in any other place. And I am well aware that those who do not share this faith can find it difficult to comprehend – they might even misunderstand something a man says in the dark night of the soul.' Jessica looked at Rachel. 'Do you understand what I am saying?'

As she listened, Rachel felt her old anger rising. Again she felt Jessica was attacking her, more or less telling her to stay away from Edward, that she was harming him. What did the woman expect her to do? Disappear? Not only was Edward very dear to Rachel – possibly her only friend in the area – but she believed that she could help him. Hadn't Edward implicitly acknowledged this to her, hinting in his own way that Rachel could help him where perhaps his own wife could not?

'Unless I'm mistaken,' Rachel replied, 'I believe you're telling me to stay away from Edward.'

Jessica caught the tone of indignation. 'I know you're trying to help Edward,' she said, the friendliness in her voice sounding false, 'but I can assure you, you are not. I know you mean well . . . but as you've shown before, meaning well and doing it are two different things.'

Now Rachel really was angry, but she decided to listen and gather some ammunition before replying. Jessica was talking about the way Edward had taken Anne Fraser's death to heart, how he had been very close to Anne; and then about how Edward had been very upset about Gabriel's attempt at suicide; then she made another long speech about the church and the need for a man to question his faith without *interference* from outside. As she listened, Rachel suddenly remembered the scene she had witnessed the day after Anne's funeral: Edward saying a prayer for Anne's baby, how upset he had been. She remembered, too, Edward's words from the pulpit the day he had broken down, the way Jessica had reacted, which had seemed odd at the time. In an instant Rachel knew that Anne had been carrying Edward's baby and that Jessica was worried in case Rachel found out.

'Jessica,' Rachel interrupted suddenly, 'this is about Edward and Anne Fraser, isn't it?' Jessica looked so shocked that Rachel knew she was right. 'That's why you are telling me to stay away from him, isn't it?'

Jessica hesitated. 'Edward . . . told you something about Anne Fraser?'

Rachel chose her words carefully. 'Don't you mean

told me about Anne's baby?' she asked, and tried to make the question sound significant.

Jessica looked at Rachel for a long time. 'What *exactly* did Edward tell you?' she asked at last.

Rachel couldn't resist it. 'What do you *think* he told me, Jessica?' she said, harshly.

'Don't play games with me, Rachel!' Jessica hissed.

The ferociousness of Jessica's expression increased Rachel's certainty. 'I can assure you I'm not playing games!' Rachel replied, surprised by her own vehemence. 'Edward and I are very close. I . . . feel for him. He has spoken to me in confidence. I have not repeated any of it. Not even to Gabriel.' Rachel was trembling, terrified suddenly, because although she knew she had a hand to play, she was not quite sure what was in it.

Then Rachel realised that the look on Jessica's face was not, as she had first thought, one of anger, it was fear. Jessica was perched anxiously on the edge of the pew, looking tired and ill and frightened. Rachel felt her confidence return. 'But you were right about one thing, Jessica,' she said. 'Church is not really my place. And I think you're right that it's probably wise for me to stay out of your world. And . . . I'm willing to do so, too. On one condition.'

For a while they sat there in the semi-darkness. Rachel held her breath. Was it possible that she had stumbled upon something that could make Jessica release her grip on her son? Was it possible that they were having the conversation Rachel thought they were having? Rachel's head swam. She was threatening Jessica, but did she really have anything to threaten her with? Did Jessica even know she was being threatened? It was impossible, surely, utterly mad. But then why did Jessica look so worried?

At last Jessica spoke. 'What's the condition, Rachel?'

It's true! Rachel thought. 'I'll leave Edward to you, Jessica, if you leave Gabriel to me.'

Jessica's mouth tightened. 'Gabriel is my *son*!'

Rachel raised her eyebrows. 'Gabriel is my *husband*!'

There was another long silence until Jessica said, 'You're a very determined woman, Rachel.'

Rachel laughed coldly. 'And so are you.'

Jessica snapped into polite mode again, as if she had this sort of conversation every day. She nodded and smiled, then she stood. 'I don't want to keep Edward waiting too long,' she said.

Rachel said, 'No, I understand. Goodbye, Jessica.'

As soon as she got back to the house, Jessica took Mary into the drawing room.

Jessica was shaking with anger. Mary poured her a sherry which she drank in one go, shuddering as she did so.

'She's a snake, Mary, a snake! Something has to be done about her!'

Mary nodded gravely. 'He telephoned her at work, just now.'

'Who? What?'

'Edward telephoned Rachel just now. I found him in the study, on the telephone. When I went in he went quiet, so I listened in on the upstairs extension.'

'What was he saying?'

'Oh, nothing. I think I caught him early. He was just apologising for letting her down. At work, I think he meant.'

Jessica stood stock still. 'What happened?'

'Well, before he could say anything I went back into the study and stood over him. Huh, he wasn't on long after that. But he did say that he'd call in and see her.'

'What did she say to that?'

339

Mary shrugged. 'I don't know. Nothing.'

'Snake!' Jessica said again. 'How has she managed to worm her way into his confidence. Why?' Again Mary shrugged. 'I'll tell you why,' Jessica said, 'because she's out to destroy us. She'd do anything to get Gabriel away from us, she said as much today.' Jessica cursed to herself. 'Without her interference we could save Gabriel and Edward, but . . .' Her shoulders drooped. 'I'm lost, Mary. We're lost.'

'No,' Mary said, firmly. 'No. We must control Edward until he can control himself. I've given him some more of my pills. They're very strong – I've put some more in his food. I'll go and get more this evening. We must be patient. We must fight.'

Jessica nodded and took a deep sigh, looking sadly at Mary. 'I must surrender Gabriel,' she said. 'I must surrender him.'

·21·

G ABRIEL WAS HAVING his morning injection as usual.

'Aren't you worried about Charlie, mum?'

'Of course I'm worried. But what am I supposed to do? I tried everything to stop you going down the path she seems determined to tread, and it never did anything. Until you came crawling back, there was nothing I could do.'

'Charlie's not like me, mum.'

'Oh, she is.'

'No, mum, she's a girl.'

'Well, if she comes crawling back looking for help, I'll do my best.'

'She might not come crawling back.'

'You did, Gabriel.'

'Yes, but only because I found Rachel.' Jessica looked at him. He went on, 'It's different for girls, mum. Guys get it one way, it's completely different for girls. A lot worse. There's less of a chance she'll come back.'

Jessica sighed. 'Do you think I should call the police?'

Gabriel shook his head. 'I'm going to look for her. Today.'

Jessica nodded.

Gabriel was amazed. 'Aren't you going to try and stop me?'

'No, Gabriel. This is the end of the road for me and you. From now on you do your own thing.'

He looked at her uncertainly. 'What do you mean?'

'I mean, if you want to risk everything looking for your sister, that's up to you. This is the last time I'm going to do your injection, Gabriel. When you go, you can take this stuff with you. Ask Rachel to help you.'

'No, mother.'

'I can't keep hold of you. The family falls apart the more I try to hold it together. Now I have to hold myself together. And your father. You have a wife who loves you. I don't want to come between that.'

'But you haven't.'

'Rachel believes I have.'

Gabriel shook his head. 'Then I'll talk to her.'

'No, Gabriel. She's right. She's your wife and she shouldn't be cut out of standing by you. It is your world and hers. I don't want to be a part of it any more.'

Gabriel felt tears welling up.

'Go away from here, Gabriel,' Jessica said. 'Go and look for Charlie if you must, but then get out of here. Go away, both of you, somewhere that you can breathe. And survive. Please survive . . .'

'Mum, you've got it all wrong.'

'Yes, Gabriel, and this is the only way to put it right. Now, hold still,' she said, and pressed the plunger of the syringe.

Stunned by the drugs and by the news he had just received, Gabriel hardly noticed that Lenny was talking to him at first.

342

'Gabriel, did you hear me? I'm leaving this afternoon. With Mark. We're going back to Oxford.'

He looked at her. 'Going?'

'Yeah.'

Gabriel shook his head. 'I didn't even know you and Mark had made it up.'

'Oh, right, Mr Ear-to-the-Ground.'

'Sorry, Lenny. I mean, that's great.'

'Yeah.'

'Me and Rachel are going too.'

Lenny was staggered. 'Going? Where to?'

Gabriel shrugged and then laughed at his own absurdity. 'Huh, dunno – away.'

Lenny put her hand on his arm. 'Good,' she said. 'How's mum taken it?'

'She suggested it.'

Gabriel and Lenny looked at one another as if the sun had just come up green.

'What about Charlie?' Lenny asked when she'd digested this information.

'I'm going to find her.'

'Take her with you.'

'Huh,' Gabriel laughed again. 'I doubt she'd come.'

Lenny put her hand on Gabriel's arm again. 'We've *all* got to get away from here – seriously. It's lethal.'

Gabriel nodded.

When Gabriel returned to the Lodge, he told Rachel what his mother had said. She pretended to be surprised.

'Zing go those apron strings.' It wasn't hard for her to pretend because she was so pleased.

'At first it terrified me, injecting myself again,' Gabriel said. 'But then I realised she's right. I realised how much of a strain it's been for her. You should have seen her face.' He looked down. 'I wish I'd realised it myself.'

Rachel put her arm on his. 'I'll help.'

He looked at her. 'Will you help me? I know I'm asking a lot. But I really do feel I can make it.'

'You've said that before, Gabriel.'

Gabriel shook his head vehemently. 'No, Rachel. It's different this time. This time it'll just be you and me. I don't want to be dependent any more. I mean, it'll be you and me, together, as equals.'

Rachel smiled. Gabriel was irresistible when his eyes shone with hope like that. 'And we'll go away?' she said.

'We can pack as soon as I get back.'

Rachel looked at him. 'You're still going to look for Charlie?'

Gabriel nodded. 'I'm going now.' Rachel looked at him. 'Trust me, Rachel.'

She nodded. 'I'll start packing straight away.'

Gabriel smiled. 'Right.'

Rachel said, 'By the way, where are we going to live?'

When Gabriel shrugged, they both burst out laughing.

Jessica was downstairs, when someone knocked at the door.

It was Patrick Harris, retiring bishop; the last thing Jessica needed. With a great effort she stretched her face into a smile and shook his hand. 'Patrick, what a pleasant surprise.'

'Yes, Jessica, I was passing and I wondered . . . I mean, I wanted to see Edward, if I may.'

'Er, I'm afraid he's asleep upstairs. The doctor has given him a sedative and strict instructions to rest.'

The old bishop smiled kindly and shifted awkwardly from one leg to the other. 'Oh, yes, yes. I should have telephoned ... only ... I did want to speak to him personally. He seems very troubled.'

'Impossibly so, I'm afraid. I'll tell him you called.'

'Have you any idea what might be troubling him, Jessica?'

Jessica nodded sagely. 'It's the children. I mean, you've seen for yourself the suffering poor Gabriel has been through. Edward thought his son was dead, and now Charlotte, our youngest daughter, she's going through her own difficulties ... Oh, not the same thing, no. I mean, you know adolescents ...' Jessica was aware that she sounded jumpy, but felt powerless to correct it. She felt as if she were saying: I'm begging you, don't write Edward off, he must have that job! 'I mean, Edward took his secretary's death very badly, they were very close ... and of course our other daughter has been living with us, but things are working out and she'll soon be returning to Oxford to resume normal married life ...'

She had to stop. She was sounding ridiculous. She looked at the old bishop imploringly, but saw something in his face that she didn't like: doubt, or was it pity?

'Well, Jessica, I understand, of course. Family life is never simple, as I've learned myself.'

'Yes, it's never easy, and of course Edward is very much looking forward to taking up his new duties. I do feel that a new job will give him something to occupy ... to help him restructure his life ...' Again she trailed off.

The old man spoke firmly. 'I'm afraid decisions regarding Edward's future have been put on hold for the time being, Jessica, until such time as Edward is fully recovered. I had hoped to tell Edward myself.'

Jessica tried to reply but had to make do with a stiff nod.

'Yes, well, Jessica, I must be going. Ellen sends her regards. God bless.'

And God bless you and yours! Jessica thought bitterly, as she watched the old man retreat down the path and climb hastily into his car.

Gabriel knew this part of the city of old.

The drab old buildings that remained among the so-called regeneration seemed all the more bleak now, surrounded as they were by the gleaming, sinister façades of the new-age buildings. He thought how the reflective glass of the new towers gave them the smug impression of a uniformed man wearing mirrored sun-glasses.

He knew where to look for Charlie, among the caravans and green-and-black painted trucks parked up in one of the squares of the vast, drab, concrete concentration-camp, hidden away behind the motorway flyovers, billboards and shuttered-up shops of the dense, grey cityscape.

He walked the way he would have walked all those years ago when he first started using drugs, when he was tantalised by the lights and the promise of scoring, ducking under the subways and kicking through the walkways, eyeing the graffiti and the teenage girls. Heading for trouble or fun, which in those days seemed to be the same thing.

There was a flat with boards across the windows, exactly as it had been then. One of the boards had been wrenched from its setting and was now rotten, hanging grotesquely away from the window. There were messages scratched into the wood: 'Ian came and left again.' Gabriel remembered that one. Surely it hadn't been this dirty when he was here? Had his flat in London been this dirty? He hoped not. This was a flat where people came not to score, but after they had scored. Junkies knew that they could use here, if they gave the tenants a hit out of their bag.

They were pleased to see Gabriel and said they'd missed him, even though they hadn't thought about him once since the last time they'd seen him. No one offered Gabriel a hit – heroin wasn't like that – but someone said they knew where you could get a good deal. Gabriel asked where, and asked after Charlie. He knew Charlie would have been here, because he had brought her here once, years ago, and made her sit outside while he went in to find out where you could score. She had thought it was dead cool. Gabriel had been annoyed with her even then.

Someone said they'd seen a girl answering her description at one of the squats. Gabriel promised he'd be back and left with a grim expression on his face. He called at the squat where he found Charlie upstairs, asleep, in a dirty bed.

Rachel heard the door to the Lodge open.

She turned to find Edward standing there.

'Come in, please,' Rachel said, and then saw the expression on his face. 'Are you all right?'

Edward shook his head. 'Anne?' he said.

Rachel stared at him. He looked so weak, as if his legs might fold beneath him. 'Edward, it's Rachel.'

He seemed to awaken slightly. 'Rachel, ah, Rachel, yes.' She guided him to an armchair. 'Forgive me, Rachel . . . I think . . . it's the drugs.'

'*Drugs?*'

'Yes . . . drugs . . .' His eyes were rolling, under heavy eyelids.

'You've taken drugs?' Rachel thought he had taken an overdose.

Edward shook his head. 'I've been given drugs. By Mary . . . and Jessica.'

Rachel could hardly believe what she was hearing.

Edward struggled to make himself understood. 'I'm sorry, Rachel,' he said brokenly.

'It's no problem, Edward.'

'They are trying to make me sleep . . . for ever.'

Rachel wasn't sure if this was an attempt at a joke. 'I'll make you some coffee.'

Edward smiled. 'Yes, coffee. Please. Strong.'

After drinking it, Edward tried again to speak. Rachel wasn't sure if the coffee had had much effect, for his speech was still hesitant.

'I've always liked you, Rachel . . . and I know . . . at least, I think, you like me well enough . . .' Rachel nodded. 'Yes. I thought you did . . . but, unfortunately, I think you would . . . like me less . . . I think you *will* like me less . . . when you know the truth.'

Rachel felt a sudden fear. She was sure her suspicions about the baby were true, but perhaps the situation was even worse than she had thought.

'It *was* your baby, wasn't it, Edward?'

Edward looked at her through the fog and nodded. 'You knew?'

'I guessed, but that doesn't make me . . . it doesn't mean I like you any the less.'

'Oh, Rachel, if only that were the whole of it.'

Rachel froze. Again she felt that pit of fear in her stomach. Now she didn't want Edward to tell her anything in case it threw her into conflict with Jessica all over again. That was the fear, she realised: she was afraid of Jessica.

'What is it, Edward? Do you want to talk to me about it?'

Edward nodded, sadly, painfully. 'Jessica and Mary will

not . . . they won't . . .' He sighed. 'Rachel, I killed Anne. I pushed . . . *threw* her down the stairs . . . and then I left her there to die.'

Rachel was calm. 'Edward, are you sure about this? I mean, you're not telling me this because of the drugs? You're not imagining it?'

'Rachel, believe me. I killed Anne. I wanted to tell someone I . . . Jessica won't let me.'

'Why haven't you gone to the police?'

Edward began to cry. Great sobs shook him and he buried his face in his hands. Rachel did not reach out to comfort him. 'I can't . . . I couldn't do that. Not myself . . . Jessica wouldn't listen . . . I told her I wanted to confess . . . Mary and she . . . Rachel, I can't . . . I need help . . . please . . . I'm weak . . . I don't know why . . . or how I came to be this way.'

Edward cried for twenty minutes while Rachel sat and watched him. Jessica's behaviour was beginning to make sense. She *had* to speak to her.

She left Edward at the Lodge, still crying.

Charlie woke to find her brother sitting in a chair looking at her.

She immediately got up and rushed at him, sneering angrily, kicking and slapping him as hard as she could. She screamed that he was a bastard, that she hated him, that he should leave her alone.

Gabriel took the assault full on. He held her wrists to stop her hitting his face, but still she kicked and spat at him and called him every foul name she could mouth before he wrestled her down on to the vile bunched-up blankets and sheets that had made up her bed. Finally she gave herself up to tears and cried like a little girl.

Gabriel held her to him and she sobbed into his chest.

349

'Why, Charlie, why would you want to follow in my footsteps?' he asked, over and over.

'Because I hate you!' she screamed.

Gabriel was stunned. 'What?'

'Everyone loves you, Gabriel,' Charlie spat. 'Everyone. Even Thomas. No matter what you do, no matter how bad you get, everybody loves you.' She continued to sob. 'I felt so disgusting, I wanted to be disgusting. That's how I am. That's how everyone sees me.'

'What have you done, Charlie?'

She looked at him. 'Everything.'

'What? Heroin?'

She nodded. 'That's the best bit.'

Gabriel looked at her. 'What's the worst bit?'

She wouldn't look at him.

'Charlie, what?'

'The men,' she said.

'What? You? Charlie, couldn't you have . . .? I mean, there are other ways . . .'

'They weren't disgusting enough,' Charlie said.

Gabriel produced the bag of heroin he had bought.

'What are you doing?' Charlie asked.

'I'm going to show you how much I love you,' he said.

Charlie didn't look pleased as Gabriel took out his needle.

'Do you use one of these?' Gabriel asked.

Charlie shook her head, somewhat hesitantly.

Gabriel said, 'You should. You don't want to be messing around with foil and stuff. That's for the amateurs.'

'Gabriel, what are you doing?' Charlie said, more seriously this time.

'Well, if you're following in my footsteps, I'm coming with you. We'll crawl around in the gutter together.'

Charlie shook her head. 'No, Gabriel.'

'Why not? If that's what you want, I'm not going to let you go there on your own. How could I? Not when you're doing it for me – because of me.' Charlie stared at him. 'I'm serious, Charlie. Go and get me a spoon.'

'What about Rachel?'

'What about her?'

'You love her.'

'Yes, but I love you, too.'

Charlie looked puzzled and very worried.

Gabriel shrugged. 'Rachel won't die. You probably will.'

Charlie was shaking her head again. 'Don't Gabriel . . .'

'I'm serious!' Gabriel shouted. 'Go and get me a spoon.'

'No, Gabriel. Please. I'm not . . . I've only done it a few times . . . I . . .'

'I thought this was what you wanted? This gets *really* disgusting.' Charlie didn't know what to say. 'Get me a spoon.'

'Gabriel. I don't want it. I . . . don't know what I want.'

Gabriel looked at her. 'You can have this with me, if you want.' He held up the bag of heroin.

'No,' she said.

'Are you sure? I'm up for it. I've got a needle. It's a lot better with a needle.'

She shook her head. 'I don't want you to.'

'Then throw it away,' Gabriel said. 'Here . . .' he held out the bag again, 'take it and throw it away.'

Understanding him at last, Charlie smiled. Without hesitation she took the bag, went into the grimy bathroom, turned on the tap and poured a quarter of a gram of heroin down the plug-hole.

Charlie and Gabriel hugged, crying tears of pain and of love, promising always to love and protect each other.

Gabriel told Charlie he loved her more than he loved himself and Charlie laughed, saying that was how she felt about him.

Eventually, Gabriel said, 'Home?'

When Rachel arrived at the house, Jessica and Mary were waving to Ben, Lenny and Mark.

As Rachel approached the car, Mark stopped and they said their goodbyes. Lenny said she'd phone and speak to Gabriel when they got home. Rachel hardly paid any attention to them. Lenny kissed her and shook her head sadly. 'Get away from here, both of you,' she said. 'It's the only way Gabriel's going to get better.'

Rachel smiled as best she could and nodded. 'Good-bye,' she said vaguely.

When the car had swept away, Jessica and Mary remained. Looking at them, Rachel was again struck by that image of them as clones; their stance was identical, their expressions matched. The two women returned her stare. Rachel asked Jessica if she could have a word with her.

Jessica said, 'In private? Come to my room.'

Upstairs, Rachel stood by the bedroom door, reluctant to enter.

'Is Gabriel back?' Jessica asked.

Rachel shook her head.

Jessica nodded. 'As I thought.'

'He phoned last night. He's found Charlie,' Rachel said, without feeling. 'They decided to stay over. They'll be back later.' Jessica nodded again. 'We're leaving, Jessica. We can't stay here.'

Jessica had never seen that cold look on Rachel's face before. With a hesitant step she went over to the dresser and took out some ampoules and a few syringes. 'You may as well take these,' she said. 'I was keeping them here in case Gabriel lost his supply.'

Rachel was still in the doorway, staring.

'Come in, Rachel. I'll run through the procedure one last time,' Jessica said, a little more firmly. 'It's better to be sure. The first couple of times are the worst. Stabbing a needle into someone you love is hardly something one can relish, but when you understand what it's for, the revulsion passes.' Aware of Rachel's gaze, Jessica fiddled with a syringe and the ampoules as she spoke, clumsily sucking in fluid and air through the needle. 'Don't forget, the most important thing is to avoid getting air in the syringe . . . that is literally fatal, it can bring death in seconds . . . it's life we are talking about, remember . . . it's life . . . all of our lives . . .' She broke off and looked round at Rachel. Her tone changed. 'Edward has told you, hasn't he?'

Rachel was relieved that Jessica had raised the subject herself. She nodded.

Jessica nodded too. 'He didn't kill her. I know he didn't kill her. It was an accident . . .'

Rachel felt sad and confused to hear Jessica deny it. 'I think the police might take a different view.'

Jessica looked mightily shocked. 'What are . . . I don't see . . . nothing could be served by going to the police!' she stammered, before going on, more firmly, 'Whatever Edward did, or did not do, it was an aberration, totally out of character, a possession. The woman possessed him! She suffocated him! He couldn't breathe! He had to force her off him, he had to – or be killed himself.'

Rachel looked at Jessica as if she had just committed a crime, but then softened and sat down on the bed next to her old adversary. 'Is that for us to decide, Jessica?' she asked quietly.

'Who else? Who else can understand?' Jessica said, desperation showing on her face.

Rachel suddenly felt very calm. At last Jessica had lost any power she had over her. 'I understand, Jessica,' she said, as if she were talking to a child. 'I understand you sacrificed possession of your son to me, because you feared that I would discover the truth from Edward. At first I thought it was the pregnancy you didn't want me to discover – huh – you put me on to that yourself when you tried to warn me away.' Rachel put her hand on Jessica's arm. 'I don't *blame* you, Jessica. I think I might even have done the same thing myself.'

'Then you know why we must protect Edward,' Jessica said.

Rachel shook her head, sadly. 'This is . . . this might be murder, Jessica. A woman is dead – and so is her child. That goes beyond a family battle. There are decisions which cannot be made within these four walls.'

'What good would it do?' Jessica said. 'Why persecute him? Don't you think he is already in hell, don't you think the woman possesses him even from the grave?'

Rachel suppressed a shudder. 'I don't know about that, Jessica. But I do know that Edward will not be free of her by evading the truth. And neither will any of us. In one way or another it would operate like a cancer running through the family.'

'Oh, you know, do you?' Jessica said with great bitterness. 'You're suddenly the one who knows what's best for us all?'

'Yes, Jessica. Unfortunately, yes.'

'So what do I do?'

'You must persuade Edward to confess.'

'Don't you think Edward has confessed enough?'

'No, I'm sorry. I don't think that's for us to decide.'

Jessica sighed. 'And if I don't ... persuade him to confess?'

Rachel's face made a reply unnecessary.

Jessica looked away, seeming to capitulate. 'Yes, yes. You're right, Rachel.'

'I wish I wasn't.'

Jessica's shoulders slumped and her face fell into an expression of despair so awful that Rachel immediately felt a great wave of pity for her. Her mother-in-law looked old suddenly, haggard even, as if the curtains had been drawn exposing a vampire to the deadly rays of dawn. Tears came to Jessica's eyes and Rachel reached out to embrace her, feeling Jessica's body like a dead weight in her arms. Then she felt Jessica's arms about her and held her all the more tightly.

'I'm sorry, Rachel,' Jessica was saying. 'I'm so, so sorry ...'

Jessica pushed the syringe full of methadone and air into the back of Rachel's head, at a steep angle so that the needle would insert itself directly into her brain. She felt Rachel jolt violently and held on to her, quickly pressing the plunger.

'I'm sorry ... so, so sorry ...'

Rachel shuddered briefly, her expression as much one of surprise as of horror.

Rachel died there in Jessica's arms, quivering painfully as she did so.

As Rachel died, Jessica held her almost lovingly and said, 'Forgive me. You have to understand, I can't have the family destroyed. I can't sit back and watch those I love destroyed. You understand that, don't you, Rachel? Of course you do ... of course you do.'

Jessica called for Mary who came and stared at Rachel's still twitching body on the bed.

'Go down to the Lodge, Mary,' Jessica said. 'Pack a bag

355

of Rachel's belongings. We must be quick, before Gabriel returns. We can bury it with her.'

Mary nodded.

Jessica collected up the remaining syringes and ampoules and placed them back in the drawer. 'Rachel left,' Jessica said. 'Just as she said she would.'

·Epilogue·

Six months later

THE LANDSCAPE WAS cold and bare.

Two young people were walking arm in arm by the lake. The golden winter sun flashing through the trees, laying a glistening carpet over the lake and seeming to make the birds call out in praise of the day, did nothing to lessen the weight of the burden pressing down on the young man's shoulders.

'Isn't it beautiful, Gabriel? Like one of your paintings.'

Gabriel laughed cynically. 'It might be beautiful to you, Charlie, but to me it's torture . . . like a cold fire when you're freezing to death.'

Charlie stopped and looked at him. 'Very poetic, bro.'

Gabriel didn't return her smile.

Charlie picked up a couple of stones and threw them into the lake where they momentarily smashed the golden ball of the reflected sun. She'd suggested the walk so that she could talk to her brother, but she was finding it difficult to speak her mind. 'Gabriel,' she said, 'I know it's hard, but you've got to . . .' She sighed, awkwardly. 'You've got to let her go.'

Gabriel said nothing, but out of the corner of her eye, Charlie saw his head drop forward as if to seek out some comfort in the frozen earth.

'Gabriel, she's gone. She left you high and dry.' Charlie didn't want to lay it on too thick and make Rachel out to be a demon because Gabriel would never allow that. 'She's gone and you're still here, pining away. I mean, you've done brilliantly getting clean – I mean brilliantly – there's no way I could have done it on my own like that . . . but,' she shrugged her shoulders again, 'I mean, what's the point if you're just going to be miserable, eh?'

'She'll be back,' Gabriel said. 'She'll come back and I'll be ready. I'm clean and we can start again. Properly.'

The words sounded so forlorn that Charlie wanted to cry. Yet at the same time she wanted to shake Gabriel; as far as Charlie was concerned Rachel was a bitch for leaving him, simple as that. She sighed and chose softer words than she would have liked. 'I know you think that, but . . . well, I mean, if she was going to come back, wouldn't she have left you a note, or phoned to let you know where she is, or at least that she's OK? She hasn't even contacted her best mate.'

'So *she* says. She might have told Caroline not to let on in case we go looking for her.'

Charlie was exasperated. 'Well, if that's the case she's definitely not coming back!'

Gabriel was searching the earth again.

Charlie had heard it all before and she was used to her brother's intransigence on the subject; his arguments were never rational, his position never changed. Rachel had gone, Rachel would come back. Charlie longed for Gabriel to come back to life, to let go of the past and smile like he used to. She longed for the closeness they had briefly experienced when he had come to look for her in the city, yet it was as if there was a wall around his heart with Rachel's name scratched on it, a wall too high to climb, too wide to get around.

Charlie sighed, put her arm back through Gabriel's and they set off again on their forlorn winter journey around the lake. With a faint smile, Charlie said, 'You're as loyal to Rachel as you used to be to heroin.'

Gabriel was blinking into the reflected sunlight. 'She'll be back,' he said.

Mary and Jessica were busy with the Sunday roast.

Jessica had been to visit Edward at his religious retreat where he was convalescing from his breakdown. Mary was asking after him. Jessica told her that Edward was well, that he seemed to be coming to terms with his conscience at last, but that he would be staying on at the monastery for a while longer, until he felt able to resume normal life.

They were just taking the joint from the oven and wondering whether Gabriel and Charlie were going to be late back from their walk when, through the window, they saw a car pulling up outside. A smart-looking man climbed out, youngish with side-parted blond hair. Both women thought he looked familiar.

He came up the drive and knocked on the back door.

'Excuse me,' he said, in a polite and friendly tone. 'I'm looking for Gabriel Rattigan. Could you help me?'

Something in Jessica became suspicious suddenly. 'And you are?' she asked, returning the friendly smile which froze on her face.

The man laughed, as if he had anticipated the question.

'Are you a friend of his?' Jessica asked.

'Not exactly,' the man said. 'He married my sister.'

Jessica extended a hand.

'You must be . . . (what was it) . . . Steven Whittaker? Rachel's famous absentee brother.'

The man smiled again. 'Steve. All the way from America. And you must be . . . Jessica Rattigan.'

They shook hands.

'You know my name,' Jessica said, as lightly as she could.

Steve nodded. 'I've heard a lot about you.'

Jessica laughed to cover her discomfort. 'You've seen Rachel, then?'

Steve looked at her for a while before shaking his head. 'Not since she disappeared. But she mentioned you a lot in the letters she wrote to her friend Caroline.'

Jessica nodded. 'I thought you might have come with some news. For Gabriel.'

Again Steve looked at her. 'No,' he said. 'On the contrary. I've come looking for news of Rachel. This was the last place she was seen.' He stopped. 'I wanted to see the place for myself.'

Jessica returned the look Steve was giving her and then smiled kindly. 'Of course,' she said. 'Come in. You're just in time for lunch. Gabriel has gone for a walk around the lake with Charlie. Ah, here they are now. I'm sure they'll be delighted to meet you. And this is Mary, our housekeeper.'

'Pleased to meet you, Steve.'

'You will be staying, won't you?' Jessica inquired.

'That's very kind, but . . .'

'I insist,' smiled Jessica. 'You're family.'